Praise for As the Crow Dies

"A must-read book. Both poignant and realistic."
—*Brenda Novak NYT Bestselling author of* Body Heat

"Jason Crow is a mix of Ironside and James Lee Burke's Dave Robicheaux. Plenty of twists and turns along with an electrifying ending."
—*Ken Hodgson, award winning author of* The Man Who Killed Shakespeare *(Starred review)* BOOKLIST

Other Ken Casper Books from Bell Bridge Books

As the Crow Dies
(A 'Jason Crow' West Texas Mystery - Book One)

Taking a Stand
(A Coyote Springs Novel)

Standing in the Shadows
(A Coyote Springs Novel)

Crow's Feat

A 'Jason Crow' West Texas Mystery
Book Two

by

Ken Casper

Bell Bridge Books

This is a work of fiction. Names, characters, places and incidents are either the products of the author's imagination or are used fictitiously. Any resemblance to actual persons (living or dead), events or locations is entirely coincidental.

B

Bell Bridge Books
PO BOX 300921
Memphis, TN 38130
Print ISBN: 978-1-61194-164-7

Bell Bridge Books is an Imprint of BelleBooks, Inc.

We at BelleBooks enjoy hearing from readers.
Visit our websites – www.BelleBooks.com and www.BellBridgeBooks.com.

10 9 8 7 6 5 4 3 2 1

Cover design: Debra Dixon
Interior design: Hank Smith
Photo credits:
Landscape (manipulated) © Kevin Carden | Dreamstime.com

:Lfc:01:

Dedicated to the memory of

Pres Darby, physician, adventurer, raconteur, friend and one of the bravest men I've ever known.

Garda Parker, author, teacher, inspirer, friend and whose kindness and generosity helped make the world better.

Their spirits endure.

Crow's Feat

For God will bring every deed into judgment,
Including every hidden thing,
Whether it is good or evil.
—*Ecclesiastes 12:14*

Chapter One

Tuesday, June 1, 1976

The body was slumped at the dining room table, a knife buried to the hilt in his back. I stared for several seconds, disturbed by the realization that I felt nothing. This man wasn't a friend. I hardly knew him, and what I did know about him I didn't like. His call last night had come as a surprise.

"You in charge of the Bicentennial program?" he'd asked, after identifying himself with full military title, his words slurred.

"Yes, sir. I'm the chairman of the committee."

"Hear you're gonna set up a display of military uniforms at the new mall."

"Yes, sir," I said again.

"Well, I've got one for ya." He then offered me a set of "pinks and greens," the standard Army officer's Class A uniform in WWII. I'd spoken to several older vets who acknowledged having them hanging in the backs of closets or tucked away in footlockers in the garage, but none of them had been willing to give them up, even temporarily. They wanted to be buried in them. I gazed at the corpse at the head of the table. Had he?

"Come by tomorrow and pick it up. Anytime. And when you do," he'd added before I had a chance to thank him, "there's . . . a personal matter—" his thick Mississippi drawl was exaggerated "—I'd like to discuss with ya. In confidence, y'understand."

When I asked for elaboration, he said only "Tomorrow" and hung up.

Now tomorrow had arrived. I leaned slightly forward, mindful of my balance, suddenly aware of the miasmic odor of death, and placed two fingers on his left carotid artery. He was dead all right and, judging by the coolness of his skin, he'd been that way for several hours.

I surveyed the scene. Just beyond his right hand was a nearly full old-fashioned glass, tan on top, clear at the bottom. From melted ice, I reckoned. An uncorked bottle of cheap whiskey was within reach of the other hand. The rest of the table was strewn with clean and wrinkled paper napkins, opened and unopened mail, bottles of aspirin, cough remedies and prescription drugs, as well as paper plates and plastic flatware.

At the far end of the table, draped over the back of the chair, was the uniform I'd come for, still on its hanger. His medals were emblazoned above the left breast pocket. The stylized silver oak leaves of rank adorned the shoulder epaulettes.

I pivoted back toward the kitchen of his modest house, walked beside the red Formica-topped counter to the wall phone, removed a handkerchief from my hip pocket and used it to lift the receiver from its cradle.

Most of the cops at the stationhouse knew me from my participation in community affairs—I also coached some of their kids in Little League, the only legless ex-football player and now part-time high school football coach in town—so I had no trouble getting put through to Lieutenant Burker, the head of homicide.

"What?" he snapped. "I'm busy."

So he wasn't having a good morning either. It was about to get worse.

"I'm at the home of Colonel Bartholomew." I started to give him the address in the Indian Heights section of town.

"I know where Bart lives. What about him?"

"He's not living here anymore," I said. "He's dead."

A beat of time slipped by before he replied, "Well, he obviously didn't have a heart attack or you wouldn't be calling me. How?"

"Knife in his back. I'm pretty sure it wasn't suicide."

It was a cheap shot, one I instantly regretted, a reference to eight years ago when I'd just come home from Vietnam, proud of the fact that I'd learned to walk, only to find my father had taken a single bullet to the head. Clyde Burker, the detective in charge of investigating the violent death, hadn't questioned what appeared to be obvious—that Theodore Crow had committed suicide. I'd ultimately forced him to accept my contention that he'd been murdered, but only after I'd produced the killer.

Burker now spat out a word unsuitable in the presence of women and children. "I'll be there in a few minutes. Don't touch anything." He hung up.

I replaced the receiver and scanned the room. The combination kitchen and breakfast nook ran parallel with the living room and dining area. It had a decidedly neglected feel about it. Fussy canisters shaped like owls lined one counter. Sentimental "collector" plates were spaced above the backsplash of the opposite wall. Bart's wife had passed away several months ago. Reminders of her presence in the kitchen didn't seem to have bothered him, maybe because he spent so little time there. One possibility I dismissed without a second thought was that he'd left things the way they were as a shrine to her memory.

I proceeded into the small entrance hallway and beyond it to the living room. Through the broad picture window overlooking the backyard I saw brown-paper wrapped bundles of roofing shingles dumped haphazardly under a magnolia tree along with a carelessly folded tarp and not very orderly stack of rough planks, probably to build a debris chute. Apparently the old sot was having the house re-roofed.

Burker needn't have bothered telling me not to touch anything. I had no intention of disturbing the crime scene, but I would have welcomed a chance to sit down. I was wearing new legs, a marked improvement over my old prostheses, but the left socket wasn't quite right. I had an appointment that morning to get it adjusted at the military hospital on Coyote Air Force Base. For the moment though I would have been content just to relieve the pressure. Unfortunately the rattan living room furniture was too low for me to settle onto without firmly grasping the armrests, and once seated, I wasn't sure I'd be able to get up without assistance. I wasn't too proud to ask for the help of friends when I needed it, but there were occasions when I didn't want to call attention to my limitations. Like now. The dining room chairs had armrests and would have been just right, but I would have had to move one out, and I didn't want to do even that.

Having come full circle I now had a broadside view of the dining table and the sideboard behind it, including the china collection above the counter. Prominently displayed on the top shelf was a large plate that I instantly recognized as Japanese *Imari*. It was a magnificent piece with its distinctive dark blue, deep red and bluish-white thematic patterns, all trimmed in gold. I was no expert on the porcelain, but thanks to a family trip to Japan three years ago to visit my wife's parents outside Tokyo, I knew enough to say it was probably late 17th century. That so valuable a piece was not encased or under lock and key was a little surprising, yet I approved of it being "in use" rather than hidden in a bank vault somewhere. Such objects of beauty were to be seen, not hoarded.

There was a den off the living room with a handsome stone fireplace on my left. What dominated the room, however, was the Steinway baby grand piano. I noticed the ceiling above it was badly water stained, which accounted for the roofing materials outside and the blue tarp neatly folded beside the secretary against the far wall. The piano bench would have suited me fine, except it was down two unguarded short steps. Under the circumstances I didn't trust myself to navigate them without falling, so I turned back to the living room.

Across a wide expanse of wall-to-wall carpet I now faced a television in a recessed alcove. Wired to it was a Sony Beta video-cassette player similar to the one my brother Leon had hooked up in our dad's old office in the carriage house. I would have liked to compare the two, but the colonel's was stowed in the stand under the portable TV. Ours was mounted on top of the console, so I could get easy access to it. Still looking for a place to sit, I strode towards it, then out of curiosity veered left and headed down the hallway leading to the bedrooms. Directly in front of me at the end of the narrow corridor an open door revealed a pink-and-avocado bathroom. On my right were two closed doors, to what I presumed were bedrooms. On the left, the vent in the first door told me it was a utility closet that housed the heating and air conditioning unit. Beyond it were double doors. One was open. I stepped into the master suite.

It had a stale, bedroom smell. The Venetian blinds were closed, leaving the room dim. The bed was turned down but didn't look as if it had been slept in. The decedent in the other room was fully dressed in daytime clothes. Had he been getting ready to retire for the night when the killer struck? Someone he knew, I surmised, since I'd seen no signs of a struggle or resistance.

To my left, another full bath. This one in blue. Blue asphalt tile on the floor. The cabinetry painted a darker shade. The ceramic tile of the counter matched the floor; the walls were a lighter hue. It was overpowering, and to me, oppressive. I wondered if it reflected Bart's taste or his late wife's.

I backed away from the threshold and rotated around. It was then that I saw them.

On the wall opposite the foot of the bed were a dozen framed photographs, some black-and-white, one sepia, the others in color. All were of young girls with big colorful bows in their hair. The camera man had been good, capturing innocent shyness and vulnerability, along with the poignant eagerness of a child to please. Why the bows?

I moved closer and examined faces. A couple of them, I surmised from their features and expressions, might have been related to Bartholomew. His grandchildren? I was surprised when I realized one of them was of mixed race. Her complexion was what would have once been called "dusky." I wasn't sure what to make of it. Did Bart the Bigot have a little black granddaughter?

I heard a car pull up outside and made my way back to the kitchen just as Burker came through the side door.

Six-feet tall with broad shoulders, his girth had expanded considerably in the nearly two decades since he and I had played on the Coyote Springs High School football team together. We'd competed for the same girl. I'd won, then ditched her. He'd married her and forgiven me. She hadn't.

"What were you doing back there?" he demanded, without a salutation.

"Looking for a place to sit where I wouldn't have to touch anything."

He instantly broke eye contact, glanced around at the kitchen's contents and muttered, "Heard you got a new pair of legs."

"They still need adjustment. I have an appointment—" I looked at my watch "—*had* an appointment for 11:00. Doesn't look like I'm going to make it now."

"I would have gotten here sooner," he said, "but there was a domestic murder-suicide up on the north side I needed to check out. It's a mess." He glanced at his watch. 10:45. "I can have a patrol car escort you to the base to make sure you get there on time."

I appreciated the offer. He'd sworn to me a long time ago that he wouldn't pity me, and he hadn't, but once in a while he showed concern, even deference. Like now.

"Thanks, but a short delay won't matter." I hoped. I nodded in the direction of the deceased to change the subject. "He's been dead a while."

"How is it you found him? What're you doing here?"

I told him about Bart's offer of the uniform but was tempted to leave out the part about the "confidential" matter, until I realized there was no reason to. Could it have any bearing on his murder?

"You have any idea what he was referring to?" Burker asked a minute later.

"None whatsoever."

We went to the dining room. He circled the table, examined the corpse from every angle but, just as he'd instructed me, touched nothing. I took the opportunity to note the names of the prescription drugs. Lanoxin. Lasix. Potassium. My wife was a nurse. She'd know what they were for. Finally Burker's attention fell on the uniform.

"Forensics will have to go over it before we can turn it over to you or anyone else." He popped a peppermint into his mouth, a defense, I supposed, against a variety of unpleasant smells he was inclined to encounter in his line of work. "Now walk me through exactly what you found and what you did when you got here."

It didn't take me long to explain. "I arrived at ten, figuring there was a reasonable chance he'd be up by then. When I received no answer to the front bell, I came around to the door off the carport and was about to knock when I realized it was ajar. I nudged it wider and called out, still got no response."

At the time I'd wondered if Bart might have fallen, but that wouldn't explain the open door. Maybe he'd started to go to his car, gone back for something or became ill . . . . The possibilities seemed endless, speculation idle.

"So I came in but didn't touch anything."

"The door's up two steps," he commented casually. He knew the difficulty I had with steps. I generally need handrails, canes, crutches or a human hand to lend me the balance I needed to climb or descend them.

"I grabbed hold of the doorframe," I admitted, "but you won't find my fingerprints anywhere else."

He grunted. "Go ahead to your appointment. I know where to find you if I have any questions. There is one thing though. I was planning to call you and Zack later today. I received notification this morning from Huntsville." In his brief pause I knew what he was about to say. My jaw tightened. "Bubba Spites is being released this afternoon."

I'd felt nothing at the discovery of Bart's body, but I did at this news. My reaction was complex. Bubba—his real name was Harden—Spites was the son of Brayton Spites, my dad's one-time employer and, it so happened, my mother's long-ago lover. Brayton was also my biological father. That made Bubba my half-brother. Shortly after Theodore Crow, the man who'd given me his name and brought me up, the man I loved and respected more than anyone else in the world, the only man I would ever call my dad, was murdered, Bubba Spites was arrested for assault and battery against me and Zack Merchant, my best friend and business partner. Brayton did his best to persuade us to drop the charges, but we'd refused. Months later, additional charges were brought against Bubba for dealing hard drugs. Still, the case dragged on for a year and a half, thanks to Brayton's high-priced lawyer's delaying tactics. Eventually, however, Bubba ran out of excuses, was tried, convicted and sentenced to ten-to-fifteen years in prison. Now, six years later he was being set loose.

"Considering the threats he made against you and Zack after the trial," Burker reminded me, "I'd watch my back if I were you."

Chapter Two

I missed my appointment at the hospital. The receptionist told me she might be able to squeeze me in later if there was another no-show but, seeing the number of people in the waiting room, it didn't appear likely. On the other hand, there was an opening on Thursday morning, if I could hold out that long. Realizing I might have to anyway, I chose to take the firm appointment, rather than waste hours in the reception area reading months-old movie magazines. In the meantime I'd just have to endure the discomfort or give up the *illusion of normalcy* and stick to my wheelchair.

I drove to the carriage house behind the *Crow's Nest Steakhouse* and took the outside elevator to the second floor where Zack Merchant and I had our *Restoration, Inc.* business. My father's old office to the left of the entranceway hadn't changed much. We used it principally for meeting clients. What had changed was the room to the right. It had once been the best college dorm room in the world for Zack and me. Now we called it our "drawing room" because a pair of drafting tables dominated the available space.

Zack was sitting at his, sorting through mail, when I arrived a few minutes past noon.

"You didn't get your adjustment," he observed as I crossed to my table opposite his.

"That obvious?"

"I know your stride." The only one who knew it better was my wife.

I told him about Colonel Bartholomew.

He paused for a moment, then put down the letter opener he'd been using. "Any indication who did it?"

"Nothing obvious to me." I reviewed with him what I'd seen, as well as my impressions.

"You think it might be family?" he asked.

In situations like this, in the victim's normal surroundings, where there were no signs of a break-in or struggle, suspicion automatically started with members of the family. "I reckon that's where Burker will begin."

Zack resumed sorting through the morning mail. A minute of silence went by. He looked up. "Is there something else?"

"Bubba's being released today."

My friend's brows rose, passivity banished.

"Burker suggests we watch our backs."

"We'd better do more than that," Zack said. "I'll call our lawyer about a restraining order to keep Bubba at least a mile from our homes, businesses and families."

I'd been thinking along the same lines, though I didn't imagine we'd get a radius that wide. I also recognized a restraining order was like a lock on a glass case. It kept out the honest. Paper wasn't much protection against fists and bullets. "While you're doing that—" I picked up my phone "—I'll call Michiko and have her alert Nancy to be on the lookout."

Since my wife was half Japanese and half American, it always fascinated me to see which of her cultures came to the fore in any particular situation. In this case she took the news calmly. "We knew he'd get out someday, Jason. He's had six years to think things through."

"You mean plan his vengeance."

"He's not stupid, Jason. I'm sure he realizes by now there's nothing to be gained by going after any of us."

But I knew the woman who'd taken me for better or worse and accepted me the way I was. I could hear it in her voice. She wasn't scared, not in the conventional sense, not for herself and, I liked to think, not for me. I wasn't helpless, as she well knew. Bubba had learned that lesson the hard way. Nonetheless, she was justified in her unspoken concern that he might try to get to Zack or me by attacking our families. I hoped the ex-con understood doing so would make things even worse for him. I took my roles as provider and protector seriously. Nor did missing limbs hinder the rest of me from keeping fit. No way would I run from a fight.

"Just stay alert," I told her, "and remember, if he starts following you, don't try to outrun him—"

"I know, Jason. Head for the police station or any cop car."

"Exactly. Don't forget to let Nancy know what's going on."

"Jason . . ."

"We probably ought to get the family together tonight and discuss what to do if he decides to take the low road."

"A cookout then. Steaks and burgers by the pool."

When I was growing up we used to go swimming in a stock tank on my grandfather's ranch. A year after taking up residence there following my father's death I had a "real" pool installed which I used regularly as much for physical therapy as enjoyment. How my world had changed.

That evening, while Zack was grilling hot dogs and hamburgers for the kids and steaks for the adults, we discussed Colonel Bartholomew and the confidential matter he hadn't gotten a chance to tell me about.

"Could it have been just a ruse to make sure you'd show up?" asked

Nancy, Zack's wife.

"But why wouldn't I?" I replied. "He was offering me something I wanted. Why engage in intrigue?"

"Because he knew you didn't like him."

"I don't know where he could have gotten that idea," I said only half-seriously. It was true, but I'd done my best not to let it show. Apparently I hadn't been very successful.

My first encounter with Lieutenant Colonel Mortimer Bartholomew, United States Army (retired), had been eight years ago at the Coyote Air Force Base officers' club on the day of my father's funeral. I'd gone there with Michiko, Zack and Ned Herman, not to drink, but to get away from the press. Bart came in and, unaware Michiko and I were sitting behind the potted palms in the lounge and could hear his every word, spewed a mixture of racist bigotry and false rumors to Zack and Ned at the bar. Eventually I'd made my presence known, but rather than punch his lights out, something my father would not have approved, I'd signed a bar napkin entitling him to a complimentary dinner for two at the *Crow's Nest Steakhouse*. A few days later, I realized there'd been an element of truth in the retired officer's inebriated ramblings. It helped me piece together what had happened to my father . . . and to me.

Those memories made me cantankerous. Loose ends bothered me, and now I sensed my sister's seven-year-old loitering close by and trying not to be obvious about it.

"Is there something I can do for you, Lavinia?" I asked.

"Colonel Bart . . . I heard you talking to Uncle Zack and Aunt Nancy about him. Did something happen?"

"He died last night, Livy."

"Oh."

Just then my son Ted called her from the other end of the pool. She looked up at me. I nodded permission; she bolted to the diving board and did a cannonball into the water, the subject dismissed—for now, at least.

"Sorry about the eavesdropping." Aaron had been watching and listening. "I'll have a little talk with her about good manners."

Tall and dark-chocolate-brown, my brother-in-law still had the flat belly and wide shoulders of the competitive swimmer he'd been in college. He and my sister had married a couple of months before Michiko and I tied the knot. I'd been his best man.

I shook my head. "I don't think that'll be necessary. Livy's curiosity is natural. We don't want to discourage her from asking questions. Getting back to Colonel Bart . . . whenever we met, I made it a point to be friendly and polite, like the night he and his wife came to the *Nest* for their free meal. I turned on the charm, even threw in a complimentary dessert."

Zack handed me a glass of half iced tea and half homemade lemonade. "Yet they never came back. That should tell you something."

"Maybe there was too much gristle," I joked, then told Michiko about the prescription medication I'd seen on Bart's dining room table.

"Lanoxin? That's digitalis. It's used to treat heart conditions. Lasix is a diuretic. Sounds like he might have had congestive heart failure." She paused to think. "He's . . . he was a heavy drinker. Based on those medications, my guess is that he had alcohol cardiomyopathy."

"What's that?" Zack asked.

"Heart disease."

"Is it fatal?"

"If he kept drinking it would be."

"So he was a dying man," I said.

"Except," Zack noted, "in this case a knife got him first."

"I wonder how many people knew he had a terminal heart condition."

"I hate to sound callous," said Nancy, "but Bart isn't our concern. Bubba is. What are we going to do about him?"

"Ignore him," I replied. "We've taken out a restraining order against him. Beyond that there isn't much we can do unless he violates it. If he does, call the cops. Burker assures me they're all aware of the situation."

"Will he be staying with his father, do you think?" Aaron asked.

"I have no idea. As far as I know Brayton hasn't uttered a word about him coming home."

Then again, I didn't imagine many parents bragged about their son being released from prison.

Chapter Three

The following morning, using my wheelchair, I accompanied Michiko to her medical appointment with Dr. Preston at the Clover Medical Center. She was three months pregnant with our fourth child.

"It feels like a boy," she told the doctor.

"You said Gideon felt like a girl," I reminded her.

"Until he started practicing football maneuvers in my belly."

"He is pretty good at dodging and weaving, isn't he?"

"And yelling and screaming."

"Yep. He's a boy all right." I grinned.

While Michiko was getting dressed, the nurse at reception congratulated me on becoming a daddy again, then added, "I read in the paper it was you who found Colonel B."

I confirmed that I had.

"How terrible. Was there a lot of blood?"

"Some, but not much."

"He must have died quickly then. At least he didn't suffer long."

I hadn't given the matter much thought, but she was right.

"I'm glad of that," the nurse said. "He was such a nice man."

"You knew him?"

"We used to play bridge with him and his wife."

"I bet that was interesting."

She laughed. "Oh, he never drank when we played cards. He was witty, though. Had a dry sense of humor. Subtle. A gentleman too. The strangest part is that he and Hazel were really good bridge partners, took the championship four years in a row. Everyone was always surprised how they could be at each other's throats—at least, she could—then the cards were dealt, and it was as if a switch was flipped and they could read each other's minds."

People were mazes of contradictions and not always what they seemed. I'd learned that the hard way. Apparently Bart hadn't been an exception to the rule.

Michiko and I had taken my pickup truck, so by pre-arrangement I dropped her off at Zack's house in Oakdale, the city's newest housing development. She and Nancy planned to go shopping for maternity and baby clothes, after which Nancy would drive Michiko home.

"Remember, if you see Bubba, he's too close. If he tries following you in a vehicle, don't try to outrun or outmaneuver him."

"I know, Jason. I know. Just lead him to the police station."

I pulled into the Merchants' driveway, leaned over and kissed her on the cheek. "Have a good time."

Backing out and waving goodbye, I proceeded directly to Davis Street and the carriage house.

"How did it go?" Zack asked the moment I wheeled into the drawing room.

"She's pregnant, no question about it."

"Congratulations, papa." He turned the page of the morning *Gazette* while I positioned myself at my drafting table.

"I've been reading Bartholomew's obit," Zack said. "I knew he'd been in the war, but I didn't realize he'd had such a distinguished military career. Not just the Meritorious Service Medal but the Silver Star with V for Valor. Impressive."

"Plus the Purple Heart. That kind of military record seems incongruous for a man teaching young kids to play the piano."

Zack nodded. "Did you know Bart's granddaughter is married to Keith Connors?"

Four years ago, fresh out of divinity school, Reverend Keith Connors had been preaching for a year or so in a little church just outside Coyote Springs when the local TV station offered him an early Sunday morning time-slot for a service-and-sermon program. Within six months other Texas stations had picked it up, and by the end of the year it had gone national. His audience was reportedly still growing.

"Not until I read it in the paper this morning at breakfast."

"Well," Zack said, "he called a few minutes ago."

"Connors? What did he want?"

My suspicious tone didn't alarm my friend. He'd been a witness to the crisis I'd had to contend with when my mother fell prey to a religious cult while I was in Vietnam. The psychological and emotional damage the self-appointed "high priest" had wrought on her was serious and long lasting.

My growing family belonged to a local church because I believed in the moral values they taught, but my commitment wasn't blind or unconditional, at least as far as "men of the cloth" were concerned.

"He has a project he'd like to discuss with us."

"What kind of project?"

"Restore the church he uses as his logo." Zack flipped the newspaper to the back page. Among the advertisements was one showing a small country church at the top of a knoll. "Apparently the building is real. I figured it was just a Currier-and-Ives-type graphic someone had created for him."

"Restore a church? Hmm. Could be interesting."

"I didn't know what time you'd be in, so I told him I'd call him back. When do you want him to come over? He'd like it to be as soon as possible."

I looked at the Regulator on the wall across from me. A few minutes before noon. "How about one o'clock? That'll give us time to grab a quick bite."

Zack made the call while I phoned over to the *Nest* and ordered a couple of BLTs.

We were cleaning up the remnants of our sandwiches when there was a knock on the outside door. It was precisely one o'clock. Zack brought the preacher into the office where I was sitting in my wheelchair behind my father's old desk. He reached across and gave me his hand. His grip was firm. He looked me straight in the eye.

I'd caught occasional glimpses of him on TV when I was visiting my mother in her sitting room, but this was the first opportunity I'd had to meet him in person. Tall and slender, he had ice-blue eyes and straw-blond hair—its color natural I decided when I spied no trace of dark roots and his eyebrows were the same shade. He also had what I called a Hollywood tan. He was considered drop-dead handsome by some women, including Mom. Observing him in person, I was inclined to accept their judgment. The thick yellow hair could have been girlish, but he didn't come across that way. How much his Prince Charming looks accounted for his ministerial and television success was anybody's guess.

I motioned him to the guest chair by the door. He set the black-leather attaché case he'd brought on the floor beside him. Zack sat parallel to him at the other corner of the desk.

"First, I'm sorry you had to be the one to find Colonel Bartholomew's body yesterday. It couldn't have been a pleasant experience. I would have come to see you sooner, but I was at a religious convention in California. My wife called me yesterday morning in tears with the news. I took the first available flight home and didn't get back until late last night. What a tragedy. Murdered." He shook his head. "There are people who didn't like him, some for good reason, but I didn't realize he was so hated. To stab him in the back . . ."

"My condolences to you and your wife. I didn't know he was an in-law."

"Not many people did. I would never have denied him, Mr. Crow, but he thought it would be better if people didn't know we were related. He was aware of the reputation he carried, and he felt it would place an unfair burden on my ministry if I were put in a position of having to explain or defend him." Connors studied his hands. "I'm ashamed to admit I went along with him. It was easier that way, but of course, that was only an excuse. He had his problems, but he was basically a good man."

"Hate the sin, love the sinner?"

His eyes widened momentarily, then he lowered his head. "The newspaper said you were there to pick up a uniform for the Bicentennial celebration."

I explained my plan to put American military uniforms from the Revolution to the present on display at the mall, and that Bart had offered his set of WWII pinks and greens.

"He was very proud of his war record. Hazel, his late wife, was disappointed that he wasn't promoted to full colonel. She was convinced he should have been a general. The problem, he explained, was that he hadn't gotten his ticket punched."

"He wasn't a ring-knocker," I said, "a West Pointer."

Connors nodded. "He also didn't have a college degree, and wasn't from a well-connected family. Under those circumstances he claimed making lieutenant colonel after the war was quite an achievement."

"You liked him."

"I did." The minister shuffled in the seat, crossed one leg over the other, and went on. "The reason I'm here is about the church building where I'm still officially the pastor. It's old and small, much too small for the congregation I have now, but to me it's symbolic, the country church where people feel they're with family. You may have noticed I use it as my trademark. Unfortunately the place is in poor condition. I mentioned to the colonel that I'd like to restore it. He suggested I talk to you. I thought that might have been the reason you went to see him."

Was this the confidential matter Bart intended to talk to me about? It made sense since he apparently didn't want to taint his grandson-in-law's reputation with his own.

"He did mention wanting to discuss a personal matter with me. Unfortunately, he didn't get a chance to tell me specifically what it was."

"I'm sure it was this. He was not himself a religious man, but he was very supportive of my ministry and quite enthusiastic about the prospect of your company doing the work." Connors again bowed his head. "Who could have done this terrible thing?"

"The police are investigating," Zack reminded him. At Connors' somewhat dubious expression he added, "Lieutenant Burker has an excellent record for successfully closing cases."

"When you say restore the church building," I ventured, "do you mean simply repairing it or do you mean reverting to an earlier configuration?"

"I want to put it back to the way it was, the way its founders intended it to be."

"How old's the building?"

"Built in 1896. Unfortunately, over the past eighty years it's been modified and changed in ways that aren't consistent with the original design. The quality of the workmanship leaves a good deal to be desired too. What I propose is that you return it to the little country church it started out as."

"It sounds like the kind of challenge we enjoy, but I'm sure you understand we can't make any commitment without seeing the property first."

Connors smiled for the first time. "Bart was sure you'd be interested."

"When will you be available to show us around and explain exactly what you have in mind?" Zack asked.

"I wish I could do it right now, but I'll be tied up this afternoon and for the next few days. There's no reason you can't go out there on your own though, look the place over. When I can break away—it probably won't be until after the colonel's funeral—we can go together." He reached down, laid his attaché case on his lap, popped it open and extracted a manila envelope. "In the meantime, here are copies of the only historical pictures I have of the place. The earliest is dated 1905. I don't know how much help they'll be."

"Photos are always useful." Zack got up and looked over my shoulder at the badly faded snapshots as they were passed to me.

"Lastly—" Connors removed a ring with half a dozen keys on it, one of them a skeleton key "—here is an extra set of keys to the building. Front door, back, belfry. Feel free to go anywhere you like."

He clicked the case closed and stood up. "My office and personal telephone numbers are on a card in the envelope. Please call me any time you have questions or ideas."

"What about a budget?" Zack asked. "How much do you have to spend on this project?"

"If you can give me what I want, Mr. Merchant, I'll pay whatever you charge. Colonel Bartholomew trusted you to be fair and honest. So do I."

"Give us a few days to arrange our schedules," I said. "Then we'll be in touch."

He turned to the door. I wheeled out from behind the desk. He glanced my way but didn't blink.

"One other thing—" he stopped at the outside door "—I haven't mentioned this to anyone. The media can get in the way of things, and I'm sure there are people on our board of directors who will object to this project for a variety of reasons. So for the time being I'd appreciate your keeping this confidential."

"Absolutely." My own relationship with the fourth estate tended to run hot and cold.

After he left, Zack and I returned to the office. As I gathered the pictures on the desk and put them back in the envelope, Zack peered out the window overlooking the courtyard.

"The Word of the Lord must pay," he commented. "He's driving a brand new maroon Chevy pickup with chrome wheels and running boards."

I picked up the envelope. "Let's take these over to the drawing room and study them more closely."

"A blank check," Zack added. "That's a novel approach."

We crossed the hall. I was about to spread the photos out on my drafting table when we heard the familiar tread of footsteps on the outside stairs. I shoved the envelope in a drawer and closed it just as Burker arrived.

Chapter Four

"Heard Michiko's pregnant again," Burker said from the doorway of the drawing room, a garment bag slung over his shoulder. "They know what causes that, you know."

"Yeah." I grinned. "So do I."

He chuckled, then grew serious. "Forensics is finished with Bart's uniform. I called his son. Junior isn't interested in keeping it, suggested I send it to you directly, and since I just happen to be in the neighborhood . . ."

"Appreciate it."

"Any idea who killed him or why?" Zack asked.

Burker hung the bag on a coat hook by the doorway and plopped down in the chair across from my desk. The wooden joints creaked. "It's early yet. He didn't have a whole lot of friends, and there's a long list of people who didn't like him for one reason or another."

"Where did the knife come from?" I asked. "The kitchen?"

"It was part of a cutlery set in a drawer by the sink."

"So the killer was familiar with the place. Points to family, doesn't it?"

Burker shook his head. "The next of kin generally go to the top of the list of suspects, especially if there's a sizable inheritance involved."

"Is there?" Zack asked.

"Bart's son says he's the executor for the estate. The house is paid off. He's not sure about the Cadillac since it's less than two years old. He doubts there's much in the bank. Claims the old man liked to dabble in penny stocks, but they were all losers. In any case it all gets divided three ways, between him, his sister Stacey and his niece Lisa. Bart's lawyer is out of town until Friday, so it'll be next week before we'll be able to get the specifics. As for the murder weapon, the kitchen drawer is the logical place to look. For that matter the old guy may already have had it on the table, or it could have been on the drain board."

"In other words, in plain sight." Zack noted. "Nancy will tell you that's the best place to hide anything from me, just stick it right in front of my nose."

"How about fingerprints?" I asked.

"The lab reports the handle was clean," Burker replied.

"So the killer had the presence of mind to wipe it," I muttered.

"Or he was wearing gloves," Zack noted.

"If he was wearing gloves," Burker corrected, "old fingerprints would still be there. This knife was clean."

"Interesting," I said, "and contradictory. The killer using a weapon of opportunity suggests an impulsive act rather than one that was premeditated, while cleaning the knife indicates cool-headedness."

"We don't know what weapon he might have brought with him," Burker pointed out. "Maybe he . . . or she . . . came with a gun, then seeing the knife decided it was quieter."

I conceded the point. "Still, I have to wonder what kind of person stabs someone to death in a fit of rage, then manages to calm down at the scene and calculate what has to be done in self-protection."

"You'd be surprised," Burker said, "what people are capable of. Psychopaths do it all the time."

"And in a sense aren't all murderers psychopaths?" I commented.

"What about the time of death?" Zack asked.

"The M.E. reckons somewhere between 9 p.m. Monday night and 6 a.m. Tuesday morning."

"Why such a large window?" Time of death could usually be narrowed down to a two-to-four hour period if it had taken place within twenty-four hours of the body being discovered.

"Happenstance. He was sitting directly in the draft of the main air conditioning duct, chilling his back, head and neck."

I remembered the coolness of his skin. "I can narrow it down a little for you. He called me Monday night at 9:30, so he was still alive then. I didn't hear anything in the background to suggest there was anyone with him. That doesn't mean he was alone, of course. Did the M.E. comment on the wound itself?"

"Entered left of the vertebra between the sixth and seventh ribs, twisted as it scraped both bones and managed to puncture the back of the heart. He died quickly. Had the knife been shorter or not pushed in as far, he would have bled out, which would have been slower and excruciatingly painful."

It wasn't a scenario I wanted to contemplate. "You reckon Bart saw his killer?"

"Probably," Burker agreed.

"Yet nothing was disturbed. There was no indication he was startled or that he offered any resistance. The conclusion seems inescapable: Bart knew his killer and didn't fear him . . . or her."

"Did anyone in the neighborhood see or hear anything unusual?" Zack asked.

Burker shook his head. "You're posing the right questions, but I'm not at liberty to answer them. This is an on-going investigation." Seconds ticked by. "Given your past help in a couple of instances, however, and a gut feeling I have that you might be able to help again, I'll answer what questions I can, but they go no further than this room."

"Agreed," I said for both Zack and me.

"We canvassed both sides of the street and the alley behind the house. Nobody remembers any strange vehicles in the area that night, but then not too many people are outdoors much this time of year."

I nodded. "People used to spend summertime evenings sitting on porches, trying to stay cool. Some even slept there. Now with air conditioners, they're more likely to be inside with the drone of window units masking outside noises. One of those unintended consequences. We gain physical comfort and lose social contact."

"In other words," Zack commented to Burker, "you don't know if the killer came on foot or in a vehicle, up the front walk or down the back alley, whether it was Monday night or Tuesday morning."

Burker didn't look happy. It was hard to pin someone down on an alibi when you couldn't specify when the crime was committed.

"Any idea what the motive was for killing Bart?"

Burker shook his head. "Motive is frequently the last element we uncover, and sometimes it surprises us, like the oil tycoon who gets blown away by his son, not because the kid wants to inherit a few million bucks, but because he's pissed at his old man for not allowing him to go to a rock concert."

"By the way," I said, "how come you knew the colonel's address by heart when I called you yesterday morning?"

Burker huffed. "Back when I was on patrol, we'd get calls from his old lady, Hazel. She was forever complaining about someone or something—that the neighbors were playing their music too loud, or someone had parked a car at the curb and was blocking the driveway by a few inches. Bart was inevitably apologetic when we showed up, and more often than not had already taken care of the problem. It made me wonder if she didn't do it just to embarrass him. The woman was never satisfied. She'd insist we charge the neighbor with disturbing the peace, or the owner of the car of being illegally parked while obstructing traffic, or whatever she could think up. A real piece of work that one. No wonder the old guy drank like a fish."

That matched my limited impression of her.

"This is all very interesting," Zack agreed, "but we have another issue of some slight importance. What about Bubba? Where is he? What's he doing? Is he staying with his father?"

"Arrived by bus late yesterday afternoon," Burker answered. "Nobody there to meet him. Took his canvas bag of personal belongings and walked over to the Conrad Arms Motel, got a key from the manager and went directly to number 27 around the corner. Five minutes later he was served with a restraining order advising him he'd be breaking the law if he came within a thousand feet of either of you or members of your families. He left his one-room efficiency long enough this morning to grab some breakfast and go to the unemployment office. He then went back to his room and has been there ever since."

"So you have him under surveillance," Zack commented.

"I told Jason I had y'all's back, and I meant it. Can't promise to have someone on his ass constantly, but we'll do our best. In the meantime I recommend everyone be alert. What's the Air Force phrase? Check six? Keep looking over your shoulder."

"Thanks, Clyde." I rarely used his given name, but there were occasions when it seemed called for, like now. Burker and I weren't exactly buddies. There was too much baggage between us for that, but we weren't enemies anymore either. "Getting back to Bart, what did you think of all the pictures he had on the wall in his bedroom?"

He shrugged his massive shoulders. "His students, I suppose."

"Anything strike you as odd about them?"

"The ribbons? Different, I'll grant you."

"And that they're all girls. He must have had some male students."

"Junior said he had a few until five or six months ago. I guess boys aren't as interested in learning to play the piano as girls."

"Their daddies may have something to do with it," Zack commented. "I mean, given a choice between sending junior to his piano lessons or to football practice . . ."

"Yeah, I see your point."

While we were talking, Zack removed the uniform from the hanging bag on the wall and laid it across the top of my drawing table. I checked the inside pockets of the blouse, as the jacket was called. Empty. The outside breast pockets were fully functional, but by tradition were not used. I unbuttoned them. There was nothing in the right one, however, but in the left I found a snapshot of a little girl in a Depression-era cotton dress, with a bow in her hair similar to the framed pictures on the wall in Bart's bedroom.

"Forensics miss this?" I asked.

"No." Burker answered, taking umbrage. "They put it back where they found it."

I showed it to Zack. He looked at it fleetingly and handed it back to me. "Cute."

"Any idea who she is?" I asked Burker.

"His daughter, I reckon. Stacey."

I nodded, then got an idea. "Maybe I can display it with the uniform, the kind of thing a lonely GI might carry with him to remind him of home."

"Yeah," Burker muttered, "be real touching. You better get permission to show it first though, if you don't want to get your butt sued for invasion of privacy and anything else she can dream up."

"Sounds like you don't have a high opinion of the lady."

He chuckled. "I'll let you decide which part of that statement I find funny."

Chapter Five

Michiko made sure I was on time Thursday morning for my second appointment with the orthotist. He had me walk in front of a wall-length mirror so he could observe my gait, asked a few questions, then motioned me to the examining table at the far end of the room.

It took him less than half an hour to make the necessary adjustment to the left prosthesis. I walked out of the office with as close to a spring in my step as I'd had in eight years.

You can walk if you really want to, Dad had insisted when the experts were telling me I'd spend the rest of my life in a wheelchair.

I wished he could see me now.

Bart's son owned *Bartholomew's,* a jewelry store downtown in a two-story nineteenth century building that had originally been a saloon. Zack and I had helped restore its architectural features four years ago. I'd been in the shop several times since its opening, usually to buy something for Michiko.

I'd purchased a piece of jewelry for my mother one Christmas too. As a younger woman she'd welcomed jewelry, diamonds especially, but the events of the last ten years had affected her in ways none of us could have anticipated. When she saw the antique gold brooch encrusted with diamond and ruby chips that Michiko and I had picked out for her, she'd frowned before seeming to remember she was supposed to be delighted. Then she only smiled. I noticed too over the course of the following year that she never wore it, even on the occasions when it would have been appropriate, so I abstained from giving her "baubles" after that and concentrated on more practical things. She never frowned at warm sweaters.

I drove by the jewelry store now only because it was on my way to the carriage house, was surprised to see Junior's bronze Chrysler New Yorker Brougham parked in the side lot and to glimpse him moving around inside the store. I pulled into a diagonal parking space almost directly in front of the building and got out. He saw me immediately, strode to the door, unlocked it and let me in. A sign in the window announced the place would be closed for ten days due to a death in the family.

We shook hands and exchanged the conventional platitudes.

"I noticed your car outside."

"Stopped by to pick up my running gear. Usually go from here to the health club after work. Like to run a few miles to unwind."

"Great release," I said. "Always enjoyed the sense of freedom, the chance to let my mind wander."

"Exactly." For a moment we experienced the bond athletes share—until he remembered he was talking to a man who no longer had legs. Self-consciousness stiffened his features and his eyes shifted to avoid mine. The reaction was all too familiar. "Is there something I can do for you?" he asked.

I reminded him he'd given Burker permission to pass the colonel's uniform to me. "Are you sure you don't want it for his interment?"

"He'll be buried in the one he wore when he retired. The police lieutenant who talked to me said you requested the old uniform for the Bicentennial display at the mall."

I explained what I had in mind. He approved without hesitation. "It's obviously what Dad wanted."

"There is one other thing." I removed the snapshot from my shirt pocket. "This was in the blouse. Lieutenant Burker thought it might be your sister."

Junior examined the slightly faded photo. "Oh, that's Stacey all right." He studied the image a little more closely. "I don't think I've ever seen this picture of her before though. I'm sure I'd remember that bow."

"It's the kind of thing a serviceman, stationed far away from home, might carry to remind him of who he'd left behind and why he was fighting for his country. I'd like to include it in the display. I'll need your sister's permission, of course."

"That's easy. She's here in the back. We were going to breakfast . . ."

I followed him past the sales counter, down a short corridor to his private office. It wasn't large. A medium-size wood-paneled desk with a matching credenza behind it. In front of it, a pair of tapestry-upholstered chairs separated by a lamp table left little room for much else. A woman with brown hair that didn't reach her collar stood in front of the desk staring down at an open copy of the morning *Gazette*, detailing coverage of the murder/suicide of the retired doctor and her husband two days before, the case Burker had been investigating when I called him about Bart's death. I'd skimmed the story that morning, marveling that a town where a year or two might go by between homicides, two murders happened on the same night.

"Stace, this is Jason Crow."

Like a teenager caught with a lit cigarette, she jumped when Junior spoke her name, quickly folded the newspaper and tossed it to the side of the desk blotter.

"My condolences on the loss of your father." I extended my hand.

She stared up at me, paused a moment, took my hand and tried to smile.

"I used to run into your dad from time to time at civic luncheons and city council meetings," I said, "but I hadn't seen him in quite a long while."

"You know Mom died a few months ago," Junior said.

"I saw it in the paper." A brief death notice. No obituary. I recalled the woman I'd met at the *Nest*, an uptight, fussy lady who'd been more patronizing than friendly. "I'm sorry."

"I hope we thanked you for the card and flowers," Stacey remarked. "They took Dad by surprise. He hadn't expected anything from you."

Why not? But I didn't bother to ask.

"Alzheimer's," Junior explained. "She died of Alzheimer's. We were lucky, I guess. It only lasted a couple of years."

"*We*? What about *her*?" his sister objected.

"She was out of it, Stace. She didn't know what was going on. She didn't even know who we were anymore."

His sister screwed up her mouth, but I could see she was conceding the point. "He put her away. Sent her to Woodbridge."

Woodbridge Psychiatric Hospital was north of town. My mother had been a resident there twice in the last eight years.

"He refused to keep her at home," Stacey emphasized to me.

"He couldn't, sis," Junior countered with annoyance. "It was the best thing for her. You agreed. She was better off there than she would have been if Dad had brought people in to take care of her at the house. You know how she wandered."

"She was our mother. She was our responsibility."

"We did take care of her the best way we knew how. Dad sure as hell was in no position to deal with her by himself. You weren't here. I have a business. What was I supposed to do? At least I visited her regularly to make sure she was being well taken care of, and so did he."

I could see emotions building. It seemed to me this was an old discussion, much repeated but still unresolved.

"I guess her illness hit him pretty hard," I observed. "Is that why he stopped going out?"

Junior smirked. "It had nothing to do with Mom. He had a little run-in with the Dairy Queen on Fennimore Rd a year or so ago. He was coming home from the commissary on base—"

"After his usual stop at the officers' club," Stacey interjected.

"He was driving west on Fennimore," Junior went on, "when he apparently fell asleep at the wheel, veered across on-coming traffic, ran into the parking lot of the Dairy Queen, sideswiped one parked car and broad-sided another."

"Anybody hurt?" I asked.

"The occupants of the car he sideswiped were shaken up but were otherwise okay."

"Sounds like he was lucky."

"You know the adage. God protects fools and drunks," Stacey said. "He was safe on both counts."

Junior scowled at her. "Fortunately he wasn't driving very fast. The investigator figured his foot slipped off the gas pedal when he dozed off."

"Dozed off. Ha!" His sister jeered. "You mean passed out."

"So what happened?" I asked. "I don't remember reading anything about this in the paper."

"Everybody knew he was sloshed," Stacey lectured. "The DQ manager called the cops. A patrolman showed up minutes later and was giving Dad a hard time—"

Or Bart was giving him one, I thought. I hoped the patrolman wasn't black.

"As luck would have it—" Junior took up the narrative "—a friend of Dad's, a lawyer he and Mom used to play bridge with, was driving by, saw the commotion and stopped. Daddy wasn't coherent. The cop claimed it was because he was drunk. The lawyer insisted he was in shock and needed medical treatment, called for an ambulance and refused to give the police further access to his client until he'd undergone a full medical evaluation."

"So a breathalyzer wasn't performed," I concluded.

Stacey smirked. "And the lab results on the blood they drew in the ER were subject to patient privilege. The cops could have obtained a court order for them, but they decided it wasn't worth the effort. Nobody was hurt. Dad's insurance company was picking up the tab for all the vehicle damage, so they let it slide. The one good thing to come out of it was that Daddy gave up driving."

Which explained why I hadn't seen him in more than a year. "What did he do with his time?"

"He was an avid reader," Junior answered, "Liked to watch old movies, too—"

"Drink, of course," his sister added.

"And the piano lessons he gave," I noted.

"When Mom was alive, he waited until the last student had left before he started drinking," Junior said. "But a few parents had come by my store to complain he'd begun drinking while their kids were still there. They wanted me to talk to him about it. I did, but it didn't do any good. At one time he had about twenty-five pupils. He's down now to less than a dozen."

Could he have had a run-in with an irate parent over his drinking?

"I have to admit," I said, "he struck me as an unlikely music teacher."

"Now. You should have heard him years ago play Dixieland and jazz," Junior replied. "I remember him jamming with some of the bands at the O club when we were stationed in Japan right after the war. Everybody agreed he was really good. Except Mom. To her it was just noise. He stopped playing after we came back to the states, until about five years ago when he realized he was facing forced retirement from civil service because of his age and would have plenty of time on his hands."

"Well, he blew that with his damn drinking," Stacey retorted. "And what he was doing now? Selling everything out from under us so he could move to Las Vegas."

"He was leaving Coyote Springs?" I hadn't heard about that.

Realizing we were still standing, Junior waved me to a chair. Stacey took the one on the other side of the lamp table, and Junior parked his rump on the corner of his desk opposite his sister.

"Last week Dad called my wife," Junior explained, "to let her know he was putting the place on the market and wanted to know if her brokerage was interested in the listing. Rhonda was flabbergasted, as I was when she told me."

Junior got up and slipped into the seat behind his desk. "Dad's family moved around a lot when he was a kid back in Mississippi. Sometimes it was to look for work. Occasionally they snuck out in the middle of the night, one step ahead of the rent collector. In the army we relocated constantly, of course. He swore once he retired he'd throw away his footlocker and stay put. That's why this sudden hightailing it to Vegas came as such a surprise."

"Every time he received orders for a permanent change of station," Stacey complained, "I'd get sick. I hated the term PCS. It meant leaving the kids I'd made friends with, changing schools, being the new girl in class and having to make friends all over again, only to lose them when Dad's next set of orders came through. I hated living that way."

And hated your father for being the cause of it? Michiko was a service brat, too, but by the time she was born her father had retired, and her life was stable, even privileged, as the daughter of a Marine Sergeant Major living in occupied Japan.

"It must have been hard on your mother too," I commented.

"She complained about it all the time," Stacey replied.

"She also loved it," Junior said. "At each new post she'd run for president of the Officers' Wives Club and win. I remember overhearing a senior officer's wife describe her as a tidal wave. It took me several years before I realized it wasn't a compliment."

26

"Mom was determined and focused," his sister countered. "She had to be."

"She was a control freak."

"That's not fair," his sister objected, "and it's not true. Somebody had to take charge—"

"Has this been the longest you've lived in one place?" I interrupted to avert a squabble between them.

"I don't think we ever lived anywhere more than two years," Junior noted.

"Mom maintained that if she'd realized we were going to stay here in Coyote Springs for good she would have found a bigger place than the one on Claremont Street," Stacey said, "something with a formal dining room so she could put all her silver, china and crystal on display."

"There's nothing wrong with that house," Junior objected. "It's not as big or as fancy as Mom would have liked, and it's had the usual problems older houses have, but it was comfortable enough."

"Yet, now, all of a sudden, just like that—" Stacey snapped her fingers "—he decides he's going to sell everything and move to Las Vegas. He didn't even consult us."

"I thought he was crazy," Junior continued, "or pulling one of his pranks. He loved to put people on, to say outrageous things just to get a rise out of them."

Was that what he'd been doing that afternoon at the officers' club eight years ago when he'd practically accused Dad's business partner of driving him to suicide? The racial stereotypes he'd employed to describe George Elsbeth, who wasn't there to defend himself, had convinced me Bart believed every vicious word he spouted.

"But he was serious about pulling up stakes and moving to Vegas?" I asked.

"Yep. That's why he was replacing the roof, not just repairing it. He was also planning to paint the whole place, inside and out. Although, I must say, at the rate Manny was working, Dad wouldn't be going anywhere soon. I'll probably be retired before that guy gets anything finished, and by then he'll have to start all over again. Maybe that was his game plan all along, job security."

"Manny? Are you referring to Manny Hollis?" I asked.

"You know him?"

"Not well." I'd hired him several years ago to paint the trim on a turn-of-the-century two-story house Zack and I were restoring, but Manny had been so slow and undependable that I'd had to let him go. "Why Vegas? Does . . . Did your father have friends or family there?"

"No," Stacey snapped, "but it has plenty of free booze and legal gambling. He told us flat out that was what he was fixing to do, throw our inheritance away."

I was tempted to remind her that it was his money and his property, which she had no legal or moral right to, but I didn't see any such remark as productive.

Thinking that a change of subject might be in order, I commented, "I didn't realize your father was a photographer too. A man of many talents."

"What?" Brother and sister said the word simultaneously and stared at me with the same incredulity.

"How did you know that?" Junior asked.

"The framed pictures on the wall in the master bedroom," I said. "They're quite good."

The siblings gazed at each other in confusion.

"You have any idea what he's talking about?" Stacey challenged her brother.

He half shrugged and shook his head.

"What kind of pictures?" Stacey asked me.

"Young girls with bows in their hair."

She drew back, a frown shadowing her face.

"Jason found a picture of you in the coat of the uniform Dad gave him for the Bicentennial display at the mall," Junior explained.

"Of me?" She seemed stunned and a little pleased. "Really?"

I again removed the snapshot from my shirt pocket and held it out to her. "This one."

Her eyes widened. Her fingers trembled as she accepted it. "Where did you get this?"

"I just told you," Junior stated aid irritably. "It was in the jacket pocket of Dad's pinks and greens."

"With your permission," I said, "I'd like to put it on display with your father's uniform. It'll add poignancy."

Stacey's face had gone pale as she stared open-mouthed at the picture of herself. "No." She slapped the photo face down on the desktop. "Absolutely not. No, no, no."

Chapter Six

I was both taken aback and puzzled by Stacey's reaction. Obviously the photo held some unpleasant associations. Or could it be the opposite? Did it represent a particularly nostalgic moment that she felt was too personal, too intimate, to share with strangers? My mother had pictures like that, ordinary snapshots of her with Brayton Spites when they were still teenagers. I'd found them hidden away, like a secret treasure, while I was cleaning out her room after her last psychotic episode. The breakdown that time had been precipitated by the rumors that her former lover was planning to marry a woman Mom had considered a friend.

"What are you so uptight about, sis?" Junior asked. "It's just a snapshot." He reached across the desk, turned over the faded photo and studied it. "One of his best, I'd say." He slipped it over toward me. "Dad was a pretty good amateur photographer years ago. *Look* magazine even bought one of his pictures. I remember how disappointed he was when they didn't run it, but I can't remember him taking a snapshot in years, certainly not since we transferred back to the states. Mom had an old Brownie Box she used until she couldn't get film for it anymore. After that she usually asked Stacey, her daughter Lisa, or me to take pictures at family get-togethers."

As I listened, I realized I was beginning to see a different Bart from the image I'd created of him. A drunk, yes, but also a skilled musician, a talented photographer, an effective teacher. Even a quirky humorist. A maze of contradictions, because he seemed also to be a hen-pecked field-grade officer, a loud-mouthed bigot and a man without close friends.

"I want to see those other pictures," Stacey announced. "I also want to get what's mine out of that house before it walks off. When are the cops going to let us in?"

"Stace," Junior implored, "What's this all about?"

Burker and his people would keep it out-of-bounds for as long as they needed to collect whatever they thought might be evidence. Once they removed the yellow tape from around the crime scene, however, anything they subsequently gathered from the house would be challenged in court as tainted.

"This is a nightmare," Stacey grumbled. "Damn it, I want to see those pictures."

I hesitated to interfere, but she was so insistent and so clearly upset that I was eager to take another look at that wall to determine if I'd misinterpreted what was there. Using the phone on Junior's desk, I called Burker at the police department. He wasn't in. The desk sergeant suggested I try Colonel Bart's place and gave me the number.

A minute later, Burker came on the line. It took less than thirty seconds for me to explain that I was phoning on behalf of Junior and his sister and why.

"Good timing. I was fixing to notify him we're almost finished. If he gets here before we leave, I'll turn the keys over to him. Otherwise, he can pick them up at the station."

I relayed the information to Junior and his sister, then told Burker, "We'll be there shortly."

"You obviously have an in with the right people," Stacey commented with a smile as I hung up. "I guess I'll call you next time I get a speeding ticket. Oh, damn. My car's in the shop. I asked Junior's garage to take care of the simplest thing, and the next thing I know they're telling me they've discover something else that needs attention." She turned to her brother. "I'll have to ride with you."

"That's fine." He frowned at someone tapping on the plate glass in the front door. "Whoever it is apparently can't read."

We followed him out to the salesroom. A man wearing bib overalls and holding a tool box stood with his free hand raised as he peered into the showroom.

"My electrician," Junior mumbled. "I forgot I called him about replacing the light switch in the back room."

"I don't imagine that'll take long." I turned to Stacey. "I'll give you a lift. Your brother can join us when he's free."

"If you don't mind, I'd appreciate it." Junior's attention was already on his repairman. "I'll be there as soon as I can."

Stacey and I left.

My twenty-year-old Ford pickup was only a few yards away. By long-ingrained habit I went to the passenger-side door and held it open. Stacey seemed surprised by the courtesy.

I circled the back of the truck, got behind the wheel, started the engine and backed out of the diagonal parking space into the stream of traffic on Coyote Avenue.

"My father was impressed by you," she remarked as we proceeded west toward Indian Heights.

"Why's that?"

"He said your first meeting was rather unfortunate, but you never held it against him."

It was an encounter I preferred not to dwell on. My emotions had been raw that day.

"Dad was even more impressed," Stacey added, "when he found out you'd recommended him to tutor your niece."

I hadn't done so enthusiastically, but I didn't tell her that. Eight months ago my brother-in-law Aaron, a classical pianist, had been signed up for a nation-wide holiday concert tour. He was concerned his eldest daughter, Lavinia, who was showing signs of being a musical prodigy, would lose ground while he was away. Finding someone competent to drill her in increasingly complex exercises wasn't easy.

I'd been more than a little incredulous when the people I consulted unanimously lauded Colonel Bartholomew as the best piano coach in town. Aaron had received similar recommendations. I suggested to Debbie and Aaron that they visit him together. If they picked up any bad vibes as a mixed-race couple, they could find someone else. They'd hired him, and Livy's proficiency continued to improve.

"He's a good drill instructor," I commented.

She laughed. "The army DI."

I had to smile myself at my ironic choice of words.

Between lunchtime traffic and having every signal light against me, the trip was stop-and-go. Stacey probably thought I didn't notice her watching me manipulate the hand controls on the old pickup. I wondered why people thought they had to do so surreptitiously. Why not just ask the obvious questions: was manual driving difficult? Was it hard to learn? Few people did, however, as if they were afraid that by doing so they'd remind me I was different. It was laughable, but I'd come to accept that people didn't always act rationally.

"Thanks for the ride," she said. "Junior needs to attend to business, but it sure can be inconvenient at times."

"Glad to be of service." I tooled along Fennimore Road past the Dairy Queen her father had crashed into. "When was the last time you saw your dad?"

"I used to drive up from San Antonio every two or three months to visit my mother. After she died, I didn't see much point in making the trip."

So she and her father weren't close. That was pretty obvious. "The last time?" I prompted.

"Christmas. The family got together for dinner at my brother's. It was right after Mom died. Not exactly a festive time. Funny part is, Dad didn't drink at all that day, not even wine with dinner. I don't know what he did when he got home, of course." She paused. "Junior called me last week about Dad's crazy idea of moving to Las Vegas. I figured I'd better come up and see if I could talk some sense into him."

"So when did you get in?"

"Monday night after my shift at the hospital." She looked over at me and grinned. "If you're looking for my alibi, Junior or Rhonda can probably tell you more precisely. I reckon about eleven."

We arrived at Bart's house. The uniformed cop and civilian standing outside smoking cigarettes didn't stare at me when I got out of my pickup, but I could feel them surreptitiously watching. Being gaped at wasn't a new experience. Since I turned fourteen, I'd been something of a curiosity. I was nearly six feet tall by then. I topped out at six-six-and-a-half when I graduated from college eight years later, literally head and shoulders above about everyone I encountered. Inevitably people gaped, usually with admiration, occasionally with envy, but sometimes with trepidation too. For some, my size in itself was intimidating.

Vietnam changed my life in a way I'd never anticipated. January 31, 1968, the first day of the Lunar New Year, the beginning of the Tet Offensive. Nothing would be the same after that. I continued to be a curiosity, but there wasn't a lick of admiration or envy when people saw me sitting in a wheelchair, a man with no legs. Now, after seven years of marriage to a beautiful woman, three children and a fourth on the way, I liked to think the bitterness and resentment for my fate was behind me, that I'd come to terms with being a double amputee. For the most part I felt confident I had. There were moments though, flashback glimpses of another reality, that twisted my gut. Seeing men in uniform and civilian clothes unselfconsciously strolling back and forth outside Bart's house, carrying satchels and cardboard boxes, was one of them.

Bart's daughter and I reached the side door of the house where a sentry intercepted us. Another flashback. This one to the day I came home to find cops all over the grounds of the *Crow's Nest*. The rookie upstairs in the carriage house had tried to block entry to my father's office. I'd bulldozed my way past him. This time, however, I politely asked for the lieutenant. He must have been within earshot because he appeared almost instantly.

Chapter Seven

"Where's Junior?" Burker looked behind me.

"Nice to see you again, too," I said. "This is Colonel Bartholomew's daughter, Stacey—"

"Ogletree."

Burker extended his hand to her. "I'm sorry—"

"I'd like to see my father's room."

Through the breakfast nook window I saw the Chrysler halt behind my truck and Junior rush up the driveway to join us.

"We've met," Burker noted after the two men had shaken hands. "I bought jewelry for my wife at your store just before Christmas."

"A jade-and-turquoise necklace and matching earrings," Junior said. "I hope Janet liked them."

"Very much."

I was impressed by Junior's precise memory, but on reflection realized I shouldn't have been. Jewelry and personal service in selling it was his stock in trade. I was inclined to think of people in terms of the restorations we'd done for them. The Greek Revival mansion on Mirabeau, the Craftsman house on Hickory, the Art-Deco on Laredo.

"Thank you for coming so quickly." Burker made it sound as if they were doing him a favor. "We're about finished inside, taken a few things. I'll have an inventory of them for you to sign before I leave. If you notice anything missing that isn't on the list. Or if something is misplaced, please let me know."

"Lieutenant," Junior said, "I'm not sure how much help I can be. I haven't been past the dining room and kitchen in several years."

"Neither have I," Stacey added. "As I told Jason, I live in San Antonio and rarely get up here."

"Nevertheless," Burker went on patiently, "I'd appreciate anything you happen to notice that seems out of place."

"You think it could have been robbery?" she asked.

"We're not excluding anything."

Which in my estimation was a non-answer. Recalling the death scene, I'd seen nothing that indicated active opposition to whoever had stabbed the old man in the back. Of course the murder could have been preemptive, killing him before taking whatever it was the thief was after. What might that have been? It didn't have to be big or prominent. A piece of jewelry, for example. But what would make it worth taking a man's life, while leaving behind other objects of value, like the *Imari*? Unless, of course, the thief didn't realize its value. Still, robbery seemed farfetched.

While Burker stepped into the living room to give one of his men instructions, I observed the son and daughter of the deceased as they perused the place. Neither of them appeared nostalgic, much less disturbed by what they saw. I followed them down the hallway to the master bedroom and almost ran into the back of Stacey when she stopped abruptly just inside the double doors. She'd turned toward the wall of photographs.

"That son of a bitch."

"What's the matter?" Junior had preceded her but had veered left, toward the bathroom. He looked over his shoulder, then turned and gaped. "Who are the kids?"

"Students of his?" I asked.

"That's Casey Wabash." Junior pointed to a girl of perhaps six in a ruffled pink dress. "Her dad Billy was in the store just last week, wanted me to restring his mother's pearls."

"That miserable son of a bitch," Stacey repeated angrily.

"What are you so upset about?" Junior asked. "They're just pictures."

"You don't understand. Those bows – they were . . . his fetish."

I watched Junior pull back, not so much physically as mentally. I felt the same instinct. I didn't want to believe what I thought I might be hearing.

"Fetish? What do you mean fetish? Surely . . . you're not su-suggesting—" He stammered, unwilling to complete the thought.

"You never figured it out, did you?"

"Figured what out? What the hell are you talking about?"

"He liked little girls. They turned him on. He liked them wearing big bows in their hair."

"No-o-o. Stacey, don't say such a thing." He shook his head vigorously. "That can't be. Not Dad. He wouldn't—"

She expelled a short, harsh burst of sound. "He molested me, you damn fool. It started when I was about six and went on for years, until . . . until I had my first period. Then he lost interest."

My stomach felt suddenly empty, sour. I'd had good reasons for disliking the man, but this went beyond that.

"I don't believe you," Junior said.

She regarded him with disdain. "Frankly, dear brother, I don't give a damn whether you believe me or not. I know what happened. I know what he did."

My pulse throbbed with anger. For several tense seconds I observed the dead man's two children. Junior stood absolutely still. I'd sensed tension between them earlier. Now I was aware of something different. Rage would have been understandable, but what I saw on her brother's face was contemplation, doubt.

"Well, that explains a lot, doesn't it?" he said. "I can't believe it, but it almost makes sense now. He always gave you whatever you wanted, whatever you asked for, at the same time you disrespected him. I never could understand it. Now I guess I do. It all fits. You were blackmailing him."

"I was making him pay for what he did to me."

The two stared at each other. For the moment at least I realized they'd forgotten I was there. "Did Mom know?" Junior demanded.

"No one did." She turned away, wringing her hands. "It was just him and me."

"And I suppose you convinced him that if it was going to stay that way he had to give you your way, even take your verbal abuse."

She spun around and laughed, but it was more a bitter, contemptuous rasp. "You make *him* sound like the victim. He abused *me*, Junior. Shall I tell you what he did?"

"No!"

"You mean you don't want to know what it felt like when he—" She stopped abruptly when she realized I was standing there, witnessing. In the span of a heartbeat I glimpsed a little girl with tears in her eyes, her lips quivering with humiliation, pain wracking her. Just as quickly the vision evaporated along with the nascent tears. She stepped across the room. Her hands trembled, however, as she gripped the back of a chair. "It was a long time ago."

Plainly, however, she'd never gotten over it. The thoughts, the images going through my mind nauseated me. Young innocence stolen. What should have been the best years in her young life had been corrupted by the man who was supposed to be her staunchest protector. Then the question hit me. What about my niece? What about Livy?

"Tell me about the bows," I prompted to break the charged silence and to dispel the sick taste welling up inside me. I needed movement, action. I shuffled over to the built-in chifferobe.

Stacey took a deep breath, made a visible attempt to rein in her emotions and turned to me.

"It started out as a game. He'd bought me a pretty ribbon and made it into a bow, and he asked me to put it on for him. He liked to see his sweet little girl all dolled up, he told me. He made me feel so special. The next time he asked me to put on a different bow. It was more elaborate, so he had to help me with it. I paid no attention to the touching. It didn't mean anything.

After that came the games and the tickling. The next step . . . well, the next step—"

"Stop, Stacey. Please, stop it," her brother begged.

But she didn't. Maybe after so many years she couldn't. "Then came the fondling, rubbing his hands against my skin, stroking his fingers in places . . ." Another deep breath. "That was followed by the—"

"I said stop it!" Junior shouted. "That's enough. Be quiet."

"You think he did that to all these girls?" I asked and caught a glimpse of Burker in the hallway outside the doors. He saw me but the others had their backs to him.

"Of course he did." It seemed only then that the implication of what she'd said dawned. "I didn't realize he was still doing it. I swear. I thought it had been just me. He stopped with me. I asked him not to do it anymore and he stopped."

"And you believed him?" Junior scoffed.

I didn't remind her that she'd stated earlier it was because of her maturing. My stomach ached. I needed to sit down, not because of my prostheses. I wasn't even aware of them at that moment, but because of the repulsive mental images she conjured up.

Junior turned his back on her, his shoulders raised and stiff. For a moment I thought he was crying.

Suddenly fear, dread possessed me. I began to check drawers. In the top right one I found socks, handkerchiefs, underwear. Nothing unusual. All well-worn to the point of being threadbare. I suspected he hadn't bought any new clothes since his wife became ill.

"Jason—" Burker stepped into the room "—what are you doing?"

I opened the left drawer. A pile of loose photographs.

"Crow, what the hell's the matter with you?" Junior asked.

They were all moving toward me—Burker, Stacey, her brother.

"For God's sake," Junior exploded.

I was staring at more young girls. These weren't the blond-haired, blue-eyed variety. At least one wasn't.

I had to grip the edges of the drawer to maintain my balance. I was staring down at a portrait of Livy, my sister and brother-in-law's oldest daughter, my seven-year old niece with a big yellow ribbon in her hair.

Chapter Eight

"What did you find?" Burker came up beside me and looked over my arm. "Oh, Jesus."

"Livy's picture is here and you didn't tell me?" I was furious and straining not to show it.

Burker knew, of course. We'd had enough encounters for him to be able to read my mood.

"The officer who searched this room told me there were more pictures in the drawer like those on the wall. I scanned the top ones but didn't go any deeper." It wasn't his habit to explain himself.

"You should have."

He didn't reply.

"Michiko needs to see this."

"Who's that?" Stacey asked.

"His wife," Junior answered.

"She's also a pediatric nurse," Burker added.

I made my way over to the bedside telephone, got a nod of consent from Burker, sank into the armchair beside it, lifted the handset and dialed home. She answered on the second ring.

"Clyde Burker and I are at Colonel Bartholomew's place, and we'd like your expert opinion on something . . . Yes, it's important. You know the address. How soon can you be here?"

After a few more exchanges, I hung up. "Half an hour, tops."

We were fortunate to have a live-in housekeeper who adored our kids and who was adored in return. Lou Flores was also Brayton Spites' sister and therefore my biological aunt.

Stacey asked, "Why are you having your wife come here?"

"I don't know who all those kids are," I replied, "but if, as you suggest, they are victims of molestations, they'll need counseling when we identify them. My wife can help. As for Livy—"

"The black girl in the top photo?"

I set my teeth. Was this woman her father's daughter? Why black? Why not just girl? But it wasn't the racial word I found offensive but the way she emphasized it. I saw Burker's lips tighten. We didn't always think alike. His attitudes toward race had been close to old Bart's at one time, and maybe under different circumstances he would have asked the question in the same way, but for the moment we were in sync.

"She's his niece," Burker told the others. "Lavinia Elsbeth."

"Elsbeth? Aaron Elsbeth's kid?" Junior asked. "Oh, Christ. I had no idea she was one of Dad's pupils. Why is she? I mean, her father's a concert pianist."

"He was on the road last fall," I explained. "He needed someone to supervise Livy's practice while he was out of town. It wasn't for long, a few weeks."

"Dad wanted to teach me to play," Stacey said almost nostalgically, or maybe she was just grateful for the opportunity to change the subject. "But I wasn't interested. He taught Junior, though."

"Or tried to," her brother commented, his irritation showing. "I was never very good."

"Livy started playing when she was four—" I couldn't help bragging "—and she is good."

We spent the next twenty minutes passing around the photos from the drawer, twenty-three of them. Junior was able to identify one more, Burker three. I didn't recognize any of them, neither did Stacey.

"Boss, Mrs. Crow's here."

I swiveled in my seat and looked over my shoulder. Michiko circled around the uniformed officer who'd just announced her and strode up to me. Her beautiful face was a porcelain mask of concern. After eight years it still irritated the hell out of me that I couldn't jump to my feet when a woman entered the room.

She bent and kissed me on the forehead. "What's going on?"

I motioned to Burker who handed her the photograph.

"Livy? I don't understand. That bow, I can't imagine Debbie—"

I watched horror widen her dark eyes as Burker and I explained the situation.

"My God!" She bit her lips. "Livy?" She surveyed the wall of framed photos. "All these?"

"That's not the half of it." I pointed to the drawer in which I'd found our niece's picture.

"Your people found those pictures and didn't think there was anything suspicious about them?" Michiko challenged Burker.

"There was no reason they should. One of the two bedrooms across the hall is a photographic studio. The other is a dark room."

I turned to Junior. "You said your father didn't own a camera, and now we find all this. What the hell's going on?"

Burker stared at him as well.

"I told you I haven't been past the living room in years. Why should I?

This isn't my house. I don't live here. He must have put all this stuff in after Mom became too out of it to object."

"Those were our bedrooms," Stacey turned toward the door. "What's he done with the things that were in them? Some of the collectibles were valuable."

I rose. The four of us trailed Burker out into the hall. He opened the door of the room on the left and flipped the wall light switch, revealing the studio he'd mentioned. The two windows in the far wall were covered with aluminum foil to keep out the light. Between them a canvas backdrop showed a bucolic pasture with shady woods in the distance. In front of it a diminutive park bench. Draped on the wall to the left was a blank white sheet, used no doubt for basic portrait shots.

"The dark room is next door," Burker informed us.

I'd dabbled in photography when I was in high school. Nothing original or particularly imaginative. I'd been more interested in the science of it than artistic content. I recognized the equipment, the trays, the bottles of chemicals. It brought back pleasant memories but no particular nostalgia.

"This abusive behavior of his," Michiko said, "how long's it been going on? Since he put in this studio?"

"A lot longer than that," I answered. "He molested Stacey when she was a child."

"She says he molested her," Junior objected. "All these years later, when he's not around to defend himself. Just because she says it doesn't make it true."

Michiko stared at the woman. I saw daggers in my wife's eyes and wondered if the others did. "Who did you report him to?"

"No one. He stopped," Stacey insisted. "I told him to stop and he did."

"You're a nurse—" I started to say.

"A nurse?" Michiko exclaimed. "You've received medical training? Then you're aware that sexual predators don't just stop." She breathed hard. "You knew your father preyed on little girls and you did nothing to stop him? What the hell's the matter with you?"

Michiko rarely used strong language. I decided I'd better intervene. I turned to Burker.

"If what we suspect is true—"

"You're jumping to conclusions," Junior complained.

"If what we suspect is true," I repeated, "those children have to be identified and their parents informed of what may have happened."

"I'll talk to the chief. I reckon he'll want to set up a special task force to find out who they are and interview each of them. Might take some time."

"Chances are they know each other. This isn't Dallas or Chicago. Coyote Springs is still a small community." Which made me wonder how this could have gone on for so long without word getting out.

"Why didn't you report your father to the authorities?" Michiko challenged Stacey.

"Daddy warned me if I told anyone, he'd hurt them. Besides, he said, nobody'd ever believe me anyway. People would call me a liar, and they wouldn't like me. I wouldn't have any friends." What a terrible threat to make to a young girl. Such sadistic cruelty was unforgivable.

"Did you talk to your mother about what was going on?" I asked.

"Mom didn't know."

"Wrong," Michiko said sharply. "She knew. Your mother knew. She knew or at least she suspected."

"She didn't," Stacey protested angrily. "She never knew."

"How dare you," Junior erupted at Michiko. "You weren't there."

"But you were." I watched my wife stare him down. The room was dead silent for the next few seconds.

Finally I spoke up. "They'll need professional help."

"Dr. Kershaw at Clover has been recognized as one of the best child psychologists in Texas," Michiko said. "I'll talk to her about counseling for Livy and the others."

"I hope she's better than Webley was. Stacey went to her for years. Nobody would ever tell me why, but you can see how much good she did her."

"Shut up!" his sister shouted. "Just shut the hell up."

"You were one of Dr. Webley's patients?" Burker asked.

"Clients," she corrected him. "That was fifteen years ago."

"In the meantime, I'll have my people go through this place again," Burker announced. "I saw a bunch of 8mm movies in a bookcase. Let's see if they're what the labels say they are."

"I'll call my sister," I said, "and tell her we have to get together." I just hoped she wouldn't hate me when she found out what I had to say, that I may have been an accessory to her daughter's rape.

Chapter Nine

My wife's father was from Alabama. She'd spent her childhood summers with his family there and could be as laid back as Scarlet putting off till tomorrow what inconvenienced her today or be as aggressive as a hound dog on a foxhunt. Despite her beauty, the slant of her eyes meant she didn't quite fit neatly into the black/white social divide, and of course the Japanese had been the enemy, as if a child had been responsible for the Second World War. The sting of her American cousins' words and attitudes resulted in her developing a special affinity for my sister Debbie who was married to a black man and whose kids were seen as all black, not half white.

I sat by and listened with one ear as she spoke with Debbie on the phone and arranged for us to have dinner at their house. My sister was naturally on the alert. I didn't have to hear the other end of the conversation to figure out what was going on.

"I don't know that anything's wrong, Deb. Just some things we need to talk about. Would you mind calling Nancy and inviting them over too."

Debbie said something else I couldn't hear.

"Don't worry about it. How about fixing your Salisbury steaks on Kaiser rolls?" Hamburgers by any other word. "Yep. We'll see you around six."

While I was monitoring Michiko's half of the conversation, I was also listening to Burker tell Junior and his sister they were free to leave. I had to hand it to the professional cop. Despite what he'd admitted earlier, that he didn't think highly of Stacey Ogletree, his manner was completely neutral when he informed her that because of the new evidence he wasn't releasing the house to the family yet. It was still a murder scene and possibly the scene of other crimes as well. She and her brother would be advised when the status changed. In the meantime they were to take nothing from the premises.

Stacey wasn't pleased with the decision and didn't hesitate to voice her displeasure. Burker let her comments slide.

"She's a regular Jekyll and Hyde," I remarked after they'd left. "She was pleasant enough on the drive over here with me."

"Why'd she come with you?"

"Her car's in the shop."

"The Mercedes? I thought those expensive German cars were invulnerable."

"Apparently she took it in for something minor, and they found something else."

"Ain't nothin' easy or cheap. Especially on a Mercedes." He smirked. "I stopped her years ago when I was still on patrol. She was driving a Continental at the time. Different husband, different car. Tried hard to convince me it was in my best interest not to give her a ticket. I did anyway. Two days later I stopped her again. She ranted, insisted I was out to get her, made a few threats. I called her bluff, told her if she didn't calm down I'd take her in and let her cool off in a holding cell. She shut up only when I removed the cuffs from my belt. If she'd had a scalpel in her hand at that moment, I'm convinced she would have cut out my heart."

It sounded like she took after her mother in the sweet and cuddly department.

Michiko ended her phone call and joined me. "How many husbands has she had?"

"Four, the last I heard, but there are so many more expensive cars to experience."

There was nothing to keep us at Bart's residence. Michiko and I left, she to go to the hospital, where she would contact Dr. Kershaw to arrange, we hoped, for the child psychologist to interview and counsel Livy sooner rather than later. I was on quite another mission.

Bart had been giving piano lessons for around six years, an occupation that gave him repeated opportunities to come in contact with children. If, as Stacey claimed, the hair ribbons were his fetish, it seemed unlikely over so long a period he'd be satisfied with merely seeing pretty ribbons in their hair. He'd want to touch. The question was had he?

Child Protective Services would have a record of any complaints that had been lodged against him, as well as any actions, legal or administrative, that had been taken. Their office was in one of the oldest municipal buildings in town, an unpretentious, badly eroded but tasteful embellished edifice. I pulled into a parallel parking slot not far from the front door.

The three-story building had no elevator. Fortunately the CPS office was on the first floor, behind the marble and iron staircase. It looked very much as I'd expected. Crowded, run down and chaotic. The person I wanted to see was Lena Trace, the head of the department. The receptionist, a woman in her early thirties, looked harassed in the maelstrom of noise created by two crying infants and a manic toddler, who was slamming toys from a box in the corner against tables and chair arms. The young Anglo woman, presumably her mother or guardian, sat reading a movie magazine a few feet away.

"I'd like to see Ms. Trace," I told the woman behind the desk.

"I'm sorry, she's not available right now."

There was a crash behind me. The receptionist winced but took no action to discourage the offensive behavior.

"When can I see her?"

The door to my right opened and a man and a woman emerged.

"That's the third time she's been stopped for drunk driving," said the woman, probably in her mid-fifties, "and the third time she's left the baby alone. She's blessed with good neighbors who obviously care about the child more than she does. The judge will sign the protection order this time, then take the kid. We'll see if mama even notices he's missing."

"Ms. Trace?" I stepped forward.

She ignored me and continued her conversation with the man. "Start the paperwork to permanently remove the child from her care."

"What about the father?" he asked. "He's been trying to get custody since the baby was born. Shouldn't we give him a chance to decide if that's what he really wants?"

"All he's interested in is getting back at the mother. He doesn't give a damn about the kid. They never do. It's a game to them."

I wondered who "they" were.

"Ms. Trace, my name's—"

"Call me if you have any problems with his honor," she instructed the man, then turned to go back into her office.

"I'd like to speak to you," I said, raising my voice over the hammering sounds behind me.

She finally acknowledged my existence by spinning around and glaring at me. "Do you have an appointment?"

"No—"

"Get one." She again turned away.

"Ms. Trace, this will only take a minute."

She stood stock-still, her back to me, inhaled and breathed out. "Oh, very well. Come in, but leave the door open."

Knowing the emotional issues she dealt with, I understood the order. Inside the room she waved me to a chair across from her desk. "Are you here to file a complaint? My receptionist can help you with that."

I explained the purpose for the visit, that I had reason to believe Colonel Bartholomew had molested little girls who came to him for piano lessons, and that I would like to know if any complaints had ever been filed against him.

"I can't help you, Mr. Crow. You are free to file an official request, and naturally I'll comply . . . in due course—"

"Bartholomew is dead, Ms. Trace."

"But whoever may have complained about him presumably isn't. I have an obligation to protect the privacy of any victims he may have had."

My blood was beginning to boil. "How are we supposed to protect children, Ms. Trace, if everything is kept under wraps?"

"I understand your perspective," she replied. "I hope you can see mine. My duty is to protect the living victims of predators. There aren't too many ways we can hurt the miscreants who abuse women and children. The best I can do is help protect them from being further victimized."

I wanted to ask her how she was protecting those victims when she was hiding their victimizers, but I'd beaten my head against enough bureaucratic stone walls in the past ten years to know they were hard and impenetrable.

A funk of frustration shrouded me as I climbed into the cab of my truck. I'd been looking for the easy way. Now I decided to go about the task the smart way.

Chapter Ten

I drove home to the ranch, all the while dreading Debbie and Aaron's reactions at being informed their young daughter might have been sexually molested. The stages of grief applied to more than just death and mutilation. We all experience them to varying degrees upon receiving bad news, but even death and mutilation paled in comparison to the corruption of youth, the violation of innocence.

I stripped off my shirt, washed up, put on a clean polo, then drove over to the Elsbeths' house in the Cottonwood district. The two-story Dutch colonial on Conklin Street had been built in the mid-1920s on a double lot. Over the years it had been erratically maintained and generally neglected—until Aaron bought it three years ago. Zack and I spent four months renovating the inside, including removing several walls to enlarge living spaces. Next year Aaron planned to install a swimming pool.

I parked in front of the detached two-car garage and was met at the open back door of the house by my sister and brother-in-law.

"What's going on, Jason?" Aaron stood behind Debbie, his fingers lightly touching her shoulders. From the music room I could hear crisp arpeggios being repeated in quick succession. At almost eight, Livy could play better than I'd been able to after six years of lessons.

"Has Michiko called?"

"You haven't answered my question."

"I'll explain it all as soon as she and the others get here."

He frowned. "So mysterious. I hope it's good news."

I stepped inside. Debbie was about to close the door behind me when Michiko pulled up the driveway and parked her yellow-and-tan Dodge station wagon next to my pickup. Zack and Nancy were behind her.

"Were you able to talk to Kershaw?" I asked as Michiko approached.

"Yes."

"Kershaw?" Debbie asked. "Dr. Kershaw, the child psychiatrist?"

"What's going on?" Aaron was generally a laid-back guy, but there was no mistaking the tension.

"Let's go to the kitchen," Nancy suggested, then asked Debbie, "Need help with anything?"

"Everything's ready. Just light the grill and put on the burgers."

The six of us sat around the breakfast nook table. Debbie had set out a tray with a pitcher of tea and glasses filled with ice.

"We're waiting," Aaron said to me after everyone was served.

I took a deep breath. "As you know, Colonel Bartholomew was killed two days ago, stabbed in the back with a kitchen knife."

"You found the body," Aaron reminded me. "Yes, we know."

I told him about walking through Bart's house while I was waiting for Burker and noticing in his bedroom a wall of framed photos of young girls with big bows in their hair.

Aaron was getting restless with what seemed to be meaningless information.

I explained about finding a similar picture in the colonel's uniform coat, my establishing that it was of his daughter Stacey, and her reaction when I asked for permission to display it with the uniform.

"This is all very interesting, Jason. At least I guess it is," Aaron finally interrupted, "but what's it got to do with us?"

"She claimed those bows were her father's fetish, that he'd used hers as an opportunity, an excuse to fondle her, that for several years he continued to abuse her."

"What's that got to do with . . ." Debbie's words trailed off as her green eyes widened. "Oh, my God! Are you telling me—"

"In a drawer in his bedroom," I said quietly, "I found photos of other little girls wearing bows in their hair." I paused. "Among them was one of Livy."

For a moment nothing happened. Then came the explosions.

Debbie jumped to her feet, knocking over the chair she'd been sitting in. "No, no, no. It's not true. Nothing happened. I was there . . . the whole time . . . except . . . " Her words faded.

Aaron turned to her. "You didn't leave her alone with him, did you? You were always with her, right? So nothing could have happened." The relief in his voice was palpable, yet tinged with anxiety.

"I was with her the whole time," Debbie replied shakily, "except for a few minutes on the last two visits."

"What?" Aaron's black eyes widened, became fixed. "You left her there alone. You took her over there and left her with that dirty old man!"

Debbie cringed, as if he'd slapped her. Her cheeks grew red. "I didn't," she cried. "I didn't leave her alone with him. The housekeeper, Rosa, was there. She promised she'd watch her."

"Why didn't you stay?" Aaron was breathing hard. "What was so God damned important that you'd leave our daughter with a stranger?"

"Bart wasn't a stranger. Not after a while. Rosa isn't a stranger either. We'd talked whenever she was there during the lessons. She told me about her family, about how proud she was of all of them. Her oldest daughter's a lawyer."

"Why did you leave her?" Aaron demanded again.

"I had grocery shopping to do. I was gone about forty-five minutes each time."

"Forty-five minutes is plenty of time—"

"Hey y'all, take a deep breath and calm down. Now's not the time . . ." I glanced toward the other end of the house where Livy was practicing a *fortissimo coda* on the piano. "Let's figure out if it happened, then . . ."

Aaron glared at me, his powerful arms folded across his chest. "You recommended him. You said . . . Are you sure this happened? Are you absolutely certain?"

"No, I'm not." I was still sitting at the table. I stood up. "It's speculation, Aaron. That's all. Speculation based on what Stacey claimed happened to her nearly forty years ago. The police will identify the other girls and interview them, and Rosa, the housekeeper, too, to find out what he did, if he did anything."

"Isn't it strange that in all these years no one's come forward with a complaint?" Nancy muttered. "I mean, wouldn't you expect someone to have said something?"

"I went to CPS to see if any complaints had been lodged against him," I said, "but the woman in charge refused to give out any information."

"Lena Trace," Michiko said. "I could have told you that you wouldn't get anywhere with her. Fortunately I have a friend in CPS. Wendy's been there longer than anyone else and should have gotten Trace's job, but that's not important right now. I talked with her this afternoon. She hasn't heard of any complaints against Colonel Bart, but she'll check the records to make sure and let me know."

"Chances are this is nothing," Zack said. "You haven't noticed any difference in Livy's behavior, have you?"

Both parents shook their heads, but I could see in their expressions that they were second guessing themselves.

"I don't know about Bart's daughter Stacey," I went on. "What she's saying may or may not be true. It supposedly happened when she was a little kid. It could all be a figment of her imagination, a misunderstanding. Or she could be lying. Livy didn't react to the news of Bart's death. I think she would have if he'd represented a threat of some kind."

"What do we do now?" Aaron demanded. "Tell me what I have to do. I'll do anything." Tight fists made the veins in his arms bulge.

I understood what he was going through, the feeling of utter helplessness, the unquenchable thirst to return to the world he'd left only minutes earlier. I could have told him there was no going back. There's no bargaining with destiny. No retreat.

We make the best of the hand fate deals us.

"For now," Michiko said, "you do nothing. I spoke with Dr. Kershaw this afternoon. She's handled hundreds of cases of sexually abused children."

Her choice of words, while necessary and unavoidable, provoked Debbie into a new spasm of crying.

"Go on," Aaron prompted through clenched teeth.

"She's agreed to perform a forensic interview with Livy to determine whether any criminal activity took place. She's also agreed to give Livy therapeutic counseling if necessary."

Aaron turned around and slammed the bottoms of his fists on the kitchen counter. I didn't have to see his eyes to know there were tears in them. His shoulders trembled. At last he filled his lungs with air and turned around again to face us. His dark skin had taken on an ashen pallor I'd never seen before and wouldn't have thought possible. He'd aged ten years in five minutes. He was leaning against the sink counter in such a way that made me wonder if he could have remained upright without its support.

"When? How soon?" His voice was stronger than I'd expected it to be.

He gazed at Debbie, whose head was still cradled on her arms. With what seemed like a supreme effort, he straightened up, squared his broad shoulders, walked over and stood behind her chair. Uncurling his long fingers, he began to gently massage her neck.

"I shouldn't have sent her to that man." He kneaded her shoulders. "I didn't like him, but he had all the right answers. He knew music. He had a decent piano, and when I asked him to play something, he chose a ragtime number by Scott Joplin that wasn't easy. I'd taken a little known piece by Franz Liszt which I asked him to sight-read. He seemed more amused by the request than insulted. He played it competently, made a couple of mistakes which he accurately acknowledged. If I hadn't known his reputation as a drunkard and a bigot, I probably would have liked him."

"Did he do or say anything that disturbed you?" I asked.

"Nothing. I was frankly hoping he would, so I'd have an excuse for not hiring him, but he was gentlemanly, courteous and professional. He wasn't patronizing or condescending. One sidewise glance and I would have happily rejected him."

"Me, too," Debbie said.

"I had no doubts about his musical qualifications," Aaron concluded. "My big fear was that Livy would be subjected to racial innuendoes that would be hurtful."

"Not that she hasn't heard them before and dealt with them." Debbie's words were muffled by her crouched posture. She raised her head and straightened in the chair, a signal to Aaron to stop. "I didn't like him at first either, but I couldn't think of a single reason for Livy not to go there for her lessons. After all, it was only for an hour, and I would be with her the entire time. I was, except for those last two sessions."

"You did due diligence," I reminded them. "You personally interviewed the man, saw where he lived, asked questions and got character references from parents of his other pupils. You did everything you reasonably could."

"Obviously it wasn't enough," Aaron snapped.

"Don't beat yourself up," I said. "There's only one person responsible for what happened, *if* it happened, and that's Bart. He alone bears the guilt."

"The key is *if it happened*," Michiko reminded him. "We don't know that anything inappropriate took place, so let's not jump the gun."

"Don't we?" Debbie retorted sharply. "You told us his daughter said—"

"That he molested *her*," Michiko emphasized, "and I have to admit her story is compelling, if not completely convincing."

"What do you mean?" I asked.

"She said she was molested," Michiko explained, "but she never told her mother, and her brother seemed to be taken completely by surprise by her announcement."

"Junior also said it explained a lot in hindsight," I reminded her.

"That she was able to blackmail him with the threat of going public shouldn't be a surprise," Michiko said, "but it doesn't make the underlying allegation true. Bart was a military officer on active duty. If his daughter came out with such an accusation, his career would have been over. He never would have recovered from the charge. You've reminded me more than once, Jason, that you can't prove a negative. If a woman yells rape, there isn't a damn thing a man can do to prove he didn't do it."

"Is she really that much of a bitch," Debbie asked, "that she'd lie about something so serious?"

"Even if it's all true, what does she gain by ruining the man's reputation after he's dead?" Nancy asked. "All she's doing is making herself look weak."

"It makes her a victim," I replied. "We need to get as much information as we can before we—"

"Someone's going to have to ask Livy what happened," Aaron said. "Oh, God, I can't. I can't ask her if he did . . . what he did." He covered his face with his hands. I wanted to weep for the man. If anyone touched my daughter Rachel . . ."

"That's what a forensic interview is for," Michiko told him.

Still blocking her eyes with her hands, Debbie said, "You used that term before, forensic interview. What does it mean?"

"It's a technique used mostly with children to determine if they've been mistreated in any way. Most commonly it's about sexual abuse, but it could be any kind of mistreatment."

"Interrogation," Aaron declared angrily. "You think my daughter has been sexually abused, and now you want to interrogate her, like she's the criminal."

"Aaron," I cautioned.

"It's not like that," Michiko said patiently. "Livy won't get the third degree. She'll be questioned, yes, in a friendly place where she won't feel as if she's being blamed or punished for anything. With young children it's frequently in a school room where they can draw with crayons or play with dolls. The interviewer, if he or she is any good, asks indirect questions and works a subject until the picture becomes clear. Sometimes it takes more than one session, but that's all right. The child needs to feel comfortable telling his or her story."

"Will she have to testify in court?" Debbie asked.

"Not in this case. Bart's dead. There's no one to prosecute. This interview will be to find out if he actually did anything wrong so that Livy can receive counseling."

"Let us be ever thankful to God that Mortimer Bartholomew is dead," Aaron muttered, "because now I won't have to go to prison for the rest of my life for killing the son of a bitch."

There was a moment of silence.

"Can one of us be there with her?" Debbie asked. "I don't want her to face this alone. She needs to know everything's all right, that no one is mad at her."

"The interviewer has to talk to her alone," Michiko explained. "You can understand why. Even when there's a strong, healthy bond between parent and child, the child will be reluctant to admit something happened for fear of being blamed for disobeying some rule. It's better for the child to be alone, under no sense of pressure."

"She couldn't have done anything wrong," Aaron objected. "She's not even eight years old."

"But she may blame herself if something bad happened," Michiko said. "That's the way kids are. They want so much to please their parents that when something goes wrong they think it's their fault."

"None of it's her fault," Aaron insisted, his voice raised. "It's my fault for insisting she go there to practice."

I interrupted them by asking Michiko, "When did Kershaw say she could interview her?"

"Tomorrow afternoon. She wasn't sure where yet. Said she'd call or leave word where to take her."

"I still think one of us should be with her. Debbie's right," Aaron said. "Livy'll feel more secure if one of us is by her side. What about us? When does Dr. Kershaw interview us?"

"She probably won't," Michiko replied. "She's only interested in what Livy has to say."

"But—" Debbie raised her head "—that doesn't seem right. How can she understand what Livy is telling her if she doesn't know what she's like? Who knows her better than we do?"

"She's trained to read body language," Michiko explained. "She'll be able to evaluate it better is she doesn't go in with preconceived notions of what to expect."

"Ignorance might be bliss," Aaron snapped, "but it's still ignorance."

Chapter Eleven

I wasn't one to sit around and wait for people or information to come to me. The first thing I did Friday morning after my swim, shower and shave was call police headquarters in Coyote Springs. The desk sergeant told me Lieutenant Burker wasn't in yet. I left a polite message, requesting he call me at his earliest convenience. Then, I hoisted myself into my wheelchair and was making my way to the kitchen for breakfast when the phone rang.

"Burker." Michiko held the receiver out to me as I rolled up to the table in the bay window. I'd hung up the extension less than two minutes earlier.

"What do you want, Crow? I'm busy." It had become a mantra.

"First—" I humored him "—to say good morning."

"Yeah, same to you. Now get on with it."

"I'm wondering if you'll be in this morning because I'd like to stop in to see you."

"About what?"

"Your prognostications on the game between the Boston Celtics and the Phoenix Suns this evening." In other words I'll tell you when I get there.

"You're rooting for the Celtics, I suppose."

"So you're a Suns fan. I suspected you might be."

"Come on in. I'll be here all morning. Probably. Subject to change without notice, of course."

Fifty minutes later I pulled into the parking lot in front of police headquarters.

I found Burker at his desk, elbow-deep in paper. He glanced up from the formal-looking documents I recognized as autopsy reports. He didn't try to obstruct the identities of the descendants: Webley.

It took a second for me to place the name. "The murder/suicide on the north end of town?"

"The same."

"What happened?" I asked.

"Erma Webley was a retired psychiatrist. Had her license yanked about twenty years ago. Seems she had a tendency to write too many mind-altering prescriptions and convince her patients they had non-existent conditions, among other things. She went into some sort of counseling service after that. Still called herself doctor and hung her medical degree on the wall, but she never officially practiced medicine again."

"Was she the victim or the suicide?"

"Victim. Shot in the chest at point blank range by her husband, Sylvester, who then turned the gun on himself."

"Any idea why?"

"Not a clue. At least not yet. We found some fresh tire tracks that indicated they'd had a recent visitor, but we have no idea who. Haven't been able to identify them yet. Could be a delivery van. If we find out who they belong to, that person might be able to shed light on the Webleys' frames of mind. Doesn't really matter. The case is a slam-dunk."

He'd said that about my father's death, too, and been wrong. He could be wrong now. I refrained from reminding him, though, because a glance told me he was having similar thoughts. Appearances can be deceiving.

"The Webleys were notorious for having loud, if not violent, arguments," he continued. "Sylvester, who was a good ten years younger than Erma, had been her patient years ago."

"Isn't that an ethics violation, having an affair with a client?"

"She discharged him six weeks before the nuptials. Supposedly they became involved only after that." Burker shook his head. "He may not have been mad as a hatter, but the consensus is that he was a little more than eccentric. Definitely liked to do outrageous things, like streak through Coyote Park, butt-naked, on Sunday mornings. Claimed he was communing with God. The unkind rumor at the time was that she married him so she'd always have someone to practice on."

Burker closed the folder and opened the one beneath it, studied the top page, working his lips as he did so. "That's interesting."

Since I refused to ask the obvious, several seconds elapsed before he gave me the answer.

"Bart had a terminal heart condition. Would probably have been dead within six months if somebody hadn't accelerated his departure."

"Digitalis," I said. "I saw the pills on the table when I found him. Six months isn't very long, but apparently somebody couldn't wait. Any idea who that someone might be?"

"It's a process of elimination at the moment. We know it couldn't have been Keith Connors. The rev was at an evangelical conference in California. That's confirmed. As for the others, Junior and his wife Rhonda had friends over at their place for a light supper and bridge. They played until almost eleven. No question about that. Junior's sister Stacey showed up from San Antonio just as their guests were leaving. She parked her car in front of the garage where Junior keeps his Chrysler. A neighbor saw him go out running around midnight. Apparently he's an insomniac and does that fairly often. Stacey's car and Rhonda's Caddy were still in the same places in the morning."

"Didn't the M.E. say the time of death was anywhere between 9 p.m. and 6 a.m.?"

"He's since revised that. Based on your telephone call from Bart around 9:30, he says now it was probably between 9:30 p.m. and 2 a.m. The a/c duct blasting directly on the body complicates matters."

"What about Lisa, Stacey's daughter?"

"Apparently she's not a bridge player. She was home alone."

"So except for Connors, none of them has a firm alibi. What else have you been able to find out?" I asked.

"Those 8mm films of his were twenty years old, judging from the clothes. Amateurish family stuff. Why do people buy movie cameras, then pose in front of them like statues? Anyway, there was nothing there."

"What about the pictures on the wall?"

"His current students."

"Find any boys?"

"In another drawer. All wearing baseball caps turned sideways."

"Another fetish?"

Burker shrugged his massive shoulders. "Anything's possible. Perverts get some funny ideas. What turns them on probably wouldn't do a thing for the ordinary heterosexual male."

It was a subject I'd just as soon not contemplate, except now I had to. This wasn't about my comfort zone, but about Livy's well-being.

"Have you talked to any of them, boys or girls?" I asked. "Were they able to help?"

"Not yet. We found a typewritten list of his students, complete with addresses and telephone numbers, in a drawer of the secretary in the den. We'll be setting up forensic interviews for them." He checked his wrist watch. "In fact, a couple of them should be underway as we speak. It'll take a while to get through the entire list."

"Livy's scheduled to be interviewed this afternoon."

"With Kershaw," he confirmed. "That's good. The sooner the better. Kershaw's the best. You were lucky to get her."

"Can I sit in?" It was a foolish question since I knew the answer, except I hated feeling out of control, and I was desperate to learn everything I could about the situation. In spite of what I'd said to Aaron the evening before, that Bart alone was to blame for what he may have done, I couldn't help feeling I shared some of the responsibility. Nothing was more precious than the innocence of a child and, unwittingly though it had been, I'd contributed to Lavinia's going to the home of a man who may have robbed her of that blessing. "I think Livy would feel more comfortable, and I know her parents would."

"Jason, you know damn well that's not the way we do things. If I let you or any other member of the family sit in on the interview it'll distort the responses we get from her, because she'll either be afraid to tell the truth, or she'll give answers she thinks will please you, not to mention that every other family will want the same consideration."

He paused and looked me straight in the eye. "If I were in your position, I'd want the same thing, but trust me, Dr. Kershaw knows what she's doing. I've seen her interview dozens of kids, victims of violence and witnesses to it. She's good. She knows how to develop rapport with them, steer them to the important points without getting the kids upset. You'll just have to trust me on this, Jason."

I didn't doubt his sincerity or his good will, but . . . "You said you'd witnessed Dr. Kershaw doing interviews," I remarked.

He knew instantly that he'd volunteered too much. To his credit he didn't compound the error by trying to backtrack. "The room she uses has a one-way mirror, like a police interrogation room, except that it's kid friendly."

"You monitored her interviews."

He huffed. "The interviews are monitored and recorded since they may be used in court as evidence."

With his cautious nod I could see he knew what I was about to say next. "Let me watch this one too."

"Me and my big mouth." He got up from his chair. "Let me talk to Kershaw and the D.A."

He excused himself and left the room. Almost half an hour went by before he returned.

"Okay." He closed the door behind him. "They've agreed to let you witness the interview, but there are a couple conditions. First, Livy's not to know. You're not to tell her before or after. Second, you keep absolutely quiet throughout the interview. No comments, no explanations or corrections. The people responsible for monitoring the interview are not to be distracted."

"Thanks, Clyde. I really appreciate this."

Chapter Twelve

It was close to ten o'clock when I reached the carriage house. I gave Zack a rundown on the forensic interview Livy would have to go through—alone.

"Makes sense," he commented. "As a parent I'd go crazy listening to one of my kids recount what some bad man did to them."

"That's the question," I said. "We know Bart was a bigot. The question is whether he was a pervert too. He obviously liked kids. Did he like them too much, in the wrong way? If he had a weakness for touching little boys and girls, how did he manage to keep it secret all his life?"

"It wouldn't have been too difficult in the military, where he moved around a lot."

I nodded. "Junior says they never stayed in one place more than two years until they came to Coyote Springs, but he lived here fifteen-plus years. If he was accosting kids, wouldn't someone have caught on?"

We speculated for a few more minutes, got nowhere, reached no conclusions. Zack called over to the *Nest* and asked them to deliver a couple of grilled steak salads, an innovation George had added to the menu a couple of years ago to an enthusiastic reception.

During lunch our conversation migrated to a more pleasant subject: Hilltop Church.

"Let's check the place out this afternoon," I said. "I hope it's salvageable, but a little-used eighty-year-old wooden building may not be."

"You want to get changed?" In other words, was I going to remove my prosthetics? Ironically I could do more without them, bend, crawl and climb, for example, but there was the inevitable tradeoff. I couldn't carry things that didn't fit into my pockets or belt.

"For now I just want to do a walk-around."

We took my pickup a few minutes later.

"I can see why Connors uses the place as a logo," Zack said when we reached the picturesque landmark. "Must be downright inspirational at sunset with the light behind it."

Hilltop Church was an exaggeration on both counts. It was more a chapel than a church, capable of seating fewer than a hundred people; and the hill was more like a mound in the middle of a wild mesquite-crowded prairie that extended for perhaps a mile in all directions.

I pulled up in front of the modest white-clapboard building. We got out.

Zack brought his clipboard and graph paper as well as the envelope of photographs Connors had given us. The view from directly in front of the story-and-a-half frame structure hadn't changed in eighty years, though the grounds had. The sapling oak trees in the oldest picture were gone, as was the shrubbery in the most recent photos.

Zack got down on his hands and knees and examined the raised stone-and-concrete foundation. "Looks good. No cracks. No patches."

I wasn't surprised. Buildings of that age often survived because they were overbuilt by modern minimalist engineering standards. Consequently they survived better than the newer more scientifically built ones.

The main entrance was beneath the steepled belfry. Zack got out the ring of keys Connor had furnished us. The lock on the narrow double doors needed some jiggling but finally clicked open. Gripping my friend's shoulder for balance—there was no handrail—I mounted the three steps.

The foyer was small and windowless, the bell rope tied to a peg on the right. The nave beyond was daylight-lit by six crusader-arch windows, three on each side, and a rose window above the choir. Flanking the choir were two alcoves, one a vestry, where the backdoor was, the other a combination pantry and cupboard. I opened a few of the built-in doors and drawers.

"Bibles, prayer books, linens and candles," I noted.

Zack unclipped the 25-foot measuring tape from his belt and called out measurements, while I sat on the choir riser and sketched out a rough floor plan.

On the drive back to town, Zack scribbled additional notes on the graph paper as we talked.

"What's your overall assessment?" he asked.

"I like it. I think it'll be a fun project. A few challenges. At least two of the window frames and three of the sash windows need to be replaced. We'll have to be extra careful to save the thin, wavy glass, but the building itself seems to be solid."

"There's dry rot on the north side under the vestry window."

"I noticed that. The wiring will have to be completely replaced, of course."

Electricity hadn't been available in West Texas in 1896. Some farms and ranches still didn't have it fifty years later.

"The post-and-wire circuitry that's there now was probably installed in the 20s," I said.

"Funny, old Bart pushing for us to get the job of restoring the place," Zack mused.

"Maybe he considered it repayment for my recommending him to

Aaron and Debbie for Livy's piano lessons." A recommendation I might regret for the rest of my life.

We'd just entered the drawing room at the carriage house when the phone rang. Zack picked it up at his desk.

"Jason, it's for you. Nelson Spooner."

I recognized the name. Spooner was an attorney in Coyote Springs. I'd never met him, but he was well-known and had a good reputation.

I picked up my receiver. "This is Jason."

"Mr. Crow, this is Nelson Spooner. I represent the estate of the late Mortimer Bartholomew. I'm wondering if you could possibly stop by my office on Monday at 2:00 p.m. If that isn't convenient, tell me what is, and I'll do my best to accommodate you."

I quickly flipped through the appointment book under the lamp on the desk. "Monday at two is fine. Can you tell me what this is regarding and how long it will take?"

"Not on the phone. Monday is time enough. I recommend blocking one hour. I look forward to seeing you. Good bye." He hung up.

"What was that all about?" Zack asked.

"I have no idea."

Chapter Thirteen

Livy's forensic interview was scheduled for 4:00 o'clock. When I picked her up at home that afternoon, I followed the script Burker had passed on to me, that a doctor was looking into Colonel Bartholomew's death, and since Livy had gone to him for piano lessons, the doctor wanted to talk to her about him.

The precocious, seven-year-old was skeptical. I could almost hear her thinking, "Why me?" After all she'd been to his house maybe a dozen times and always with her mother, but she was a good kid and didn't argue.

"Will you stay with me, Uncle Jason?"

"The doctor wants to talk to you privately," I replied, "so I won't be in the room with you, but I won't be far away. You can leave any time you want." As if even a precocious child, especially one brought up to be polite and respectful, were likely to get up and walk out on an adult.

We arrived at an elementary school that was out of session for the summer. Three unmarked cars were in the parking lot, plus a police cruiser. I pulled up the horseshoe driveway to the front door, hung my handicapped tag from the rearview mirror, got out and escorted Livy to a room about halfway down the central corridor. Dr. Kershaw was there to meet us. I reckoned her to be in her late fifties. She had short, wavy russet hair, hazel-brown eyes, and wore large, bulky but colorful jewelry. The three of us chatted for several minutes about school, Livy's family and music. A spinet piano sat in the corner. I wondered if it was a normal part of the room, or if it had been brought in just for this interview. Either way, having it available was a smart move.

Dr. Kershaw invited Livy to play something for her, which was my signal to leave. I was gratified to see my niece had taken to the woman and didn't seem disturbed by my announcement that I was stepping outside.

In the hallway Burker met me and ushered me into a dim adjoining room. A picture window gave us a complete view of the classroom I'd just left. He didn't introduce me to the man and woman already there, sitting on stools. A stool had been set out for me too, but I couldn't use the tall ones, so I stood, watched and listened.

"Where did you learn to play the piano so well?" Dr. Kershaw asked.

"From my daddy. He taught me."

"He must be awfully proud of you."

The glow of pride on Livy's face was unmistakable, but she remained silent, as if she were content to bask in the warmth of the compliment.

"Did Colonel Bartholomew teach you too?"

"Uh-uh. He just helped me practice."

"How did he do that?"

"Told me to go faster. He said being able to do a proper *accelerando* was important."

I smiled at the controlled expression on the doctor's face. She probably hadn't encountered too many seven-year-olds who could let *accelerando* roll off their tongues as easily as the words ice cream.

The questions that followed were broad and innocuous. "What else did you practice when you were with Colonel B?"

"Exercises, but sometimes he would let me play songs and things from a list Daddy had given him."

"Was Colonel B a good teacher?"

"He was all right. Daddy's better. He makes it fun."

"Did Colonel B ever give you candy or cookies?"

"He didn't, but Mrs. Garcia, the lady who cleans for him, did. She brought fruit empanadas sometimes. They were yummy."

They talked more about Colonel Bart, about his house, about having her picture taken.

After a while, Kershaw's questions became more specific, more focused. "Did anyone ever come to Colonel B's house when you were there?"

"A man called Manny did sometimes. He asked Colonel B questions about what to do around the house. Colonel B talked to him, then sent him away."

"Was your mommy with you the whole time you were there?"

"She sat in the corner and read a magazine or just listened."

"Did Colonel B and your mom talk to each other?"

"Not much. Sometimes, when I was doing drills."

"So you couldn't hear what they were saying?"

"Uh-uh, except that they laughed a lot."

"Did Colonel B ever get mad at you when you didn't get things right?"

"He would tell me I could do better, that I had to try harder. He would ask me if there was something I didn't understand about what I was playing, then he'd make me play it again."

"How did that make you feel?"

"I didn't like it, but it felt good when I learned to do it right."

"Did he praise you when you got it right?"

"He would say well done, then have me play something different and come back to it again."

At last came the more disturbing questions. I didn't like them being asked, but I also realized they had to be. They were the reason we were there.

"Did he ever give you a hug or a kiss for doing well?"

"Colonel B? No. Daddy does sometimes."

"Were you ever completely alone with Colonel B?"

"Maybe sometimes when Mommy had to go to the bathroom."

"Did he ever touch your clothing, your hair or your skin?"

"He brushed my hair back if it got in my eyes."

I breathed an emotional sigh of relief. Nothing Livy had said suggested anything inappropriate had taken place, or that Livy was ashamed or embarrassed about her association with him. Dr. Kershaw didn't stop, however.

"Did your daddy ever spank you?"

Whoa! Where was this coming from? I was confused.

"A long time ago, when I was little."

"Did it hurt?"

When had the interview switched gears from Bart to her father?

"Not much," she answered. "He said he would never hurt me, and he didn't."

Where was Kershaw going with this? It rubbed me the wrong way.

"Did he make you cry?"

"Only because I was sorry I made him mad."

"How often did he do that?"

Livy shrugged. "Not in a long time."

"When was the last time?"

She shrugged again. "Before school."

"Did your daddy ever touch you in places where Mommy said he shouldn't?"

Now I knew. That bitch!

"Why would he do that?" Livy asked, her brow wrinkled. I saw fear in her expression.

"That's it." My heart was pounding.

"Wait," the man said above the whisper he'd been using with his colleague. "You know the rules." He stood in my path.

"Get out of my way." I took a step forward, only to be blocked.

"You're staying right here. Dr. Kershaw isn't finished."

"Yes, she is." I tapped on the glass, not hard enough to frighten the young girl in the other room but loud enough to interrupt what was going on.

"You just ruined everything," the woman cried angrily.

"No, Dr. Kershaw did. This interview was supposed to be to determine if my niece had been inappropriately touched or molested by Colonel Bartholomew. It wasn't supposed to turn into a witch hunt."

"I'll have you arrested for interfering with a police investigation," the man said.

I don't take lightly to threats. He apparently didn't know that. "Are you a cop?"

"I'm a—" In other words he was not.

I turned to the woman. "Are you a cop?"

"Well—"

In the other room Dr. Kershaw was facing the window separating us. Livy, still sitting on the piano bench, had also swiveled to face what to her was nothing more than a framed mirror.

I tapped on the glass again. They couldn't hear us talking, but I figured it would be enough of a distraction to halt further discussion or interrogation between the doctor and Livy. In fact, Kershaw walked to the door and opened it.

Ten seconds later Burker burst into our room. "What the hell's going on here?"

"This guy—" the man started to reply.

"We're leaving." I lurched forward. Standing still for so long had made me stiff. Concern momentarily lit Burker's face. I took a second step. The man again tried to intercept me. I wasn't sure he knew who I was or the reason for my clumsy advance. It didn't make any difference. He wasn't going to stop me. "Get out of my way."

"You have just screwed everything up. She was about to tell us—"

I ignored him and addressed Burker. "I want the names of these two people and their roles in this investigation."

"You have no right—" the woman started.

"If I have to jump through legal hoops to get the answers to my questions, madam, so be it, but be advised it will be a lot more painful for you if I do."

"That's a threat. You just threatened us," the man stammered.

"Jason," Burker said, "I don't know what's got you all fired up, but you're out of line, and you're really beginning to piss me off."

My chest was pounding more violently than ever. "Save the lecture and the wounded pride, Lieutenant. Livy and I are leaving. I want the names and—"

"You're making a big mistake—"

"Not my first and probably not my last." I stared at the man. "Will you get out of my way, or do I bring charges of unlawful detention?"

"Jesus." He looked at Burker, who nodded. The man stepped aside, affording me a direct path to the door.

I felt them staring at me as I moved forward. Outside the interview room, I sucked in a raggedy breath, let the oxygen cool my blood, took a more relaxed breath, reached forward, turned the doorknob and entered the classroom.

Livy jumped off the piano bench and ran to me, wrapping her arms around my hips.

"What's going on?" Dr. Kershaw glanced past me to the others who'd followed me but stayed outside in the hall.

"I'm so sorry to interrupt, Doctor," I said, "but we've run out of time."

"I don't understand." She seemed genuinely baffled and kept shifting her attention to the people now in the doorway. "We were supposed to have at least an hour."

"One of those mix-ups, I'm afraid," I explained. "Livy, have you got all your things?"

"I didn't bring anything, Uncle Jason. Remember? You said not to."

"Oh, yeah, right. Well, let's go then."

"But we aren't finished," the doctor objected.

I smiled. "Yeah, you are." I leaned slightly toward her and whispered in her ear. "Don't ever come near my niece again." I straightened and extended my hand. "It's been very enlightening meeting you, doctor. Have a pleasant day."

Her handshake was limp, her expression one of total bewilderment.

I rested a hand gently, reassuringly on Livy's shoulder and guided her out of the room.

"Y'all have a nice day now, hear?" I said in my best West Texas twang, as we walked by the others. They were all pissed at me. Burker was seething, but I had to hand it to the guy. He didn't deck me, which I suspected he would very much have liked to do and might have done if Livy weren't there.

Livy was quiet as we climbed into my truck.

"How about some ice cream?" I asked. We exited the circular driveway.

"Okay." Ice cream was always welcome, but my precocious young niece wasn't going to be bought off that easily. "Why did we leave early?"

I turned onto Fennimore Rd. The Dairy Queen was less than half a mile down the road.

"Dr. Kershaw had already asked the questions she needed answers to." We rode on in silence. "What did you think of her?"

"She was all right, I guess."

"But?" I prompted.

"I think she wanted me to say bad things about Colonel B and Daddy, and I didn't want to."

"That's why we left early," I explained. "I didn't want you to have to answer those questions either."

"Do I have to see her again? When someone tapped on the mirror and she stopped asking me questions, she said we might have to continue another time."

"Do you want to?"

"No." There wasn't a second's hesitation.

"Then you won't."

"Uncle Jason, did I do something bad?"

"Bad? Like what?"

"I don't know, but the way she was talking to me, I felt like I did something bad."

"You didn't do anything wrong, sweetheart. I was proud of the way you answered her questions. You did absolutely nothing wrong."

I pulled over to the side of the road, "How about a big hug."

She threw herself against my chest and hugged me so tightly I was afraid she would squeeze tears from my eyes.

"That's better," I declared, when we both started to relax our holds. "I love you, Livy, just like your mommy and daddy and Aunt Michiko. I don't want you to forget that, and if you ever want to talk to any of us about anything, you can. Okay?"

She wiped her eyes and nodded. "Okay."

I got underway, pulled into the Dairy Queen, where we pigged out on two banana splits with an extra cherry on each.

I dropped her off at home, told her parents everything went fine, not to worry and that I'd fill them in on the details later.

"In the meantime," I said, "I need to talk to Burker. I'll see you later at the house."

Chapter Fourteen

Every few minutes I realized my hands were gripping the steering wheel so tightly it was painful, and I had to make a conscious effort to relax. I was angry, frustrated.

I wanted to think nothing untoward had transpired between Bartholomew and my niece, but could I be sure? If Livy had been molested and was so burdened with guilt that she was convinced she had to hide it—"Uncle Jason, did I do something bad?"—what were her chances of long-term recovery? At the same time, we had to be careful not to plant that very notion in her head. If she got the message that confessing to something that hadn't taken place would please us, we could be doing more damage to the girl than the situation ever warranted. Bend and distort a child's mind so early, and it might not be possible to straightening it out again.

From Livy's account nothing sinister had happened. Her sessions with the old man had been exactly what they were intended to be, piano lessons. Had he touched her improperly? He certainly wouldn't have gotten away with it in my sister's presence. The least indiscretion and she would have kneed him where it hurt the most. No mother would be more ferocious in defending of her child than Debbie.

The only alternative, therefore, was that something had happened when Debbie wasn't there.

The picture of Livy with the big yellow ribbon in her hair, according to what she told Dr. Kershaw, was taken on the last visit. She said Rosa, the housekeeper, helped Livy put it on. Bart hadn't even been present.

But was it true? Could Rosa have been a party to the molestation? It seemed preposterous.

I'd spoken to Debbie in private last night before leaving their house. She reiterated that she'd been with Livy the entire time at every session—except the last two. She'd excused herself on those occasions because she felt comfortable with Bart, had actually come to like the old geezer, as she called him, and because the housekeeper was there to look after Livy.

"Why did you have to leave at all?" I asked.

The first time was because the local supermarket was having a sale on veal, one of Aaron's favorites but something rarely available in West Texas, in spite of it being cattle country. The second time was because a local stationary store was having a going-out-of-business sale on school supplies.

Where was the line between protecting your children and being paranoid?

My intent, following the forensics interview, had been to drive directly to the police station and confront Burker, but my automatic pilot homed to the carriage house.

Sitting at his drawing table, Zack regarded my arrival with intense scrutiny. "Burker called. He asked me, no, he told me to call him the minute you came in. I told him I didn't think you'd be stopping here, that you would probably be going straight home. He didn't seem particularly interested in my opinion, just repeated, 'Call me,' and hung up. My impression is that he's somewhat annoyed with you."

"Pissed, you mean." I grunted. "Call him and tell him I'm here."

Zack waited for an explanation. When none was forthcoming, he dialed the number from memory. "He's here," he stated, then added, "Okay," and hung up.

"Okay what?"

"He said not to let you leave, that he'll be here within ten minutes."

The child in me wanted to rebel, walk out the door to spite him, and I guess it showed on my face because my friend said, "You haven't told me what's going on. Whatever it is, I hope you both calm down enough to express yourselves coherently, if not unemotionally."

I sat in the swivel chair at my desk. "We got sandbagged. Livy and I. We . . . I thought they just wanted to find out about Bart's activities, but it turned into a fishing expedition, except in this case—"

The pounding tread of footsteps on the stairs outside stopped me in mid-sentence. Zack went to the foyer to admit our guest, only to find Burker had already entered, slamming the door against the wall in the process.

"Stop right there," Zack ordered.

"Get the f—"

Zack planted himself directly in front of the head of homicide. All five-foot-two of scrawny muscle against six-feet of sweaty corpulence.

"I said stop and I mean it." Zack's voice was raised.

"Move your skinny little—"

"You take one more step, Lieutenant, and I swear by all that's holy I'll defend myself against an assault to my person and will prefer charges for trespassing, abuse of police power, violation of my civil rights as well as the fourth Amendment to the U.S. Constitution. And while the police chief is trying to figure out what to do with a rogue head of homicide, I'll hire a lawyer to think up a few more offenses, civil and criminal, to charge you with."

"Jesus H. Christ. You two are a pair." He turned in a rage and put his fist through one of the panes of the outside door, which had automatically closed behind him.

I'd watched this showdown from the drawing room doorway. "I'll get bandages."

I went to the bathroom off the office and returned with a role of gauze and another of adhesive tape, as well as a tube of antiseptic. Burker's hand was bloody, but his fist had moved so fast the glass had spewed in front of it. He'd only sustained a couple of cuts pulling back. Fortunately they weren't deep.

"You want to go to the ER, see if you need stitches?" I asked. Zack applied pressure to the cuts.

"Screw you, Crow."

While Zack held a gauze pad firmly against the two cuts I wrapped more of it around his knuckles and taped it securely.

"In the movies they always offer brandy about now. Want some?"

"Drop dead."

"That's what I thought."

I sat in my father's leather desk chair, swung around to the credenza and got out the bottle of Courvoisier that had been there for at least ten years, removed three crystal snifters, wiped the dust off them with my handkerchief and poured generous drams in each.

Zack handed Burker his and picked up his own glass. I couldn't remember the last time I'd sipped cognac in this room. It had to have been with my father. I put the thought aside.

Burker slugged a mouthful of the aromatic liquor, spewed half of it out and choked on the rest. His face became so red I began to worry, then he calmed down and fell against the back of the chair.

"Jason, goddammit, don't you ever put me through a day like this again. I went to the mat to bend the rules to accommodate you. As a friend. Instead, you've—I swear . . ."

He let the words trail. The adrenalin was waning. In a few minutes he'd be weak as a kitten, but I didn't tell him that, figuring he'd find out for himself when the time came.

"You embarrassed the shit out of me today." He swirled the cognac, almost spilling it.

"I'm sorry."

"You humiliated me in front of people I have to work with."

"I'm sorry."

Zack appeared from the foyer with a glass of ice water, which he gave to our guest. "Jason says you sandbagged him."

"Not quite," I objected. "I said we were sandbagged. I'm unaware of Lieutenant Burker having anything to do with it."

He gulped down the water. "I didn't."

"Good," I declared, "then we can still be friends."

Burker took a more conservative portion of brandy, let it linger on this tongue a moment, then swallowed.

"What the hell happened today?" Zack asked from the other chair.

I told him about the interview, that everything seemed to be going all right until Dr. Kershaw started asking questions that clearly implied she thought Aaron might be molesting his own daughter.

"Not might be," I corrected myself. "Was molesting her. Worse, and the reason I put a stop to the interview is that Kershaw was about to plant seeds of doubt in Livy's mind about her father."

"Corrupting youth," Zack muttered.

"I don't know anything about that," Burker said. "I don't have any idea where she was coming from. I've seen her interview kids before and—" his voice faded until it was almost a whisper "—she doesn't normally ask leading questions."

I studied him and exchanged eye contact with Zack.

"What're you thinking?" Zack asked him.

"I'll have to do some checking." He spoke slowly, distractedly.

"On what?" I asked as quietly.

"She doesn't work much with black kids, not in her private practice. But in her public service counseling . . ."

I closed my eyes. "I bet she finds an unusually high incidence of abuse by—"

"It's probably nothing." Burker didn't sound particularly convincing.

"By their fathers?"

"Or stepfathers, uncles, brothers, male cousins, mama's boyfriends."

"So what are you going to do about it?" Zack asked.

"I don't know." Burker polished off the last of his drink. "That stuff's not bad. Better not serve me anymore, though. I can't afford to become an expensive drunk." He climbed heavily to his feet. "Whew."

I didn't bother telling him he would have been lightheaded even if he'd only drunk the water. Zack and I both accompanied him to the outside door. On the landing he turned back to Zack.

"Did you mean it about charging me?"

"Every word of it. I'm a lousy poker player because I don't bluff. If I have the ace, king, jack and ten showing and I raise, it's because my hold card is the queen."

Burker shook his head. "I'll have to remember that. By the way, when

I drove up here there was a beat-up car parked across the street that isn't there now."

"So?" I asked.

"The windows were darkened to the point you couldn't make out the driver's face, but I ran the plates."

"One of those cop feelings?"

"Yeah, the car's owned by Brayton Spites, Bubba's daddy." Burker held the banister as he descended the stairs.

Chapter Fifteen

What we'd planned as nothing more than a cookout at the Elsbeths that evening to bring everyone up to date turned into a slumber party for the children, which didn't surprise any of the adults, though the kids were ecstatic at having come up with what they thought was their own idea. It allowed us adults to sit and talk as late into the night as we wanted without having to worry about hauling sleeping children home and getting them resettled.

Aaron's two-story house didn't have an elevator, so I'd bade Ted, Rachel and Gideon good-night in the living room and sent them upstairs with their mother. I missed the traditional fatherly role of carrying my young children when they grew tired and hauling them sleepy-headed into our house from the family vehicle after a busy day.

Aaron and Zack came down a few minutes later, the ladies right behind them. We went to the music room across from the library.

"Kids often put up pretty good facades to others," Michiko was telling Debbie, obviously continuing a conversation they had started upstairs, "and after a while manage to repress the truth. Then maybe years down the road, something triggers a breakdown."

"Great," Debbie murmured.

"What are we supposed to do in the meantime," Aaron asked, "sit quietly with a fine, single-malt Scotch whisky and wait?"

"Stay alert," Michiko advised, "but constantly bringing up the subject to Livy is a bad idea. We'll either be putting her in a position where she thinks she has to admit to something that didn't happen in order to satisfy us, or she'll bury the experience so deep she may never completely recover from it."

"Let it go for now," I advised. "If later she runs into behavioral problems be aware that this may have something to do with it—or not."

"That's a great help," Aaron muttered.

"The point is we have to be careful not to contribute to the problem and make it worse," I said.

"You're right, of course."

"Wendy, my contact at CPS, stopped by this afternoon," Michiko said. "She wanted to give me a more complete report on what she told me yesterday. It took her a while because she had to work around Mrs. Trace."

"I understand rules and regulations," I said, remembering my encounter with the imperious woman. "They're intended to get the job done in an orderly fashion, not be used to obfuscate."

"Yeah, well, everybody has a rice bowl to protect," Michiko mumbled.

"So what did Wendy have to say?" I asked.

"She was right. There is no file on Bart, but ironically there is one on his wife Hazel. Wendy knew about it because she worked the case."

"What kind of case?"

"One of Bart's young male students complained that Hazel kept walking into the bathroom when he was using it and made remarks he found embarrassing."

"So what happened?"

"Wendy was sent to investigate. She'd hoped to interview Hazel alone, but Bart was home and insisted on remaining present. Hazel in fact didn't say anything, just smiled and left it to him to explain that the boy looked remarkably like their son at that age—the kid was twelve—and that Junior's mom got confused sometimes."

"He said that in front of her and she didn't get upset?" I asked.

"She didn't say a word, just kept on smiling. Bart assured Wendy that's all it was, an unfortunate misunderstanding. He apologized profoundly if the kid felt uncomfortable and promised it would never happen again."

"When was this?" I asked.

"About three years ago. A couple months later Wendy learned that Hazel had been diagnosed in the early stages of Alzheimer's."

"Stacey, Bart's daughter, was very critical of her father for sending Hazel to Woodbridge," I said. "She felt he should have kept her home. Stacey didn't challenge her brother though when he insisted Bart took good care of her."

"It's a difficult disease to deal with," Michiko said. "You can't let your guard down for a second."

"Do you think it's true then—" Aaron sat down at his Yamaha grand, a fifth wedding anniversary present from his father, George "—that Bart didn't do anything?" He started playing Gershwin's dramatic opening of *An American in Paris*.

"Probably." I wheeled up to the bay window, gazed briefly at the last ribbons of gold and violet in the western sky, then swung around to face the others. "But that's my uneducated evaluation. The experts might come to a different conclusion."

"That wouldn't make them right," Zack said from the wet bar on the other side of the room. "Chances are if you presented the case to six of these so-called experts they'd come up with six different opinions."

"Which makes me wonder why they're called experts," I added. "Anyone can have an opinion."

"Four." Nancy settled into a corner of the couch. "That's how many options are available in this case. The victim was molested by person or persons unknown. She was molested by the accused. She was molested by a known person other than the accused, and finally, she was not molested at all."

"Thank God you stopped Kershaw when you did. What a nightmare!" Aaron added from the bench.

The phone rang in the hallway. Aaron kept the ringer disabled in this room. Debbie went over and picked up, then held the instrument out to me. "It's for you. Burker."

I wheeled over. "Jason," I said into the mouthpiece.

"Just thought I'd let you know we've identified all but half a dozen of the twenty-three photos we retrieved from Bart's house. Only four of them have been interviewed so far by shrinks. None by Kershaw. All four girls claim to have been sexually molested by Bart."

Chapter Sixteen

Until Burker's call we could believe the charge of molestation was a figment of Stacey's overactive, even twisted imagination. Now we were forced to reconsider.

"We have nothing but a photograph to indicate physical contact between Livy and Bart when Debbie wasn't present," Zack stressed. "Her absence was only for two brief periods of time, and there was a third person on hand."

"We can't be sure right now if the housekeeper was with her the entire time," Nancy pointed out. "She could have been running the vacuum cleaner at the other end of the house."

"When was the photo taken?" Aaron asked.

"Livy told Dr. Kershaw it was during her last lesson," I replied. "Whether he intentionally waited until Debbie was out to take it—"

"He had no way of knowing I wouldn't be there," Debbie objected. "I didn't know myself until I saw the ad in the paper just before I drove over to his place. Besides, Rosa Garcia, the housekeeper, was there to watch Livy for me. We can ask her if she was with Livy the entire time and if she's aware of any agenda on the old man's part."

"Assuming she wasn't part of it herself," Aaron said.

"Impossible," Debbie responded without hesitation. "I can't believe she's like that."

"Why didn't anybody tell you about the picture taking?" Zack asked.

I answered for my sister. "When he took her picture, Bart asked Livy not to say anything about it because he wanted to give it to her mother as a present."

"So why didn't he?" Aaron asked.

"We'll have to ask Rosa. Maybe she knows."

"If Bart really was touching any of his young students inappropriately and their parents found out," Zack offered, "wouldn't that put all of them on the most wanted list? What greater motive can you imagine than a parent defending, or in this case, avenging the loss of a child's innocence? I'm sure Aaron's reaction isn't unique. In fact, I know it isn't."

Nods all around.

"There's something I still don't understand," Nancy said. "We're assuming Bart touched little girls on a recurring basis. Why didn't any of them speak up, yell out, even fight back?"

"Some of them may have," Michiko replied, "but their parents didn't believe them or simply withdrew them from lessons rather than confront the man and cause trouble."

"Those that did follow-up," Zack added, "could also have been bought off in one way or another."

"Good points," Michiko agreed. "However, other elements factor in as well. Abusers pick on kids they feel are most vulnerable to intimidation. Except to a few really sick perpetrators, they don't want opposition. They want compliance. They don't want a fight. They want cooperation. So they pick the shy ones, and very often these perverts are willing to play a waiting game. For them the anticipation is itself stimulating. It emboldens them to gradually escalate their involvement."

I watched the faces of the others. The discomfort and disgust in their expressions was unmistakable.

Michiko pressed on. "From initial innocent, inadvertent contacts, if the victim doesn't immediately object—and they're not likely to because the molester doesn't make his intent clear and no harm is done—contacts increase and intensify. *I rubbed your neck last time and you didn't mind. I thought you liked it. That's what you said.* And so on. Sometimes the child does like it. The gentle massage of a sore muscle feels good, not to mention the satisfaction of getting close, positive attention from an adult. Experienced child molesters know how to use comforting gestures and reassurances at each advancing level. *Everything's perfectly all right, darling, but let's keep it our little secret.*"

I saw the expressions of outrage and anger on the faces of the others and shared their disgust.

"Bart couldn't possibly have had the time or opportunity to go through all these stages with Livy," Debbie objected. "It's not as if we lived next door to each other."

"Which is one reason why I don't think anything happened," I said.

Aaron bowed his head and breathed. "Please, God, let it be no more than a misunderstanding."

"In this case, I agree with Jason," Michiko said. "With more aggressive predators, however, the situation eventually accelerates from persuasion to intimidation. Prepubescent kids who have no real understanding about what's going on, who have received no moral training, who possess no intellectual sense of what's right and wrong, whose only barometer for wrong may be a vague awareness that what's happening doesn't feel right, isn't fun anymore, if ever it was fun, that it leaves them feeling dirty . . . those kids are the most at risk."

Everyone turned stone-faced.

"No." Debbie shook her head. "Bart wasn't like that."

"I hope he wasn't," Michiko responded. "I hope he turns out to be nothing more than what he seems, an old man who gave piano lessons. I'm simply trying to warn you that predators can be experts at deceiving people."

Chapter Seventeen

Michiko and I attended the memorial service for Mortimer Bartholomew, Lieutenant Colonel, United States Army, Retired, Saturday morning at ten o'clock in the chapel on Coyote Air Force Base. As a veteran Bart was entitled to burial with full military honors in a national cemetery, but at the time of his wife's death he'd made pre-arrangements with Eldridge's Funeral Home to be buried beside her in Coyote Springs, the town in which he'd lived longer than anywhere else in his life.

The simple wood-frame building, not unlike Hilltop Church but bigger, was barely half full. I was in something of a quandary. I hadn't liked the living man and now had reason to further question his moral behavior, yet I felt an obligation to show respect for the soldier's contribution to the defense of his country. He'd been no coward in battle and deserved the martial accolades heaped upon him.

I looked around the chapel at those in attendance and recognized a few senior officers, not the commanders themselves but their deputies, in addition to several civilian employees.

I saw a Hispanic couple in their late fifties or early sixties, sitting in the back, off to the side, away from the rest of the congregation. The woman was short and round, the man stocky and not much taller. The Garcias, I presumed. Rosa, I'd learned from Junior, came to Bart's house every day except Sunday to dust and clean, to fix his lunch and leave a cold plate for his supper.

Across the aisle from them I was surprised to see Manny Hollis, sitting by himself, looking very gentlemanly in a dark blue suit, white oxford shirt and black tie. The only incongruity was the huge, sculpted Afro hairdo. I nodded to him. He nodded back.

The congregation rose. A military guard of honor, resplendent in ceremonial uniforms and white gloves, preceded the flag-draped casket, now on rollers, up the chapel's center aisle.

Behind it, Junior Bartholomew was accompanied by his wife Rhonda, his sister Stacey and a younger woman I presumed to be her daughter Lisa.

The minister for the funeral service wasn't a military chaplain but Lisa's husband, Reverend Keith Connors.

The entire ceremony lasted little more than half an hour.

I was pleased when Michiko and I got outside to find that Manny was still there. We shook hands.

"The police have been looking for you," I said.

"They found me. I told them everything I know, which is nothing, about the old man's death. I also gave them my alibi for that night. I was in Austin, playing jazz in a nightclub."

"I didn't know you were a musician."

"There's a lot about me you don't know, Mr. Crow." He didn't say the words offensively, but the message was clear. *Mind your own business.*

"Weren't you working on the colonel's roof? Do you plan to finish the job? Because if you don't, I can recommend someone to Junior—"

He snuffled. "I don't know why I told the old sot I'd do it in the first place. Tell Junior to get someone else."

The relief I heard in his voice had me staring at his dark face. That's when it struck me. "My God. You're afraid of heights." Just like Zack.

He sucked in his cheeks and looked away.

"That's why you didn't finish the painting job I gave you."

"I'm sure you'll be able to find someone who's up to the task." He said the words without irony—until I caught the twinkle in his black eyes. I chuckled. He walked away.

From the base chapel, the funeral cortege wended its way under a police escort to the cemetery on the outskirts of the city.

The family, along with a smaller number of friends and dignitaries than at the chapel, took their seats around the polished wood casket beneath a white canopy that spanned the open grave. Michiko and I were offered seats in the second row for no other reason, I was sure, than as an accommodation to me. The casket was covered once more with the national flag.

The preacher rose, opened his book but recited from memory the words of the twenty-third Psalm:

"The Lord is my shepherd; I shall not want . . ."

While others had their heads bowed, I studied those gathered. Twenty people, not including Michiko and me. Separated from the group, watching from three rows of tombstones away was the single black man, his hands in his pockets, slouching against a granite mausoleum. The expression on Manny Hollis's face, as best I could read it at that distance and in the shade, was contemplative, as if he couldn't quite figure out what to think. This time we didn't exchange nods, though I was sure he'd seen me watching him.

As those seated rose to their feet and those standing began to shuffle quietly toward their vehicles, Junior announced a reception at his home in Woodhill Terrace, immediately following.

"I hope you and your wife will join us," Junior said to me, once I'd escaped the tangle of folding chairs.

"Thank you." I had no desire to attend the social hour, except that, it seemed to me, there was a reasonable chance the murderer would be there too. I looked around again. Manny Hollis was nowhere to be seen. I extended my arm to Michiko. "Thank you. We will."

Chapter Eighteen

My attendance at veterans' gatherings was something of a predicament for me. I was regarded as a war hero by some, as a war criminal by others. Technically I was a combat casualty, having been wounded during a crucial battle in a war zone. I'd been formally awarded the Purple Heart. Months later I'd felt undeserving of it since my injuries hadn't resulted from combat with the Viet Cong or the North Vietnamese Army or even friendly fire. The man who hated me would have found a way to kill or cripple me regardless of the war.

I'd never gotten a chance to discuss it with my dad. By the time I'd learned the full story, he was dead. I did talk about it at length with my best friend. Ultimately Zack counseled what I was convinced my father would have as well. *Let it go.*

Those assembled around the casket began their retreat to the roadway where their cars and trucks were parked, some with their engines running to keep the air conditioning going. I set out in the same direction, Michiko at my side, but at a crosswalk I took the right fork. Michiko didn't follow. I turned to her. She gave me the merest nod. No explanation was necessary. I resumed my way down the path.

I don't know where she acquired her wisdom. She seemed to instinctively know when to touch me, when to withdraw; when to argue and when to accede. She left me alone in the graveyard that day as I moved with a steady gait toward a modest tombstone that rose only a few inches higher than the ones around it. I halted at its base and read the inscription:

Theodore Crow
1917 – 1968

A breeze rustled through the oak and elm trees. Somewhere close by honeysuckle was in bloom, lending its sweet fragrance to the hot summertime air. Birds twittered. I gazed at the headstone and waited, but my father's spirit wasn't hovering. He'd never been to this place when he was alive. Why should I expect to find his ghost enchanting this particular locale now?

I wasn't a cemetery visitor. I'd come to this gravesite only once in eight years, on the afternoon of my first child's birth. I'd named the boy Theodore Isaac after my dad and my best friend. To "Ted," his grandfather would forever be a mythological ancestor rather than a real person. I had to smile. Dad would have chuckled at being dubbed a mythological ancestor. I wished so much he could have met my children, that they could have gotten to know their grandfather.

I retraced my steps to where Michiko stood in the sprawling shade of a live oak tree. She didn't smile. She didn't say anything. She simply took my hand. Together we strolled to her station wagon. I got in on the passenger side.

The driveway at Junior's home in Woodhill Terrace was already filled with cars and trucks when we arrived. The curbs on both sides of the street were jammed bumper-to-bumper.

"I'll drop you off in front," Michiko said, "and find a place to park."

I wanted to say no, that I could walk like everybody else, but of course that wasn't true. The distance wouldn't be extraordinary, but it would be foolish of me to pretend that shorter distances weren't preferred to longer ones. The day was warm, West Texas warm, the temperature in the mid-90s. Since I expended at least twice as much energy walking as a healthy two-legged man, by the time I reached my destination, I'd be sweat-soaked.

"Thanks," I said. "I don't want to stay long."

I hoisted myself out of the vehicle, negotiated the single step of the curb and proceeded up the slight incline toward the front door. It opened before I reached it.

"I'm so glad you're able to join us," a twentyish woman with long light-brown hair said in greeting and stepped back. "We haven't met." She thrust her hand out to me. "I'm Lisa Connors, Bart's granddaughter."

"It was a beautiful service," I said. "Your husband did very well."

"He's good at ceremonies," she replied.

I wondered if there might be a note of sarcasm in her comment. "My condolences on your loss."

She gave me a little ironic smile. "Some people didn't like him. I know he wasn't always a nice man, but he treated me okay."

"Were you close then?"

"Not as close as we should have been. That was my fault, not his. I should have stopped by more often, but he never seemed to need anyone."

I didn't get a chance to pursue the subject because Junior joined us as Michiko turned up the path. We were ushered into the living room, a large, cathedral-ceiling space. The furniture was traditional and high quality, the colors vivid and varied but not garish, yet the room struck me as staged.

Considering Junior's wife, Rhonda, owned the largest and most successful real-estate agencies in Coyote Springs, it didn't seem unlikely that it had been professionally decorated.

Our hostess was a tall, heavy-set, buxom woman, famous for her trademark wigs. No one knew exactly how many she had, but estimates ran as high as a hundred, in every color, hue, style and length imaginable. She was talking with a group of women in a far corner. When she saw us enter, she excused herself from her other guests and joined us.

"Thank you so much for coming." She was wearing a black wig today, suitable no doubt for mourning. "There's plenty of food. Please help yourself. We have wine, beer and mixed drinks, if you prefer." She nodded toward a portable bar that had been set up beside the massive stone fireplace. I recognized the man in a starched white cotton jacket, white shirt and dark tie from the chapel. Oscar Garcia, I assumed. They hadn't been at the cemetery.

"Orange juice, if you have it."

"Lemonade for me," Michiko added.

Rhonda crossed to the bar, put in our orders and returned. Michiko complimented her on the house and what she'd seen of the grounds. The bartender brought our drinks.

"Let me show you around." Rhonda was clearly pleased with the compliment, but also the inveterate real estate agent.

The house was indeed impressive. Two stories, almost five thousand square feet combined.

"A lot of house for two people," I observed when we reached the game room.

"We bought it as an investment, of course. In the next ten years the prices of homes here in Woodhill Terrace will go up faster than average. We'll be able to get twice what we paid for the place."

"The three rules of real estate," I quipped. "Location, location, location."

"Exactly." She invited us to see the master suite upstairs.

I politely declined. She was clearly disappointed, until she realized why.

"Oh, the stairs. Of course. I forgot. I'm sorry. Oh, dear." She spun around, as if she were looking for a place to hide. "How thoughtless of me. I hope you'll—" She stopped and was staring at my legs or rather at my thighs, probably trying to determine where flesh and blood ended and artificial limbs began.

I'd run across the reaction before. I was occasionally able to convince the embarrassed party that by forgetting my handicap they'd actually paid me a compliment, but I didn't see that happening with Rhonda Bartholomew. Apparently neither did Michiko. To divert attention she began peppering our hostess with questions about the den's Saltillo tile floor, the rustic beamed ceiling, the pool table and the glass-fronted gun cabinet. It was similar to the one in my father's office but twice as big.

"You shoot?" Michiko asked.

"I grew up on a ranch in the San Joaquin Valley," Rhonda replied. "Carrying protection against varmints was mandatory. Junior's the marksman though." She pointed to several awards he'd gotten in various categories, ranging from shotgun to rifle to handgun, including black-powder antique weapons.

Michiko wandered over to a *Pachinko* game in the corner. She and I had spent hours playing the Japanese pin-ball machine when we first met in Tokyo ten years ago, before I deployed to Vietnam.

"What was your father-in-law like?" I asked as we stepped from the game room onto the screened-in patio. The sun was glinting off the heart-shaped pool beyond.

Rhonda smiled. "I was wondering when you'd get around to asking me that. I guess the best single-word description would be complex. I'm not suggesting he was schizophrenic or in any way unstable. Let's just say his personality was . . . multifaceted. A chivalric gentleman of the old school, an uncouth country boy, a well-read, highly intelligent man and a narrow-minded bigot. Take your pick. He was also very secretive. For the most part I liked him, but I never felt I knew him."

"I'm sure you've thought about this. Who do you think killed him?"

She shook her head. "I honestly don't know. Some people disliked him, but I can't think of anyone who had reason to kill him."

"Who profited by his death?"

Her head shake this time was dismissive. "No one, Mr. Crow. He lived modestly because it was his choice, but also because it was what his means allowed. I never heard him express an interest in greater wealth or more possessions. He was not an avaricious man."

"What was his wife like?" Michiko asked. "I only met her once briefly, by chance when they came to the steak house."

Rhonda laughed. "If he was multifaceted and secretive, she was secretive and two-dimensional."

"What do you mean?" Michiko asked.

"She was the one with the split personality. She could be pleasant enough, but she had a mean side, too, an almost vicious streak."

"Can you give an example?" I asked.

Our casual tour had brought us through a side garden to the front of the house. Parked in front of the garage was the huge, brilliant lavender 1975 Fleetwood that was her trademark. I couldn't imagine Junior or any other man driving it. Sort of made it invulnerable to theft, too. We circled back.

"Bart wanted Junior to become a doctor," she said, "preferably a surgeon. Hazel said from the beginning Junior wasn't cut out for blood and gore or listening to people's woes, not to mention the crazy hours. She seemed almost pleased when he flunked out of med school in his freshman semester. The jewelry business was her idea. She was absolutely convinced it was where he'd make his fortune."

"And she seems to have been right," Michiko concluded.

Rhoda smiled crookedly. "I guess she was."

"What do you think of Stacey's contention—"

"That her father molested her when she was a child? I don't know what to make of it."

"Do you believe her?" I asked.

"No." She paused. "Unless . . ."

"Unless what?"

"Unless it was the reason for his drinking. A guilty conscience? Or maybe a means of impulse control. After all, if a man is plastered . . . I mean . . . he can't, well, you know."

"That's an interesting observation," Michiko said. "It would certainly help explain his various moods."

The tour ended in the back yard under the covered patio. On the other side of the swimming pool was a strip of perfect lawn, its farthest edge delineated by a row of tall poplars. To the farthest left was the garage, behind it an added carport which could be accessed only from the back alley.

"I'm so glad you stopped by, Mr. Crow," Rhonda repeated. "I'm hoping I might talk you into working on my late father-in-law's house. We want to sell it, but before we do, I'm sure you noticed it needs a good deal of attention, and I don't know of anyone who does better quality work than you and your company."

"That's very kind of you," I said, "but what the house needs, as far as I've been able to see is standard maintenance and a fresh coat or two of paint."

"Well, that's certainly true, but—"

"There are several people I can recommend for the job."

"Not Manny Hollis, I hope."

I smiled. "I figured you were looking for someone else. "My first choice would be Fernando Amorado. He's good, reliable and honest." I pulled my notebook and ballpoint pen from the inside pocket of my suit jacket. "He's not listed in the yellow pages, but here's his home number. Tell him I recommended him. I think you'll be pleased with his work."

Rhonda Bartholomew studied the paper, then folded it. "Thank you so much. If he's as good as you say he is, I'll have plenty of work for him."

"May I ask a question?"

"Certainly."

"The master bathroom in your father-in-law's house. All that blue—"

She laughed with genuine humor. "Hideous, isn't it? Bart loved blue. Hazel hated it. After he tucked her away in the local loony bin last year, he had Hollis paint it blue. It originally had a gray-and-white motif. Changing the color scheme was one of Hazel's first projects. She re-did it in yellow and brown. I'll have Fernando—" she conferred her piece of paper "—do the walls and cabinets in white."

More guests arrived. Rhonda ran off to greet them while Michiko and I stepped out of the doorway. The short, round woman we'd seen at the church came up to us with a paper-doily-covered tray of hors d'oeuvres.

"You must be Rosa." Michiko reached for a stuffed mushroom cap. "I understand you and your husband took care of Colonel Bartholomew."

The woman's brown eyes blinked once, but the tray didn't waver. "Yes, ma'am. For about six years, since before his wife took sick."

"Alzheimer's. That's what Stacey told me," I commented. "Terrible disease."

"He was good to her. People don't give him credit for that, but he was. Ms. Bart wasn't always nice to him."

"In what way?" I asked.

"She was a nagger, forever telling him to do things, then complaining that he didn't do them the way she liked."

"Did you make these?" Michiko asked, taking a second mushroom cap. "They're delicious."

"They were his favorites. Them and my hot tamales."

"You liked him, didn't you?" Michiko smiled sympathetically.

Just then Rhonda called Rosa over to serve other guests.

"I knew Hazel for thirty years," declared a woman sitting in a wingback a few feet away. I turned to acknowledge her statement, and she continued. "Our husbands were frequently stationed together. Hazel had her qualities, but, well—" She extended her hand to me. "I'm Dominika Kowitz. Forgive me for butting in, but I couldn't help overhearing. I can tell you, Hazel was one of the best organized women I've ever met, but there was a dictatorial element too. Sort of a Napoleon complex with a very strong sense of entitlement."

A younger woman brought her a martini to replace the empty glass at her elbow. Dominika nodded her thanks and made the introductions.

"Hazel set her sights on Bart the first time she saw him in uniform," Dominika went on after her daughter had left to talk with other guests. "This was during the Depression, remember. A man with a job and a steady income counted for more than youth or good looks back then. She was sure he'd be a general someday. Everything she did was practice for when he put on a star. She never forgave him for not fulfilling her dream."

"You ready, Gram?" The young lady was back. "Sorry to rush off, but I didn't realize what time it was. We're supposed to meet friends at the country club." Dominika took a final sip of her martini, and the two women hurriedly left.

"Can't say I'm surprised about Bart's wife," I told Michiko. "She gave him attitude even when they were having dinner at the *Nest*."

"Not a pleasant way to live. Do you think it was payback for what he'd done to Stacey?"

"Could be, even though Stacey insists her mother didn't know. You disagreed. Why?"

"You heard Mrs. Kowitz," she answered quietly. "Bart was Hazel's meal ticket."

"Do you think she knew Stacey was blackmailing him?"

"She would never have used that word, but yes, I think she may even have encouraged it."

Rosa returned with a fresh plate of canapés. "You asked me if I liked the colonel. I did. He was troubled though, unhappy."

"About what?" I asked.

"Don't rightly know. I thought after his wife passed away he might cheer up and stop drinking. That sounds bad, but the old woman was the kind of person who sucked the fun out of everything, even when she wasn't there."

"Maybe he loved her," Michiko said.

Rosa lifted her shoulders, suggesting more doubt than confirmation. "He made sure she was taken care of. I grant you that, but I think it was because he was her husband and it was something he was supposed to do. That's what I mean, him being a good person. Not many men would."

"I heard he liked little girls, maybe too much, inappropriately."

"That's nonsense, and that's what I told the police. I can't imagine why anyone would say such a nasty thing." Rosa was indignant. "I have daughters and granddaughters, Mr. Crow. I wouldn't have worked in that house if I thought for a moment Colonel Bart would do anything to hurt young children, mine or anyone else's. The very idea, it's disgusting."

"You were there when Livy came for lessons," I commented to Rosa.

"Such a nice child. So smart and polite, and what a wonderful piano player. Colonel Bart said she was the best student he'd ever had, that someday she will be famous."

I hoped it was true. I knew Aaron thought it was.

"On their last two visits, when Debbie went to do some shopping, did you ever leave Livy alone with the colonel?"

Rosa's demeanor seemed to slow, as if she were trying to figure out how to react. She glanced at her husband who was busy preparing drinks.

"I told you," she finally said, "those rumors. They're not true. He said things sometimes that were . . . He didn't think about other people's feelings."

"Like what?"

"He said Livy had natural talent, that she got it from her father, that . . . *they* . . . all had natural rhythm."

My pulse accelerated. "Did he say that to her?" This was exactly the kind of remark Aaron had been afraid of.

Rosa shook her head. "No, no. He said it to me one day after she and her mother went home. I told him he shouldn't say things like that."

"What was his reaction?"

"He laughed, said I was probably right, even though it was true."

I was ready to ask her about the ribbons and the pictures when Stacey's voice carried over from the other side of the room.

"Mom wanted me to have that china, Junior. *And* her jewelry. You know it as well as I do."

"Stace, keep your voice down. This isn't a barroom."

"The china and jewelry belong to me."

"If mom had wanted you to have them," Junior persisted in what amounted to a stage whisper, "she should have said so in her will. It doesn't matter what she may have told you privately. It's what she put in writing that counts, and that was nothing, so it all went to Dad. If he didn't specify who gets what, it all goes into the common pot and gets divided among the three us, you, me and Lisa."

"Don't play games with me, dear brother. You're the executor. That gives you discretion."

"I said keep your voice down. As for discretion, I'm going to exercise it. As soon as we can make the house presentable we put it on the market and sell it. The contents too. If there are particular pieces of furniture or other items you want, you can buy them at fair market value."

"Buy them? Why, you son of a—"

"Mom, please." Lisa had run to Stacey's side and reached for her hand, but she refused to submit.

"You shouldn't refer to our mother like that, Stacey. It's disrespectful." Junior contemplated the drink in his hand. "Besides, I don't understand what you're complaining about. If you think about it, you'll really be buying things at a thirty-three-and-a-third-percent discount, since we'll be divvying up the proceeds from the sale."

"Don't give me that crap—"

People had ceased their conversations and were watching, some with amusement, others with bitten lips.

"Mom," Lisa pleaded, "will you just leave it alone for once? We just buried Grandpa. Like Uncle Mort said, can you show a little respect at least for today? Oh, that's right, now that he's dead and can't defend himself you're telling the world he raped you."

Someone gasped. Even the tinkling of ice cubes ceased.

Stacey turned her head slightly aside, seemingly oblivious to the eyes staring at her. "I didn't say he raped me. I said he molested me."

Lisa lowered her eyes, took a breath, gazed up at her husband who'd just moved to her side and shook her head in frustration. She handed him her glass. "I'll see you at home," she told him, "after my kinesiology class."

Keith straightened his shoulders and nodded, eyes momentarily closed. "Wait . . ." His eyes sprang open. "I thought you were going to get your assistant to teach this week."

"He couldn't make it. Family problems of his own."

Another nod. "I'll see you at home later then." They kissed briefly on the lips.

Lisa wended her way toward the door to the hallway, then turned back to her mother. She was obviously on the verge of saying something, when she shook her head and strode out the door.

Silence prevailed for several more seconds after she left, then, as if a signal had been given, everybody started talking at once.

"Reverend Connors," I said to his back.

He came around slowly and extended his hand. "Please call me Keith. It was good of you to come today."

"Zack and I went out to Hilltop Church yesterday to look around. Wonderful potential for restoration."

"That's what Rhonda said when she showed it to me a few years ago. It had been on the market for some time. It's small, and I reckoned I'd quickly outgrow it—at least I hoped I would—but it's so picture-perfect and the price was right."

"If it's too small for your congregation, what exactly do you have in mind for it?" I asked.

"Ceremonies like weddings, and I'm considering doing my Sunday morning television programs from there. You have to admit the setting is beautiful. It's all still in the planning stages, of course."

"With that information we can work up some ideas with various options and cost estimates."

We touched on his future plans for a church big enough to accommodate the size of congregation he envisioned. He'd done some traveling in the last couple of years, seen some of the iconic cathedrals of

Europe. As much as he admired their monumental architecture, he admitted his personal tastes ran much closer to the tasteful simplicity of Williamsburg. It was a conversation I would have enjoyed pursuing, but we were interrupted by other guests eager for his attention.

I looked around. The Garcias were busy serving food and drinks. I didn't see much chance for a private conversation with either of them. None of the brief exchanges I had with those nearby went beyond the polite amenities.

"Shall we go?" I asked Michiko a few minutes later. "Zack and I have a meeting with Ned this afternoon to discuss the vineyard."

Ned Herman had been my hooch mate in Vietnam. Descendent from a long line of Spanish and Italian wine growers and vintners, he'd been the moving force behind Zack and me starting a vineyard in West Texas.

Michiko and I thanked our host and hostess, and despite Michiko's offer to get the car, I walked the block to it with her.

Chapter Nineteen

Zack and I had been laughed at eight years ago when we told people we were fixing to grow wine grapes. They didn't realize there'd been 150 vineyards in Texas before Prohibition. Only a few of them had survived the experiment in social engineering, mostly by producing sacramental wine, grape juice, raisins and alcohol for commercial use. The culture of wine-drinking had been lost in the Lone Star state. Texans, we were earnestly reminded, were beer, bourbon and tequila drinkers.

Following Ned's advice, we'd started off with one acre as a test, six hundred plants. The first year produced healthy Chardonnay vines but no fruit. The second year brought a plentiful harvest. The third year we expanded to cover five acres. The numbers had astounded us. By the end of the fifth year we were harvesting eight to ten tons of grapes per acre. Now we had twenty acres of grape vines: five each of Chardonnay, Riesling, Sauvignon and Zinfandel, a grape I'd never heard of, but which I discovered produced a hearty red wine I'd come to appreciate.

We sold what we produced to other wineries and to commercial producers of "jug" wine, the uniformly blended mediocrity that's identified neither by the type of grape nor vintage year, what the French would call *vin ordinaire*. It paid the bills, sometimes with a profit. Ned also pressed a small batch from each harvest for our own experimental private reserve. It ranged from moderately good to undrinkable.

The two familiar red cars, Zack's '66 Mustang convertible and Ned's beloved '68 Karmann Ghia, were parked in front of the ranch house when Michiko and I arrived. We found their owners sitting at the glass-topped table out on the patio overlooking the swimming pool. Michiko said hello to the "boys," then retreated into the house. I urged her to take a nap.

I sat down and nodded at the glasses lined up in neat rows on the sideboard. "What do we have here?"

"I'd like us to taste some wine," Ned said. "Four Chardonnays."

Zack brought the tray on which were three rows with four different white wine glasses in each row, while Ned went to the under-counter refrigerator beside the wet bar and removed a single green bottle with a plain white label marked A.

We sniffed and sipped less than half an ounce of the chilled wines, spat out what we tasted into small individual buckets and cleansed our palates with unsalted soda crackers. After we'd sampled all four, Ned asked which I liked best.

"C."

He asked Zack.

"I agree. C."

I couldn't help smile at the expression on Ned's face. He was pleased, but he was also proud. "That's our wine," he announced, trying to be cool about it. "It's young, a '74 vintage. Give it two full years of aging, and it'll be award-winning."

"What do you recommend?" I asked. "That we plant Chardonnay grapes on the remaining ten acres we have available there?" The current location was hemmed in by a rim of boulders, rocks and a caliche mesa. Once the plat was fully cultivated, we'd have to establish a new, separate plantation.

"Definitely," Ned replied, "but that's only half of it."

"You think it's time for us to start bottling Caliche Caverns wine, don't you?" The excitement in Zack's voice was unmistakable.

My heart skipped a beat as well.

"You tasted it," Ned reminded us.

"What were the other wines?" I asked.

He grinned again, opened the cooler and removed three labels on the backs of which he'd written the letters corresponding on the bottles we'd just tasted from.

"Mondavi, Sebastiani and Gallo? I believe Gallo," I said. "But Mondavi and Sebastiani. I'm impressed."

Ned poured us each drinkable quantities of *our* wine and removed a small platter of Dutch cheese and sliced Fredericksburg peaches from the beer refrigerator. He held up his glass. "To Caliche Caverns."

We'd discussed a variety of names, ranging from Chateau Crow to Merchant & Crow, which I preferred over Crow and Merchant, and finally hit upon Caliche Caverns for the table wine.

Over the next hour we sipped Chardonnay, nibbled cheese and juicy fruit while we discussed the pros and cons of becoming vintners.

"If we keep our grapes for processing instead of selling them," Zack pointed out, "we give up the income they would have earned us at a time when we'll have the significant expenses of producing, bottling, distributing and marketing our own wine."

"We're going up against entrenched interests in what is now a small market, but that will grow over the next decades," Ned assured us. "Americans are ready for wine, so delay won't be to our advantage."

"More vineyards are being established here in Texas every year," Zack noted.

"And the ones in California are expanding," Ned added. "The competition will be getting better, which is why we have to break into the market now and establish a name that people will recognize, respect and be loyal to."

"But you're also advising us to expand our current acreage," I reminded him. "Another expense with no offsetting income. We won't be producing a profit for years."

"Not for the next three to five years at least," he admitted.

"How much do you estimate this expansion enterprise will cost?" Zack asked Ned.

"I've worked up some rough figures." He stuck his fingers into the shirt pocket, withdrew a wrinkled paper and read off a litany of purchases: storage tanks, a crusher, vats for fermenting and aging, tubing, corking and labeling machines—"

"How much?" Zack asked.

"About fifty-thousand dollars."

Zack frowned.

"Ten percent on either side, but it could be double," Ned ventured.

The patio remained silent for a long minute.

"I don't know how short you are cash-wise," Ned finally said, "but you have three choices. Put this off until you feel fiscally comfortable. The problem with that is prices keep rising and competition getting more intense. The brass ring may remain forever out of reach."

I couldn't argue with that assessment.

"Option two—borrow the money."

"I don't like borrowing money on speculation," Zack said, "hoping a gamble will pay off."

"The third option," Ned ventured. "Let me invest in Caliche Caverns or whatever you decide to call it for a percentage of the profits." He'd wanted to be an investor in our vineyard from the beginning but hadn't had the cash.

"Invest how much and for what percentage?" Zack, the accountant, asked bluntly.

"Twenty-five thousand dollars, half of what you need to establish your own label in exchange for fifty percent of the profits."

"Fifty percent? Out of the question," Zack said without hesitation.

The expression on Ned's face was one of shock at Zack's instant rejection. I, too, was a little taken aback by my friend's bluntness.

"Not fifty percent?" Zack replied. "You're failing to consider the investment we already have in the vineyard. There's the value of the land, which is Jason's contribution, and the investment I've made in cash and unpaid services. What you bring to the table now constitutes approximately one-sixth, not one-half of its total value."

Ned's jaw muscles flexed as he gazed up at the patio ceiling. "Sixteen percent," he muttered, clearly displeased.

"I'm thinking more like twenty percent," I said.

Ned stood up. He was trying to maintain his cool, but after almost ten years I recognized anger under the genial façade. "I'm leaving for California in a few hours, be gone all week, back late Sunday night or early Monday. You can let me know then what you decide, where we stand."

Chapter Twenty

At church on Sunday my mind kept wandering. I thought about the twists and turns my family had taken since my high school days. I was a sophomore when my grandfather died shortly after my father had opened his first steakhouse with George Elsbeth. The following year Dad sold our house in town to raise money to buy the *Crow's Nest*, and the family moved out to the ranch. With Dad's unpredictable hours at the restaurant, Mom's involvement in clubs and charity work, and the long bus ride my brother, sister and I had to school every day, we rarely had a chance to get together as a family except for Sunday dinner at the *Crow's Nest* with the Elsbeths: George, his wife, Lavinia, and son Aaron.

Lavinia Elsbeth died of cancer when I was in Vietnam. George didn't remarry. Still, our extended family had grown. Zack and Nancy Brewster tied the knot and had so far produced two children. My sister Debbie and Aaron Elsbeth joined in holy wedlock and had four kids. Now Michiko and I were expecting our fourth child.

Sunday dinner at the *Crow's Nest* these days was a boisterous affair with children playing happily and the adults talking and arguing. It was now up to me to keep the momentum going. Following my father's example, I kept a provocative question or two in reserve on the off-chance there was a lull in the conversation. I rarely had to play my trump.

Today my mother was extolling the virtues of Reverend Keith Connors, whose picture had appeared in the paper as the clergyman who officiated at Colonel Bart's funeral. Mom went to church with Michiko, the children and me most of the time, but she also watched the rebroadcast of the evangelist's program on Sunday afternoons.

At 55, Julia Snodgrass Crow had settled for the most part into a quiet passivity to the world around her, but her treatment of people was directly and unmistakable influenced by her deep-seated concept of their "racial purity." She'd come to accept Michiko, who was half Japanese, but never as warmly as she did Nancy, Zack's wife, who was a "true, blue American." I realized a year or so after our wedding that Mom accepted Michiko, not because she saw the error of her ways, but because she couldn't dominate her, and if it came down to my having to choose between the two women, Mom would lose.

She was pleased to have grandchildren, but she was disturbed that ours were not wholly desirable, each showing varying degrees of their mother's Japanese heritage. As for my sister's kids, the situation was even more complicated. Their mixed race was unmistakable. It baffled me that my mother could be so prejudiced, so narrow-minded. If Dad were alive he'd hug each of his grandkids without hesitation or discrimination.

"You're quiet," Michiko said as I lay down my knife and fork after only one piece of beef tenderloin, medium-rare, with just a hint of garlic.

"Thinking." That Dad should be here. He'd be almost sixty now, still a young man by modern standards. I could picture him smiling at the discussions underway and positively gloating over his grandchildren. How would he handle this situation with Livy?

"Oh, no," my mother was telling Debbie who was sitting across from her midway down the long table, "your father never was able to appreciate the joy of receiving the Lord's grace. Poor man."

I saw my sister's features tense up and instinctively started to rise to Debbie's defense, but Michiko tugged on the back of my hand. "Let her be, Jason." She was referring to my mother. "You can't change her. You know that." Then she came to my rescue by shifting the conversation. "Did you see Johnny Carson Friday night, Mrs. Crow?"

How to address my mother had been something of a conundrum for a while after Michiko and I got married. Michiko was willing to call her Mother, Mom or Ma, but my mother had rejected all three. "After all," she'd pointed out, "I'm not your mother." I supposed I ought to be grateful to her for being so diplomatic for a change. Implied was: *you don't look like us.*

I suggested Michiko call her Julia, but Michiko rejected that, saying it was inappropriate and disrespectful for a young woman to address an older woman—one old enough to be her mother—by her first name. The result was that Michiko and Aaron had something in common; they both addressed their mother-in-law as Mrs. Crow.

"You mean the skit about the fortune-teller?" Mom asked, referring to the Johnny Carson Show. "Oh, that was so funny."

"He's mastered the secret of comedy," Michiko continued. "Timing. He reminds me of Jack Benny."

"Oh, the Jews are experts at laughter. After all, they've been laughing at us all the way to the bank for centuries now."

"Nice try," I mumbled to my wife.

"Lavinia, get your elbows off the table, and act like a civilized girl instead of an African monkey."

"Mother!" All movement at the table stopped. "You owe both Lavinia and her parents an apology. Now."

"That won't be necessary." Aaron pushed back from the table. "It's time for us to leave. Let's go, kids."

"But we haven't had dessert," Emmet complained. "Grandpa made us his special peach crumble."

"Aaron, let's stay, please," Debbie interceded, then glared at our mother. "It's not fair to spoil the children's treat because their grandmother lacks good manners."

"Deborah," Mom objected with an exaggerated uplift of her chin.

"Mother," I repeated firmly, "please apologize so we can go back to enjoying our dinner."

"Oh, for heaven's sake. I'm sorry. All right? Ruffled feathers smoothed now. I don't understand what everybody's so upset about. All I said was—"

"We know what you said," I interrupted before she made it worse. "That's the problem."

"Tsk, you're just like your father, making mountains—"

"Why, thank you, Mother. I can't think of a nicer compliment than to be told I'm just like Dad."

Mom turned her face away from me in a pout.

"Tell us about your preparations for the bicentennial, Jason," Nancy urged.

We managed to get through the rest of the afternoon without further incident, thanks largely to Nancy's keeping my mother distracted by a constant change of topics.

Shortly before dessert was served, the peach crumble Emmet had been waiting for, Michiko rose and excused herself. "The duty nurse at the hospital called right after we got here," she explained for everyone's benefit, "asked if I could fill in for the first two hours of her shift. Her parents arrived in town unexpectedly, just passing through, and she wants to spend as much time with them as possible. Of course I agreed."

"Must you go this minute?" my mother asked. "Dessert hasn't been served yet. I don't know what it's like in your country, but in ours it's considered poor manners to leave before the end of a meal."

"Here in *my* country," Michiko retorted conversationally, "honoring one's word is more important than dessert. So, yes, I'm afraid I do have to leave now, since I have to drive home to change clothes before reporting in at the hospital. I'm sure Uncle George understands."

"Of course." He rose from the other end of the table. "If you wait one minute, I'll have the cook pack you a big piece of the crumble to take with you."

"Thanks. That'll be great."

"What about the children?" my mother asked, not ready to give up. "Surely you don't expect Jason to take them home in that ridiculous truck of his."

I smothered a sigh. As a ranch girl Mom had no problem with pickups, but she thought they should be traded in every year for the newest model. Mine was nearly twenty years old and becoming a classic, but all Mom saw was the faded paint and the usual dents and dings work vehicles accumulate.

"I'll take the kids with me, Mom," Debbie said. "Michiko can pick them up on her way home."

"Probably be around eight," Michiko told her. "If it looks like I'll be much later, I'll call you."

"They can stay over. No problem."

"Can we?" Sarah begged.

This was hardly the first time we'd improvised schedules. It was one of the things I loved about having a big family. There was always someone willing to lend a hand.

"Yeah, can we?" Ted echoed. "Me and Emmet can sleep in the tree house."

"Emmet and I," Mom corrected him.

"Are you going to sleep in the tree house too, Grandma?"

Everybody's breath caught as they smothered laughs.

"Don't be impertinent, young man."

He looked at me. I winked, and he lowered his head with a grin.

An hour later the busboys were clearing dishes, Debbie and Nancy were instructing the kids to go to the bathroom one more time—*and don't forget to wash your hands*—when I heard my name called. George was walking toward me with a telephone. He plugged its long cord into the jack in the wall a few feet away.

"It's Clyde Burker." He handed me the instrument.

"What's up?" I asked into the handset.

"It's Michiko. She's been in an accident."

Cold terror raced through me. *Dear God, not Michiko. Don't take her, too. Please God, not her.*

"How bad? Is she all right? She isn't . . ." I couldn't say the word "dead." Not Michiko. Please God. Not Michiko. My hands started shaking. The phone base in my left hand tumbled to the flagstone floor. "Tell me," I demanded.

Chapter Twenty-One

"Tell me what happened?" I repeated before he'd had a chance to answer me the first time.

"A traffic accident, Jason. Some jerk in a pickup decided to make a right turn from the left lane. Michiko's a little bruised, but she's all right."

"Where is she?" And what about the baby? Oh, God!

"Clover Emergency Room. As soon as the doctor gets finished, I'll—"

"I'm on my way. No. Wait. Let me talk to her."

"She's in an examining room. There's no phone in there. She's okay, Jason."

I wanted . . . I needed to believe him, but the acid in my stomach was eating away the walls.

"I'll be there in a few minutes." I hung up.

"I'll drive you," Zack volunteered.

"I can drive myself."

"Maybe you can, but I'm not about to let you." He stood in front of me. "Jason, I'm your friend. You know that."

I thought about Burker on Friday, how lightheaded he became when the adrenaline rush had worn off. "I'm okay." In fact I was furious and . . . scared.

"Michiko will be all right," Zack assured me. "But she won't be if you mess up." He waited a moment. "Come on."

We walked side-by-side out to his Mustang. It sat lower than I liked, but it had two offsetting advantages, moveable bucket seats, and it was a convertible.

"Jason, she'll be fine." Zack started the engine.

"How do you know?"

"The way you and Burker were yelling at each other, I and everyone else could hear his every word. Like she's a little bruised but not seriously."

Those may have been Burker's words, but they didn't match my mental image. My mind was filled with dread at the thought of losing her. The death of my father had left an empty space inside me I was only now beginning to fill with family. The loss of my wife would leave a chasm even family couldn't compensate for.

Zack put the transmission in gear, and we were on our way. Then it

97

came to me. Why was the chief of homicide getting involved in a traffic violation?

Within minutes we arrived at the ER. Zack pulled up to the entrance, jumped out, came around to my side of the car. I'd already opened the door and was shifting around in the seat. One at a time I repositioned my legs and placed the feet flat on the pavement. Without my asking, Zack extended his hands. We grabbed each other's wrists, and he pulled me upright.

Burker was standing at the nurses' station, chatting with a candy-striper, when I walked through the extra-wide entrance.

"Where's Michiko?"

"Room two," the young lady replied eagerly before Burker had a chance.

"Come on." Burker led me to a cubicle a few yards away.

She was on a gurney, her head and shoulders raised. Her pale face brightened the moment she saw me. The glow in her eyes sent my blood racing. The streak of dirt on her left cheek froze it.

I marched directly to her, intent on swallowing her in a bear hug until I realized doing so might hurt her. Instead I clasped her hands in mine and kissed her on the temple.

"You all right?"

"Except for a couple of cuts, contusions, abrasions and bruises, I'm fine. I look like hell now. Tomorrow I'll probably hurt like hell." She was trying to make light of it.

"The baby?"

"The baby's fine, Jason. Relax."

"What happened?" I continued to hold her hand.

"I was driving west on Texian in the right lane because I'd stopped at Mangrove's Nursery. I was lucky to catch them as they were about to close. When I pulled out into the street, a faded blue pickup started tailgating me. All of a sudden, just as I was coming out of the arroyo, he dropped back for a moment, then came flying up on the outside, his engine roaring. That wasn't a problem . . . until he decided he wanted to turn down Cuthbert. He pulled a ninety-degree right directly in front of me. I slammed on my brakes and still had to veer sharply right to avoid hitting him. That's why I ended up in the bar ditch."

"So how'd you get injured?" I peeked under the sheet covering her legs and almost wished I hadn't. Both showed cuts and scrapes.

"The garden tools I'd just bought were on the seat next to me. The rake and hoe sliced right into my thigh and calf and the paper sack of pruning shears and other tools joined them. It seemed like everything was flying. My injuries really aren't as bad as they look, Jason. The doc tells me

I'll be gardening again inside a week."

"Did you get to see who was driving the truck?"

She broke eye contact and replied the way people do when they know the answer to a question but don't want to give it. "I'm not sure."

"Michiko?"

"I think it may have been Bubba Spites."

I wanted the world to stop spinning, or at least slow down. I was growing weary of surprises, of things going wrong, of feeling out of control.

"You told me—" I glared, tight-jawed at Burker "—you had our backs."

He ignored me and turned to Michiko. "What make of truck was he driving, any idea?"

"A Ford F-150. Light blue. 1962, I'm pretty sure. The hood and fenders were faded. The right side of the front bumper was also out of alignment. Looked like it had been that way for some time."

I was fuming, yet I had to smile. Like most women, my wife was more tuned in to color and details than men generally were, and like many ranch wives, she was familiar with truck makes and models.

"Good," he said. "That's very helpful."

"Are you going to pick him up?" I asked Burker.

He held up a hand. "What was the license plate number?"

"I have no idea," Michiko replied.

"Was it a Texas plate?"

She thought a moment and shook her head. "I really don't know."

Burker nodded, then addressed me. "Here's the problem, Jason. Michiko's description of the truck is good, better than most, but there are more than sixty light-blue Ford pickups in Spring County alone. I know because I checked when she told me the first time I asked her about the other guy."

"It sounds like the same truck Bubba was driving eight years ago," I said.

"Six of those blue trucks are '62s," Burker rattled on, ignoring my comment. "I checked that too. If we extend our parameters, there are approximately two hundred within a fifty mile radius of Coyote Springs. Of course, we don't know if this particular truck was from Texas. I don't want to think about how many there are just in neighboring states, not to mention nationwide."

"Okay, I get the message," I said. "In other words, you're doing nothing."

"No, Jason, I'm doing what the law allows me to do, collect evidence. Unfortunately in this case there isn't a whole lot to collect. Michiko's station wagon and the pickup didn't come in direct contact, so we don't have any paint scrapings, for example."

I knew he was right, but I'd had a scare that left me feeling helpless, which in turn fed my anger. For all my posturing, I respected Burker as a cop. He knew his job, took it seriously and did his best. I didn't always agree with his premises or approach, but I didn't question his honesty or integrity. I also recognized he had rules to follow. Maybe it was time for me to back off.

"Any eye witnesses?" I asked.

"Several neighbors came out after Michiko ran into the bar ditch, but none of them saw the actual accident."

"So we're nowhere."

Burker crooked an eyebrow at me, recognizing that my saying "we" was a sort of white flag of truce. Before either of us could pursue it, however, the ER doctor joined us.

Though we'd never met, he came directly to me, offered his hand and addressed me by name. That wasn't unusual. Over the years my picture had been in the papers a few times. Initially as an athlete, then as a war casualty and most recently as a successful businessman.

"Mr. Crow, I'm Dr. Case. The first thing I want to assure you is that your wife and baby are fine." He then reviewed the medical situation. "I had to put in a few stitches on the right leg—"

"Will I have a scar?" She sounded more curious than concerned.

"I'm pretty good with a needle," he replied, "so I doubt it. If you do have one, it'll be hardly perceptible and will fade with time. No one will notice it."

I thought about my own scars. They were barely discernible after eight years.

"The bruise on your left thigh will probably bother you more," he went on, "at least for the next few days. You don't have to stay off it. In fact I recommend that you continue with light exercise, walking is enough, just don't overdo it. I'll give you a prescription for pain medication."

"When can she leave?" I asked.

"I'll sign the discharge order now. You can leave any time."

It took another twenty minutes, however, before someone brought a wheelchair so she could be transported fifty feet to the circular driveway where Zack was standing by the Mustang. While we waited, I made a telephone call to the *Nest*, assured everyone Michiko was all right, confirmed Aaron would take the kids and Debbie would drive Mom home.

Michiko's wheelchair arrived. She was in no shape to squeeze into the cramped backseat of Zack's car, so I settled there and stretched my legs across the hot black leather upholstery.

When we arrived at the ranch house, Zack and Lou Flores assisted

Michiko out of her seat while I extricated myself from the confined space behind it. Only after he was satisfied everything was under control did Zack bid us goodnight.

I quickly removed my prostheses, then helped Michiko undress and settle onto our bed, a futon on the floor, Japanese-style. Lou returned a few minutes later with a large tray. Knowing I wasn't likely to leave my wife's side, she brought two bowls of soup and two chicken sandwiches.

After some squirming, clenched teeth and gentle persuasion, Michiko gave in and took a pain pill. She quickly fell asleep.

The evening was young. I had no place to go. I picked up the book I was reading—I invariably had two or three books, fiction and non-fiction, on my side of the bed. *Fire in the Lake* by Frances Fitzgerald was an attempt to explain Vietnam and our involvement there. When Michiko saw me reading it, she advised me to leave it alone, that I wouldn't find the answers I was seeking there, but I almost never stopped reading a book once I'd started it. This subject was torturous yet fascinating. Tonight, however, I needed something less intense, less provocative. I needed to be distracted, so I brushed aside *Fire in the Lake* and picked up the novel I'd been reading, Rex Stout's last Nero Wolfe mystery, *A Family Affair*.

Wolfe, the titular hero, the brilliant detective who used cold logic to solve crimes, never left the house on business, but it was Archie Goodwin, the glib, common, man of the world, who was the star of the show. I envied Archie's carefree independence, but of course he lived in a fictional world. The fat man's lips were working in and out, in and out, a sure sign he was connecting the dots in preparation for solving the seemingly unsolvable mystery, but my eyelids were growing heavy. I wanted answers but the words on the page were floating, fading . . .

"So he cut off his legs," Wolfe says, *"because it seemed the right thing to do, the act that would balance the scales of justice. His enemy deserved to spend the rest of his life a double amputee, a helpless cripple."*

"It wasn't his fault those things happened," I try to protest. "He wasn't responsible for the tragedies that took place."

"It doesn't make any difference," Wolfe rejoins. "The scales of justice have to be balanced."

"But that's not fair."

Archie laughs. "Fairness has nothing to do with it. When are you going to wake up?"

Of course, that's the answer. Just wake up. I stir. I have to wake up, and when I do, I'll be sitting up in my bed at home. I casually look down at myself and gape in horror. Where are my legs? What happened to my legs? They must be here somewhere. I look around the room.

The door opens, and I behold the most beautiful woman in the world. Sloe eyed with perfect features, peaches-and-cream complexion, wearing a nurse's starched white uniform.

"Looking for something?" she asks.

"My legs. Somebody took my legs."

She laughs. "They're not important. Believe me. You'll get along without them."

"But—" I started to argue with her, then realized she's sitting in a wheelchair. I look down. She doesn't have any legs either.

I scream. "No-o-o."

"Jason, wake up. Wake up, Jason. Wake up, sweetheart."

I opened my eyes and gazed at Michiko. The cover's been thrown back, showing her long legs and the bandage on the right one where the doctor had put in a few stitches. The bruise on the left thigh was even more colorful than it had been earlier. Purple and green.

"Are you all right?" I asked her.

"I'm fine, but what about you? You haven't had a nightmare in a long time. The same one?"

Almost. I couldn't possibly have told her that in this one she had no legs either. The bad dreams were far less frequent than they had been when I first came home, but the nightmare would never be over. I recalled my father's words: *We make the best of the hand fate deals us. We're not quitters, you and I.*

"If Bubba ever hurts you again," I said with a calmness I didn't feel, "I'll kill him."

Chapter Twenty-Two

Monday morning I wheeled into the kitchen to find Zack sitting in the breakfast nook sipping Lou's excellent coffee and reading the morning *Gazette.*

"Something up?" I asked.

"No. I just thought I'd stop by and see how you're doing after all that happened yesterday."

"She called you." I gave my wife a questioning glance.

"Yes," she said, while he just shrugged.

I had to laugh at the expressions on their faces. "I suppose she told you she's worried about me."

"Something like that."

I snorted. "Well, you can both relax. I'm not loading my shotgun and going after Bubba, much as I'd like to."

Lou poured me a cup of coffee. I thanked her.

"Since you're here," I told Zack, "let's talk about something else."

We spent most of the morning discussing the vineyard, our vision for it, and Ned. He'd always been an integral part of our plans as well as crucial in making our vineyard a success. That wine grapes would grow in West Texas was no longer in doubt, thanks in some degree to us, and the venture was expanding. The still limited number of wine growers in the Lone Star state were all mutually supportive—for now. The time wasn't too far distant, however, when we would see each other as competitors.

The big stumbling block to offering Ned a slice of the Caliche Caverns pie was that Zack and I were equal partners. That meant we had to mutually agree on any change we wanted to make. If one of us couldn't persuade the other, it probably wasn't a good idea and was to our mutual advantage to find another solution.

If we gave Ned stock, it would come from both of us and could eventually become a wedge between us, effectively making him a spoiler. In a dispute, he'd have the swing vote, even if it was only by two percent.

"How about preferred stock?" I proposed over breakfast.

Zack knitted his brows, studied me for several seconds before the light went on. "You mean non-voting stock?"

"Why not? He has his salary. We can boost that a little, plus offer him twenty percent of the vineyard's profits."

Zack stroked his chin. "Twenty? He asked for fifty."

"He couldn't possibly have expected that. He'd have as much as both of us combined. You don't think he'll go for twenty?"

"No, but I agree we can start there. We'll probably end up giving him twenty-five percent in compensation for his not having a voice in management, but I think that's fair."

"Will it keep him?" I asked.

He thought for a moment. "For pride's sake. He could leave us and go with someone else, but then he'd be effectively competing against himself."

"When do you want to discuss it with him?"

"The sooner the better. As soon as he gets back from California next week."

It wasn't until mid-morning that I was willing to leave Michiko. Not that she would be alone and abandoned. My mother and Lou were there, and we'd received a call from Debbie who planned to come over around lunchtime. I rode into town with Zack and at the carriage house transferred to my old pickup. Until then I'd never noticed how many light-blue Fords were on the road. I was beginning to wonder if Burker's count of sixty blue pickups in Spring County might be low.

At ten minutes to two I parked in front of a 1920-vintage two-story red-brick house on Niall Street, one block north of the Coyote River. Like so many of the old residences downtown it had been converted to commercial use. The tasteful sign on the front lawn indicated three lawyers had their offices within.

There was no ramp up to the front porch or any sign that a more convenient entry was available at the back of the house. At least there was a sturdy handrail. I used it to mount the six concrete steps, paused at the top and completed my journey to the front door. The reception area had been created by partitioning the wide central hallway. What I supposed was the foot of a staircase was hidden behind a blank sheetrock wall with a cheap, hollow-core door that was completely at odds with the tasteful, more ornate, older interior design. I scanned the ceiling. The original molding had been shamefully and amateurishly defaced when the hallway was divided.

"May I help you?" asked a woman by a filing cabinet, who only half turned at my entrance. I judged her to be in her fifties. She could have doubled for a schoolmarm in a silent movie.

"Jason Crow to see Mr. Spooner."

"Do you have an appointment?"

"Are you his secretary?"

This time she did face me, her hands folded primly. She wore several rings. The ruby on her right hand gleamed more brightly than the others.

"I'm his receptionist and personal assistant."

"And you don't know if I have an appointment with him?"

She pursed her thin lips, clearly not used to being challenged, and for several long seconds glared at me. Finally her eyes narrowed. "What did you say your name was?"

I let a couple more seconds tick by. "Jason Crow."

"Oh, Mr. Crow. Of course. Yes, two o'clock. You're early. If you'll take a seat—" she nodded to a tiny sitting area by double sash windows "—I'll see if Mr. Spooner is ready for you."

"Thank you, Mrs.—"

"Gartner. Ethel Gartner. And it's Miss." She scurried through the door to the back hallway.

The chairs didn't look particularly inviting, and since I didn't expect to be kept waiting for long, I remained standing and indulged in one of my favorite pastimes, examining the old building's design and decor. It must have been a charming and commodious residence once, the proud achievement of someone who was probably only a generation removed from frontier settlers. I wondered if Spooner was one of their descendants and, if so, what they would think of what he had been done to their home.

"Jason, I'm Nelson Spooner," said a voice from behind me.

I turned and faced a man in his forties. He had his hand out. I took it.

"I'm sorry to keep you waiting. Let's go back to my office. Would you like something to drink? Coffee? Soda?"

"Nothing, thanks."

"Ethel, hold my calls."

"Yes, sir."

I followed him through the doorway. The hardwood floor had a worn runner on it. The wainscoting was original but butchered in a number of places where external electrical conduit had been amateurishly added. We arrived at a set of double doors on the left and entered what I imagined had once been the dining room. Spooner's desk was positioned in front of two pairs of narrow windows that looked out on the back yard. Unfortunately, a metal garage now obscured what might once have been a view of the Coyote River.

"Beautiful house," I commented.

He waved me to the guest chair and took his place behind the desk. "It probably makes you cringe to see what's been done to it."

"Your family's?"

"Indirectly. My wife's grandfather built it in 1922 after he struck oil. Her uncle inherited the place but had no desire to live here, so he turned it into offices. I bought it two years ago. Would love to restore it someday."

"Whenever you're ready," I said, "let me know."

"Good. I will. But before we go any further, let me apologize for the steps outside. Perhaps before you leave you can advise me on the best way to make the place more friendly for the handicapped."

"Be glad to, but that's not why I'm here. Why am I?"

He reached across to the right corner of his desk for a file. "It must have been quite a shock to discover Colonel Bartholomew's body last week." He opened the folder, then looked up and met my eyes. "Mortimer Bartholomew was a strange and enormously interesting man. Charming, crude, bigoted, staunchly patriotic, and in spite of appearances, nobody's fool."

I smiled. "That's the prelude. What's the punch line? He left me his original copy of *Uncle Tom's Cabin?*"

Spooner chuckled softly. "As far as I know he doesn't own an original. What he did was make you the executor of his estate."

Chapter Twenty-Three

"He did what?"

"He made you the executor of his estate. Obviously he didn't bother to tell you."

"No," I said. "He didn't."

"I'm not surprised. I imagine he figured if he did you'd turn him down."

My mind was spinning. Restoring Hilltop Church wasn't the confidential matter Bart had wanted to discuss with me. This was. I thought about my father changing his will only days before he died. Had those changes been known, he might not have been murdered.

"When did he do this?" I asked Spooner.

"Six months ago. Until then his son was his executor."

I remembered Junior's statement to me the first time we met and his argument with his sister at the reception after the funeral. *You're the executor,* Stacey had shouted at her brother. *That gives you discretion.* I had no reason to doubt he honestly believed he was still the executor, which meant Bart hadn't told him either.

"Why the change? And why me?"

"Six months ago Bart was diagnosed with severe cardiomyopathy, a chronic and ultimately fatal heart condition brought on largely by his heavy drinking. He wasn't morbid about it. To be honest I detected no change in his personality or attitude. He was one of the few people I've met who seem to accept the prospect of death philosophically. I'm not suggesting he was happy about it, but he wasn't unhappy either."

"But why make me the executor?" I persisted.

"Bart didn't think Junior would be able to stand up to the pressure or temptation this new will would place on him. He wanted a man of integrity, someone who knew what injustice is and who would make sure the major provisions of the new will were implemented. He was convinced you were that man."

Spooner still wasn't answering my question, at least not in terms I could understand. "What are those provisions?"

"Instead of his estate being divided between Junior, Stacey and Stacey's daughter Lisa, this new will bequeaths to Junior and Lisa only token amounts. Stacey receives nothing. Bart made it clear she'd soaked him when he was alive. She wouldn't profit from his death as well. Now the bulk of his estate is to be to be given to a child abuse organization or organizations of *your* choice. He was convinced you'd choose wisely."

The old curmudgeon was full of surprises. Was this choice a tacit admission that he was a molester? Was this his *mea culpa* from the grave?

"Why child abuse agencies?" I asked.

Spooner leaned back in his chair and became thoughtful. "Some years back," he began, "his daughter Stacey told him that as a result of psychotherapy she'd come to realize he'd molested her as a child. He denied it, but she rejected his defense."

"What was he supposed to have done?"

"He was an ardent photographer and had taken many snapshots of her. Apparently he had some talent and had decided to open a portrait studio. He needed examples of his work to put on the walls and asked Stacey and a couple of her friends to pose for him."

"With ribbons in their hair."

Spooner raised his eyebrows. "So you know about that."

"Did she complain at the time? Did any of the other girls complain?"

"She claimed he had manipulated, even threatened them into silence."

"Do you believe that?"

The attorney's reply wasn't knee-jerk but thoughtful. "Mort had his problems, heavy drinking being the primary one, but I never found him to be anything but a gentleman, on an individual basis or with a group of people."

He obviously hadn't been privy to any of Bart's racist rants. No point in dwelling on them here. Racism wasn't the issue.

"So Stacey cried rape," I summarized, "but in a whisper, not a shout. Did she ever tell her mother?"

"According to her he warned her not to."

I frowned. "This is what he told you?"

He nodded.

"Have you ever discussed it with Stacey?"

"My client was Colonel Bartholomew, not his daughter. I had no legal or ethical right to question her, and frankly no reason to question the old man's veracity. He was telling me he had been accused of a heinous moral crime. No man in my experience would confess to that gratuitously."

Should I tell him that his client's current piano students have also accused him of touching them?

"He trusted you, Jason. With his money. Even with his family, who, as you can imagine, will fight you tooth and nail for what they consider to be their birthright."

"You've given me a lot to think about, Mr. Spooner."

"You'll have unlimited discretion in the use of his money to fight legal claims and to recover any expenses you might incur in the performance of your duty, but Colonel Bart awards you only a single dollar for your services."

I smiled to myself. So much for putting a high value on my integrity and dedication. "There's still one important point you haven't told me yet. Exactly what is the estate of Lieutenant Colonel Mortimer Bartholomew worth?"

He paused dramatically. "Approximately four-point-four-million dollars."

Chapter Twenty-Four

I whistled. "$4.4 million! How did he get that kind of money? Certainly not as an army officer. Was the family wealthy?"

The corners of Spooner's mouth rose. "Not since the war, was how he put it, referring of course to the War of Northern Aggression." The attorney leaned back in his chair. "He told me only that he'd been very fortunate in some of his investments. I know he liked to dabble in penny stocks. As you may be aware, ninety-nine out of a hundred go under, and fifty percent of those that survive never pay a dividend, at least, not in the first ten years, but there are a few that make it, and a smaller percentage that make it big. If you happen to pick the right one, I guess you can become a millionaire."

"He liked to gamble," I observed.

"He'd be the first to admit his picking a winning stock was far more luck than skill. He compared it to shooting craps. Eventually you'll hit a winner, if you can wait long enough."

"Who in the family knew about this?"

"No one. He swore me to secrecy, though it would be unethical for me to discuss his personal affairs with anyone, in or out of the family, without his express permission. His wife had been disdainful of his playing the stock market, and his kids were convinced he was a first-class sucker, so when his investments began to pay off, he didn't bother to tell them."

That was cold and lonely. "So they have no idea he was worth millions."

"None whatsoever. That'll be one of your biggest challenges, dealing with them."

Spooner had run off a copy of Bart's will, which he handed to me. He then went through it with me line-by-line. It wasn't particularly long. Once we got through all the boilerplate, the heart of the document was only a couple of pages, and it was remarkably clear.

"How difficult will this be to break?"

"No document is absolutely ironclad, but I think this is nearly so."

We talked for another half hour. Some of it to clarify legal points, but I was also interested in the lawyer's impressions and opinion of the man.

"He was something of an enigma," Spooner summarized. "Intelligent, definitely. He could also be charming. Strangers at social events invariably found him pleasant and interesting, but he was an extraordinarily private person. His reclusiveness after his car accident didn't surprise me, especially in light of his wife's deteriorating condition."

"What did you think of her?" I asked. "And what was their relationship like?"

He rubbed his chin. "One is not supposed to speak ill of the dead. On the other hand, she wasn't my client. I met her only a few times, and to be honest, each time I did I found her unpleasant and overbearing. As for their relationship, I never understood his tolerance of her. Their feelings for each other were obviously complex. I don't know how else to explain them except to say on some primitive level, I sensed genuine affection for one another."

"One last question, Mr. Spooner. What happens if I decline this honor?"

"In the event you should turn down this opportunity to do good—"

"His words?"

He nodded. "The alternate executor of the will is his granddaughter Lisa. Should she decline, it'll be left to the court to appoint someone."

"Did he give any explanation why he chose her, someone so young and inexperienced, when he has older kids who are more worldly-wise?"

"He said he felt he could trust her. The others would do their best to milk the system. He knew it would be a difficult task for her to stand up to her mother and uncle, but he also maintained she's stronger than she appears, having already experienced some child abuse herself."

"Can you elaborate?"

"I don't know any details, and I wouldn't be at liberty to discuss them if I did, but I will remind you that her mother Stacey has been married four times."

Stepfathers probably were at the top of the list of household members who abuse children.

"Does she know she's the alternate executor?" I asked.

"No. Bart was clear that he didn't want her to know unless and until you could not or would not accept the role."

"So," I concluded, "either I say yes or I force an inexperienced twenty-two-year-old preacher's wife into the hot seat."

I left Spooner's office without giving him a decision. It was late in the afternoon when I arrived at the carriage house. Zack's Mustang was still in the courtyard. I rode the elevator up to the second floor. My best friend and business partner was hunched over his drafting table, muttering to himself. Before looking up, he circled something on a piece of the paper beside the architectural drawing of the old church.

On my way to my drawing table I glanced at the figures he'd isolated. "Problem?"

"The numbers don't compute. I'm not sure if I measured incorrectly or if I transposed numbers when I wrote them down."

"Is the discrepancy significant?"

'Not really, but it makes we wonder how many other mistakes I've made."

"Measure twice and cut once."

"I'll run up there tomorrow or Wednesday," he said. "I have a list of other things I want to check on anyway."

He was meticulous in planning, borderline obsessive, but if I had to have a partner with a complex, I couldn't think of a better flaw.

"How's the proposal coming along otherwise?" I asked. Reverend Connors had indicated we'd have a blank check, but we would still give him a formal estimate and stick to it. Nobody likes surprises, and we didn't want any misunderstandings.

"I haven't been able to find a roofer. It's a relatively small job and for those they want to stay closer to town." He looked up at me with a smile. "You interested?"

Except in the broiling heat of summer I enjoyed roofing, whether it was cedar shake or composition shingle. Not having legs was actually an advantage in that kind of work. I didn't have long limbs that got in the way or the backaches associated with constantly squatting and kneeling. My chances of slipping were also minimized, not to mention scuffed knees and twisted ankles. There were disadvantages, too, of course.

"If you can get me a reliable helper to fetch and carry, I'll do it."

"You're hired. So what did the lawyer have to say?"

I told him.

"More secrets," Zack remarked. "Why would anyone want to keep good news to himself? Bragging, it seems to me, is a human impulse."

"It wasn't out of greed. As far as I can tell, the money didn't enrich the old man's life one iota."

"How does his money play into his murder?" he asked.

"Apparently it doesn't, since he told no one about striking it rich, including his wife who was still *compos mentis* at the time."

"What a strange person."

"Who? Bart or his wife?"

"Both, I guess. She seems to have been pretty cold, and Bart, well, we know what he was like."

"Do we?" I asked. "The more I find out about this guy, the more mysterious he becomes. Will the real Mortimer Bartholomew please stand up? Was he a bigot, a child molester, a generous guy, a tightwad, a loud mouth or an actor?"

On my drive home, I kept mulling over the significance of Bart's change of will. Was his leaving almost all his money to help abused children an admission that he was guilty of molesting them?

I found Michiko tending the flower beds in front of the house.

"You should be relaxing, taking it easy."

"I am," she replied. "What's more relaxing than pulling weeds and trimming flower beds." She gathered her tools into a wicker basket. "How did your meeting with the lawyer go?"

I walked with her to the potting shed on the side of the garage. "Interesting and a little confusing." Together we put things away, then entered the house by the back door into the kitchen.

She brewed a pot of hot tea and got out the oatmeal-raisin cookies Lou had baked the day before. Over the afternoon snack I explained Bart's will and the unpaid role he wanted me to assume.

"You want to do it, don't you?"

"On one level, yes, of course."

"What's stopping you?"

"Timing's rotten. You're going to have a baby. Zack and I are talking about expanding the vineyard and bottling our own wine. We have a big restoration job coming up that I'll need to be there for. As I say, the timing is terrible."

She gave me one of her little grins. "When has timing ever been right? You keep so many irons in the fire that every new job, every new challenge is supposedly more than you can handle, but somehow you do."

"What about spending time with you and the kids? And our new baby? My first obligation is to my family, not to strangers or to a dead man I didn't like when he was alive."

"Jason, what he's asked you to do isn't about him. It's about kids who've been mistreated, abused, some of them severely."

"The counter-argument is that I can't solve all the problems of the world. I could pour my heart and soul into this effort, and there will still be kids who are mistreated and abused."

She bowed her head and nodded slightly. "You're right about that."

I stirred the hot tea. "I have no doubt Bart's money can make a difference in the local area, and beyond family, that's where our first duty lies, close to home, with our neighbors. I'm also aware that I'm not the only one who can enforce the provision of Bart's will. The money won't go begging because I'm not attending to it. But I can tell you that whoever takes on the role of executor is going to be in for a time-consuming and probably acrimonious fight with Bart's family, especially when they find out how much the old man was worth."

"I imagine he was going to live high in Vegas in the months he had left," she said.

"I wonder." I slouched, reached forward with my right hand and curled a finger through the cup handle. "I don't know who he was, Michiko. My image of him keeps changing."

"What does your gut tell you?"

"That I'm going to spoil my dinner if I keep eating these cookies."

She didn't smile.

"I'll call Spooner in the morning," I said. "I just hope I'm not making a serious mistake."

Chapter Twenty-Five

Even while I was speaking to Nelson Spooner on the phone the following morning, I was second guessing my decision to accept the position of executor of Colonel Bart's estate.

The lawyer was pleased with my decision and had no objection to my stopping by his office immediately to sign the necessary paperwork. Bart had also left a package to be hand delivered to me when I accepted the executorship. Clearly he'd been confident I would.

I needed to inform Burker that I, not Junior, was the executor. I called his office.

"What now, Jason?"

"Wondered if you've been able to find the truck and the driver yet?"

"Jason, there are hundreds of old blue pickups in this county, including yours. We're looking, all right? When we find it I'll let you know. Now, if there's nothing else—"

I told him I had some news I wanted to talk to him about, but not over the phone. I could picture him at the other end shaking his head.

"So when and where do you want to meet?" I persisted. "You busy now?"

"You'll have to come here. It'll be some time before I can get away."

"I'll see you in about ten minutes."

"I'm blessed."

I drove to his office. As usual he was half-hidden behind stacks of paper. He'd received an award a couple of years ago for the number of crimes he'd solved. It definitely wasn't for neatness while doing it.

"Caleb," he called out when he saw me, "bring one of those arm chairs in for Mr. Crow."

Three minutes later, after I was seated and given stale coffee in a Styrofoam cup, I told him about Bart naming me as executor of his estate and about the estate being worth approximately $4.4 million. Naturally he had questions, the same ones Michiko and I had discussed the night before. My answers today weren't any better than they had been then.

"I might have more information when I get access to his bank records and checking account," I said without much conviction, then added, "A man who lives modestly but is secretly worth millions is stabbed in the back

115

in the middle of the night for no apparent reason, without ever putting up a struggle. Nothing is disturbed or missing, even though valuable art objects are within easy reach. We're missing something, Clyde."

"When you figure out what it is, let me know."

"How soon will you be able to release the house to me? There's a lot to be done before I can put it on the market."

"I was fixing to call Junior this morning," he said, "but since you're the executor, I can turn it over to you now. I'll have somebody go by and take down the tape."

I thanked him and pushed to my feet.

"You're walking better," he commented. "More natural. Are the new legs more comfortable?"

It was the most personal and straightforward reference to my missing limbs he'd ever made, almost as if he'd finally accepted me the way I was. Progress.

"A lot better than the old ones. Advances in prosthetics are being made all the time. One of these days you and Janet will see Michiko and me out dancing."

He stood up. "Good. I look forward to that."

We did something then we hadn't done in a very long time. We shook hands. I didn't question why, but I sensed we'd just passed a milestone.

I returned to the carriage house to find a note from Zack saying he'd gone to Hilltop Church to start a detailed list of repairs that would have to be made immediately and that I had a package in the office from Bart's attorney. On my father's desk was a canvas bag with a leaden security seal, addressed to me.

As eager as I was to find out what was inside, I decided it could wait a little longer.

I called Bart's accountant. Fortunately he was someone I knew and respected, explained my position and set up an appointment to visit him later in the week. I'd never seen a portfolio worth $4.4 million. That in itself would be an interesting adventure.

I flipped through the notes I'd jotted down at Spooner's office and located the telephone number for the Garcias. Mrs. Garcia answered on the second ring. I identified myself and told her I was the executor for the colonel's estate—

"You? But I thought Mr. Junior—"

"So did I," I said. "I'd appreciate it if you'd keep this to yourself until he's been officially notified."

"Sí . . . of course."

I explained my reason for calling. "Are you and your husband available to clean the old man's house and pack things up in preparation for selling it?"

"Sí . . . yes, sir. Mr. Junior said he would contact us about that, but he has not. I was afraid he had changed his mind. We will be very glad for the work."

She then explained that her nineteen-year-old grandson had been in a car accident. His friend who was driving was killed and Felipe was left a paraplegic. They had a lot of medical bills and needed to buy him special equipment. I sympathized and arranged to meet them at the colonel's house so I could go over specifically what I wanted them to do. It would also give me an opportunity to continue the discussion I'd started with Rosa at the funeral reception.

My next call was to Fernando Amorado, the handyman my father had introduced me to years before. Zack and I had hired him on a couple of our restoration jobs and had been pleased with his work. I made arrangements to meet him at Bart's place as well.

Those details attended to, I tackled the courier package.

I used my pocket knife to slice through the hemp cord. Inside the bag were two boxes, each about the size that hold file folders. Both held large manila envelopes. Having no idea of their contents, I went to the outside door and locked it.

I spent the following hour poring over the contents of the three envelopes in the first box. What I found was disturbing as well as surprising. The one marked Stacey contained documentation of all the money Bart had given her over the years. I didn't take the time to add up all the cancelled checks or scraps of paper on which he'd noted cash amounts, dates and cryptic memos, but the bottom line must have been well over a hundred thousand dollars. Adjusted for inflation over a thirty-year period, it had to be considerably more.

The contents of the envelope marked "Junior" pertained to his jewelry business—a list of precious and semi-precious gem purchases Bartholomew's had made at inflated wholesale prices, thereby on paper showing less profit for retail sales than was actually realized. The IRS would have loved to see those receipts. In addition, Bart identified two numbered Swiss bank accounts, where presumably Junior had squirreled away his ill-gotten gains. Did Junior know his father's true worth or that he'd been collecting information about the jewelry store? The combination would give him a powerful motive for murder, especially if, as his tax evasion suggested, he wasn't as successful a businessman as he seemed. Why? Another woman? Bad investments?

I had no way of verifying any of the information. Was it true? In the case of the payments Bart had made to Stacey, she would argue they had all been "gifts" freely given. How and why Bart obtained copies of his son's business records wasn't clear. Perhaps when I examined his bank statements I'd find payments to an investigative service.

The last envelope, marked Lisa, did surprise me. A small collection of eight-year-old medical bills showed that when she was sixteen she'd undergone a procedure and was hospitalized in San Antonio for three days. It didn't take a medical degree to figure out it was most likely for an abortion. Considering she was now married to Reverend Keith Connors, public release of that information would be devastating for both of them. Did the televangelist know his wife had had an abortion? Who was the father? Did it matter? Did Lisa realize her grandfather had been collecting the information? And underlying everything I had spread out in neat piles on my desk, I had to ask myself how Bart had acquired it?

One big happy family.

I'd just packed the documents back into the first box and was getting ready to open the second when the hurried tread of feet on the outside stairs warned me I was about to be interrupted. I shoved everything into the canvas bag, placed it in the well of the desk and went to answer the pounding on the outside door.

Chapter Twenty-Six

Junior Bartholomew stomped into the entryway looking as if he wanted to beat the crap out of me. His sister Stacey stood behind him. Her expression wasn't friendly either.

"Spooner says my father made you executor of the estate, not me."

"That's right."

"Why?" Stacey asked sharply.

"I have no idea."

"Bull," Junior bellowed.

"It's true. I don't know why he picked me."

"How much are you getting out of this?" she demanded.

"One dollar."

"I don't believe you."

I fought the temptation to argue with her, to take umbrage at being called a liar.

"How much was he worth?" Junior asked.

"I don't know that either." Which was technically true. "We'll find out when I have his accounts audited. What do you think he was worth?"

"Counting his car, the house, its contents, I reckon close to a quarter of a million dollars. Divided three ways, that's eighty-thousand-plus each, but he was also into stocks. They must be worth something."

"Stocks?" Stacey appeared to be genuinely surprised. "I didn't know he was into the stock market?"

"Why should he tell his blackmailer? Besides they weren't Big Board stocks, not exactly blue chips. Penny stocks."

"How much?" she demanded.

"If we're lucky, maybe a few thousand dollars."

Boy, were they in for a surprise. Not only was the total value of the estate off by a few million, the amount they would each receive was off by hundreds of thousands. That might prove to be a hardship. My impression was they'd spent all or most of it already.

"How do you know about his investments?" I asked. "Did he discuss them with you?" "It's not important."

"I need that money," Stacey admitted, confirming my conjecture. "It isn't easy making ends meet when you're a single woman by yourself." She glared at me. "Try to hold any of it back and we'll sue."

"I wouldn't do that, if I were you."

Her eyes nearly popped. "Why the hell not?"

"Because your father left me ammunition to use against you."

Perplexity turned to fear as she considered my words. "What kind of ammunition?"

I shook my head. "You'll find out if you challenge your father's will. I don't recommend it. You'll lose."

"He's bluffing," she told her brother. "He hasn't got a damned thing." She didn't sound overly confident. "If we don't watch out he'll steal us blind."

"That's the second unfounded accusation you've made against me, Ms. Ogletree. I don't like being called a liar and a thief." I turned to her brother. "Did you know about your father's predilection for little girls?"

"I told you I didn't. Until Stacey told us about the bows and the pictures, I didn't have a clue."

"That's for sure," she mumbled sarcastically.

"But *you* knew he liked touching little girls," I reminded her. "You were one of them, and you did nothing, and because of your silence other girls may have been abused."

"You can't blame that on me."

"You were an accessory, and I take that very personally, because one of your father's victims may have been my niece. You could have done the right thing and exposed your father as a pervert if that's what he was. Instead you chose to keep silent so you could blackmail him—"

"Just a minute, Crow," Junior tried to intervene.

"Shut up." My blood pressure was rising. "You were more than an enabler." I pointed to Stacey. "You actually profited from your father's depravity. You want to challenge his will, go ahead. Try it. I'll destroy you."

She backed up, goggle-eyed. What I felt wasn't pleasure or even satisfaction, but sick that we were discussing such things, that I was losing my temper.

"As for you—" I peered at Junior "—you're hardly less guilty. You turned a blind eye on a situation that you must have recognized as unwholesome, but you chose to ignore it, to do the easy thing."

"I didn't know. I swear to God. I didn't know." It was an old defense, valid on its face, if you didn't take into account willful ignorance.

"Do either of you have keys to your father's house?"

"I do," Junior said before he'd thought about the implications.

"How about you?" I asked his sister.

"He never gave me one."

I believed her. "Hand over yours," I told Junior.

"You have no right—"

"Wrong. I'm the executor of the estate. I'll have the locks changed in any event, but I'm requesting your keys now."

I saw in his eyes the urge to fight back, the uncertainty. He reached into his pocket and extracted a chain with three keys on it. "Front, back and side."

"Thank you. Now get out of here, both of you."

They nearly slunk out of the office. I listened to their retreating steps as they descended the outside staircase, then locked the door again. In the office I retrieved the courier bag from under the desk, removed the two boxes, put aside the one I'd already examined and concentrated on the other. It contained three envelopes as well, two of them thin, one of which was addressed to me by name. I used the letter opener on the blank envelope.

Inside I found two facsimiles.

The first was of a death certificate issued by Sunflower County, Mississippi, dated June 17, 1972. Name: Beulah Hollis. Age: 60. Cause of death: heart failure. Manner of death: natural.

The second was of a birth certificate issued by the same county on August 31, 1928, for one male child. Born: August 30, 1928. Name: Manfred Hollis. Mother: Beulah Hollis. Father; unknown. Race: Negro.

I opened the thick, unmarked envelope and found page after page of hand-written numbers in neat columns. The meticulousness of the record was impressive, but what was astounding was what they documented. If it was reading the data correctly, starting in April, 1928, and continuing until June, 1972, Mortimer Bartholomew had sent Beulah Hollis a check every month. Ten dollars was the earliest and smallest amount. The last checks had been for three hundred dollars.

The conclusion seemed obvious. Manfred (Manny) Hollis was Bart's natural son.

Just when I thought I'd reached my quota for surprises, life dealt me another. I sat dumbfounded for several minutes, idly shuffling through the papers before me, while my mind raced. By my calculations Bart had been nineteen when he impregnated a fifteen-year-old black girl, then left her to bring up the boy by herself. Given the time and place, he probably hadn't had much choice. Nowadays a black man could marry a white woman with legal impunity. Witness my sister and Aaron. But in Mississippi in 1928, the mixing of the races could have gotten them both killed. Yet Bart hadn't completely abandoned her. For almost forty-five years he'd helped support her financially even though his legal, and probably his moral, obligation for child support would have ended when Manny turned eighteen.

Had the teenage lovers ever seen each other again, and what was their relationship like if they had? It would be easy to dismiss a white teenage male having sex with an underage black girl as a passing phenomenon, a twisted sort of rite of passage, a cruel dare, even rape, but for the forty-five years of financial support. Was it possible he'd loved her? Had his leaving Sunflower County, Mississippi, been abandonment or an act of protection for the mother of his child and for the child himself? Was it social ostracism by both races that had ultimately turned him into the bigot I'd encountered?

Lastly, did Hazel know about Beulah? About Manny? When had she found out? After their marriage? The wisdom of Sir Walter Scott came to mind: *Oh, what a tangled web we weave when first we practice to deceive.*

I also noted that shortly after Beulah died, Manny showed up here, and Bart hired him as his handyman. Extortion? Technically it wouldn't have been, since Manny performed work for the money he received and seemed to be fairly competent at what he did—except for the roof.

The third manila envelope with my name on it contained a single sheet of bond paper, a letter, typewritten and signed in blue-black ink.

March 18, 1976

Dear Mr. Crow,

Thank you for taking on a task which I'm sure you find onerous. I realize that you harbor no fondness for me, deservedly so. Please be aware that I hold you in the highest esteem. It is precisely because of your integrity and commitment to what you hold dear that I am entrusting you with information and actions regarding my final wishes for the disposition of my worldly estate. If you have any questions regarding the legality of my actions, please consult my attorney, Mr. Nelson Spooner. If you have any doubts regarding their propriety, please consult your conscience. You are in control.

Enclosed you will find documentation with which to fight my children when they try to break my will. And they most assuredly shall. When you find yourself tempted to give in to them, remember it will be at the expense of children who truly need champions.

You're asking yourself if I molested my daughter. For what my word may be worth, the answer is no, but she believes I did. Have I ever molested a child? Again the answer is emphatically no. You must protect children, not just from the molesters but from those who would corrupt them by implanting false notions. I trust you, Jason Crow,

```
to do just that.
     Perhaps in another life we can be friends.

Sincerely,

Mortimer Bartholomew
Lieutenant Colonel, USA (ret)
```

I wished I'd had this piece of personal correspondence when the question of Livy's victimization had erupted. In itself it didn't prove anything. It wasn't exactly a deathbed confession, more a deathbed protestation of innocence, but such lack of guile coming from a dying man made a powerful statement.

The relationship between Bart and Hollis had serious implications. I'd have to bring it to Burker's attention, but first I had to meet with the Garcias and get some other questions answered.

Chapter Twenty-Seven

Rosa and Oscar Garcia were already at the colonel's house when I arrived a little while later. She explained that they had a key to the side door but hadn't gone inside. She'd offered it to Junior right after they'd learned of Bart's death, but he'd said not to bother, that he would be changing the locks as soon as the police left. I'd brought the keys Burker had given me, as well as Junior's, and was about to ask Rosa whether she'd been present when Bart photographed Livy and how the two of them had gotten along, when Amorado pulled up to the curb. His faded tan pickup was almost as old as mine but looked the worse for wear. He was early. My questions for the Garcias would have to wait. Sitting on the bench seat beside Fernando were his two young boys.

"Stay here," he told them in Spanish, "while I speak with Mr. Crow."

"Sí, Papa," the boys answered in unison.

"They can wait inside or in the back yard," I told Fernando after shaking his hand. "It'll be much cooler under the trees."

He waved to them and they sprang from the truck. He introduced them formally. Jesse was eight, his brother Miguel six.

Fernando looked around the area, his expression betraying disapproval of what he saw. "Jesse, there's a magnet on a long string behind the seat. Use it to pick up as many nails as you can find. Miguel, you get one of the plastic buckets from the back, go around and pick up shingles—" He pointed to several small pieces of roofing felt and asphalt shingle, some of them on the hedges under the bedroom windows.

"Sí, Papa."

"We will clean the place up, Mr. Crow," Armando assured me.

The boys happily raced to the truck and within a minute were busy at work.

"Be careful of the nails and the sharp edges of metal," Fernando warned.

"Sí, Papa."

"Such good boys," Rosa commented. "So polite."

"Our boys are polite, too," Oscar reminded her.

"They better be, but I'm talking about Nando's boys. And so handsome."

"They look like their mother," Fernando said modestly, but he was unable to hide the pride he had in his sons. In fact they were striking copies of their father. Lanky, with shiny, thick, black hair, olive complexions, and features that hinted of Native American.

"When you are finished here," he called out to them, "come around to the back. I bet there's more there."

Rosa shook her head disapprovingly. "Manny is a slob. I tell him over and over to pick up after himself. You'd think a man his age would have better sense. He's worse than a teenager."

Fernando stepped back to the curb and scanned the roof of the house from his left to his right and back again. "It doesn't look too bad from here, Mr. Crow. Is it leaking anywhere?"

"In the den," Rosa commented. "Over the piano."

"Colonel Bart keeps a tarp there to cover it when it rains," Oscar added.

"Fortunately there's no rain in the forecast," I said.

Fernando laughed. "This is West Texas. That can change any minute."

Which was absolutely true. "First thing you need to do," I told him, "is patch the spot that leaks. With no one living here, we can't take a chance of a surprise shower."

He nodded and walked around the side of the house to survey the roof from the back. I ushered the Garcias inside. As we walked through the house I identified what I wanted them to do. Clean out all the closets, pack usable clothing to give to charity, dispose of the rest, put aside anything they had questions about. In the kitchen and dining room I asked them to segregate the china, crystal and silver for an estate sale.

"Colonel Bart said those Japanese plates are valuable, that his wife bought them cheap when they were in Japan at the end of the war."

"They are," I agreed. "The big one is about two hundred years old. The other two are about the same."

"I will be very careful with them," Rosa promised. "Also with the china tea sets and crystal."

The Bartholomew collection, while eclectic, was impressive. No wonder Stacey was anxious to lay her hands on it. Did she and her brother realize precisely how valuable it all was? Junior was certainly in a position to find out. I'd have to talk to him about getting formal appraisals. They could be sold at auction instead of in the glorified garage sale called an estate sale.

"The things in the small bedrooms?" Oscar interrupted. "The photographic equipment. What about all that?"

"It all goes."

"I have a cousin who might be interested in buying it."

"Tell him to give me a bid."

I'd been wanting to ask Rosa about the hair ribbons and the promise Bart had made to Livy to send a copy of the photograph for her mother. Now was my opportunity.

"He didn't like the way the picture of Livy turned out," Rosa explained, "so he didn't send it."

I would have liked to go look at it, but Burker's people had taken all the photos with them. Was the answer as simple as the maid made it sound, that the quality of the work was below standards? I tried to recall it. What I could distinctly remember, however, was a rather stiff pose of a dark-complexioned girl with a yellow ribbon in her hair. But for the ribbon, the portrait possessed no special quality. It lacked the spark I'd seen in Bart's other photographs.

We went over a few more house-cleanup details. I'd have a locksmith come out that afternoon and give them new keys, so they could come and go as they pleased. I knew they had a reputation for being honest.

I went out the back door. Fernando was up on the roof. Ironically, if I weren't wearing my prostheses, I could have climbed the ladder and joined him.

"This leak is very bad. The decking is rotted through. I must tear out more shingles, patch the hole, put down new felt and re-shingle," he explained. "It'll do for a little while, but there's also plenty of old hail damage. The entire roof needs to be replaced, Mr. Crow."

We discussed a timetable. Fernando had another job to finish first, but he didn't think it would take more than a day, two at the most, then he'd get to work on this.

"What about Manny Hollis?" Rosa asked as I was leaving. "Colonel Bart hired him to do the roof. What happens if he comes back?"

"He told me he doesn't want the job, to get someone else. If the colonel owed him money—" I gave her a couple of my business cards "—tell him to call me and I'll settle things with him."

I returned to the carriage house. The note I'd left Zack was still on his desk. I phoned police headquarters. Burker was out. They didn't know when he'd return.

"Please ask him to call me at the carriage house at his earliest convenience."

I sat at my drafting table and tried to concentrate on the layout of Hilltop Church and how best to go about restoring it. Too many stray thoughts, however, kept getting in my way. I finally gave up, put in another call to Burker, left word that I could be reached at home—he had the number—amended the note for Zack, locked up the place and drove out to the ranch. Halfway there I started to relax, partially I suspect because of the anticipation of seeing my wife and kids.

The house was redolent with the tantalizing aroma of cookies in the oven. Chocolate chip. Naturally the kids were in the kitchen with their mother. She was wearing jeans and a yellow blouse. I remembered the sight of her bruised legs that morning when she went to take her shower. I'd vowed to love, honor and protect her. The first two were easy. I'd have to work harder at the last one.

My children gathered around me. Gideon, the youngest, wrapped his little arms around my left leg. At three he was getting to be a chatterbox. Sarah, five, was more reserved, but not by much. She put her arms around my other leg.

"I'm glad you're home, Daddy. Can we go swimming?" She loved the water.

"Can we, Dad?" At seven Ted took his role as big brother very seriously.

I mussed his dark hair. "Can I have a cookie first?"

"Just one," Sarah cautioned. "You don't want to get a cramp in the pool."

Michiko said very seriously, "I think Daddy is big enough to have two cookies."

"He's not so big when he takes his legs off," Sarah said.

Michiko sputtered, caught my eye, and we both laughed.

"You better eat them now while you're still big, Daddy," Sarah advised me.

"It doesn't make any difference if he's wearing his legs, stupid," Ted mocked her. "They only make him look bigger."

"Ted—" I called him aside "—I don't want you talking to your sister like that. Don't let me hear you do it again. Is that clear?"

He hung his head. "Yes, sir."

"If your sister doesn't know something, tell her. If she doesn't understand it, explain it, but don't belittle her."

"Yes, sir. Are we going swimming now?" He'd watched me devour the last of the second cookie.

I chuckled. "Yep. Go get changed, but don't go in the water until I get there."

As they disappeared to their bedrooms, I snagged a third cookie. Michiko came over, wrapped her arms around my back and gazed up at me. "I don't want you getting a cramp now either."

I groaned. "I love my kids, but—"

She backed away. "I think maybe you should go change too."

I chuckled. "Later."

I spent the next couple of hours with the kids, having fun, playing games. Not surprisingly, I gave out before they did.

I'd showered, dressed for dinner and was about to wheel from the bedroom to the dining room when the phone rang. I picked up the receiver from the stand by the door. "Jason."

"Thought you might want to know," Burker said, "Rosa Garcia was just found on the living room floor of Bart's house. Unconscious."

Chapter Twenty-Eight

"Is that where you are?" I asked.

"Yep."

"I'm leaving now."

"Figured that." He hung up.

On my drive into town I thought about the kind woman I'd talked with earlier in the day. A heart attack? Stroke? Burker didn't know. What about the questions I'd postponed asking. Would I get answers now?

I trudged up the slight incline of the driveway to the carport. Bart's year-old Cadillac Seville had been moved back a few feet from where it had stood that morning, probably so Oscar could access the storage areas in front of it. I pictured the spaces crammed with long forgotten "stuff" that barely qualified as junk.

A uniformed officer opened the side door of the house a few seconds before I got there. I didn't have a choice but to put my hands on the doorframe as I worked my way up the two steps. He watched but didn't object.

"The lieutenant's in the bedroom," he said.

I strutted the length of the kitchen, which, I noted, had been stripped of the owl canisters and memorial plates, and down the hallway. At the end I turned left into the master suite.

"Is this where she was found?" I asked.

"The dining room. I'll show you." Burker circled around me and headed for the door I'd just come through.

I followed. "What are you doing here? This is a medical emergency, isn't it?"

"The dispatcher recognized the address of the 911 call and notified me. I understand you hired her and her husband to clean out the place."

"Called them this morning after I left your office. Since they'd been working for the colonel, I figured they were the best qualified to separate the junk from the salvageable. At least they know where things are. I also found out they needed the work. One of their grandkids was in a car accident, so they've got a mountain of medical bills."

"Felipe Garcia. Rotten situation. I'm sure God has a reason for punishing the innocent, but I can't figure it out. Maybe someday he'll explain it to me."

The quandary of the ages.

We crossed to the dining area. I looked around. Cardboard boxes were scattered about, old newspapers beside them. Knickknacks and figurines were missing from tabletops and shelves. Boxes cluttered the dining room table, pieces of glass, crystal and china next to them, along with more newspapers for packing.

"Two tragedies in the same house," I observed, "in the same room within a few days of each other. Figure the odds. Selling this place now is going to be doubly difficult. People will say it's jinxed or cursed."

"Slight difference between the two incidents, though." Burker went to the space between the dining room table and the china hutch. "The first victim was murdered. With Rosa it looks like natural causes." He pointed down at the gray Berber carpet. "She was found here on the floor. No sign of trauma or injury, but there was a broken plate at her side."

"Plate? What kind of plate?"

"Big, fancy Oriental thing. Blue, red and white. Had some gold trim."

I looked at the top of the sideboard. The *Imari*.

"Don't know at this point if she dropped it and had a seizure," Burker continued, "maybe a heart attack, or if she had a seizure and dropped it. Either way, it broke."

"Who found her?"

"Her husband. He called 911. No telling how long she'd been out. She was still unconscious when they loaded her into the ambulance."

"Where's Oscar now?"

"One of his daughters and her husband came and got him and his truck, took him home a few minutes before I called you."

"No foul play?"

"No obvious signs of it. She was overweight," he said, his back to me as he examined the remaining contents of the china cabinet. Burker himself was probably a hundred pounds overweight himself. "Had diabetes and high blood pressure. According to her husband and daughter, she wasn't always punctual about taking her medication." He looked around the room. "We're ready to shut down here."

"You need anything from me?" I asked.

He shook his head. "There was one other thing I wanted to talk to you about though," he said when we were alone. "It wasn't Bubba Spites who ran Michiko off the road Sunday night."

I turned and stared at him. "Then who was it?"

"Don't know yet."

"If you don't know who did it, how do you know it wasn't Bubba?"

"Because we've had him under surveillance since he got here last

Wednesday."

"The whole time?"

"Jason, I don't have that kind of manpower available, but enough of the time to know he didn't go anywhere Sunday evening. His truck was parked in its usual spot the entire afternoon and evening."

"Why didn't you tell me this sooner?"

"The patrolmen I needed to verify it with were on break. I wasn't able to get hold of them until this morning. Jason, it wasn't Bubba."

I was about to argue that just because his truck was there didn't mean he was, when logic kicked in. Michiko had identified a truck that looked like Bubba's, but it obviously couldn't have been if his was parked outside his apartment.

I tried to imagine Bubba sitting by himself in a motel room doing nothing. I couldn't. The guy I remembered didn't read books or listen to classical music. He raised Cain with his buddies. After six years in the slammer, however, he might not have many friends left in Coyote Springs. So if he wasn't out causing trouble, what was he doing? A couch potato? Solo? The image didn't quite fit, but what he did with his time was his concern, not mine. As long as he wasn't trying to harm my family, I really didn't give a damn where he went or what he did.

"You're sure his pickup was there?" In this case the truck was the key. If it was parked at his place he couldn't have run Michiko off the road.

"That's what I'm telling you, Jason. Bubba's truck was outside his motel the entire afternoon and evening, and he was in his apartment. It wasn't Bubba Spites who ran Michiko off the road."

I wanted to believe him, wanted to be confident my family wasn't being targeted for disaster. Given the twists and turns my life had taken in the last ten years I felt justified in being skeptical. "Then who did?"

"We're working on it."

"I've got something for you."

He peered at me curiously. "What?"

I told him about the courier package, the envelopes and their contents.

"Whoa! You're telling me Manny Hollis is the illegitimate son of Colonel Bart?"

"It looks that way."

Burker's expression now morphed into ironical humor. "I guess I missed the family resemblance." He snorted and grew serious. "I've suddenly got a lot of questions for Mr. Hollis. Like did he know the old man was a millionaire? And did he expect to be included in his will?" He made eye contact with me. "He isn't, is he?"

I shook my head. "Spooner showed me the will. Hollis isn't even mentioned, and I'm willing to bet he wasn't in the previous will either. I have a feeling he regarded Hollis about the same way he did Stacey, that they'd already gotten all they were going to get out of him."

"Either way," Burker commented, "Hollis had a motive to kill the old man—to gain his inheritance, if he thought he was named as an heir, or in retribution for being left out, maybe in fury for never being publicly acknowledged." Burker shook his head. "I'll up the level of the alert for Hollis."

Chapter Twenty-Nine

I stared at the headlines of the Wednesday morning gazette: "Garcia Arrested for Wife's Assault." I thanked Mrs. Flores for pouring my coffee, said yes to her offer of breakfast, and plunged into the lead story.

> Oscar Garcia, 62, was arrested at his home late last evening by the Coyote Springs police based on evidence that he struck his wife over the head hard enough to crack her skull.

I was stunned but kept reading.

> Earlier yesterday Oscar Garcia reported finding his wife unconscious on the floor of the residence of the late Mortimer Bartholomew, where they had been cleaning and sorting in preparation for an estate sale. The initial assumption that she had collapsed from a stroke or heart attack changed dramatically last night when medical personnel examining the 58-year-old woman discovered she sustained a fractured skull. The resulting subdural hematoma, a blood clot on the brain, necessitated surgery to alleviate the pressure. It will be some time, days, even weeks, before the extent of Mrs. Garcia's injuries can be fully assessed.
>
> A subsequent investigation at the scene of the assault enabled the police to identify the weapon used as a 17th Century Japanese plate found at her side. A forensics examination of the broken antique porcelain revealed only one set of fingerprints, those of her husband, Oscar Garcia. A neighbor told the police that the couple had a verbal altercation in the front yard which culminated in Mr. Garcia getting into his 1965 Ford pickup and speeding away. According to the neighbor who witnessed the heated exchange, he returned about three hours later, discovered his wife unconscious on the living room floor and called

911.

The article went on to say further details were not yet available, except that Mr. Garcia was reportedly refusing to answer questions by the police on the advice of his daughter, Graciela Brooks, who was an attorney.

I picked up my coffee cup to take a sip only to find it empty. I didn't remember drinking it. A moment later, Mrs. Flores poured another, then served me a generous plateful of pork sausage, scrambled eggs, hash browns and biscuits.

"What's this?" I asked. Except on Sunday I had only cereal, juice and coffee in the morning.

Michiko laughed. "Lou offered you a full breakfast. You said fine. Maybe in the future," she told Lou, "you ought to wait until after he's finished his first cup before asking."

"Do you want me to throw it away?" my aunt asked.

"Waste good food? Not on your life. I'll just have to go without lunch for the next few days." I watched my weight carefully, not out of vanity but necessity. Every extra pound meant additional pressure on my prostheses, as well as additional strain on my elbows and shoulders when I maneuvered my wheelchair or hand-walked.

"What do you make of the assault on Rosa?" Michiko was having granola with sliced peaches from Fredericksburg.

"Strange and sad. The couple we met Saturday didn't strike me as the violent type. I wonder why it took so long for the medics to realize she'd been struck on the head."

"She has very thick hair. That could easily have hidden a knob. She wouldn't necessarily have had any external bleeding. The hemorrhaging could have been all inside the skull."

Zack could verify that. When he'd been struck on the head in Vietnam while searching for me on the night the Tet Offensive began, he hadn't bled either, but the concussion had put him to sleep for three days.

"What are you going to do?" Michiko asked.

"About Rosa? I don't know that there's anything I can do."

But the idea of doing nothing didn't sit well, especially since Rosa wouldn't have been in Bart's house if I hadn't hired her and her husband to clean the place out. I'd felt no particular sense of responsibility for Rosa's collapse when I thought it was natural, the result of poor health and unhealthy habits, but this was an assault, the intentional infliction of pain, suffering and perhaps permanent disability. That hit too close to home.

Considering the situation in those terms made me realize I didn't believe Oscar had struck his wife, and having reached that conclusion, I now had to delve more deeply. Once again I recalled an adage of my father's, that feelings and emotions can tell us something is wrong, but they can't tell us what or why. That required logic, the clear and inevitable progression from cause to effect.

My father had also taught me to be suspicious of coincidences. In this case the odds of two people independently suffering violence in the same place a few days of each other seemed astronomical. What did Colonel Bartholomew and Rosa Garcia have in common that made them threats to a third party? Was the key to uncovering Bart's murderer finding Rosa's attacker?

"I'll give Burker a call, see what he'll tell me," I said. "Then I'll call Oscar's daughter—" I checked the paper for her name "—Graciela Brooks."

Michiko got up from the table. "I'll see if her number's in the telephone book."

Chapter Thirty

I phoned the police station and asked for Burker. He wasn't available, but if I would leave my name and number . . . . Obviously a rookie. I left the information, then dialed Bart's house.

"He's here, Mr. Crow, talking with the crime scene people. Want me to get him for you?"

"Just let him know I'm on my way there."

"Sure thing."

Fifteen minutes later I climbed into my pickup and drove into town. What possible motive could Oscar have had for attacking his wife? Was there a history of violence between them?

Had Burker found a connection between the murder of Bart and the assault on Rosa? A couple of the typical motives for murder seemed completely laughable. One was that Rosa and Bart had been having an affair and Oscar found out. Another was that Oscar found out she'd been facilitating Bart's molestation of young girls. The latter made even less sense. If Oscar were willing to knock his wife unconscious, wouldn't he be the more likely candidate to molest little girls?

I had no proof that either conjecture was right, but my instincts and my gut told me the woman I'd met, the mother of six and grandmother of eight, was happily married to her husband, that morally and culturally, infidelity was unthinkable for her. As for Bart, I couldn't imagine him being interested in, much less attracted to a little old married lady. My sixth sense also told me Oscar was exactly what he appeared to be, a good man who loved, honored and cherished his wife.

I could be wrong, of course. There was the adage that opposites attracted, and some of the most enduring legends of evil had to do with shattering the *illusion of morality*. Nonetheless, I still didn't believe it. The Garcias I had met were honest, decent people. On the other hand, good people had tempers—and occasionally lost them.

I found Burker in the master bedroom staring at the wall where the framed pictures had hung.

"Any more information on the kids?" I asked.

"Last I heard, only two or three hadn't been identified. Those who have all took piano lessons from the old man, and nearly every one of them admitted to being sexually harassed."

"Harassed? That's a bit different from being molested."

"The shrinks say it's the first step in acknowledging they are victims. They start by denying anything happened—"

"Maybe because nothing did."

Burker eyed me. "Then they admit he made them uncomfortable, then that he made overtures, followed by actual touching—"

"And eventually they'll all admit he did dirty things with them and forced them to do dirty things with him."

"Look, you're still pissed about Kershaw—" he held up a hand to forestall my interrupting "—and you have every right to be—"

"She's one of the best, remember? And if I had let her continue she would have poisoned the relationship between Livy and her father."

"They've suspended her from performing any more forensic interviews—"

"And will they hold her accountable for the lives she's already ruined?"

My anger was building. I had to get it under control if I wanted Burker to continue giving me access to his investigation.

"Sorry," I said. "I keep thinking of something Stacey told me, that her father warned her not to tell anyone about what he did because no one would believe her, that she'd be blamed for telling lies. Now I'm wondering if, in the case of these forensic interviews, that might also be the case, but in reverse?"

"You mean the kids feel compelled to tell adults what they want to hear, even though it didn't happen?"

"Adults are authority figures. Fear is a powerful weapon. As a pediatric nurse Michiko's been privy to plenty of cases of child abuse. She says kids get caught in the middle and become victims twice in the tug of war between their abusers and the people who are supposed to be helping them. The physical damage from sexual abuse, if any, is usually temporary. It's the psychological and emotional damage that often lasts a lifetime."

Burker nodded. "I don't know what we can do about Kershaw. We'll have to wait and see what the department and the medical board decide."

I resisted the urge to say "Nothing."

He studied me for a moment, then asked, "Why are you even here, Jason? What's your interest in this case?"

"If the Garcias hadn't been here working for me, Rosa wouldn't be in the hospital, and Oscar wouldn't be in jail, accused of assaulting her." I shook my head. "You're going to tell me that doesn't make me responsible for what happened to her, and I'd agree with you in principle, but—"

Burker exhaled. "What do you want to know?"

"Exactly what happened? Do you seriously think Oscar attacked his wife?"

"My feet are killing me. Let's sit down in the living room."

I led the way, smiling to myself about the remark about his feet. It had taken a long time for him to be so at ease. He settled on the couch. I took the upholstered wooden chair on the other side of the coffee table.

"Here's the sequence of events, as best I can piece them together," he said. "After you left them yesterday morning they started clearing away junk. From our search of the place after Bart's death I can tell you there was a lot of useless stuff stuck in closets, cabinets, drawers and just sitting around. No worse than most—I'd hate to have someone go through my house—but still, there was plenty that could be thrown away and never missed."

I waited for him to get on with it. I knew about packrats. My mother was one.

"Around two o'clock Manny Hollis showed up."

"Where had he been?"

"Don't know. He didn't say. He's taken off again. We're looking for him. Rosa was in the back yard when he drove up the alley. Apparently it took about thirty seconds for them to get into a shouting match. Then he grabbed his stuff, took it to his pickup, and peeled off."

"What were they arguing about?"

"According to the neighbor, Rosa was giving him a ration of shit about his not finishing the roofing job, accused him of stealing by taking the old man's money and not doing anything for it."

"Okay, so Manny left. What happened next?"

"According to the neighbor, everything was quiet for about half an hour. Then Rosa came out of the house and starting giving Oscar hell about something."

"What?"

Burker shrugged. "Don't know. That exchange was in Spanish. The neighbor doesn't speak Spanish. And Oscar isn't talking. All I know is he went inside, they shut the door and maybe two minutes later, he came stomping out, yelling in English this time that he was taking a load of crap to the dump and would talk to her later after she calmed down."

"Is that where he went?"

"They keep track of license plate numbers at the dump. His was on the list. He came back here three hours later, found Rosa on the floor and called 911. My sources at the hospital tell me it wasn't a moment too soon, that any further delay, and she would have been a goner."

"You found your friend just in time," the doctor had told Zack. "We were able to save his life, but we couldn't save his legs. We had to amputate both of them above the knees."

"It doesn't take three hours to unload the back of a pickup," I observed. The dump wasn't more than twenty minutes away. "Where was he all that time?"

"Claims he was so pissed over the fight with his wife that he bought some booze and went off to drink it."

"Did he?"

"He appeared and smelled drunk when I met him here."

I thought of Bart's incident at the Dairy Queen. A good attorney would argue he was actually in shock, which might have been partially true, but it didn't explain his reeking of liquor.

"That was one reason I called his daughter to pick him up," Burker explained. "No way was I going to let him get behind the wheel of his truck."

"Oscar Garcia has a fight with his wife," I summarized, "hits her over the head with a heavy plate so hard he puts her into a coma, then goes to the city dump. After that he buys booze and gets drunk. Eventually he comes back here and acts surprised to discover his wife is right where he left her. You paint the picture of a very sly, cold-blooded sadist. Are we talking about the same Oscar Garcia?"

Burker shrugged. "It was enough to convince the D.A. and a judge."

"I don't buy it, Clyde. I don't claim to know the Garcias well. I met them only a couple of times, but I can tell you with certainty that Oscar Garcia is not the ruthless brute you make him out to be. He would never leave his wife unconscious on the floor, then go out and get snockered."

"Here's the thing. The doc in the ER says Rosa may not have been unconscious when he left her. It's not unusual for trauma victims to act completely rational for a short period of time immediately following a blow on the head."

I didn't question the medical assessment, only who wielded the plate. It wasn't Oscar Garcia. "Have you checked the alibis of the people involved in the case?"

He rolled his eyes. "Yes, Jason," he said patiently. "I've checked alibis. At least I've asked for them. Haven't had time to verify them yet. Junior was at his shop. He's reopening tomorrow and was busy all day getting ready for all the people who will be coming in out of curiosity. Told me he was setting up a display of inexpensive things people could buy to justify their visit."

"Good business practice," I murmured.

"His wife was researching property listings after lunch for some people from out of town. Her lavender Queen Mary was parked out in front of her agency all afternoon. Stacey was at their house trimming roses. Lisa was out shopping. Meanwhile her husband was cloistered in his office writing a sermon for Sunday."

I was impressed with the extent of his investigation thus far and was about to say so when we heard a knock on the side door. The cop on sentry duty answered it. A few seconds later a woman with coal-black hair pulled back and tied at the nape of her neck stepped into the room.

"Jason Crow? My name is Graciela Brooks. Oscar Garcia is my father."

I struggled to my feet and offered my hand. "I'm sorry about your mother, Ms. Brooks. Any news on her condition?"

"She's still unconscious."

"Any idea how this could have happened?"

"My father didn't hit her, Mr. Crow. He loves her. He would never hurt her."

"I believe you."

"He's not helping himself by not cooperating with the police," Burker said. "What did he and your mother argue about?"

She shook her head, showing frustration. "He refuses to tell me or anyone else."

"Why?" I asked.

"Because whatever he has to say will make matters worse," Burker stated categorically. "Get your father to talk, Ms. Brooks, if you want to help him."

She studied him, then turned to me. "Would you speak to him, Mr. Crow? He knows what you've been through. He respects you, trusts you."

"Trust me above his own daughter?"

She shrugged. "Sometimes it's easier to talk to a stranger." When I hesitated, she went on. "You loved your dad, Mr. Crow. I love mine. My father isn't well educated or sophisticated or as financially successful as yours was, but he's honest and good. He would never hurt our mom. Never. Whatever his secret is, it can't be worth the shame of being accused of nearly killing the woman he's been married to for almost forty years. Please, Mr. Crow."

She knew what strings to pull and she was tugging hard.

I addressed Burker. "Okay if I visit him, ask him a few questions?"

He pursed his lips and blinked thoughtfully. "Just as long as everybody understands he's been read his Miranda rights. Anything he says can be used against him."

Chapter Thirty-One

My impression of Graciela Brooks was that she was of a self-disciplined, intelligent woman. I suspected she was also a formidable attorney, coldly logical and pugnacious. This morning, however, she was mostly scared. Her mother was in critical condition. Her father was accused of inflicting the pain and suffering.

She made two telephone calls, the first to her office to let her law partner know what was going on and—I noted—to tell him she had talked me into seeing Oscar. Then she called her husband and reminded him to cancel their attendance at a dinner party that evening. He'd apparently already taken care of it. At that point, she lowered her voice and mumbled something she didn't want me to hear. The entire conversation was in English, suggesting to me that, consistent with her last name, Brooks, her husband was not Hispanic. Having ended the conversation, she turned to me.

"Would it be possible, Mr. Crow, for me to ride with you? I can ask someone at the stationhouse to bring me back here for my car or I'll call a taxi. If we travel together, it'll give us a chance to talk."

"No problem."

She watched me get settled behind the wheel, start the engine, shift into gear and pull away from the curb. "Was it hard learning to use hand controls?"

"Took me about two minutes." I smiled to myself. "When you want to do something badly enough, and it's within your capabilities, it doesn't take long to meet the challenge."

"My cousin was in a car accident several months ago. It left him paraplegic. He's only nineteen."

"Your mother told me about him. I'm sorry."

"Maybe you could meet him sometime and convince him the world hasn't ended, that he can still do things like drive and play sports."

"Be glad to." I turned onto Fennimore Rd and headed east toward the downtown area. "Burker doesn't think your father did it, you know."

She stared over at me. "Why do you say that?"

"He didn't have to agree to let me visit your dad, and he made it abundantly clear what the status of any conversation with him would be."

"He wants the information he thinks you can get to use against my father."

"He wants the truth."

"He's a rare cop then. Most just want to get their man. Any man . . . or woman."

The cynicism surprised me. I wondered what her experience with the police had been, and if it was the reason she'd gone into law. Perhaps eventually I'd find out, but this wasn't the time to probe.

"Tell me about your dad, Ms. Brooks."

"Please call me Graciela or Grace. And thank you for taking an interest in this . . ." she didn't finish the sentence. "My father is a simple man, Mr. Crow—"

"Jason."

"Jason. By simple I mean he's uncomplicated. He's not devious or cunning or two-faced. He's a good man, works hard, doesn't complain. He and Mom grew up together. As far as I know they never even dated anyone else. It's always been just the two of them. He never finished high school. Had to work on the family farm. They ended up losing it anyway during the Depression. He'll be lost without her." She paused a moment. "I just hope . . ."

"Don't get ahead of yourself," I advised.

"He wouldn't tell me much when I saw him last night and again this morning. He and Mom had a fight. Afterwards, he went off and got drunk. It must have been serious because I've never seen my father drunk. Tipsy a few times on happy occasions. But intentionally getting drunk . . . it's not like him. It's completely out of character."

"The police will claim it was from a guilty conscience for hitting her, but you're saying it was because whatever they argued about was serious."

"Yes," she replied unhappily.

We arrived at the police station. The county jail was next to it. I pulled into the parking lot in front of the two buildings, into a space as close to the jail entrance as possible.

I turned off the engine. "Another woman?"

"No way. My folks aren't perfect. They argue once in a while, usually about silly things, like Dad not taking out the garbage and it stinking up the kitchen, or my mother borrowing one of his tools and not putting it back. Petty stuff. But they're devoted to each other. Sure, Dad's a man, and men, well . . . some men wander . . . but not Dad. Besides, when would he have had the time? They're always together. One other thing. If Hollis told Mom that Dad had been seen with another woman, she wouldn't yell and scream at him. She'd cry. She wouldn't say a word. She'd just cry."

That rang true. "Did you instruct him not to talk to the police?"

"When he called and told me what they were charging him with, I told him not to say anything without a lawyer present. I didn't tell him not to cooperate. I got there as soon as I could, but he refused to talk even to me about the argument."

"It doesn't sound like the police have a very strong case against him. There's more, isn't there. What else happened?"

Her eyes widened slightly, then she nodded. "The neighbor the police keep talking about, the one who overheard my parents arguing, says she heard a vehicle come down the alley less than an hour after my father left for the dump, enough time for him to go there and return. She looked outside, but by then it had gone behind the tall, photinia bushes. She figured it had kept going, but then a few minutes later she heard a vehicle start up in the alley and practically spin its wheels leaving."

"But the police have no positive identification that it was your Dad's truck?"

"According to them, the woman is totally convinced it was him, even though she only heard it."

"Do you think your father came back?" I asked her.

She shook her head. "If he had, he and Mom would have made up. They never stay mad at each other very long, but the police think he returned, they got into another row and this time he hit her over the head with the heavy plate. He panicked, ran off and came back after getting drunk, then acted as if he'd just discovered her on the floor."

Strangely, this version sounded more reasonable, especially the part about panicking. I could see why his daughter was unnerved. There was still the question of what they had fought about to begin with. It had to be really serious to provoke the chain of events that followed, and if the second vehicle wasn't Oscar's truck, whose was it?

We got out. She came around the front of the pickup and escorted me to the jail.

Chapter Thirty-Two

I'd been in the jailhouse only once before, to confront my father's killer right after he'd been sentenced to life in prison. That was eight years ago. Of course I'd thought of the murdering bastard many times since then, but rarely did I picture him behind bars, even though I knew that was where he was spending his days and, if I had my way, would spend the rest of his life. Whether that term ended abruptly, peacefully or violently, or it dragged on for decades, mattered little to me, as long as the son of a bitch never got out. Vindictive? Yes. Some might even say sadistic, but that was the way I felt about him, and I made no apology for it.

Eight years, yet nothing in the building seemed to have changed. There was still a sour smell overladen with disinfectant, cage-like holding cells, claustrophobic visitation rooms. As I passed them I realized they were exactly the same. The same drab gray walls on top, the same drabber olive-green on the bottom. Who selected these colors? Did they hold contests for ugly and depressing?

How a human being who'd spent any time within these confines could allow himself to return to them was beyond my comprehension. Yet the recidivism rate among first time offenders was incredibly high. Maybe having experienced it once they decided it wasn't all that bad compared with the uncertainty of freedom outside. At least here their lives were predictable.

But I was letting my mind wander.

The case at hand was Oscar Garcia, who was undoubtedly innocent of the crime he was accused of. Having met him, his wife, and now his daughter, I wanted to think so. The challenge at hand was whether I could induce him to help us help him. I had an idea what I would find and wondered how I could get past the gates of Oscar Garcia's depression.

I was shown to an interrogation room remarkably like the one in which I'd met my father's killer. It might even have been the same one. It didn't matter. I sat on the hard metal straight-back chair and waited. Behind me was a one-way mirror through which we would be observed. For now at least, Graciela stayed there.

The door on my right opened slowly. A moment passed before a man in prison garb entered the room. When he saw me there was a flicker of light in his eyes. I'd seen men who were down before, men who'd lost body parts and had given up hope, but I don't think I'd ever seen a man as downtrodden as the one who came in with shackles on his wrists and ankles, a marked contrast to the energetic man I'd dealt with the day before. I'd credited him with being capable and strong, though not in the ostentatious way my friend Ned Herman was, but the man I saw before me now had shrunken to a gnome.

"Rosa? Is she . . . ?" His voice was a whisper.

"She's still unconscious, but she's alive, Oscar. She's still alive."

He gazed at me. "Will she recover?"

I couldn't lie to him. "I don't know. No one does."

He hung his head then and made no further attempt to establish eye contact. The guard gave an order and Oscar did exactly as he was instructed, which was to sit facing me, his hands on the table.

I knew the guard. His son was on the little league softball team I coached. "Can you take off the cuffs?"

"I'm not supposed to."

"I know," I said, "but if you can do it without getting into trouble, I'd appreciate it."

He considered my request for a moment, went to the door, exchanged a few words with someone on the other side, returned with a ring of keys and unlocked the manacles.

"I was told to give you privacy," he said, "but I'll be watching you from outside, so if there's any trouble—"

"Thank you. I'm sure there won't be."

I offered my hand to Oscar. He hesitated, then gave me his. To my surprise his grasp was firm, in spite of his beaten-dog demeanor, like a drowning man clinging to a rescuer. A good sign, I decided.

"Your daughter and the rest of your family are worried about you."

He didn't respond.

"Nobody in your family believes you hurt Rosa, Mr. Garcia. Graciela wants to help you. Why don't you let her?"

"There is nothing she can do."

"You insult your own daughter? Is that how you brought her up, to be useless?"

It was hard to explain the expression that came to his face. Shock but something else. Not quite humor. More like pride, definitely appreciation and a hint of hope.

"Graciela is a good girl. Smart," he said.

"Then let her use her smartness and her goodness. Give her this opportunity to follow the commandment to honor her father and her mother."

He looked up then, clearly jarred by my reference to one of the Ten Commandments.

"I respect you, Mr. Crow. Bad things have happened to you, but you are still a man, a man of honor. I will tell you what you want to know. Then you will understand why I am not."

I wanted to tell him not to crown me with sainthood quite yet. I'd been thinking about how to approach the situation with him and decided to take a page from the way Dr. Kershaw had conducted her interrogation of Livy: focus on someone else before getting around to what he may have done. The questions began.

"Tell me about Manny Hollis." The response was as I had hoped.

"That one! A lazy man who could have made something of himself with a little effort, but he would rather pretend to work, leave a mess for others to clean up, then get drunk. Rosa was always on him to pick up after himself. For all the good it did. Most of the time she and I ended up doing it. No respect for his tools. Good tools, too. He leaves them laying around. He's lucky we don't get much rain, or they would all have rusted away a long time ago."

"Yesterday, what happened?"

"There was so much stuff inside the house to cart out, so much to scrub and clean. We worked as fast as we could—"

"When did Hollis show up?"

"Around 2:00 o'clock."

"Did he say why?"

"To get his tools. Said someone else was doing the roof. He didn't care, but he wanted his tools back."

"What happened then?"

"Right away Rosa started yelling at him. I wanted to tell her to be quiet, that it wouldn't do no good, but when she gets all wound up, there's no stopping her."

"What was his reaction?"

"He pretended she wasn't there at first, then lost his temper and yelled back that she shouldn't be so self-righteous. He said something else to her, but I couldn't hear it. Rosa's face got real red. I would never do a thing like that, she told him."

"Where was this," I asked. "And where were you?"

"We were in the back yard. I was bagging some of the trash the Amorado boys had piled up nice and neat, so I could take it to the dump. I was watching and listening to what was going on. Rosa was doing fine. She would have gotten mad at me if I had tried to come to her rescue, but I wanted her to know I was there in case she needed me."

"Go on."

"Hollis laughed at her and got in his truck in the alley where he's always leaving it. The neighbors kept complaining that he blocked their way, but he did it anyway."

"Did you ask her what he said?"

He lowered his head. "She said it wasn't worth repeating." He kept rubbing his hands together. "Later I was working in the carport, loading junk from the outside storage closets into the back of my truck, when Rosa called me inside. She was standing by the TV, real mad, said she'd put in a movie to watch while she was cleaning and packing. She thought it was a regular movie, but—"

"What was it?"

"A man and a woman were . . . having sex. I turned away. I don't want to see such things."

Pornography? I had to fight to control my surprise. Oscar was staring at his own hands so he didn't notice.

"Then what happened?" I asked.

"She started yelling at me, that what Hollis said was true, that I had been bringing Colonel Bart dirty movies. She was angry, more angry than I've ever seen her before. I tried to tell her I didn't know what was on the tapes I got for him, but she wouldn't listen. She started crying. I tried to go to her, to tell her it wasn't so bad, but it was no good. She kept saying I had disgraced myself, disgraced our family. That made me mad, so I went outside to the truck. She followed me. I yelled at her that she didn't mind when I brought extra money home, so we can buy Felipe the kind of wheelchair he needs because he can't walk no more, can't feel anything like a man.

"She yelled back that even Felipe wouldn't want money from people who—" Oscar's voice dropped to a nearly inaudible whisper "—who did . . . that for people to see." He looked up, his eyes were glassy.

"Were you speaking English or Spanish?"

He thought. "I don't remember. Spanish probably. We usually speak Spanish when we get excited." That confirmed what the neighbor had told Burker. "I reminded her she'd seen some of the movies I got the old man, although he hadn't played any when we were around in a long time. I didn't think anything of it, but I guess I know why now. It's true," he murmured. "My family will hate me."

"No," I tried to assure him. "They're upset right now because of so many things are happening that they don't understand, but they don't hate you. Give them time."

"What about Rosa? Suppose she dies. I will have killed her. Or if she lives and is not the same person. Some people here, they're telling me she may survive, but she could be a vegetable or maybe she'll be blind or can't talk or take care of herself. It'll be all my fault because I'm supposed to protect her."

"What happened next?" I was eager to direct his attention elsewhere.

"I told her I was taking the junk in my truck to the dump, that when she would listen, I would explain to her."

"Did you go there?"

"Yes."

"And then you returned to Bart's house?"

"Not right away. Rosa was angry. I was angry. I thought it would be better if I stayed away a while so she could calm down. Me too. She was yelling at me when I left, telling me I had disgraced our family, and when someone came and hurt her, I was getting drunk."

It was an image he would have to live with for the rest of his life. There was nothing I could do about that. I had to live with a similar burden.

"Then where did you go?"

Chapter Thirty-Three

"I went to a liquor store and bought a little bottle of tequila and a six pack of Pearl, even though I don't like beer and tequila makes my head hurt."

"Did anyone see you?"

"The fat lady behind the counter, and there were some people in the store, but I didn't recognize any of them."

"How did you pay for it?"

He shrugged. "Cash. Three dollars and seventy-six cents with the tax."

"Did you get a receipt?"

He huffed. "They don't give receipts."

"Where did you go from there? Home?"

"To the state park. It was close. I drank some of the tequila but not much. I shouldn't have wasted good money on bad liquor, not when Felipe needs things."

"When did you go back to Bart's house?"

"It was about six, I think. I'd been away for hours. I thought maybe Rosa wouldn't still be there, that she had called one of the children to come get her and take her home." He paused. "I swear on the Virgin Mary, Mr. Crow, Rosa was fine when I left her."

"Tell me what you found when you returned to Bart's house."

There was anxiety in his brown eyes as he faced me. I was asking him to relive one of the worst moments of his life. He drew himself up, took a deep breath and began, almost like a narrator of someone else's story.

"I came in the side door like I always do, and . . ." His voice trailed off.

"Was it open, closed, locked?" I asked.

"It was closed, but it wasn't locked. I was going to scold Rosa for not locking it when she was there alone. She forgets sometimes, because we don't lock our doors at home."

"Go on."

"I went in and called out her name. I was hoping she would sing out like usual and that all would be forgiven, but I got no answer. I went into the living room. I thought I'd find her cleaning out a cabinet or maybe moving furniture. But it was like I'd left it. I turned to the dining room . . . That's when I saw her." Oscar stopped.

I pressed on. "I know this is difficult for you, but I need you to tell me everything you saw and heard, all the thoughts and impressions that went through your mind. Do you understand?"

He nodded once.

"She was on the floor by the china cabinet. Not far away was the big plate the colonel told us was worth a lot of money."

The *Imari*. "Was there any blood?"

"No, no. I thought she had broken the colonel's plate and fainted. I rushed to her, called her name, expected her to turn to me, maybe groggy. It didn't look like she was breathing. I was scared, didn't know what to do. Then I remembered to check her pulse. I couldn't tell if there was one or not. I tried to blow air into her lungs, but nothing happened."

"How long did you try?"

He shrugged fatalistically. "One minute? Five? I don't know. I tried to get up, but I was too weak. I sat there holding her hand, telling her I was sorry that we fought, that I needed her to come back." He wiped away the tears coursing down his face. "But she didn't move."

It wasn't his fault, but telling him that would have been a waste of words. I waited for him to get control of himself.

"What did you do next?"

He took another swipe at his cheeks. "I crawled over to a chair and I pulled myself up, sitting first, then stood and walked to the phone in the kitchen and called 911."

"What did you think had happened to your wife?"

"She'd asked me to take the plate off the top of the china hutch and put it on the table so she could clean it. I figured she'd picked it up to move it and it fell from her hands and broke. She would have been very upset, that she got so excited she had a heart attack."

"It never occurred to you that someone might have hit her?"

"Why would anyone want to hurt Rosa? She is a good woman. She never hurt nobody."

Where was Hollis? He'd precipitated the battle between husband and wife by telling Rosa about the porn. Could he have come back to the house a second time, maybe he'd left something, a tool, the porn itself, and ended up having another argument with her. Maybe this time he completely lost his temper, picked up the plate and smashed it over her head?

"If I'd been there, I could have protected her," Oscar said. "She would not have been hurt."

I gazed at him sympathetically. "You'll drive yourself crazy talking like that. I've been there, Oscar. You can't change the past, and you can't know the future. Why didn't you tell all this to the police?"

"It doesn't matter. Rosa is hurt and it's my fault. Whatever they do to me—"

I needed to get him out of the downward spiral he was in. "Did you ever see any of the videos you got for Colonel Bart?"

He nodded. "When I first started getting them for him he would play one right away. He liked the old movies, not too many of the new ones. Then right after the holidays he stopped watching them when me or Rosa was around. I still got them for him, but he just put them aside. Most of the time I was working outside in the afternoon so it didn't make no difference to me, but Rosa liked to hear the music in the background when she was dusting and cleaning."

"Did either of you ever ask him why he stopped playing them when you were there?"

"She wanted to but I told her it wasn't our place." He studied his folded hands. "The colonel paid us good. Gave us cash for our grandson. He's only nineteen and . . ."

"I know," I said. "Rosa told me about him. What about the pictures in the bedroom?"

"I was in there only a few times to fix something in the bathroom. Real nice. Rosa said they were his students."

"The ones I saw were really good," I said. "Did you know he took them?"

"Rosa told me. She said he used to be a photographer. I recognized some of the girls. They were real pretty, even prettier with their bows."

Clearly the man had no idea of the significance of the bows. There was no point in bringing it up.

"Were you or Rosa there when he gave piano lessons?" I asked.

"Sometimes. Rosa didn't want me making noise when they were there, so I usually went to one of my other jobs."

I rested against the back of the metal chair. "That was a real nice video player the colonel had. How long has he had it? Did he buy it himself?"

"Last summer I drove him to the TV appliance store on Texian Trail to buy it. Hollis hooked it up for him."

"And the movies . . . Where did he rent the movies?"

Oscar rattled off the names of several book and record shops. "But most of them had the other kind that didn't fit his machine."

"VHS."

"Yeah, or they had only a few of the colonel's kind. The best place for Beta is the used bookstore on North Mirabeau. It's called *Old Reads*."

"How did that work? Did you go there and pick whatever you thought the colonel would like, or did he give you a list?"

"He did at first, then after the holidays he decided *Old Reads* had the best selection, so he would call Mr. Leser, who ran the place, and send me to pick them up. Usually they were already wrapped when I got there, but a few times I had to wait while he got them off the shelf in the back room and wrapped them."

"Do you remember the names of any of them?"

"Mostly musicals. *My Fair Lady, Call Me Madam, Annie, Get your Gun, Singing in the Rain.* I figured since he played the piano—"

"You never saw him watch any of them after the holidays?"

He bowed his head. "I suspected there was something wrong with them."

"Why?"

"Because they didn't have regular movie pictures on the cases. Just typed words. I figured they were copies that Leser made illegally."

It was a reasonable assumption. Videos for the home were new and in short supply. Buying one and making multiple copies could be very profitable but would have to be done on the QT.

"How did Bart pay for them?"

"He gave me cash. Said he didn't like to write checks when he didn't have to, but he paid all his house bills with checks."

"If he didn't drive and didn't go out of the house anymore, how did he get cash?"

"He sent me to his bank with a check about once a week."

"How much did he have you get?"

"Usually two hundred dollars."

"That's a lot of money for someone who didn't go anywhere. What did he spend it on?"

"Booze mostly. I bought him a bottle of whiskey almost every day." Oscar shook his head. "He liked the cheap blends. I got him a bottle of what the man at the liquor store said was better whiskey one time, but Bart told me not to bother, said the cheap stuff had more flavor."

"Was he angry with you for buying it?"

"He said he appreciated why I did it, but that it was a waste of money. After that I always got whatever was cheap or on sale. He didn't mind the better bourbon if it was on sale."

Eight years earlier, when we met for the first time at the officers' club on Coyote Air Force Base, he drank vodka and tonic, mostly vodka, because it didn't leave a smell on his breath, since he still had to drive home. Once there, where that wasn't an issue, he obviously preferred whiskey. The common denominator, of course, was alcohol. I had to wonder if the man had even been able to taste it in the end. Years of drinking rotgut had probably destroyed his taste buds. Did he never have hangovers from the swill he drank?

"When was the last time you picked up movies for him?"

"On Monday he had me take back the four I'd gotten him on Friday and get three more."

"Was that unusual?"

"Sometimes he held them for two or three days, but mostly he had me take them back the next day, except weekends. The only one he ever bought and kept was about six months ago. The others I figured either weren't good movies or they were copied so many times they were no good to watch."

I hadn't planned to ask the next question, yet it seemed a natural one when I did. "What did you think of Colonel Bart?"

Oscar thought a moment before answering. "Mostly I felt sorry for him. He was lonely. I think he had been lonely for a very long time."

"Since his wife died? You worked for him when she was still alive, didn't you?"

"For five, almost six years, ever since he retired from the base. But him and Hazel weren't close, not like Rosa and me. He was lonely when she was alive too. She was proper and polite to me and Rosa, but not real friendly, and she talked down to him, like he was stupid or a child. I don't think they loved each other. When she got sick he took good care of her, though."

He laced his fingers on the table, then separated them.

"His children weren't real nice to him either. Junior came over maybe once a month, stayed for ten-fifteen minutes, sometimes told him what he should do, then left. I never heard him ask what he could do for his papa. And his daughter, Stacey . . . she showed up every few months, told him she needed money, complained if he didn't give her enough, then left without even saying thank you. If one of my daughters talked to me like that, I would throw her out of the house without a penny. I think he wrote the checks so she would go away and leave him alone."

I reflected on my first meeting with the brother and sister. Stacey had made it very clear she not only expected money from her father, but that she needed it. Junior hadn't been as transparent, but the impression I received was the same.

My next question was another one I hadn't anticipated asking. "Did Junior ever ask his father for money, that you know of?"

"I heard him ask once about three years ago, and the colonel said no."

"How much did he want?"

"Ten thousand dollars."

"That's a lot of money. Did he say why?"

"That they'd break his legs if he didn't pay them."

Whoa! That sounded like a mob threat. Had he borrowed from a loan shark and failed to make the minimum payments? Was he a gambler? I'd have to check with Burker. "What was Bart's reaction?"

"Said he got himself into his fix without help. He could get his way out the same way."

Tough love. "What happened after that? Did Bart eventually give him the money?"

Oscar shrugged. "I never heard them talk about it again. Mr. Junior didn't get his legs broke."

"I guess he solved the problem then. How did Bart treat you and Rosa?"

"He was real good to us, always gave us little things. Extra money at holidays. He knew our birthdays and gave us money then, too. After his wife died he gave some of the things she'd collected to Rosa—tea cups, smaller cups for rice wine. I didn't know you could make wine from rice. And little Japanese statues they bought when they lived over there. He gave me a dagger and a collection of buttons he said his great-grandfather wore in the War Between the States. Sometimes he called it the War of Northern Aggression, never the Civil War. Somebody told me the buttons might not be brass but gold. I never took them to find out. I was afraid if they were I might be accused of stealing them."

What a different picture of the man from the one I'd had. This one kind and generous. "If you ever want to find out, let me know and I'll go with you."

His eyes lit up for a second, then dimmed again.

"Graciela is waiting to see you, to talk to you."

He lowered his head like a boy being chastised. "Her mama's in the hospital, and it's my fault."

"It's the fault of the man who hurt her," I insisted. "No one else's. Let your daughter help you."

He nodded sheepishly.

Almost immediately the door opened. Graciela hurried up to her father and wrapped her arms around him. The guard appeared in the doorway. I could see the indecision in his eyes. Should he interfere, remind them they weren't supposed to have any body contact beyond a handshake.

"Thanks." I shuffled toward him, my butt sore from the hard seat.

I wasn't surprised to find Burker outside in the hall.

"How much did you hear?" I asked.

"Most of it."

"Any idea where Hollis is?"

"We have a bulletin out for him."

"How about *Old Reads Book Store*?"

"It's being placed under surveillance. We plan to pick up Leser for questioning when he shuts down tonight."

In the meantime, I thought, they'll keep track of who patronizes the place. What surprises might that produce?

"What do you make of the mob-like threat?"

"He could have had a cash-flow problem and borrowed unwisely," he said. "But it could have been gambling debts too. He flies to Vegas two or three times a year, claims he does well, but then not many people admit to getting shellacked. He was a regular in a high-stakes poker game here in town till about three years ago when he ran into some problems paying the bill. They banned him until he settled the tab, then told him not to come back."

"How much?" I asked.

"My sources say around twenty-five grand."

"No wonder he wanted his share of his daddy's estate."

It also explained why he was playing with false invoices and maintaining Swiss checking accounts. He couldn't have much in them, however, since he had to go begging to Daddy.

"What's his current status, do you know?"

"He's been going to Acapulco on a regular basis. They don't play friendly when you lose down there. Haven't heard of any visits from strangers, though."

"Would you?"

He didn't answer.

Chapter Thirty-Four

"Before we go any further," Burker said to me, "I have something to tell you. We've found the truck and the driver who forced Michiko off the road."

"Bubba?"

"I told you before, Jason. It wasn't Bubba. Did you think I was lying to you?"

"You could have been mistaken."

He studied me for several seconds, then chose to ignore my comment. "Michiko's description of the truck was completely accurate. Faded blue '62 Ford F-150 pickup with the front bumper warped on the right side. We've impounded it. Michiko's description of the driver was pretty good too, and I have to admit he does resemble Bubba, or the way he looked eight years ago. Same build. Same coloring. He's in custody. When this promising young college student finally sobers up, he'll find he's in a world of hurts, and I'm not referring to his hangover."

I was about to say thank you when Burker rambled on.

"Just so you know, we don't normally put the entire Coyote Springs police force on alert for a minor traffic violation in which no one was seriously injured and no property damage was sustained. As for Bubba, except for going to a few job interviews—strangely, nobody wants to hire him—he's kept to himself, maybe because when I personally welcomed him to Coyote Springs upon his arrival in our fair city, I assured him that the smallest violation of a law, ordinance or road sign would be sufficient to land his ass in jail for a night or two or maybe in the state pen to finish out his ten-to-fifteen. My point, Jason, is that I said I'd have your back, and I've done my best to fulfill that promise."

"Thank you," I said, when he stopped long enough to take a breath.

He shook his head and actually grinned. "You're welcome." He resumed his march toward the building's front door. I tagged along.

"You got a lot out of old Garcia. Good job." His passion was spent. "There are a number of problems with his story, however."

"You don't believe him?"

"Oh, I believe every word he said. Proving it is all true may be more difficult."

"Such as?"

"The booze. If he paid cash for it, there won't be any record of the sale, and even if a clerk happens to remember him, it'll be tough verifying the time."

I thought about that for a moment. "I should have asked him where he bought it. If it was where he usually got Bart's bourbon, I bet the proprietor or sales clerk will remember selling it to him, since it broke his usual pattern, and the shopkeeper probably knows Bart's dead."

"Good points. Since Garcia has agreed to be cooperative, I'll ask him."

We'd reached the main entrance. Burker went to the desk sergeant and used his phone. Two minutes later he came back to me.

"Garcia said he didn't buy it at the usual place, didn't want to be seen there and have people asking him about Bart's murder. So he went to the place on Landfill Road and South Heyward. He didn't know the name of it, but I do. *Cherry's. Sour Cherry's* to those acquainted with the fat woman who runs the place."

"Which of us has a better chance of getting a straight answer from her, you or me?"

Burker nodded. "Call me later. Oh, one other thing. Just in case you wondered how Hollis knew about the porn, his fingerprints were all over the player."

I thanked him again and left the smelly, depressing building.

I drove from the jail to Heyward Street and headed south. I hadn't been to the city dump in several years. It was a dangerous place for someone whose balance was precarious on uneven ground, so after one visit I let other people dispose of the debris our restoration projects accumulated. I had a vague recollection of the intersection of the main highway and Landfill Road. The city of Coyote Springs was dry, but Spring County was not, and the dump was on county land. The liquor store was located just past the city limit sign.

The inside was cramped and not very clean. It also made me uncomfortable. Sidestepping around cases and bottles that partially obstructed aisles would have been a challenge for a man my size in the best of circumstances, but now if what I wanted happened to be on a lower shelf, I'd have to ask someone to retrieve it for me. Bending wasn't something I could do without auxiliary support. There were plenty of Pearl and Lone Star beers in the cooler. I checked to see if there was a wine section. There was. Mogen David and Thunderbird. I noted the price, then I selected a bottle of Gallo Burgundy, *vin ordinaire*, and took it up to the checkout.

The woman behind the cash register wasn't just fat, she was obscenely obese. Loose wattles of skin hung and swayed from her upper arms as she packaged the purchase of the man in front of me. Behind her, prominently displayed in a frame was a newspaper article, yellowed with age, of a much younger and slimmer woman standing beside the same cash register with a .45 semi-automatic in her hand. The caption read: *Liquor Store Owner Defends her Goods.*

I would have liked to read the story, but the man ahead of me completed his transaction and left. I could feel the woman appraising me as I shuffled to the counter. She took the bottle of wine, glanced up at me and placed it in a paper bag.

"Anything else I can get for you?"

"Do you have a small bottle of tequila?"

"Half pint." She gestured to the shelf behind her where a variety of half and full pint bottles were displayed. "Ninety-five cents."

I mentally added it to the price of the beer. With tax it came out to the exact amount Oscar had mentioned. "Is that the only brand you have?"

"Got fifths and quarts of a couple of others on aisle two, but you said you wanted a small bottle. This is it. You taking it?"

"No, thanks."

"Wise decision. Dollar eighteen."

I gave her two dollars, received my change, grabbed the wine and returned to my truck.

Opposite the turnoff to the dump was the road to the state park. I'd never been there. What I found was typical West Texas prairie, gently undulating, rocky land dotted with stands of live oak and cedar, separated by dry patches of native grass. It was a study in dull tan at the moment, but a rainstorm would turn everything green virtually overnight. Wild flowers would bloom, pretty enough for a *Texas Monthly* centerfold. It'd be back to sepia the next month. West Texas was like that, full of surprises.

Oscar had given me clear directions to the particular picnic area he'd gone to as an escape from his doghouse status. I found it without difficulty, though it was one of the more remote sites. He'd sat there for about an hour and a half, he'd told me, alternating sips of vile-tasting tequila and warm beer, until finally he decided he'd had enough. He'd capped the liquor, tossed the bottle in a trash barrel along with three unopened cans of the six-pack he'd bought.

There were two trash barrels at the site. I stepped to the one on the right, stirred its meager contents with the walking stick I'd gotten from behind the driver's seat. No tequila bottle or beer cans. I moved to the other barrel but didn't have to stir anything to see the objects I was looking for.

Now I was in a quandary. If I left and someone came along and disturbed the scene, the evidence would be lost. But I was alone. If the park was patrolled, it must be infrequently, because I hadn't seen a single vehicle, official or otherwise, since I'd arrived. As I sat at the picnic table, trying to work out a solution, I realized something else. Burker was right. Even if I was able to get the police to collect the bottle and cans and they had Oscar's fingerprints on them, there was no way to prove when the objects had been put there. I seriously doubted the liquor store proprietor would be cooperative, and even if she was, I didn't expect her to make a very creditable witness on the stand.

Suddenly, a flash caught my eye, coming from the other side of the draw that probably marked the boundary of the park.

There it was again.

This time I was able to pinpoint its origin. A lone single-wide trailer on the edge of a wasted mesa overlooking what was now a dry channel.

A third beam of light. I was being observed by someone with binoculars. A witness. My next problem was how to get to him.

I had no choice but to abandon the picnic area and the barrel with the evidence that could conceivably free Oscar Garcia. I drove as fast as safety allowed back to the liquor store. The fat lady hadn't moved. She observed my return with amused dispassion.

"Forget something?"

"I was just in the state park." I explained that I'd seen a trailer home on the hill across from where I was and wondered if there were any lots there for sale, and by the way, how do I get there.

"I can tell you how to get there," she said, "but it won't do you no good. Old Trina ain't gonna sell ya an inch of her land. You go there you're more likely to get a belly full of buckshot."

"She doesn't sound very friendly," I commented.

"Mister, she ain't never been friendly, especially to Anglos and cops. You don't look or act like a cop, but there ain't no doubt you're a white man. I suggest real strong you forget about going to see our sweet Trina."

"How do I get there?"

She shook her head. "Remember I warned ya." She gave me directions.

Trina's home hadn't been more than about five-hundred yards from the picnic table I'd sat at, but I had to drive a full two miles to get to it, the last three-quarters of a mile on an unpaved road that would have served as an inspiration to any washboard.

Halfway there I made a calculated decision. I reached behind the passenger seat and retrieved the crutches I carried for emergencies and proceeded to my destination.

Chapter Thirty-Five

The single-wide sat alone on a slightly domed ledge above the dry wash. A ten-year-old Chevy sedan was parked off to one side. The location was beautiful, and because it abutted the state park, the view wasn't likely to change. No housing developments or businesses enterprises would mar the landscape. I would have liked to explore it, but I knew I had very little time in which to accomplish my mission.

I opened the door of the truck, positioned my feet on the ground and reached for the crutches, then stopped in mid-motion. I could justify their use. The ground between my pickup and the mobile home was coarse and uneven. Falling was a major hazard for me. Unless I had something to grab onto, a chair, a table, a cane or crutch, I couldn't get back on my feet. On this treeless expanse, I would be reduced to crawling.

I left the crutches in the truck.

I hadn't advanced more than ten feet when the trailer door opened and a middle-age woman with long, gray-streaked black hair appeared on the wooden platform that served as a porch. She was clinging to a double-barrel shotgun in a manner that convinced me she knew how to use it and wouldn't hesitate to do so if she felt threatened. At her side stood a large dog of indeterminate pedigree. It didn't growl or bark, but its eyes never left me.

She leveled her gaze at me. "Get off my land," she said in Mexican Spanish.

"Senora, I wish you no harm," I said with equal fluency. "I come for information only and will leave you undisturbed."

"Crawl back into your truck, drive away and do not return," she ordered.

"Senora, a man's life is at stake. I come to you on his behalf. You may have information that can save him."

"I said get—"

"His name is Oscar Garcia. He is accused unjustly of hurting—"

"Do I have to say it again, mister? Get off my land."

"Or what?" I questioned in English. "You'll shoot me? Go ahead."

I saw her dark eyes shift for just a second to my legs, and I realized she'd watched me getting out of the pickup and had noted my laborious gait.

"On Monday," I said, reverting to Spanish, "a man went to the picnic table across the way, drank tequila and beer, then left. The police have now put him in jail for assaulting his wife during that time period. You alone are witness to his being there. If you speak up, the police will have to let him go, and he can return to his family. If you do not, the police will keep him locked up until he is tried and convicted. A judge will then sentence him to a long time in prison for a crime he didn't commit."

I rocked my hips to reposition my boots on the uneven ground. The dog studied my movement. The woman stared at me. I tried to read her thoughts but her face was blank, yet I thought I saw what might have been compassion in her shadowed eyes.

"What do you expect me to do about it?" she asked.

"Did you see him?"

"It's a long way from here."

"Not with binoculars."

I doubt she realized her eyes widened, but they did.

"If it is true that he was over in the state park where you could see him Monday afternoon between around 2:30 and 4:30, drinking, and that before he left he threw the tequila bottle and the beer cans into the trash barrel, tell the police. I'm not asking you to lie or to fabricate a story, senora. Only tell the truth."

"And the truth shall set him free," she said in unaccented English, then reverted to Spanish. "Call the police. If they come I will tell them what I saw, and it will be the truth."

"Muchas gracias, Senora."

"I knew your father, Jason Crow," she said, again speaking in English. "He was a good man. I mourned his passing." She lowered the shotgun and started to turn, then changed her mind. "I'm glad you didn't use the crutches. I will do what is right because it is the right thing to do, not because I feel sorry for you. Call your police. I will be here." She snapped her fingers. The dog turned and they retreated behind her door, which she closed quietly.

I stood there for what must have been almost a minute. I'd nearly done something I'd sworn I'd never do, use my handicap to gain pity, to manipulate people. Oscar said I was an honorable man. What would he say if he knew about this?

What would Dad have said?

I drove back to town in a funk and arrived at the police station at shift change. The place wasn't chaotic, but it was hectic.

"Is Lieutenant Burker still here?" I asked the desk sergeant.

"In his office, I think. Want me to check?" He lifted the phone and put it down a few seconds later. "He said go on back."

I walked down the narrow corridor. Burker was standing by a wall map in his office with an older man in civilian clothes. He waved me to the armchair I'd occupied on my last visit. "Have a seat. I'll be with you in a minute."

"So what's the M.E.'s problem with the Webley case?" the other man asked. "I thought it was open and shut."

My mind went into overdrive. Webley. I'd heard or seen the name before, recently.

"It should be," Burker said. "Sylvester shot his wife, then turned the gun on himself. He had a long history of mental instability, but the M.E. is questioning the suicide nevertheless. Apparently Sylvester was left-handed but the suicide shot to his head was right-handed."

"Unusual but not unheard of. Maybe he was ambidextrous? Or his left hand was hurting him. Arthritis or a cut of some sort. There are a dozen ways of explaining it."

"Ask around," Burker said. "See what you can find. Give the M.E. something he can use to close the case."

"You got it."

They turned almost in unison from the map board and only then seemed to remember I was there.

"Jason Crow, Detective Roy Lambke."

Lambke was about sixty, medium build, a minimal fringe of gray hair, a shiny crown and eyes that were as sharp as any I'd encountered. We shook hands.

"What have you been up to?" Burker asked me.

"I found a witness who'll vouch for Oscar being at the state park during the hours when his wife was attacked."

"I'm listening." His face became more contorted as my narrative progressed.

"Trina? Surely you don't mean Trina Alvarez," Lambke said.

"I'm told she has a reputation for not talking to Anglos or cops."

Lambke huffed. "That's her. She talked to you?"

"She recognized me—" I may not have become the great football star I'd dreamed of, but I was still well known and easily recognized in town "—said she knew my father."

I recounted what I'd found, based on my discussion with Oscar and my meeting with the old woman.

"She's outside the city," Lambke reminded Burker. "Whoever you send better take someone from the sheriff's office for backup."

Chapter Thirty-Six

The next morning the *Gazette*'s headline announced that Oscar Garcia had been released from police custody. So Trina had kept her word and spoken with the cops.

My night hadn't been completely sleepless, but it hadn't been restful either. I had a collection of dots and was looking for the links.

Among his vices, it appeared Old Bart was addicted to pornography. Manny Hollis's fingerprints were all over the tape player, but Oscar said Hollis had installed the machine. There was no telling how old the fingerprints were.

I had to wonder if Rosa would recover sufficiently to answer questions reliably. Burker and I knew the likelihood of her being able to identify her attacker was extremely small. Concussion victims often had no memory of the trauma that caused it.

Other dots kept popping up, obstructing a clear vision of what was going on, instead of filling in the picture. The knife that had been expertly rammed into Bart's back then wiped clean. The plate that had been shattered over Rosa's head, having only Oscar's fingerprints on it. He'd admitted handling the plate when he got it down from the sideboard for his wife. That meant the assailant had used something readily available with which to grab the plate—dust cloths seemed a strong possibility—or he was wearing gloves.

Using the plate seemed opportunistic rather than calculated. Who would be wearing gloves in the summertime? Answer: a workman.

Hollis's fingerprints on the video player. Gloved hands wielding the plate. Hollis fit the bill on both counts, but why would he violently assault Rosa? I had no doubt the blow to the head had been an attempt to kill her. What possible threat could she have posed to him?

I was missing something.

After breakfast Michiko and I drove into town separately and rendezvoused at Clover Hospital. Her shift in the pediatric ward started at noon. Rosa was still in the intensive care unit on the fourth floor. We went to the waiting room where members of the Garcia family had been holding an all-night vigil. Oscar Garcia got up from a chair in the corner where he'd been sitting by himself and greeted Michiko and me the moment we stepped through the doorway. He didn't look much better than he had yesterday, except he was wearing clean civilian clothes instead of a prisoner's jumpsuit.

"Thank you for all you've done." He introduced the other members of the family. My interest was especially drawn to the young man in the wheelchair in the far corner. By himself. Felipe. I knew exactly how he felt. He hated being there, stared at, ignored.

I went over and extended my hand. "I'm Jason Crow. I reckon you're Felipe."

His handshake was clammy and limp, not because he didn't have the strength but because it was his way of demonstrating that he didn't exist anymore, that he was a non-entity.

"Anyone sitting here?" I indicated the chair at a right angle to him.

"Does it look like anybody's sitting there?"

"Good." I settled onto the seat. "That's better."

He was watching me, trying to figure out what I was up to. "You here to lecture me, tell me everything is going to be fine, that I'll get used to being a cripple?"

"Nope. Lectures don't work. Believe me, I've had my share of them. And if you mean by fine that things will go back to the way they were? Nope again. They'll never be the way they were. As for getting used to being a cripple, I'm afraid not. You'll learn to accommodate yourself to your handicap and respect your limitations, but they'll still be there."

He gaped at me. "Everybody tells me—"

"These people . . . are any of them paraplegics sitting in wheelchairs?"

He shook his head.

"Then they really don't know, do they?" I let a moment pass in silence. "What did you want to do before the accident? Did you have any career ambitions?"

He looked away. "Gary and I were going to open a restaurant together. I was signed up for chef's school."

"Hmm. I don't imagine you can do that too safely or efficiently from a wheelchair."

"Gary's dead, so it doesn't make any difference anyway."

"I wanted to be a football player, quarterback for the Cowboys."

"I heard. Bummer."

"You like to swim?"

"Sure. Well, I used to."

"No reason you still can't. Why don't you come out to the ranch Sunday? We can go swimming together?"

"You kidding? I'll sink like a rock."

"How about horseback riding then?" Before he could object, I said,

"Hey, if I can do it with no legs, you should be able to do it with two."

"They're dead, man. Useless." He pounded his right thigh to demonstrate its insensitivity.

"Come on out anyway. You can watch me bounce in the saddle."

"You're serious."

"The first time is the hardest. After that it's just difficult, but it's worth the effort."

I stood up and extended my hand again. When he took it this time his grip was more firm. I rejoined the others.

"It's so frustrating," Graciela said. "The doctor stopped by a little while ago, but all he told tell us was that Mom is still in a coma. We asked for how long, and he said for some time. What does that mean? For some time?"

Michiko rested a hand on hers. "It means he doesn't know. The effects of concussion are hard to predict. Let me see if I can find out anything more for you."

While she was gone, Graciela and her relatives exchanged views with each other in that unique combination of English and Spanish called Tex-Mex. I quietly asked Oscar if I could speak to him privately.

"Of course. Anything."

We moved over to where he'd been sitting but remained standing.

"Yesterday you said Bart rented the videos you got for him and that he usually returned them within a day or two."

"Sí . . . "

"Except for one movie you brought him by mistake six months ago that he decided to buy. Is that correct?"

He nodded.

"What was the name of it?"

He thought carefully. "I didn't recognize the title." He furrowed his brow and pinched the bridge of his nose. "Not the name of a musical or play I've ever heard of . . . *Sugartime*? No. Something Sweet? *Sweet Somethings.* That's it. *Sweet Somethings.*"

"But you never saw what was on the tape?"

"After he bought that one, he stopped watching videos when we were around."

I shook his hand. "You've been very helpful."

Michiko returned a few minutes later. Everyone crowded around. They knew she was a nurse and that she could find out things they couldn't.

"Your mother's still sleeping," she reported, "but she's shown some restlessness in the last hour or so. That's good for a couple of reasons. First it indicates she's coming out of the deep coma, and second, she still has motor skills."

"So she won't be paralyzed like Felipe?" asked Margarita, Felipe's mother.

"I don't want to give you false hope. Until she wakes up completely nobody can say how much impairment there might be, but at this point any movement is a positive sign."

Murmurs followed.

We stayed for almost an hour. Michiko explained all the problems associated with severe concussion. She was careful about what she said, but at the same time she didn't pull any punches. They needed to be prepared for the uncertain future.

Before we left I talked to Felipe's parents, gave them our phone number and directions to the ranch.

"Don't push him," I recommended. "The more you do, the more he'll push back."

"You and Felipe seemed to get along all right," Michiko said as we rode the elevator down to the first floor.

"He doesn't believe it right now, but he's going to make it."

We kissed goodbye in the lobby. I watched her march off to start her shift, then I ambled out to my truck on my prosthetic legs, grateful that I had them, grateful for the most precious gift of all: life.

As I started the engine the question that took prominence in my mind was: whatever happened to *Sweet Somethings?*

Chapter Thirty-Seven

After leaving the hospital, I wasn't exactly in the mood for matching wits again with Clyde Burker, but I needed information, and since he was my only source for it, I drove to the police station. He was on his way out the door.

"Make it quick. I'm supposed to meet the M.E. in half an hour." He motioned me to the wooden chair facing him.

"How did you make out with the proprietor of porn?" I asked.

Burker snorted. "He pointed out that he's been in business for a long time. Years, in fact, and that among his list of collectors of rare books are some very prominent people in our fair city, people with power to put substantial pressure on the chief, which would most likely result in yellow rain getting me all wet."

Burker wasn't normally prone to flights of symbolic eloquence, which suggested to me he was feeling rather smug about the encounter.

"To which you replied that they had a lot more to lose than you did, so he'd better cooperate, right?"

Burker chuckled. "Something like that."

"Did he change his tune?"

"Sang like a jaybird."

"Sounds suspiciously like jailbird."

"Maybe I did mispronounce it a little." He smiled.

"Do you have an inventory of the videos you found at Bart's place?"

"Sure." He shuffled through a stack of papers on the side of his desk and pulled out a single sheet. "What are you looking for and why?"

"*Sweet Somethings.*"

He ran a finger down a short list. "Nope. Should it be here?"

"According to Oscar it was the first and only video the old man bought. All the others he rented and returned. It probably doesn't mean anything except he took a special liking to it. I'm curious why."

"I'll have vice check around. Porn merchants never make just a single copy."

"Any luck finding Hollis?"

"He has a reputation for disappearing on benders for weeks at a time. Since he doesn't have a family or a steady job there isn't anyone who misses him."

"What does he live on then?"

"Nobody seems to know. He always has ready cash. The place where he hangs his hat isn't luxurious, but it's not a dive either."

"How about a criminal record?"

"Some petty stuff in Mississippi. Drunk driving. Disorderly conduct. Not exactly a model citizen but not on the Most Wanted list either."

I told Burker my gloves theory.

"For once I'm ahead of you. Also, the size and weight of that plate or platter or whatever you call it—"

"*Imari.*"

"If you say so. Its size and weight, as well as the angle of impact, means it almost certainly had to be wielded by a man. The M.E. reckons someone at least five-ten."

"That leaves Oscar out. What about the vehicle the neighbor heard in the alley between the time he left for the city dump and when he came back and found his wife on the floor?"

"We don't know if it has anything to do with the attempt on Rosa's life," Burker reminded me. "For that matter, we don't know if it was a car or a truck, what time it was there or for how long it stayed. The neighbor who's been the source of most of our information claims she heard it, but none of the other neighbors recall seeing or hearing anything after Hollis left. They remember him making a racket then. Like a teenager having a temper tantrum."

"You have Trina's testimony that Oscar was at the state park during that period."

"A good prosecutor would tear it to ribbons."

"I'm not talking about lawyers now, Clyde. Knowing her background, do you think she's lying?"

"Why wouldn't she? She hates cops. Hates lawyers too. That's no secret. She openly admits to it. This is her chance to get back at them and at the same time protect one of her own."

"You mean she would lie for Oscar Garcia, a complete stranger, simply because he's Hispanic?"

Burker laughed. "People have lied for less, believe me."

His comment came across as prejudiced, which it was, but that didn't make it false. The truth was people did act out on their prejudices.

I shifted on the hard seat and would have liked to get up and pace, but the room was so cluttered it would have been hazardous.

"It's been a week now," I said. "A murder and an attempted murder in the same house, in the same room a few days apart. We don't know for sure what the motive for either killing was, whether the second assault was even intended. The first one . . . .. It's sort of hard to argue with a knife in someone's back that it was an accident."

"Or self-inflicted," Burker muttered to remind me of my initial jab.

"But we still don't have clear motives for either crime." I rose to my feet. "I hope you'll let me know when you find that video."

"You bet. We can watch it together. You bring the popcorn."

I drove over to Bart's house. Where was *Sweet Somethings*? Why had Bart bought that video instead of just renting it? And why was it missing?

I began searching the house, all the time wondering why I thought I could find it when the police forensics team, who were pros at searching crime scenes, had been unable to. The foremost reason that came to mind was that they weren't looking for it.

I had the disadvantage in my rummaging around of not being able to gain easy access to lower cabinets and shelves. That didn't mean I couldn't. I would have been smart to go home and put on my stubbies. I considered doing so, but I'd learned to be flexible over the years, and with nobody around I didn't have to consider other people's sensitivities—or my own—so I sat in a chair, lowered myself to the floor and hand walked backwards to complete my search.

Nearly two hours went by before I was willing to accept what I'd known in my gut from the beginning. *Sweet Somethings* wasn't there. The day, however, had not been a complete loss. While going through the secretary in the corner of the den, I'd come across a carbon copy of the list of Bart's students Burker had mentioned that gave their addresses and telephone numbers. I took it with me.

It was still early in the afternoon when I arrived home. Restless and feeling stodgy, I needed exercise. I exchanged my full prostheses for stubbies, simple extensions that I strapped onto my stumps. They allowed me to amble at about the same speed and dexterity as people did on their knees. I walked out to the room beside my workshop where I had weight-training equipment set up. An hour or so of pumping iron and tightening muscles inevitably raised my spirits. No one around today to spot me on the bench, so I concentrated on high reps, low resistance. Solitary workouts also afforded me the escape I used to get from running, a chance to set my mind free.

I'd been at it nearly two hours when I finally called it quits. I hadn't solved any problems, but I did feel better.

I retraced my way to the house. Walking around in the stubbies was easier than using my wheelchair, so after cleaning the field dirt off them I went to my home office, pulled myself up onto the swivel chair and was reaching for the day's mail when Lou tapped on the doorframe and stood there waiting for me to acknowledge her, which I did immediately.

Our relationship was complicated. She and her brother had parted ways thirty-five years ago when she married a Mexican national. He'd since died, and her only child, a son, had been killed in a motorcycle accident years ago. She was a meek and gentle person, a quiet, hard worker who, in spite of being treated harshly by life, had retained an instinctive goodness.

"Can I talk to you a minute? Privately?"

"Sure," I said, and hoped to God she wasn't about to announce her resignation. "Come sit down."

Chapter Thirty-Eight

After I'd uncovered my father's murderer, the man who was also responsible for her son's fatal accident, Lou Flores had been at loose ends. During that same period my mother was experiencing serious emotional and psychological problems. Recognizing Lou's patience and compassion and my mother's need for that particular combination of virtues, I'd hired Lou to be our housekeeper as well as a companion for my mother. The two women had known each other growing up, though Lou was four years my mother's senior. The housekeeping part was easy for her. She was thorough and orderly, traits my father and I appreciated and shared but my mother had never demonstrated.

It was the companionship aspect of her job, however, that had surprised Lou as much as it had my mother and me. Lou had, I suspect, been lonely most of her life. She told me several months after she'd moved into the ranch house that she'd had few friends as a girl and no close women friends later, especially after she'd broken the social taboo of marrying a Mexican who was younger than she and could barely speak English. Living with us, she said, was the closest she'd ever come to feeling part of a family. It was a sad commentary, but it gave me satisfaction to know I had in a small way brought something positive to her life.

"What's this about, Lou? Is something wrong?"

She sat on the chair across the desk from me but didn't settle into it. "It's about Harden."

"Bubba?" I couldn't remember anyone ever calling him by his given name.

She broke the tenuous eye contact she'd made with me. This meeting was difficult for her, and I wasn't making it any easier.

"What about Harden?" I asked.

"The restraining order you and Mr. Merchant have against him . . . . The police won't leave him alone. They watch him day and night."

I thought that might be an exaggeration. Burker said he had people keeping an eye on him, but he certainly didn't have the manpower to keep the ex-con under surveillance twenty-four hours a day.

"Harden made violent threats against Zack and me and against our families before he went to prison," I reminded her. "I haven't heard of him

171

retracting those threats."

"That was six years ago. He's different now."

I studied the woman in the old-fashioned housedress, her gray hair set on the top of her head in a bun. Glasses hung on her nearly flat chest from a chain around her scrawny neck.

"How do you know that, Lou?"

"Because—" she stared at her hands in her lap "—because I went to visit him every month while he was in prison."

Unconsciously I pulled back in my seat. This was the first I'd heard of it. "You went to Huntsville every month for six years?"

She nodded. "Nobody else did."

I felt certain she wasn't indicting me but her brother. Brayton had paid for the lawyers who defended Bubba, but he'd avoided personal contact with him. Since Bubba wasn't living with his father now, I assumed they still hadn't been reconciled.

"For the first several months he refused to see me," she continued. "I went anyway and sat in the visiting room waiting for him to come out. I knew the guards or the other inmates would tell him I'd been there. Finally he showed up. He wasn't happy that I was there. At least that was what he said, but I knew different. I told him I understood what it was like to feel all alone."

Probably unaware she was doing it, she started to relax. "He stood me up a couple of times after that, but then it became routine for us to spend an hour together every month."

"You never said a word to me. Did you tell anyone else?"

She shook her head. "It was my time, my decision, and nobody else's business."

I wanted to ask her if she'd ever considered telling me, but it would have been an unfair question, the implication being that I was somehow entitled to her confidence.

"He's changed, Jason. I know you don't believe that. You have no reason to and plenty of reasons to dislike and distrust him. Under the circumstances that's understandable and probably wise."

"You obviously want something from me, Lou," I said. "What?"

The unintended sharpness of my question gave her pause. I was about to apologize for it—after all, I had no reason to be angry with her—when she pressed on.

"He had a difficult time in prison, Jason. You might say it's supposed to be hard, and I won't disagree with you, but it also gave him time to think. He's not stupid. He knows he brought many of his troubles on himself. He wants to prove now he can do better. Give him a chance to do the right thing."

"Lou, I'm not holding him back. What he does with the rest of his life is up to him."

"He wants to get a job, but no one will hire him, not when there's a police car sitting outside every place he applies. He can't go down to the quick stop for a loaf of bread without a cop following him."

I crooked an eyebrow, essentially asking her to get to the point.

"Talk to the police, Jason. Tell them to back off. That's all I ask. I know why they're hounding him. So does he, but how can he return to society when the police won't let him? I know they're there to protect you, but can't they do it without harassing him?"

She was asking me to call off the dogs. In Bubba's circumstance I'd want that, too, but did I dare? It wasn't me they were protecting. I had a disadvantage in a physical confrontation, as Bubba had witnessed firsthand when I'd been knocked off my pins and forced to sit in a pile of garbage while he'd stood over me laughing and hurling insults with impunity. He'd also seen me sitting legless on the floor. That time, however, he'd felt the jet stream of a bullet passing within a few inches of his skull. I wasn't helpless, and I wasn't easily intimidated.

"He's not interested in hurting you or Zack or anyone else, Jason. I wouldn't say that if I didn't believe it to be absolutely true. Just ask the police to ease up, give him a break."

"I can't make any promises, Lou. All I can say is that I'll consider it. No promises. Just some thought."

Chapter Thirty-Nine

The next morning, Friday, I finally had a chance to sit down with Zack in the drawing room and bring him up to date on what was going on. I'd turned Bart's typewritten list over to Michiko the night before. She wanted to talk with some of the mothers of Bart's students to get their perceptions about the man. The first thing she'd done was to call Debbie and Nancy and ask for their help. They jumped at the chance.

I looked over Zack's shoulder at the diagram of Hilltop Church he'd been working on.

"Quite a list you're developing." I noted the actions to be taken and the bill of materials they would involve.

"Nothing out of the ordinary, considering the age of the building."

I pointed to the northeast corner. "Structural problem?"

"I'm not sure yet. Remember I told you after our first visit about dry rot there. I went to check on it yesterday. By the way, I saw Junior pulling out onto the back road just as I topped the rise."

"What was he doing up there?"

"With the jewelry store temporarily closed, the funeral over, and him not being the executor of his father's estate as he'd expected, I imagine he's bored."

Suddenly restless myself, I stood up, retrieved the coffee pot and topped off our mugs. I again peered over Zack's shoulder and pointed to a space he'd striped off between the paneled wall in the choir and the inside wall of the closet behind it. "A secret compartment?"

"If the cabinets weren't empty, I doubt I would have noticed that they're shallower than the space available. So I measured the inside and outside dimensions."

We'd seen it before. Drawings that didn't match actuality; closets that should have been deeper than they were, like this one, floor compartments that weren't identified in drawings, occasionally cellars that weren't marked. All were handy places to hide money, valuable items, guns and people.

"How is it accessed?"

"Don't know. It's not obvious. The workmanship of the cabinetry, by the way, is as good as I've seen. But I had another appointment, so I wasn't able to check it out completely."

I nodded. "Reverend Connors should be able to enlighten us."

"I called him. He doesn't know anything about a secret compartment, but the real estate agent who handled the deal told him there were stories about the place being used by rum-runners during Prohibition. Revenuers supposedly searched the place a couple of times but never found anything."

"That just means the secret was well kept," I said.

"You know, of course, that his real estate agent was Rhonda Bartholomew."

"Connors told me the first time we talked. Why not? She owns the largest brokerage in Coyote Springs."

We heard the unmistakable sound of someone climbing the outside stairs. I had no doubt from the halting pace who it was.

"I wish he'd take the elevator," Zack muttered. "It's going to be hell getting his corpse off the stairs if it gets wedged when he collapses of a heart attack from the exertion."

He was making a joke of it, but the concern was real. My former high school football teammate was in dangerously bad shape. He appeared at the door a minute later out of breath.

"I can see the headlines now," I told him. "Police lieutenant drops dead climbing stairs to visit legless football player. Probably earn the *Gazette* a Pulitzer."

"Very funny." Burker collapsed into the chair by the door.

Zack brought him a glass of water and was surprised when he received a thank-you.

"What brings you to these ethereal heights?" I asked, once his respiration appeared to have leveled off.

"Vice has checked all their sources and can't find anything by the name of *Sweet Somethings*. You sure you have the title right?"

"I know that's what Oscar told me. The names of all the others were correct, weren't they?" At his nod, I said, "I don't have any reason to think he got this one wrong, unless he's purposely giving us false information. I can't imagine why he would."

"Considering what we already know about Bart," Zack ventured, "and the title *Sweet Somethings*, you reckon this flick involves children?"

"Child pornography?" I shuddered. "God forbid."

"Let's hope," Burker said, "it's no more than a collection of outtakes from forgotten masterpieces of Hollywood's Golden Age. W.C. Fields kissing Mae West."

"Anybody ever tell you that you have a warped mind, Clyde Burker?" Zack said.

I laughed. "That footage, I imagine, would be worth a fortune."

"Vice will continue to look for *Sweet Somethings*," Burker said, "but I wouldn't count on them finding it. We can't be sure the title's accurate. I'm questioning Garcia's recollection, Jason, not yours. We don't know what the flick's about, whether it's clean or dirty, straight or gay, adult or child, or a combination of any or all of them. The truth is, we can't even be sure it's what Rosa was watching when she got all bent out of shape at Oscar."

It was also likely she wouldn't be able to tell us either. Burker was right in his summary of the facts, but my gut told me he was mistaken in his supposition that the flick wasn't behind the assault.

"In the meantime," he went on, "we're checking alibis."

"What have you come up with?"

"Junior was at the jewelry store all afternoon getting ready for its reopening. No witnesses. He was by himself. Rhonda was going over listings for a client at her office. Her lavender behemoth was in its usual parking space the whole time. Stacey was at the house in Woodhill Terrace, taking it easy. Lisa was shopping alone at the mall, and Keith was writing a sermon in his church office."

"Nothing very solid," I noted.

"What about Manny Hollis?" Zack asked before I had a chance.

The phone on my desk rang. I answered it and handed the instrument to Burker. He grabbed it, identified himself, then all but barked into it, "Confirmed?" There was something about telephones, I decided, that definitely brought out the man's uncivil side.

A moment later he commandeered a pad and pencil from me and scribbled a few notes, hung up the receiver and tore off the top sheet from the pad.

"That's the other thing I came to tell you about. Manny Hollis's body was found a few hours ago in his truck on a county road off Loop 241."

"Hollis dead? Well, obviously it was by foul play," I said, "otherwise you wouldn't be involved. How did it happen? Where? Who did it?"

Burker scanned the notes he'd just taken, folded them coarsely and shoved them into his pocket. "I can answer two of your three questions, which isn't a bad start."

He took another sip of coffee. "Just after sunup a rancher was hauling a truckload of cattle to market on Farm Road 936, when he noticed a pickup on the opposite shoulder of the road, the driver hunched over the steering wheel. He remembered passing the same pickup in the same spot two days before when he was going in the other direction. He hadn't had any reason to stop then. To his best recollection the engine had been running, making the rancher think the guy had just pulled over for some innocuous reason, maybe to read a road map."

Zack brought in a fresh pot of coffee and walked around refilling mugs.

"But he pulled over this time," I prompted.

"He could see the driver was still hunched over the steering wheel and decided to investigate. As soon as he opened his cab door he knew the other guy was beyond help. The stench was overpowering. His cattle didn't like it either. The rancher drove on to the nearest convenience store and called it in."

"How was Hollis killed?" I asked.

"One shot in the head, through the temple."

A shiver ran down my spine. Like Dad. Burker had said suicide. I'd said execution. I'd been right. He'd been wrong.

"Suicide or execution?" I wondered what possible reason the guy might have had to kill himself?

He shook his head. "Not suicide. One little detail missing. The gun. No gun was found at the scene. The windows were up, the doors closed but not locked. It's possible, I suppose, that someone came along shortly after he'd offed himself and took the gun as a souvenir. Wouldn't be the first time, but—"

"Fingerprints on the door handle might tell you something," I proposed.

"That's one of the bits of information I just received." He nodded to the telephone. "Door handles were wiped clean."

"Completely clean?"

"Completely. Not even a smudge."

"Like the knife in Bart's back," I commented. "These murders have to be connected. In all likelihood they were committed by the same person. We just don't have that many killers running around in Coyote Springs. At least I hope we don't."

"A killer who uses three different weapons," Zack reminded us, "a knife, a plate and a gun. What caliber?"

"The M.E.'s still doing the autopsy," Burker replied, "but he sent out word it was a .45."

"More a man's choice of handgun," I remarked, then remembered the yellowed newspaper clipping at the liquor store of Sour Cherry caressing her .45 Springfield semi-automatic. "But not necessarily," I added. "Time of death?"

"Can't determine time precisely. Based on the condition of the body—rigor mortis had already come and gone—he reckons sometime Wednesday."

"The day after Rosa was attacked. You didn't find the video with him by any chance?"

Burker laughed. "You figure I was holding out on you? No, no tape. I can tell you this though. We searched his apartment and found shelves full of pornography."

"But no *Sweet Somethings*," I ventured.

"No *Sweet Somethings*."

"Two murders and an attempted murder of three people who were associated with each other," Zack muttered. "Obviously they're related, but how?"

"What was Hollis doing up at that end of town anyway?" I asked.

"Don't know," Burker replied. "His apartment's on the south side. Nothing much up where he was found. It's ranch country. We'll ask around. It's possible he had friends up there or was doing a job for someone."

"Not likely," I commented. "From my limited dealings with him, Hollis had no particular skill or talent. The kind of odd jobs he did most farmers and ranchers do themselves or have their regular hired help do."

"His death turns things on their head," he conjectured. "I had him pegged as Bart's killer, either in greed, if he found out about the old guy's millions, or out of bitter disappointment, if he discovered his biological father had essentially disowned him."

"Which raises another question," I said. "Did the family know who he was, that he was one of them?" I didn't really expect an answer.

Burker picked up on the thread. "Could one of them have murdered him because they thought he might inherit *their* patrimony or because they shared their father's prejudice against blacks?"

Zack shook his head. "Doesn't make sense. If they knew about Hollis before, why wait until after the old man's death to kill him? If they didn't know about him till now, who told them?"

"He's right," I said.

"I know he is, dammit," Burker replied.

Zack got up and refilled our mugs for the third time. It was enough of a break for me to change the subject. "How's Bubba doing? Keeping his nose clean?"

Burker's eyes momentarily narrowed. "A model citizen. Maintains a low profile. Quiet as a church mouse. Doesn't bother his neighbors. Downright scary, Bubba being a good boy."

"Is it possible he is?"

"What? Being a good boy? We're talking about Bubba Spites, right?"

"I want to see him." I'd been thinking about it ever since my conversation with Lou.

"What the hell for?" Burker asked. From the expression on Zack's face, he was equally surprised by the request.

"Humor me."

Burker didn't often give me that you're-out-of-your-mind look, but he did then. "When?"

"Anytime. At his convenience . . . and yours. Half an hour will do it."

"It means violating the court order," Burker pointed out.

"Can Jason petition the judge for permission?" Zack asked.

"Of course he can, and the judge will grant it, but then she might also lay down some conditions, like it has to be under court supervision."

"No," I said. "This meeting has to be personal and private. I don't want anyone else there. I don't want anyone listening in on us either."

Burker glared at me. "I think you're asking for trouble, Jason, but . . . okay. I'll set up something and let you know. You're assuming, of course, that he'll want to see you."

"He will," I said with complete confidence. "If only out of curiosity."

Just after one o'clock that afternoon, I received a telephone call from Burker. I was welcome to drop by Bubba's apartment in the Cavalier Arms at four o'clock that afternoon.

Chapter Forty

The *Cavalier Arms* was located one block south of Texian Trail behind K-Mart. It had been the *Widow's Roost* when I was in high school, the place where all the newly divorced women in town took up residence and tried to get their social lives back in order. Its better days were over, however, and though it was hardly a flea bag, it seemed to be headed in that direction.

I arrived precisely at four o'clock and had barely finished my ra-tat-tat on the hollow metal door when it flew open.

Bubba . . . Harden Spites had been flabby when he'd been sentenced to prison six years ago. He'd taken off a considerable number of pounds since then, but he was big-boned so he wasn't inclined to shrivel from the loss. It was equally clear that he'd worked out with weights during his absence. He didn't fit in the same class as Ned, who could have been featured on the cover of *Fitness and Health*, but Bubba Spites was definitely in better shape than when we'd last met. Under different circumstances and with almost anyone else, I would have remarked on his improved physique and complimented him on getting in shape, but I wasn't there to be friendly.

"What do you want?" he demanded, sounding remarkably like Clyde Burker. He kept one hand on the doorknob, his six-foot frame planted firmly in front of me.

"To come in for a start. I don't want to talk to you out here."

Whether the pause that followed was calculated or mere indecision, I couldn't tell, but it took several seconds before he stepped back and let me pass. While he closed the door, I looked around. One room about the size of a two-car garage. To the right of the entry was a small kitchenette, a bathroom, and beyond it a closet. The furniture in the room was worn and shabby, the olive-drab shag carpet stained by the kitchen area and threadbare by the bathroom.

Bubba walked around me, parked himself in a corner of the sagging, nappy brown couch and waved me to the upholstered wooden chair across from him. I wondered if he was aware that higher, firmer seats were easier for me than low, soft ones. Perhaps Lou had told him. If so, it was a positive sign that he was willing to make allowances for me.

"I understand the police are giving you a hard time," I said.

"They're harassing me. Staying close but never actually interfering with anything I do, but whoever I'm with at the moment knows they're watching, listening, taking notes."

"You sound paranoid."

He made a scoffing sound. "It's not paranoia if it's true." He glared at me. "Who told you the cops were riding me?" When I didn't answer, he did. "Aunt Lou, of course."

I tried to read his eyes to determine whether he was pleased or affronted by her coming to me about him, but he'd developed a poker face.

"I know people on the force," I said. "I'm sure I can persuade them to back off, be less visible."

"Why should you? You're the reason they're doing it, because you went to the judge and said I posed a threat to you."

"Do you?" I locked eye contact with him.

He snorted. "If I'd wanted to hurt you, Crow, I could have done it a long time ago. You'd be surprised who you meet in the pen and who they know."

His tone was menacing, but it didn't fool me. I'd learned a little about body language in the hospital and rehab, in watching people watch me. Bubba was scared. Could the attitude have always come from fear and I just hadn't noticed it? Afraid of what?

"Lou says you've changed."

"How would she know? She never had anything to do with me until six years ago, so how would she know if I've changed or not?"

"I trust her instincts." He said nothing. I plunged on. "I'll call off the dogs, Bubba, in exchange for a favor from you."

He didn't seem surprised. In the world he'd just come from I imagined every deed was a tit-for-tat. You scratch my back and I'll scratch yours.

"And what might that favor be?"

"I'm looking for a certain video tape, a piece of porn—"

"Porn?" He threw back his head, stretched his muscular arms along the top of the sofa cushions and let out a guffaw. "Pornography? Oh, that's rich. The perfect all-American boy, the wounded war hero, wants me to procure porn for him. What's the matter? Isn't Michiko—" My glare stopped him cold. He studied me from the other side of the scuffed, ring-stained coffee table. "You're serious."

"I'm looking for a specific title," I said. "If you get it for me, I'll talk to my friend on the police force and ask him to ease up on their surveillance of you." I carefully maintained eye contact. "But before you let your amusement or your imagination run away with you, I suggest you listen to me very carefully."

Again he regarded me, not sure what to expect. I watched his eyes as they shifted to my legs. He slumped deeper into the couch and in a dull, almost fatalistic tone muttered, "Go on, say your piece."

With my elbows resting firmly on the arms of the chair, I interlaced my fingers and leaned slightly forward.

"Regardless of whether you look for the video, find it or not, I'm giving you fair warning. You do or say anything to hurt me, my family or friends, I'll make you pay. Don't doubt me on this. I'll make you pay, Bubba." Then I added for emphasis. "Any pleasure you think you might derive from getting back at me for testifying against you will cost you an arm and a leg."

It was a cliché that nobody ever took literally, but my half-brother did. His brown eyes widened. He said nothing, but his gaze darted once again to my motionless legs. I saw it—the fear, the dread, the revulsion. Finally he seemed to get hold of himself enough to pose a question, but his voice shook as he asked it.

"What's the name of this flick you're looking for?"

"*Sweet Somethings.*"

"Why? What's so special about it?"

"I won't know until I see it."

He worked his jaw, his dark eyes peering intently at me. Finally he said, "Give me a few days to see what I can do."

I stood up and reached for the wallet in my hip pocket. "How much will you need for expenses? I brought cash. If it isn't enough, I can get—"

He waved the offer away with the angry fling of his hand. "Keep your damn money, Crow. Consider this restitution, payment in full for past deeds."

I was tempted to say, "If you come through," but decided to let it go.

Chapter Forty-One

"I interviewed three mothers this afternoon," Nancy said after dinner.

She'd prepared lamb chops with a red wine and brown sugar sauce, wild rice pilaf with mushrooms and pickled red beets. We'd brought our second glasses of Cabernet Sauvignon to the living room to sip while we talked. Their children were already in bed. Lou was babysitting ours tonight.

"I got to talk to the parents of three other children," Debbie announced.

"And?" I prompted.

"Of the six girls involved, only two had reported being touched. The other four girls insisted the old man kept his distance, even when he was taking their pictures. Asked what they thought of their piano teacher, one said she thought he was a nice man, two thought he was all right, and one said he was smelly, otherwise he was okay."

"I made two additional contacts," Michiko said, "and added their names to the four who claim to have been molested by Bart. A friend at the CPS did some further checking. Turns out the six had previously lodged complaints through school counselors of being sexually molested by family members. One by her father, two by their stepfathers, two by their mothers' live-in boyfriends and one by her father's girlfriend. You get the picture."

"By a woman?" I asked.

"It's rare, but I happens occasionally."

"Could they be making it up?" Zack asked.

"Kids that age don't make up stories of that kind," Michiko responded, "without foundation. What I'm saying is they were all touched, molested, even raped as they described, but not by Bart. He simply became a convenient scapegoat, an agent for transference, if you will, an opening for them to say what they hadn't been able to say before."

"It also gave them an opportunity, whether they realized they were doing it or not, to let out a cry for help," Nancy added.

"Again a different picture from the one Dr. Kershaw was trying to portray."

"There's something else," Nancy continued. "The parents of the children who said they'd not in any way been mistreated by the colonel actually had a very different opinion of him. Basically they liked him. Their mothers found him gentlemanly and charming."

"And the cynics," I commented, "would point out that the quiet men, the ones with impeccable manners, are the very ones females should be on guard against. Any man who's gentlemanly and charming must have an ulterior motive."

"Damned if you do, and damned if you don't," Zack said.

"Dad used to say there were two reasons for a gentleman to stand when a woman enters a room. The first is that it makes her feel good. The second is that it makes him feel good. Seems like nowadays any guy who acts like a gentleman is suspect."

"Whereas the abused children," Nancy pressed on, "and I must add, their mothers, betrayed an instinctive fear of him."

"Because he was a man?" I ventured.

"Yes, but more than that," Michiko pointed out, "he was a man in a position of authority."

Mother joined us at dinner at the *Crow's Nest* Sunday afternoon, the first time all week since my reprimand at the table last Sunday. I wasn't concerned by her absence, nor did I give any special significance to her return. It was not unusual for her to prefer the TV in her sitting room to our company. I made it a point to visit her every day, if only for a minute, to let her know she wasn't forgotten.

She'd been out with women friends that day, having lunch, then shopping. She was in a strange, almost euphoric mood as she gave a running account of her day's activities.

"Oh, did I tell you the latest gossip? Brayton and Dolly are breaking it off. It's just rumor now, of course, but you can be sure where there's smoke there's fire. She says he's been unfaithful." Mom snickered. "Well, I know a little about Dolly Dodge. After all, we went to school together and were practically best friends. One thing I can tell you about her is that she always accuses other people of what she's doing herself." She raised her water glass and held it as delicately as other people would fine crystal. "I'm just wondering who she's going to bed with."

Chapter Forty-Two

Late Monday afternoon a courier arrived at the carriage house with a package I had to sign for. I was alone at the time. Zack had left to meet a prospective client who wanted to discuss financing options, my partner's bailiwick. From there he was going home, done for the day. I tore off the plain brown wrapper and gazed at a video cassette. Typed on a plain white label were the words, *Sweet Somethings*. So Bubba . . . Harden . . . had come through. Quicker than I'd expected.

I wondered where he'd gotten it, but I wasn't going to ask. One of the conditions of his probation was undoubtedly that he not associate with known felons which would include business transactions with them. It seemed to me very likely that those who dealt extensively in the sale and distribution of pornography had criminal records. In essence, I'd asked him to violate his probation, thereby suborning a criminal act, and he'd done so for me, knowing I would then have it within my power to send him back to the big house. Delivery of this forbidden fruit amounted to an act of faith on both our parts.

A note came with the cassette, also typed on ordinary bond paper, but on a different machine. "Be careful what you ask for."

My original plan had been to wait until Bubba had delivered the goods before requesting the police ease up on their surveillance of him, but Burker had called Friday evening wanting the lowdown on our meeting. I hadn't told him my main purpose for the visit. He had jumped to the not unreasonable and partially true conclusion that I simply wanted to bury the past with my half-brother. The suspicious cop hadn't held out much hope of that happening, so he would have been even less sanguine about my asking the ex-con to find a piece of porn for me.

"So you guys kissed and made up?"

"I wish you'd choose a different cliché," I said. "Actually, we didn't even shake hands, but we did agree on a truce." Then, on an impulse, I added, "You can back off on your surveillance now and give him some breathing room."

"You sure?"

"Yeah, I'm sure." At least I thought I was.

"I hope you know what you're doing, Jason."

That had been on Friday. Now it was Monday, and I was staring at the video cassette on the desk in front of me. *Sweet Somethings.* Was I wasting my time on a red herring? Maybe, but I'd have to view it to find out. Then I would pass it on to Burker. Was it child pornography? The idea brought queasiness and anger.

I stepped to the hall, locked the outside door—the last thing I needed was for someone to walk in while I was watching pornography—crossed to my father's office and closed that door as well. To think I'd accused Bubba of being paranoid.

Satisfied no one was going to rush in unannounced, I turned on the TV and the VCR, inserted the cassette, made sure the volume was low and hit the Play button. When I was satisfied everything was operating correctly, I settled into the visitor's chair with the long-wire remote control.

I was amazed by the amateurishness of the initial footage, but of course viewers of this particular genre weren't obsessed with cinematic excellence or thespian skills.

The opening scene was of six women in what appeared to be a large dressing room where they were getting ready for a night on the town. Clothes came off and were put on, then taken off and replaced. Each time the stripping went a little further until all of the women had been totally naked at least once. The six females ranged in size and build from small and slim to tall and hefty. They were blond and brunette, red-headed and raven-haired. One "girl" was Asian, another a natural platinum blond, a third Hispanic. The red-head was a tall, statuesque ebony woman.

Strange, I thought, that a man who was happy to put on the face of a bigot in public would be so egalitarian in his sexual fantasies in private. But then, maybe that was the point of an imagination: it allowed a person to indulge, albeit vicariously, in what was culturally taboo and socially forbidden. Would Eve in the Bible have been drawn to the tree of the knowledge of good and evil had it not been off limits?

Let's get a move on, girls, one of the more mature women announced. *We wouldn't want to hold up the big man's performance.*

He doesn't seem to have any trouble keeping it up.

Giggles.

Ah, there's our limo driver now. Right on time too. I do like a man who's punctual.

I just like them to come on time, said the blonde who was apparently playing the role of ditz. More snickers.

I groaned and would happily have turned the machine off then and there. I hadn't seen any of the video cassettes the police had confiscated, so I had no basis for comparison, but if this was so good it was worthy of purchase instead of rent, the others had to be really bad.

Okay, ladies, another woman urged, *let's move 'em out.*

Abruptly the scene changed and the six women were sitting at a low bar facing the camera. The throbbing music had a few heads nodding, bright lights shining in their faces suggesting they were looking up at a stage. All were wide-eyed. The blonde in the middle noted that the place was really hot. It wasn't clear if she was referring to the atmosphere or the room temperature until she commenced to unbutton her blouse. A few seconds later she removed it, then her bra. A man's hand reached down and invited her to join him on the stage. She did the *Who? Me?* routine, then let him coax her up directly under the lights.

The camera receded. Still, all the viewer could see of him was his sculptured, muscular back forming a distinctive V as his wide shoulders tapered down to narrow, naked hips and small buttocks. He helped her out of the rest of her clothes. They started to dance. As the camera moved around, more anatomical details became apparent, her large, naked breasts, a beauty mark on her upper-left arm, a smaller horizontal scar on his left hip that caught the light only when she slid down to her knees in front of him.

The camera swung back to the audience. Everyone's eyes were wide and staring.

"My God, he's huge," a female voice whispered in awe.

The camera pivoted back to the stage where the star of the show, the tall, blonde, naked stud was doing a rhythmic bump and grind in front of the kneeling woman as she bobbed and weaved open-mouthed trying to catch the prize.

I stared, not at his endowment, which at a glance I had to concede was impressive, but at his face. I was staring at the beatific countenance of the Reverend Keith Connors.

The picture alternated between the outstanding parson and another stage on which a lone male, posing naked, exhibited his impressively muscular young body, the young body of my friend, Ned Herman.

Chapter Forty-Three

I couldn't say how long I sat there after the tape ended. In fact I wasn't aware of it stopping, just of looking up and realizing the screen was a blizzard, the only sound static. To say I was stunned by what I'd seen would be an understatement. My half-brother's admonition echoed in my head: *be careful what you ask for.* There was, however, no doubt of what I'd found: the smoking gun, the reason Bart had bought that particular tape: blackmail. A single video had uncovered two people who were prime targets for extortion, two people who consequently had powerful motives to murder Colonel Bartholomew, Manny Hollis and attempting to kill Rosa Garcia.

I'd been a pacer in days gone by. Crossing and re-crossing the carpet in front of my father's desk had been a favorite pastime as we discussed issues and plans. I could still pace, but it didn't offer the spontaneous ease or comfort it once had. Still, it allowed me to expend pent-up physical energy. I rocked my hips and shuffled across the room, pivoted and retraced my steps.

Ned had means, motive and opportunity to kill the old colonel, but I didn't seriously consider him a candidate for the role of murderer. For him this video would be an embarrassment but little more, certainly not enough to kill a man over.

It was Keith Connors who had the most to lose by exposure—no pun intended—of his former role as a porn star, especially since his current lucrative and growing evangelical career also gave him deep pockets.

The reverend had indisputable motive, but he'd been in California with hundreds of witnesses at the time of Bart's murder, so he lacked opportunity, which meant someone else had murdered the old man, either as his proxy or for another reason. Connors could have hired someone to do the job, of course, but that would have left him vulnerable to blackmail by his hireling. What he needed was the collusion of another person who had a vested interest in seeing the colonel dead and had the skill to wield a knife.

Connor's wife Lisa had as much to lose by the release of that video as he did, and she had means and opportunity as well. A new plethora of questions arose with that assumption. Could she have murdered Bart without Keith's knowledge? Was she being blackmailed as well? How much did she know about her husband's past? About his featured role in pornography? Had she been in the industry with him? Was that where they'd met? Was her sex career the reason she'd had to get an abortion?

I removed the cassette from the player and locked it in the safe, feeling dirty just handling it. For Ned's sake I would gladly have destroyed the damned thing, except it furnished evidence that might well identify and convict a murderer. I was tempted to call Zack or leave word for him to call me, so we could get together and consider the video's ramifications, but I wasn't ready for that yet either. I wanted to discuss it with Michiko, but she'd called shortly after lunchtime to ask if I had any objections to her pulling an evening shift for one of her friends. I would have preferred that she take a little more time off to recover from her leg injury, but I had to trust her judgment that she was ready to handle the workload. It meant I'd spend the evening alone with the kids, help Lou feed them and put them to bed, then I'd have solitary time to think. Maybe that was just as well.

And so the rest of the day went. A little after nine o'clock that evening I wheeled to the master suite, the only part of the house that was completely and authentically Japanese. Tatami floors, rice-paper walls, sliding shoji doors to the bathroom and our private garden. No TV. No radio. Only a stereo system that we rarely used. The phone was set on the lowest ring possible. Intimate serenity dominated. My intent was to listen to koto music and practice Japanese calligraphy until Michiko came home after midnight.

Exactly when I fell asleep, I couldn't say.

I run up the stairs three at a time, *fling open the outside door and call out.* "Dad?"

"In here."

He's in the office, at his accustomed place behind the desk, an open ledger in front of him. He puts down his mechanical pencil, looks up and smiles. "It's about time you got here." He motions with his hand to the other side of the room. "We have a visitor."

I spin around and am stunned to find Helga Collins standing by the far window, the light streaming in behind her. She strides up to me, her hands extended. "Jason, it's very good to see you again." Her English accent is as crisp as ever.

I bend, kiss her on the cheeks in European fashion and gently squeeze her fingers.

"Your father tells me you're getting ready to expand the vineyard and bottle your own wine," she says. "How splendid. He's very proud of you."

"He's not intimidated by life's challenges." Dad grins at me. "All you have to do is follow your instincts, son. Don't ever doubt yourself."

I grin, basking in the warmth of his praise.

"Helga's husband is being raised to the peerage," my father announces. "Henceforth Nedrick shall be known as Lord Caverns."

"*Congratulations, m'lady,*" I say.

I glance over at Dad. His smile at our guest is radiant. Yet I detect a hint of sadness in his blue eyes. He and Helga always did get along so well. They agree on just about everything. Sort of like Michiko and I.

"*It's only a lifetime appointment, of course,*" Helga explains. "*He won't be able to pass the title on to his children.*"

"*If the crown still created hereditary peerages,*" Dad comments, "*the House of Lords would be severely overpopulated and the squabbling would never end. Nothing would get done.*"

"*Quite right,*" she agrees. "*It's better this way. Nedrick gets the recognition and respect he's earned and so richly deserves. It's enough that his heirs get to enjoy his money.*"

Chapter Forty-Four

I was at the carriage house in plenty of time to make the coffee before Zack arrived, something he normally did. I'd even stopped off on my way into town to pick up donuts, a rare indulgence for both of us. I liked the raised and glazed; he preferred the powdered cake variety. I purchased two of each.

My mood was schizophrenic. I rarely dreamed about Dad and often wished I could do so more often. They made him feel closer, and even though on waking I knew he was dead, I felt encouraged by the weird encounter. In my dreams, he was ageless and I had two healthy legs which I took completely for granted.

This was the first time Nancy's Aunt Helga had appeared in one of my dreams, however. She'd been a columnist on the *Gazette* for as far back as I could remember. English-born, she'd come to Coyote Springs as the young wife of an American instructor-pilot stationed at Coyote Field after World War Two. He was killed early in the Korean War, and she elected to remain in the States. A few months after Dad was killed following my return from Vietnam, she'd returned to her native Cornwall.

Other details of the dream, however, were completely out of kilter, and I wondered why.

She hadn't remarried. I doubted she ever would. I'd learned only after my father's death that they had become romantically involved, that if he had lived he would have divorced my mother and married Helga.

I tried to make sense of the dream, which meant I had to rearrange the pieces,

House of Lords. Lord Caverns. Nedrick. Lifetime peerage. Follow your instincts.

I laughed as their subliminal meanings finally came through.

Thanks, Dad. You've revealed the answer again.

Zack arrived, looking content. "It was our anniversary last night," he said. "So why are you looking so pleased with yourself?"

"I think I've figured out how to handle the situation with Ned. I was going to call you about two o'clock this morning and tell you about it."

"I'm real glad you didn't. So what's this perfect solution?"

I told him.

"Works for me. I don't know why we didn't hit on it sooner."

"There's another matter I need to discuss with you."

He bit into his second donut. "Sounds serious."

I told him about the video, what was on it, but particularly who was in it.

He put down the donut and drank coffee, then refilled the cup. "You haven't contacted Burker yet?"

I shook my head.

"He's going to be pissed when he finds out you've been holding out on him."

"I know, but at the moment I don't feel I can do otherwise."

Zack looked at me with arched brows. One of my father's mantras was that, as unpleasant as alternatives might be, we always have a choice—a philosophy I fully subscribed to.

"Not in good conscience," I explained. "If Keith Connors were the only one involved, I'd have no qualms about turning the video over to Burker, but I can't do that to Ned, not before giving him fair warning and a chance to defend himself."

"When do you propose to do that?"

"I thought we could do it this afternoon, if he's back. First, you need to look at the tape—"

"You've told me what's on it. That's enough. I have no desire to see any of it."

He polished off the rest of his donut. "I also suggest you meet with Ned alone. You really don't need me present. A situation like this is best handled one-on-one. Less embarrassing for both parties that way."

"Thanks a lot, but you're probably right. Okay. I'll take care of it."

He drained his coffee cup but didn't reach for the carafe to refill it. Looking up at the clock on the wall, he noted, "I have an appointment with the guy who owns the Victorian on Niall Street. The usual champagne ideas on a beer budget. He seems to think we should pay him for the privilege of restoring such a magnificent old mansion."

I smiled. It was a common perception. "What's your prediction?"

"We'll pass. I'll give him a list of actions he can take to improve things, but I don't expect him to do any of them. Too bad. It really is a beautiful place."

A few minutes after Zack left, I dialed Ned's number. He'd left for California immediately after our last, unfortunate meeting and was supposed to have returned yesterday. I hadn't heard from him, so I didn't know if he was back yet. The phone rang three times; I was about to hang up when he answered, slightly out of breath.

"Did I catch you at a bad time?" I asked.

"Just got back from the gym and was taking a shower. Didn't hear the phone ring until I turned off the water."

Unwanted, my mind conjured up a picture of him naked, flexing his muscles. I wished I could destroy my memory of the images on the film along with the cassette itself. "When did you get in from California?"

"Late last night. I was going to grab a sandwich for lunch and go out to the vineyard." He tried to make it all matter-of-fact, casual, but behind the words I could hear tension and uncertainty.

"I was wondering if you could come to the carriage house. We need to talk. I thought I'd call over to the *Nest* for a couple of George's steak and onion sandwiches."

"You're on."

Ned rented an upstairs garage apartment in the Cottonwood district a few blocks away, within easy walking distance.

I had finished cueing the tape to the opening scene when he arrived.

"Sit down, Ned." I waved him to the guest chair and sat behind the desk.

He glanced over at me and sat. I hated what I had to do.

"I received this from . . ." I started again. "I have a movie I need to show you."

"A movie? Wha—"

I clicked the button on the remote controller. He studied me curiously. He had no idea what was coming. I wanted so much to turn the damned thing off, but I couldn't.

"What is this? Some sort of home movie?" He made faces at the acting in the opening scene. "Jason, this is really bad. I hope you weren't the director, because if you were—"

"Just watch."

He said nothing, clearly puzzled during the minutes leading up to the nightclub scene. I had my eyes on my friend rather than the screen. When Keith Connors finally made his appearance, Ned muttered something like, "Okay, I'm impressed, I guess." He was about to turn to me, I suspected to tell me to switch it off again, when the other image appeared on the screen.

He sat upright. "What the—But—"

For the next four or five minutes, he watched the TV screen. I watched him. Keith was being serviced by two of the women. Interspersed with those scenes were shots of Ned demonstrating the classic discus pose.

"Jason, turn it off." He bolted to his feet. "For God's sake, turn it off."

I did.

"Where did you get this piece of—" He was shaky and visibly perspiring.

"Colonel Bart had it. Have you ever seen it before?"

"No." His jaw was locked, his eyes squeezed shut. He opened them and began pacing the floor the way I used to.

I let another full minute go by. "Do you know who the stud in that flick is? Have you ever seen him before or since?"

"No." He continued to strut across the Chinese silk carpet.

"He's Keith Connors."

He stopped and stared at me. "The televangelist? You're kidding."

"The same."

"Does he know you have this? Has he seen it?"

"It's hard to imagine he hasn't seen it at some point."

"You think I have?"

"You just told me you haven't. I believe you, Ned."

He studied me, not sure I meant it. Then, in what I imagined was a combination of exasperation and resignation, he plopped down into the chair across from me, a chair I'd sat in many times while talking to my father about some seemingly world-shattering crisis. Except sometimes events really were world-shattering, like now.

Ned drew several slow, measured breaths, as if he were fortifying himself for what was to come. "When I started getting into bodybuilding in a serious way in my freshman year of college, the coach talked me into making a nude demo. Nothing dirty, he emphasized. Just classic Greek poses. The body beautiful. He was stroking my vanity, of course. I was real proud of my muscles, impressed by what I'd accomplished with a lot of focused effort. It's nice being admired for your looks. You know how that feels."

I smiled. "Yes, I remember."

"So I made the demo. I was pleased when I saw the result. A few days, maybe a week later, I realized I'd made a big mistake. I really didn't want nude pictures of me, still or motion, floating around out there. So I called the coach and told him about my misgivings. He reassured me there was nothing to worry about, that the people handling the demo were professionals."

On another deep sigh, Ned sat down before continuing. "When I persisted, he reminded me I'd signed a release and had no legal rights to the pictures. I got angry, mostly at myself for being so damned stupid, so gullible. He offered a solution. I could buy back the master, as well as all the copies they'd made so far. Buy them? That confirmed I'd made a big, big mistake. They wanted an exorbitant price, of course, but I managed to raise the money and buy the lot. At least they assured me it was all of them. Obviously they'd lied, but until this moment I didn't know that." He resumed his pacing. "Damn. That was almost fifteen years ago. It's the only film like that I ever made. I swear it, Jason. And I never did anything sexual in it. Never. Nothing."

"I know you didn't," I said. "I sat through the whole thing. The only appearances you make are like the ones you've already seen. It's clear, to me at least, that the footage of you was spliced in. It's got nothing to do with the so-called story."

"What happens now?"

"I don't know. If it was just you in it, it wouldn't go anywhere. I would have destroyed it and never said a word to you, much less anyone else. But with Connors in it . . . I have to turn it over to Burker, Ned. Please understand. I don't want to, but it's evidence in the on-going murder investigation of Colonel Bartholomew, which means—"

"It could be presented at trial. Oh, God." He hung his head.

"I'll talk to Burker," I said, "ask him to limit access."

Ned scoffed. "I appreciate the thought, but let's be brutally honest, there isn't a snowball's chance in hell that'll happen. The temptation to share this delectable piece of smut with a few close friends will be too much. Hey, look at the Reverend Donkey Dong. Muscle Boy doesn't quite measure up, does he?"

"Stop, Ned. I have no doubt some people will say things like that, but don't you be one of them. I won't, and I'm not going to show this film to anyone else."

"What about Zack?"

"He's my partner. I've told him about it, but he hasn't seen it and doesn't want to."

"It'll be better if I just resign. We've probably gone as far as we're going to go anyway. Time for new territory, new challenges. Caliche Caverns is going to do real well, Jason. In a few years you'll be competing against some of the finest vineyards in California."

"And you're going to be right here with us. I don't accept your resignation. You're more than just a part of Caliche Caverns. You're the reason it exists. I want to get into your future status a little later," I said. "We handled things badly the other day, and for that I sincerely apologize." I studied him, uncharacteristically morose, defeated. "But something's been bothering you for a while now. Mind telling me what it is?"

Head down, he nodded. "I guess it's time."

Chapter Forty-Five

He got up from the chair, crossed over to the couch and stretched out on it, his long legs extending under the coffee table, his muscular arms draped across the back of the sofa. "I have to admit I've had fun playing with people all these years." The old lighthearted Ned was back. "I guess that's about to come to an end. That's all right. It's run long enough."

I tilted my head, wondering what he was talking about.

"Oh, come, on, Jason. Don't tell me you haven't wondered. Is he straight or is he gay?"

Of course I'd wondered, but I'd never felt I had the right to ask. He was my friend either way.

"Even Leon couldn't figure me out. He finally did the obvious and asked me."

I had to smile. "Okay. So here's my question. What did you tell him?"

He laughed. The twinkle in his eyes told me he was enjoying the suspense. "I'm straight, Jason. I am unequivocally and committedly heterosexual."

It was my turn to laugh. "Good. I'm glad that's settled, but why have you kept it secret? I don't understand why you would want there to be any doubt? Why not let people know you're attracted to women?"

He shrugged laconically. "Because it made it easier to avoid them."

I shook my head. "That's not a very enlightening answer. How about telling me what this is all about."

He rested his head against the back of the sofa and stared at the ceiling. A sadness came to his eyes and mouth I hadn't seen before.

"Right after graduation from college I married the girl who'd been my sweetheart since high school. I was in the Air Force ROTC at UC Sacramento and was called to active duty almost immediately. Lindsey came with me when I was assigned to Randolph Air Force Base in San Antonio as a personnel officer. Life was good. I mean, we were young newlyweds. It can't get much better than that. Then I got orders to Vietnam, and the world didn't look quite as bright. I shipped out. She returned to California to live with her folks. A month after I arrived in-country, she wrote to tell me she was pregnant. I was ecstatic."

He'd never told me he was married. I wondered why. I thought we were friends. Why keep this secret?

He took a deep breath, folded his hands in his lap and continued. "But the letters after that grew progressively more depressing. She was having a really difficult pregnancy. At one point her obstetrician offered her the option of an abortion. She said no. Two months after Tet, I was called home on emergency leave. Lindsey had gone into premature labor."

I'd been in the Air Force Medical Center in San Antonio by then, battling with my own demons, fighting with doctors and therapists about whether I'd ever be able to walk. My plate had been full. Maybe he'd felt I didn't need to be burdened with his problems.

He continued, "The baby, a boy, had died in the womb, and they performed a Caesarian to remove it, but it was too late. Lindsey suffered a massive stroke that left her in a coma."

He bounded to his feet, turned away from me and faced the corner window on his right. I let the silence linger. The time was his.

All these years he'd kept this to himself. It was unworthy of me, but I felt offended that he hadn't been willing to share his burden with me.

"The Air Force paid the medical bills," he went on, "but I was faced with long-term custodial care which they wouldn't cover, or not at an institution I was willing to send her to. I was able to arrange for a compassionate release from active duty so I could be with her. We had a little money saved and her folks were able to chip in some. The bills kept mounting, but we still had hope she'd get better. Instead she had another stroke. The chances of a meaningful recovery vanished. I could have divorced her. Both her folks and mine urged me to, so I could get on with the rest of my life, but I'd made a vow for better or for worse, in sickness and in health. I refused.

"I'd taken on two civilian jobs since my release from active duty, but I wasn't happy with either. The virulent anti-military atmosphere at both was oppressive. I found a custodial care facility for Lindsey, not far from her folks, and left to them the heartbreak of visiting her regularly to insure she was being properly cared for, while I hightailed it to Texas, where the cost of living was lower. I went to school on the GI Bill and took every part-time job I could find to pay for Lindsey's care."

Unable to hold back any longer, I asked the question: "Why didn't you ever say anything about this?"

He shrugged. "At first, in Vietnam, because it was none of your business. I don't mean that as an insult, Jason, but I didn't know you, and I've always been a very private person. My affairs and problems are just that, mine. I think you can understand when I tell you I didn't want anybody's pity."

I could have reminded him, though, how lonely it was to carry a burden alone.

"Then Tet hit," he said, "and you had your own problems to contend with."

He spun around and faced me. "I thought about telling you, just so you'd realize other people had problems too, but I didn't see how that would be any consolation. It wouldn't give you back your legs, and it wouldn't give me back my wife and son."

"So the medical expenses were why you were always so . . ."

He snorted. "Tightfisted? Yeah, I could have declared bankruptcy, but that was just running away and stiffing people who had given me goods and services with the rightful expectation of getting paid."

"But . . . you just offered us twenty-five thousand dollars to invest in the vineyard."

"Lindsey died two months ago. I used the life insurance policy her parents had bought us as a wedding present to pay off the last of her bills. The twenty-five thousand dollars is what's left over."

"Ned . . ." I started to say.

"It was a relief really, but how could I celebrate? I'd been living like a monk for so many years, it had become a habit. My consolation prize was that I'd finally be able to buy into Caliche Caverns, but—"

"Let's talk about that," I said, relieved that I'd finally be able to make a positive contribution.

"I'll take the twenty percent you offered," he said. "It's not what I wanted or expected, but it's better than nothing. Probably cheaper than your borrowing the money from me, too."

"Hey," I said cheerfully, "don't crap out on me now. I'm about to make you an offer I hope you can't refuse."

"Please, no dead horses."

"Zack and I discussed it at some length this morning."

"Porn and profits. What a great way to start a day."

"Shut up and listen."

"Yes, godfather."

"You know why we're unwilling to offer you voting stock in the vineyard. A three way decision split can lead to chaos, and while we all agree now on what we want to do and how to do it, it stands to reason that won't always be the case. At the same time, Zack and I can't deny that you deserve to share in the vineyard's profits. We wouldn't be in business were it not for you. My offer to you the other day, however, was unworthy of us and insulting to you, and that's the last thing I intended or you deserve. We want you as a partner, Ned, even if you are straight and a skinflint."

"I might be able to do something about the skinflint part."

I laughed. "So here's our revised offer. One-third of the profits."

"I didn't really expect half. It was an unreasonable demand. One third is fair. What about voting?"

"For as long as you own the stock you have a vote equal to ours, but it's exclusive to you personally. Your successors, either by sale or inheritance will not have voting rights."

He raised his eyebrows and grinned broadly. "A good compromise. It's the kind of wisdom of Solomon resolution to a problem your father would have come up with."

The compliment was so unexpected it stunned me. "Think it over," I finally said, "and let us know."

He huffed. "I'm tight with my money, not with my brain cells. I accept." He walked over and extended his hand.

I took it, and breathed with relief. "Think we can have lunch now?"

I called over to the *Nest* and ordered our steak sandwiches with extra grilled onions.

Ten minutes later, Zack delivered them. He'd stopped by to talk to George when my call came in. While we were eating, Ned told Zack about his wife and son. Zack offered his condolences.

"I understand you declined to watch the skin flick." Ned picked up the second half of his sandwich. "I can't say I blame you, but I'd like to ask you to review it anyway. If—maybe *when* is a better word—this film becomes publicly known, you better be aware of what's on it. It's going to be embarrassing for me, but it isn't fair that you get pilloried for my foolishness."

"Let's hope it doesn't come to that," I said.

"Yeah, hope for the best, but be prepared for the worst. You found a copy of it. We don't know how many others are out there, or how many other flicks I might appear in."

He was right, of course, which only made it worse.

After Ned left, I let Zack watch the video in Dad's office while I went to pay another visit to Bubba.

Chapter Forty-Six

The door didn't fly open with arrogance when I knocked on it the second time. A moment passed, I heard a chain being withdrawn, and the steel door was opened in the customary fashion. No defiant challenge greeted me. I'd called ahead, so he wasn't surprised by my presence.

"Come on in." He stepped aside and let me pass. "You want something to drink? I've got soda and iced tea. Sorry, no beer or wine. I'm not allowed to possess or consume alcoholic beverages as a condition of my probation. So what will it be? Soda or tea?"

"If you're having something, I'll have the same, otherwise I'm fine."

"Sit down." He went to his small kitchen and came back with two cokes.

I sat in the chair I'd occupied on my first visit. He handed me the drink.

"Thank you for getting me the video," I said after a sip from the can, "and for the warning."

"A surprise, huh?"

"To me and to Ned."

"He was used. You know that, don't you?"

"Yes, but it's still dangerous. He wonders how many other flicks he's in without even knowing it. Is there any way to find out?"

"If you know the names of the flicks, you can ask for them and see what turns up."

"Suppose you don't know what title they've been put out under?"

"Then you're out of luck unless you know the name of the star performer, but they change those all the time too." Bubba rested back into the couch cushions. "I've never pictured you as being interested in watching other people get their jollies. I'm sure the virtuous Jason Crow must have some vices, nose-picking maybe, but sexual voyeurism? Mind telling why you wanted that flick? What were you expecting?"

I realized as I watched and listened to him that the comment and the question were sincere. Sarcasm notwithstanding, I sensed a genuine request for information. Did I owe him an explanation? Would it do any harm if I gave him one?

I sighed. "Child abuse. I thought the video might have to do with the sexual exploitation of children."

"Why would you be interested in child abuse?" he asked. "What's this all about?"

"What do you know about Colonel Bartholomew?"

"No more than what I read in the newspaper. A blowhard. Heavy drinker. You found his body. He'd been stabbed in the back with a kitchen knife. I guess somebody didn't like him."

"His daughter, who's now in her forties, claims he molested her for years. He had a fetish for having her wear a big bow in her hair, fondling her and taking pictures of her. There were framed portraits of young girls on the wall in his bedroom opposite his bed along with dozens more, unframed photographs in a drawer."

"And now he's dead, murdered," Bubba said. "Some people deserve to die."

I didn't disagree with my half-brother in theory. "There's a right way and a wrong way to punish criminals."

He mulled that a moment. "Except the right way doesn't always work, does it? But you're not here to discuss jurisprudence. You thought this video was going to tell you something? What?"

"I didn't know," I admitted. "Until I saw it—"

"Until the eyes see and the ears hear, Doubting Thomas."

Bubba using terms like voyeurism, jurisprudence and making references to the Bible? Maybe Lou was right. Maybe he had changed.

"Bart watched a lot of porn," I said, "after seeing *Sweet Somethings*. Rented it from a bookstore on the north side."

"*Old Reads*." At my look of surprise, he chuckled. "You're so naïve, Jason, so innocent. Old man Leser's been the porn king in Coyote Springs since before we were born. Books and magazines when we were growing up, a few 8mm films, but they were expensive, and of course you had to have a projector and screen. I reckon video cassettes are a boon to the industry. Cheap to make and easy to reproduce. Best of all, you can watch them on TV from the comfort of your bed."

I winced. He laughed again, but it was with amusement, not the mockery it would once have been.

"As I said," I continued, "Bart rented all his porn, with the exception of the first one he got by accident and bought."

"*Sweet Somethings*."

I nodded. "Problem is we couldn't find it among his videos after his death."

"You figure whoever killed him took it—"

"Actually, we didn't even know about it until his housekeeper was attacked and almost killed—"

"Rosa Garcia. I saw the story in the paper and wondered how she fit in."

I told him the scenario as I knew it: Bart's murder, the attack on Rosa and Hollis's murder. He listened patiently, thoughtfully.

Finally he asked, "Why're you so interested in Bart's murder anyway? Scuttlebutt is that you weren't exactly friends."

"I told you Bart had a bunch of pictures of little girls tucked in a drawer, girls we suspect he molested. One of them is my sister's seven-year-old daughter, Livy."

"Elsbeth's kid?" His jaw muscles flexed. Again I waited for a comment. Eight years ago he'd been generous with racial epithets. "Aunt Lou showed me pictures of your family and your sister's. They're all knockouts. I guess there's something to be said for mixing races." He rose from the couch and headed for the kitchen. "How're they doing?" he asked over his shoulder.

"Good. Aaron's career is taking off."

He shook his empty soda can. "You ready for another?"

"I'm fine, thanks."

He removed a fresh can from the refrigerator, popped the top, returned to the couch and sat down in the corner, almost as if he were seeking sanctuary. He contemplated the top of the can. "You said Bart's daughter claimed he molested her forty years ago. What specifically is he supposed to have done?"

"Fondled her for sure. She hasn't been forthcoming about whether it went beyond that, if he actually penetrated in any way."

"And he's continued to do this with other little girls?"

"She claims he loses interest in them when they start to menstruate."

"He only touches, fondles?"

"That's what the kids who've been taking music lessons from him say."

"Is that what he did with your niece?" Bubba asked.

"He didn't get a chance to go that far. Except for two brief periods of time, Debbie was there with them. When she wasn't, his housekeeper was. I can't imagine Rosa allowing him to do anything he shouldn't."

Bubba continued to study his soft drink. When he finally looked up, I sensed deep-seated distress, the kind that had been seething for a long time. "Let me tell you, brother," he said, his tone angry, mocking, "you don't know diddly about child abuse and molestation."

Now he was calling me brother. This visit was taking twists and turns I hadn't anticipated. "And you do?"

"Your old lady may be missing a few marbles," he said, "but she's still alive. Mine died when I was six. That's when things went south."

"You're not telling me your father—"

"And yours." He looked at me and smirked. "You hate the idea that you and me are brothers, don't you?"

"Harden, let's not go there."

"Harden now." He chuckled. "My old man doesn't even call me Harden anymore. Actually, he doesn't call me anything."

"Are you trying to tell me he abused you after your mom died?" I persisted.

"He didn't. He swatted me once in a while, but nothing I probably didn't deserve. Might surprise you to hear me say this, but for a while I think he tried to be a good daddy."

"So what happened?"

"My grandfather. Mom's old man. He was a sadistic son of a bitch. His girlfriend was even worse."

"A grown woman seduced a young boy?"

"Not seduced. She wasn't interested in my pleasure, only her own, and if it hurt, all the better."

"Jesus," I muttered. "Why didn't you tell your father?"

He snickered. "You mean since he was working so hard at being a good daddy? I did, and was reminded that my grandfather was a state senator. State senators didn't do things like that, and women didn't rape little boys. I went to him only one more time after that and got a beating for making up lies."

"Couldn't you tell someone else?"

"Not without my father being informed. So I kept quiet and endured it as long as I could, but the abuse kept escalating. When I couldn't bear it anymore, I started rebelling and acting out."

"I had no idea."

"I know you didn't, and I hated you for it. I got our biological father. You got a dad."

I didn't like Bubba Spites, hadn't since we were kids. I could never understand why he was so vicious. Now I did. I suspected Harden Spites wasn't a nice guy either, but at least now I knew why. He'd been molded by forces he couldn't control.

"So you see, I'm something of an expert, an authority, if you will, on sexual abuse," he said in a drone. "I don't have any formal credential, no sheepskin or engraved certificates, but I have the scars to prove it. Not just from my grandfather and his assistant, but from six years in a very exclusive men's club. One of the things I learned is that sexual perverts don't rest on their laurels. Oh, they plateau from time to time, but then they get bored and up the ante. If Bart started out fondling little girls, there's no way that forty years later he'd still be content with just touching."

"What are you saying?"

"I'm telling you he wasn't a child molester."

"That's what he claimed in a letter he left for me. But . . . .. But several girls have already admitted he fondled them—"

"They said that because it was what the interviewer wanted to hear."

I thought about the leading questions Dr. Kershaw had used, the way she kept pressing Livy. "Are you saying Bart's daughter made it all up?"

"She may have been molested by someone . . . .. What's she like? Well adjusted? Married with kids?"

"Single now. Been married four times. Has a daughter from her first marriage."

"There's a good chance she was molested then, but I'm telling you it wasn't by her father. An uncle, a brother, a cousin, even a neighbor, but not by her father."

"How can you be so certain?"

"Over the last six years I've had a lot of time on my hands. I may not have been much of a student in school, but I can read, and I did my share in Huntsville. They have a very good library system in prison, you know. They'll get you any book you want. I read everything I could lay my hands on about abuse, sexual and otherwise. About what some men do to women and to other men. What women do to each other and to men. How they trick, con, manipulate and enslave them. The human species isn't unique in its cruelty, Jason. Other species devour their young, but we seem to be unique in the pleasure we derive from pain, our own and other people's. Does a cat know it's killing the mouse it catches and plays with? There are people out there who take exceptional pleasure in hurting others, inflicting pain and torturing them to death."

Bubba Spites disappeared in this little speech, I realized. The man I saw now was Harden Spites.

"Like I said," he continued, "I don't have any formal education on the subject, but I know what I'm talking about." He said the last statement with pride I hadn't heard before.

"Thanks for your insight," I said. "It makes a difference."

"Glad to be of service." There was a hint of sarcasm, but again I noticed it wasn't intended to be offensive. "Fair exchange. Thank you for calling off the cops. They're still around, watching me. I know that, but they're being a little more low-key about it. There isn't a patrol car sitting at the curb wherever I go. Maybe now I'll have a chance of getting a job."

I left a few minutes later. He'd given me a lot to think about. If Bart hadn't molested Stacey, who had? Even more puzzling, why did Bart accept responsibility for an act so heinous, if he hadn't done it?

Chapter Forty-Seven

I left my brother's apartment even more baffled than when I'd entered it. What surprised me was that I felt full confidence in what he had told me. Two weeks ago I would have rated Bubba as having zero credibility, but today, for the first time in our lives, Harden and I had talked to each other like civilized individuals. More than just talked, we'd communicated something of value.

I'd already reached the conclusion that Bart hadn't molested his daughter, that Stacey had made up the allegation as a means of extorting money from her father. She'd apparently been smart enough to not make outrageous demands, just modest requests he could rationalize acceding to. The old man's response may not have been heroic, but it was understandable. There was no defense against an accusation of sexual abuse. Indeed, the louder a man protested his innocence, the more guilty he looked. Even if somehow he could prove the allegations to be false, he was forever stigmatized by having been accused. After all, where there's smoke . . .

My brother's other words resounded in my mind: *I got our biological father. You got a dad.*

How blessed I'd been to be brought up by Theodore Crow. I hadn't responded to Bubba's other comment, but I'd felt its sting: *Your old lady may be missing a few marbles . . .*

I didn't fully understand my mother. She'd been a good mom when I was growing up, but the last ten years had been shattering for her mentally and emotionally. The years ahead didn't promise to be any better. Nonetheless, she was still my mother.

The abuse by Harden's grandfather and his girlfriend sickened me. There were degrees of evil. Child abuse and corruption of youth were the most heinous. The only thing worse than passive enabling was active participation, and the only thing worse than active participation was being an instigator, an initiator.

I couldn't help reflecting once more on how much Brayton Spites had to answer for. I didn't think for a minute he was unaware of the kind of person the senator was. Brayton wasn't a naïve man. Did I think he approved or condoned his father-in-law's conduct? No, but he was willing to close his eyes to it. His own son was being abused, and Brayton had turned his back on him.

Michiko had insisted Hazel knew what her husband was doing. That was when we'd believed Bart was a child molester. But now, having concluded he wasn't, the question changed to whether she knew what her daughter was doing. If so why had Hazel tolerated it? I knew the answer. Selfishness.

Hazel had latched onto Bart for mercenary reasons in hard times. He was her meal ticket, her security blanket, the source of her social prominence. How ironic that Stacey was following her mother's pattern.

At the carriage house I found Zack crunching numbers. He raised the index finger of his left hand as the fingers of his right continued to skitter across the keys of his calculator. I waited as instructed. Finally the machine stopped. I expected to see a small plume of smoke rise from it. He'd already burned out two other machines in his zeal.

"So how did it go with Bubba?" he asked.

I recounted the gist of our conversation. "Did you watch the video?"

He took a deep breath and let it out. "I understand why Ned insisted I see it, but I wish he hadn't. He didn't do anything obscene on that tape, but he'll be tarred with the brush of guilty by association."

"How often lives are changed by chance." It had been a series of chance encounters that had permanently altered my life and led to my father's death.

"The Reverend Keith Connors doesn't have the same defense," Zack said. "There's no doubt he's actively involved. If ever there was a candidate for blackmail . . ."

The phone rang. I picked it up.

"Mr. Crow? Jason. This is Fernando Amorado. I'm sorry to bother you, but there's a problem. I was patching Colonel Bart's roof this afternoon. The police came. My son Jesse, he had an accident. I needed to get home right away. He fell out of a tree and broke his arm. My wife had no other way to get hold of me so she called the police."

"How is he?"

"The doctor's putting a cast on to keep him from doing more damage. It's hard to get kids his age to slow down. I can't leave him, Mr. Crow. I hope you understand."

"Of course I do."

"About the roof. I tried to find someone to finish the job for me—" he rattled off several names "—but no one's available. A storm's coming in. The piano . . . I didn't get a chance to cover it. If we get a hard rain, the ceiling over it will fall in. Mr. Crow, I don't have money to pay for a new Steinway."

"You take care of your family. I'll handle the roof. Are your tools still there?"

"Sí. When the police came I dropped everything, got into my truck and left. I'm sorry to let you down."

"Family comes first. Tell Jesse to hurry and get better." I hung up and explained the situation to Zack. He'd already figured out most of it.

"I broke my left arm at about that age," he said. "The kid'll heal fast."

Ironically, I'd never broken a bone in my life.

We made phone calls, but it took only a few minutes to realize we wouldn't find anyone on such short notice. Tomorrow would be too late. That left only one alternative.

"While I'm changing," I said, "call Nancy and Michiko and let them know we'll be late, then put your car in the garage just in case we get hail."

I went to my dressing room, removed my prostheses, donned work jeans with the reinforced seat, pulled myself into my wheelchair and descended to my truck.

The wind was growing stronger, the sky darkening. At least I didn't see the telltale signs of a tornado—purplish-green sky, rotating clouds—or hear a train coming. That didn't mean anything. Twisters were known to develop out of thin air.

"Okay," Zack said once we were on our way to Indian Heights, "we know now Ned and Connors had motives to kill Bart and Hollis and to attack Rosa Garcia, since she'd seen the damning video."

"We can eliminate Ned," I insisted. "He didn't do any of those things."

"That leaves only Connors, but he was in California when Bart was murdered, which means—"

"If he did it, he had an accomplice."

"His wife Lisa?" Zack wasn't happy with the conclusion. Nor was I, but it was inevitable.

I steered around a fallen tree branch. "She has no alibi for the night Bart was killed. Plus, she has a degree in kinesiology, which gives her the requisite skill to inflict a fatal knife wound."

"And she's physically fit," Zack added. "Strong enough to stab a man in the back and slam a heavy porcelain plate over an old woman's head."

"She also has access to Junior's gun collection," I reminded him, "if it turns out one of her uncle's guns was used to kill Hollis."

I negotiated the turn onto Fennimore Road.

"Do you think she could have acted alone?" Zack asked. "That her husband was not involved?"

I'd considered the question during the night as I lay beside my sleeping wife. What would Michiko do to defend me? Answer: anything, short of sacrificing the well-being of our children. The Connors had no children.

"I reckon it's possible," I said. "In fact she could have been the one being blackmailed without his even knowing about it. That almost makes more sense to me. She had as much to lose if her husband were disgraced. She'd pay to protect him, whereas he might have balked at the threat of blackmail and told Hollis to go to hell."

"A beautiful young woman," Zack commented a minute later. "A murderer."

"Looks," I observed, "have nothing to do with it."

I veered around another fallen tree limb, turned down Claremont Street and pulled up in front of the residence of the late Lt. Col. Mortimer Bartholomew.

"I need to call Burker." I was sickened at the thought of turning the cassette over to the police knowing Ned would be held up to ridicule, but I didn't see any alternative under the circumstances. What was the line from Shakespeare's Julius Caesar? *The evil that men do lives after them?*

Means, motive and opportunity. Means wasn't an issue. Anyone could have wielded that knife. Several people had had the opportunity, but neither of those elements carried any weight toward a charge of murder without a motive. Without the video, there could be no charge of blackmail, and without that motive there would be no charge of murder. Whether Lisa Connors acted alone or in cahoots with another party was immaterial for the moment. She alone had the means, motive and opportunity to kill old Bart. Without this evidence she would be free to murder again.

Bart's house was expectedly dark. I could see a bundle of shingles, still in its brown wrapping paper on the gable beside the carport.

I pulled up behind the Cadillac. Zack removed my wheelchair from the truck bed. I catapulted into the seat, reached into my jeans pocket, removed a key ring, selected the one for the side door and handed it to my friend.

"Call Burker. Tell him we're coming to see him as soon as we get this patch job done."

Zack ran to the door. I was barely able to squeeze through the side gate to the backyard. I positioned myself so I could see the back gable. Roofing materials were stacked around the raw patch.

When Zack rejoined me, I said, "Amorado's right. A big rainstorm will be disastrous."

"We'd better get busy then. The power and telephone lines are out."

Chapter Forty-Eight

Fernando had laid the extension ladder along the side of the house. While Zack hauled it out, I lowered myself to the ground, pawed my way to the building materials stacked neatly beneath the magnolia, found a coil of nylon rope and donned it bandolier-style over one shoulder, under the other. By then Zack had set the expanded ladder against the eave. I worked my way back to it and helped him reposition its feet at the optimum angle.

At the top I hauled myself to the critical area. Fernando had already installed new decking and felt, but the wind had caught an edge and torn it. If this were a final installation instead of a temporary fix, I'd replace it, but getting a heavy roll of the tar-soaked material topside and wrestling with it in the wind would be a comic waste of energy and time, time we were quickly running out of.

Fortunately this side of the roof was in the lee of the wind. The shingles were at hand, along with Amorado's roofing hammer. I set to work. Once I got my rhythm going, I was able to move quickly with the repairs—until I ran out of shingles.

I worked my butt up the incline, was slammed by the full blast of the wind as I crossed the ridge and fought my way to the unopened bundle of shingles at the roof's edge. A coffee can of nails beside it had tipped over. Some of them had spilled to the carport below, another picking-up job for Jesse and his younger brother. Unable to carry the heavy bundle, I had no choice but to maneuver it up the slope a few inches at a time, then down the other side.

"It's raining harder," Zack shouted up to me, as if I couldn't feel the pelting. "Come down, Jason."

"Almost finished." I was nailing the last shingle in place when lightning streaked the southern sky, the thunderclap only a second behind it.

"Jason, damn it, come down. Now."

I didn't need further convincing. I tossed the hammer to the ground below.

Another flash of lightning. I could smell the ozone.

"Jason, NOW!" Zack screamed against the howling wind.

I scurried as fast as I could to the ladder.

The rain was beating down, big, hard drops with the power to sting.
"Hurry, Jason. Damn it! Hurry!"

He was under the ladder now, hanging onto a middle rung so the wind wouldn't tear it away. I rotated onto it, my own weight adding meager stability. Time and wind-force were against me. The ladder was jiggling. I did what I'd never done before, positioned my stumps on the ladder's risers and slid down. I reached the bottom in about a third the time it would normally have taken me, but I paid a price—what felt like friction burns on the inside of my stumps.

Just as my butt hit bottom, an angry gust caught the top of the ladder. For a moment Zack tried to hang on, then, realizing it was futile, let go, falling to the ground on his hands and knees a few feet away from me.

"You all right?" I shouted.

"Fine, you?"

Together we watched the extension ladder take flight. It took the downspout on the corner of the house with it, slammed into the side fence and broke off several pickets. The wind was gale-force now. Zack had earlier folded my wheelchair and laid it on its side. He struggled to expand it.

"I can move faster without it." My shouted words were nearly swallowed by the tempest. I "loped" my torso as fast as I could to the gate and through it. Zack came up behind me, fighting, dragging the still-folded chair. He bypassed me, staggered and lifted it over the side to the truck bed. He opened the driver's door for me and held it against the vicious blast. I climbed up onto the running board, clawed myself onto the seat. The door slammed shut behind me. For a moment it was as if all sound had ceased. Zack darted around to the passenger side and jumped in. We were both dripping wet.

Zack turned on the radio. The preset local station was mostly static. He turned up the volume and adjusted the fine-tuning.

"This is a tornado alert. Repeat. This is a tornado alert. A tornado was sighted in the Woodhill Terrace area approximately fifteen minutes ago and is currently reported to be moving east toward Jordan. All residents in its path are advised to go to an interior room—"

"Jason, we need to go to my house." He was emphatic. "I have to make sure everyone's all right."

Cautiously I backed out of the nail-and-shingle-littered driveway. My heart was pounding.

"If we can get through, we will," I said, looking with dismay at the debris already cluttering the road.

Chapter Forty-Nine

The wind suddenly abated, but the rain continued to pummel Bart's roof. Would the patch withstand the beating? As I pulled out of the driveway, the wind rose again. Rain lashed the windshield like whipped sheets. A downpour on one side of the street; shafts of sunshine on the other. An eerie feeling that tingled the spine, made me aware of the tips of my leg stumps. I shivered.

"I've got to get home," he repeated. "I've got to make sure everybody's safe. If I'd thought for a minute this storm would be so violent . . . . To hell with Bart's roof."

"We're not that far." I tried to sound reassuring, but I understood his gut-wrenching fear, every man's fear, that he'll fail to protect those he loved. "We're just a few minutes away."

I drove cautiously around fallen branches toward the intersection through which we'd come less than an hour earlier. The two-story, colonial frame house on the corner had been totally demolished by the twister, the fireplace exposed, its twin chimneys amputated.

"My God," Zack exclaimed. "I hope nobody was home." In fact, we didn't see a soul about.

The glistening-wet ranch-style houses on other three corners appeared unscathed. I proceeded at half the speed I would normally drive, my course a snake line between the curbs around the debris of destruction. The tornado had torn the roofs off three houses up the next street, ripped the siding off a fourth, uprooted trees, sheared the foliage from bushes.

Zack fidgeted in his seat. "This doesn't look good. Can't you go any faster?"

Rounding what was probably designed to be a scenic bend in the road, I was forced to stop abruptly at an impenetrable wall of fallen branches, wind-driven trashcans, fence stakes and sheet metal.

"We have to find another way, Jason."

I didn't have to be told. I executed a jackknife, reversed course and drove back toward our starting point.

"I don't see lights on in any of these houses," Zack mumbled. "The power's out all over."

"Hang on." I hooked a sharp left and headed down an alley.

I was taking a calculated risk. The alleys here were unpaved, barely wide enough for the garbage trucks that came through twice a week. There was no room to turn around or even pass each other. If I met someone coming from the other directing we'd have a standoff that at a minimum would consume precious time.

I could feel my friend's glances. His knees were bobbing up and down in his anxiety. I reached the end of the narrow passage to the main road, was about to turn right when I saw an Arizona ash had been felled, crushing a car parked at the curb and completely blocking the roadway. I looked to the left. A motor home, lay on its side, an equally impassable barrier. I had no choice. I shot across the street and barreled down the next alley. I was tempting fate, but what choice did I have?

We'd entered Woodhill Terrace.

"The power seems to be out here too," Zack said. "Junior's house isn't too far. Maybe not the telephone lines, though. I might be able to call Nancy from there."

Provided we didn't run into an obstruction on the way. "He's not going to be very friendly after our last encounter."

"Screw him. That's his problem. If he gets in my way I'll deck the son of a bitch."

I almost smiled. Zack might be little, but he wasn't weak.

"Oh, shit."

I saw it too. A long stretch of the privacy fence on the right was either down, scattered about or missing altogether, exposing backyards, swimming pools, gazebos and what had probably been well-tended gardens. The houses themselves, all brick, seemed to have suffered little or no damage. The next section of fencing was intact, until we reached Junior's place.

"Oh, my God!" Zack exclaimed.

The absent fence was a minor detail. One of the six tall, spindly cemetery trees was on its side. Three women hovered over the sheared base. Under the fallen poplar lay a man, who could have been Keith Connors, face down.

I hadn't rolled to a full stop before Zack opened his door and jumped out. I was in a fix. My wheelchair was in the bed of the truck behind me. After eight years of practice, I could get it out by myself, expand it and take to it without help, but there was no way I could maneuver it over and around the labyrinth of debris obscuring my way to the pinned victim. And once I got there, what could I do?

Time to implement plan B.

I opened the door and lowered myself to the soggy dirt roadway. I was already soaking wet, so it didn't seem to matter.

"What happened?" I called out as I worked my way around the front of the pickup.

The surprise on Stacey's face quickly morphed to a dismissive glance. *What good are you with no legs?* her eyes said. For an infinitely long second the heat of resentment burned, but I refused to give it control. I heard my father's words: *We make the best of the hand fate deals us.*

Lisa's mouth dropped open at the sight of me. She tried not to gawk. I could see the embarrassed uncertainty in her expression. *What am I supposed to do or say?*

It was Rhonda who stared.

Zack had his fingers on Keith's carotid. "Steady pulse."

"You have to get us help," Lisa cried. "He can't breathe. He's suffocating. Please . . ."

"How long's he been there?" I looked around for something we could use as a fulcrum and a lever. Nothing.

"Five minutes maybe." Stacey was impatient. "He's losing consciousness from lack of oxygen. We need help fast."

I hand walked closer. "What's in the garage? Any tools? How about a chainsaw?"

Rhonda shook her head and pulled her sleeves up, revealing a skin blemish just below her left shoulder. "Pliers, screw drivers, small stuff. Nothing that'll help here."

I stared at the birthmark and didn't know why.

"How about a hand ax?" Zack asked. "We need to cut away branches."

"I don't think we have one," Rhonda replied without conviction.

"You're wasting time," Stacey complained. "My car's blocked in. Give me your damn keys." She extended her right hand to Zack, having assumed he'd been driving. "I'll get help while you two fiddle fart around."

"They're in the ignition," I told her. "Ever drive a manually controlled vehicle?"

"I'll figure it out," she snapped over her shoulder as she ran to the pickup.

My mind raced, searching for a solution. A man's life was at stake. "See if you can find bricks, planks, anything we can use to prop up the tree trunk," I told Zack. "And a shovel."

I swung myself over to Keith, felt his pulse. Steady but not strong. Stacey was right. Keith's life was slowly slipping away. "Find anything?" I called out.

"Cinder blocks." Zack emerged from the side of the garage, one in each hand. "There are paving stones back there too."

"Bring them," I told Rhonda and Lisa. "Quickly. We need to shore up the trunk by the break."

I didn't have to explain to Zack that if the sheer gave way Keith's back would be crushed.

He tried frantically to stack both blocks under the trunk. Not enough vertical space. I was useless. Even if I could have straddled the tree trunk, I wouldn't have been able to raise it enough for him to lodge them underneath it. If . . .

"Hand me the shovel," I told Rhonda, who hadn't moved, "then bring those pavers. As many as you can."

Digging deep without legs was tough since I couldn't get above the spade. Zack took it from me.

Lisa knelt at her husband's head, stroked his blond hair. "Everything's going to be all right, honey. We'll have you free in just a minute."

Since she was saying it haltingly through tears, I wasn't convinced it was very reassuring. On the other hand, he was unconscious and probably couldn't hear her anyway.

"I need those pavers," I told her. "Now!"

She jumped to her feet and ran to the garage.

I shoved a block under the horizontal trunk, but I couldn't get the second one on top of it either. I removed it. Zack dug deeper. It took three tries to force the second block into place. It offered stability but no relief.

Rhonda had retrieved six pavers. "We need at least twice that many. Hurry."

Lisa brought others. I stacked what we had a couple of feet from Keith's other side. Zack and the women delivered more pavers. I piled them as high as I could, squeezed under the trunk face-up, braced my hands on the coarse bark and heaved. I could barely raise it a fraction of an inch.

"My kingdom for a jack," Zack muttered.

"One. Two. Three." I heaved with all my might. Not enough. Connors, beside me, was developing a bluish tinge from lack of oxygen. "Build a second stack beside the first." I huffed. "Quickly. Quickly. Find something to use as a wedge. Time's running out."

The next sixty seconds seemed like hours. We built a tower outside the first. Zack found a pile of shake shingles, thin at one end, thick at the other. Perfect wedges. "Bring more."

Again I lay in place and pushed up with all my might. Zack straddled the trunk and strained to pull up as well. Rhonda slipped a shingle over the second tower. Zack and I were panting. We repeated the process. One. Two. Three. Shingle. One. Two. Three. Shingle. One. Two. Three. Shingle.

Finally Rhonda was able to get a paver on top the outer tower.

With his short legs, Zack couldn't straddle the trunk any longer. I could have once. Easily. *Don't think about it.*

I continued to heave.

A paver on the first tower.

Shingles on top of it.

A paver on the second tower.

A moan from Keith. An encouraging sign.

"We're almost there, Jason," Zack said. "One more wedge."

My arms and shoulders ached. My chest felt like it was in a vice. At least with the trunk now higher I could get better arm extension.

"One. Two. Three." I strained, grunted, breathed in short bursts.

Like a spotter standing over a weight lifter's bench, Zack shouted, "Push, push, push. You've almost got it. You can do it. It's all you. Come on, Jason. Push, Jason. Push."

I growled. My breathing became a gurgle deep in my throat. Eyes closed, I saw white spots. I gave every ounce of energy. A final shove. In my ears, the snick of wood on wood. Then the grating sound of stone on stone.

"Got it. Jason," Zack announced jubilantly. "Got it in. You can let go now, Jason. You did it. You can lower your arms."

I didn't have to lower them. The instant I relaxed the pressure, they fell to my sides like empty beer bottles.

"You did it, Jason. You did great! Can you get out by yourself?"

If in my clumsy struggle I unseated the towers, Keith would be dead. I might be too. "No."

"Okay. I'll pull you out. Just relax. Don't try to help me. Let me do the work."

I hated losing control, being dependent on someone else, even my best friend, for what I should have been able to do by myself. Zack stepped behind my head, sat on the ground, dug in his heels and slowly dragged me by the shoulders of my shirt out from under the horizontal tree.

I was clear, breathing rapidly, when I heard a crashing sound. I raised my head enough to see the makeshift towers wobble.

Chapter Fifty

A tree at the other end of the row of poplars had fallen across the yard. I could see the blackened stump, apparently the result of a lightning strike. How many others, I wondered, had been weakened and were in danger of falling?

A far-off siren, till now background noise, drew closer, more shrill. My pickup appeared in the alleyway, Stacey behind the wheel. A moment later an emergency vehicle pulled up from the other end, blocking it. Relief had arrived. My respiration slowed from overwrought panting to long, deep breaths. My chest pounded. I felt drained.

Three men in heavy firefighter's apparel burst into the yard, assessed the situation quickly and got to work. One man stuck the prongs of a stethoscope in his ears and applied a blood pressure cuff to Keith's arm. "One fifty-eight over ninety-two. Steady. Go."

A single pull started the second man's chainsaw. Two swift cuts, one at the base, the other six inches beyond the double stack of pavers, allowed his team members to remove the trunk from over Keith Connors.

Zack could barely stand still. "My family's in Oakdale, on Piney Woods Lane."

"Don't worry," said the paramedic examining Keith. "Haven't heard any reports of damage up that away. The twister's path was at least a mile south."

I watched Zack wilt with the good news. Still, he was eager to check on his family himself. I couldn't blame him.

"We'll leave as soon as we can," I told him while dragging myself out of the emergency people's way.

The reverend's color was rapidly returning. The medic looked around. "How'd you lift that thing? I don't see any—"

"He did it." Rhonda pointed to me. "It was unbelievable. So strong, even though he doesn't have—" Her eyes were again fixed on my stumps.

"With help," I interjected before she could finish her description of me.

"That tree must weigh at least four hundred pounds?"

"New personal record." Zack grinned at me nervously. He didn't want to be there. His focus now was exclusively on his family. "Your best bench press till now has been three-fifteen."

The guy shook his head. "Even that's got me beat by thirty pounds."

Zack brought my wheelchair. "You grab one elbow," he told the paramedic. "I'll grab the other."

Before I could object I was hoisted onto the seat. Zack knew I wouldn't have had the strength to raise myself on my own. "Thanks," I muttered, both grateful and embarrassed.

"You're Jason Crow, aren't you?" The fireman extended his hand. "Pleased to meet you."

I returned his firm handshake. Despite physical exhaustion, my mind was racing. Inchoate images, disjointed phrases, incomplete ideas.

In the video, Keith extending his hand to the bare-breasted woman.

"Is my husband all right?" Lisa, in tears, asked the paramedic with the stethoscope.

"He'll be fine," Stacey assured her.

"I didn't want to come over here," Lisa blurted out to her mom, "but he insisted, said it was just good manners to say goodbye in person since you're finally heading home. I hate storms. They scare me."

Stacey put an arm around her. "You always were afraid of thunder. When you were little I used to tell you it was the angels moving furniture around in heaven."

Lisa tried to smile.

"What happened, anyway?" I asked Lisa. "Why was he outside in a storm?"

"It was Mom. When we heard the warning siren we headed for the middle room, but then she remembered she'd left her car windows down. I told her to forget them, but she said now that she'd finally gotten her car back, she wasn't going to ruin all that expensive leather upholstery when all she had to do was roll up the windows."

I glanced over at the sports car under the carport awning. A Mercedes two-seater. Black. A beauty. Even with wind-torn leaves clinging to the back window and trunk lid, it seemed to glow with arrogant pride. I noticed the left front tire was new. A Michelin like the others. Only the best for Stacey. Well, maybe she'd have to get used to second best now that her soft-touch daddy was gone. She was right about one thing though: she wasn't going anywhere. A crotched limb from the neighbor's mesquite tree had snapped and was blocking access to the alley.

"Keith volunteered to take care of the windows," Rhonda chimed in. "Ever the gentleman." Was she mocking him? Why?

"When he didn't come back after ten minutes," Lisa continued, "I went outside looking for him."

"It's a good thing you did," I said. "You probably saved his life."

Stacey looked down at her son-in-law, who was being carefully turned over onto his back. He was conscious now but still groggy. One of the medics was asking him questions. Keith was trying to answer but his mumbling was unintelligible.

"He'll be fine," Stacey said with absolute confidence.

"Where's Junior?" I asked.

"At the store," Rhonda replied. "He reopened it yesterday. Says it's been busy, though he hasn't sold much. Most people coming by just want to talk."

I kept staring at the birthmark on her arm.

"Jason, you all right?" Zack was looking at me curiously.

"Hmm? Oh, yeah."

I wanted to get away from there, think, sort things out, try to find order in the chaos of information around me. Something was out of place, out of focus. But emergency vehicles still blocked my pickup. Not that it mattered. At that moment I was too wrung out to drive.

Over the next ten minutes we watched the paramedics load Keith onto a stretcher. Lisa was hovering, wringing her hands.

Stacey, who'd retreated to the sidelines and was observing, returned and scolded her daughter. "Lisa, back off and let the men do their jobs." Not exactly a warm and fuzzy bedside manner or the comforting mother of a few minutes earlier, but it achieved its goal. Lisa withdrew.

Stacey's attention shifted. "I finally get my car out of the damned shop, and now I'm stuck again. I need to get home."

Statements, images careened through my mind. *The simplest thing and it turns into a long list of other things. Appearances can be deceiving.* My pulse accelerated.

"I'm on unpaid leave now," she muttered. "If I don't get back to work soon, I'll lose my job."

"You'll hang around until tomorrow, won't you?" Lisa begged. "To make sure Keith's all right. The tornado will be on the news. Your boss will understand."

"There's nothing wrong with Keith. He got the wind knocked out of him is all."

"Stay, for Lisa, then," I said. "She needs you."

Stacey laughed. "The storm's over. She doesn't need her mommy holding her hand anymore. Keith's are much bigger and stronger. That's the way it's supposed to be."

I was having a hard time reading this woman. Warm and maternal, then cool, almost cold.

"People put up fronts," I remarked. "Of course, as a nurse, you know that. They may not say they need help, but they do. Your daughter's no exception. She'll be comforted to know you're around."

Stacey appeared completely unmoved by my appeal or her daughter's. Lisa glanced back at her as she climbed into the boxy white-and-orange vehicle to accompany her husband to the hospital. One of the paramedics closed the door behind her.

"If not for Lisa's sake," I persisted, "then for your own. It's a long drive alone in the dark, and after an experience like you've had today, you're bound to be more tired and distracted than you realize, certainly less alert than you should be. At least wait until the morning when you'll be more refreshed. You don't know what road conditions you'll run into after that storm."

As I looked over at her car I glimpsed Zack's expression. He was watching the firemen pack up their gear, apparently not paying attention to us, but I could read his body language. *What the hell's going on?*

I tried to sound both serious and upbeat to Stacey. "Your car weathered this crisis. Be a pity if it got damaged now."

Lights flashing, the boxy vehicle backed cautiously out of the driveway. The siren revved up.

Don't think about that day eight years ago when you saw the ambulance pulling out of the courtyard between the Crow's Nest *and the carriage house, its lights not flashing, its siren not making a sound.*

"I need to find somebody to remove those damn limbs," Stacey muttered.

My heart stopped beating till I realized she was talking about the branches blocking the driveway.

"It's the neighbor's tree," Rhonda said. "It's his responsibility."

Zack implored me, "Jason, we have to go, too."

The phone in the house rang, starling us all into immobility. But only for a moment. Then Rhonda and Zack dashed to the back door of the house. They nearly collided. Zack retreated just enough to let the lady precede him inside.

I wheeled after them as quickly as I could, but they were inside by the time I got there.

"We're fine," Rhonda was assuring her caller, "except for Keith."

I listened and quickly realized she was talking to Junior. She filled him in with admirable conciseness, neither making light of the situation or dwelling on what might have happened if Zack and I hadn't appeared on the scene when we did.

Zack was bouncing on the balls of his feet. "I need to call my wife," he kept muttering.

Finally Rhonda said goodbye. Zack snatched up the phone before she had a chance to cradle it, dialed a number and listened. Instead of getting

Nancy, however, the housekeeper answered the phone and informed him Nancy and the kids had gone out to the Crow Ranch even before the storm warning was issued. Another call confirmed they were there, that we hadn't even gotten rain anywhere near the house, and that everyone was fine.

Zack relinquished the phone to me.

I was almost as relieved to hear my wife's voice as Zack had been to hear his.

"We'll be there as soon as we can make it," I told Michiko, "but it might not be for a couple of hours. I still have some things to do at the carriage house." I caught the baffled expression on Zack's face. I handed him the receiver to hang up.

I wheeled myself with agonizing slowness to the door.

A moment later Zack got behind me and took over. He never pushed my chair or even offered to. It was one of our unspoken understandings. This time, however, he didn't ask, and I didn't object.

"Do you want me to drive?" he asked when we reached the truck.

I smiled ruefully. "Tell you what, if I can pull my ass up onto the seat, I will."

My arm and shoulder muscles screamed with the exertion. They'd be sore tomorrow and for several days to come. Yet I suddenly felt enormous satisfaction. I'd saved a man's life today and was on my way to solving a murder. At the moment, however, my focus was on summoning that last agonizing ounce of strength to plant myself behind the wheel. It was close, but I did it.

Zack stowed my chair in the bed behind me, ran around to the passenger side and jumped in. I backed the old Ford into the street. "Thank you."

"Nothing to thank me for," he replied, "but you're welcome. Now how about telling me what's going on in that head of yours. Why were you trying to get Stacey to stay in town another night, and why do we still have a couple of hours of work ahead of us?"

I put the truck in gear and applied pressure to the accelerator. "I had it wrong, Zack. It wasn't Lisa who killed Bart. It was her mother."

Chapter Fifty-One

"Stacey? Are you sure? Explain."

"It's still only a hunch," I acknowledged, "that has to do with a roofing nail. But first we need to block off the alley and delay any attempt she might make to drive that Mercedes out of here." I felt my friend staring at me. "I'll explain on the way back to the carriage house. Then I want to change out of these wet clothes. They're beginning to itch."

"Well," he drawled, "I get the part about itchy clothes."

I turned off San Jacinto Boulevard onto Davis Street and approached the *Crow's Nest*. "Remember Stacey said the simplest problem with her car had a snowball effect. I didn't ask about it at the time. I couldn't imagine it having anything to do with Bart's death."

Other than the streets being wet, there was no evidence of the violent storm that had wreaked such thorough damage less than a couple of miles away.

"What do you imagine is the most basic auto repair?"

Zack shrugged. "A flat tire?"

"Exactly. And she got one the night she killed her father from a roofing nail she picked up in his driveway."

"Jason, that's a mighty big leap. Can you prove it?"

"I believe I can. I have to call Burker. A lot will depend on how thorough his people were."

Upstairs in the drawing room, I went directly to the telephone. The person who answered at the police station was hesitant to interrupt his boss.

"It's important," I said.

"Hang on."

Nearly a full minute went by, then Burker got on the line. "I can't seem to escape you, Jason."

"Are you trying to?"

"What do you want?" he demanded.

"You need to come to the carriage house."

"What the hell for?"

"I'll explain when you get here."

"Just drop everything and come at your beck and call. Who the hell do you think you are, Crow?"

"Were you able to identify those tire tracks at the Webley house?"

"The Webleys'? What the—"

"Specifically Michelins with a distinctive tread. One of them had what may have been a nail in it."

"How the hell do you—Has someone at the lab—"

Since Burker was yelling and I was holding the receiver away from my ear, Zack could hear it all. He motioned to me. I handed over the phone.

"Clyde, this is Zack. Jason wouldn't be asking this if it wasn't important. You won't be disappointed." He listened for about fifteen seconds and hung up.

"Well?"

"He's on his way."

I grunted.

While Zack used the standard bathroom off the office to shower, I went to the drawing room bathroom which had been modified for me, with shower and fixtures lowered so I could use it sitting on the floor. I struggled out of my clinging wet shirt and peeled off my pants. My suspicions were confirmed. I'd bruised my leg stumps, actually cut the right one. The injuries weren't serious, only uncomfortable. They also meant I wouldn't be wearing my prosthetic legs or my stubbies for several days, maybe up to a week. Rushing it would delay healing, and I wanted to be on my feet as soon as possible.

I would have liked to sit and soak for a while, but there wasn't time. I emerged as quickly as I could, donned dry clothes, managed to pull myself up into my wheelchair, rolled over to the office and removed the video from the safe. I'd just fast-forwarded to an "action" scene when Zack sauntered into the office, a towel wrapped around his hips. He stopped when he saw the images on the screen.

"For God's sake, Jason, why are you looking at that . . . ?" His words trailed off. "Oh . . . my . . . God!"

I took grim satisfaction in having my friend confirm my suspicion, yet I couldn't help smiling. "It's so easy to get distracted, isn't it?"

Zack shook his head. "I see, and still I can't believe it."

I was ruminating on Bubba's remark about Doubting Thomas, when I heard the familiar heavy stomping of feet on the outside stairs.

"Get dressed," I told Zack. "I'll take care of greeting our guest."

"He's going to be pissed."

"Yeah, life's a bitch." I wheeled out to the entry, waited until Zack had closed the drawing room door behind him, then let Burker in.

"What the hell's this all about?" He stepped inside. "I don't appreciate being summoned like—"

I motioned him to the office and invited him to sit in the chair facing the TV screen.

"A lot of what I'm about to tell you is speculation. Some of it I can prove. Some I can back up with circumstantial evidence. And some is just plain guessing, based on logic and experience."

Burker sucked in his cheeks, pursed his lips and I suspect considered getting up and walking out. "This better be good."

Relieved, I said, "Two weeks ago Stacey Ogletree, nee Bartholomew, received a call from her brother that their father was pulling up stakes and moving to Las Vegas. Over the years Bart had been a lucrative source of income for her. If he left Coyote Springs, the gravy train was moving out of the station with him and wouldn't be back. So she drove up here Monday after work to see him. He did two things that absolutely incensed her. First, he told her she wasn't getting another penny from him."

"How do you know that?"

"I believe it's a reasonable assumption based on Bart's not leaving her anything in his will."

"Maybe," Burker conceded. "What else?"

"Second, I suspect he denied ever touching her inappropriately. He wouldn't have denied she'd been sexually mistreated as a child, but not by him."

"Who then?"

"By her mother."

Burker straightened. "Hazel? Jason, I think you're slipping. That's ridiculous. Women don't molest children, especially their own daughters."

"It is rare," I conceded, "but not unheard of. The accusation must have infuriated Stacey. She picked up a knife and stabbed him in the back with such force that she punctured his heart, killing him almost instantly. Yet she had the presence of mind to wipe off the handle. Being a nurse, she probably used alcohol, which would explain why there were no fingerprints on it."

"This is all wild speculation, Jason, not evidence," Burker objected.

"Just listen to my reasoning, then tell me where I've gone off the rails," I said. "The accusation must have struck a chord. If Hazel was the true culprit, it meant Stacey's counselor, Dr. Erma Webley, was either totally incompetent or she'd colluded with Hazel to perpetuate the lie. So after cleaning off the murder knife, Stacey set off to confront Webley. What she didn't realize was that she'd picked up a nail in her left front tire in Bart's driveway, one of many Hollis had spilled from the roof that day and hadn't bothered to clean up. Fernando Amorado's boys were still finding them more than a week later."

"You're saying Stacey killed Erma Webley? Jason, the gun had only

Sylvester's prints on it."

"Here's how I see events going down," I said. "Tell me where I'm wrong."

Zack brought in a tray with tall glasses of ice and a pitcher of tea. Until then I hadn't realized how thirsty I was. I drank down half of a glass before going on.

"Stacey has a mouth on her. Erma was also known to get into shouting matches with people. I imagine the encounter between them was right out of *Who's Afraid of Virginia Wolfe*. As it grew louder and more threatening, Sylvester, unnerved by it all, got a gun, probably with the intent of intimidating Stacey into leaving. But he had Parkinson's disease, which made him a dangerous person with a loaded pistol in his hand. Perhaps Erma tried to take it away from him. Perhaps it just went off accidentally. The result was that Sylvester fatally shot Erma."

Burker drank tea.

"Stacey, realizing her own vulnerability, decided her only way out was to leave no living witness. Sylvester had probably dropped the gun. Stacey picked it up, aimed it at his head and pulled the trigger. Being the thorough person she is, she then wiped away her fingerprints and placed the weapon in the dead man's right hand, unaware he was a south-paw. She then drove to her brother's house in time to say good-night to the members of his bridge party."

"She'd have to be one cold bitch," Burker noted.

"The next morning her left front tire was flat. Junior called his garage. The mechanic they sent to fix it discovered she had a wheel bearing problem and towed the sports car into the shop, where they proceeded to find other things wrong. We're not talking about a Ford or a Chevy here. Mercedes parts have to be ordered. It took a couple of weeks."

Burker rubbed his jaw. "It all sounds feasible, I grant you, but it's all conjecture."

"Her car is at her brother's house—or was half an hour ago when we left there—hemmed in by a broken tree branch. Zack piled some junk in the alleyway, but it'll only slow her down. I suggest you block the alley at both ends on some pretext—maybe a downed power line nearby—until you can get a warrant to impound her car."

"I have to have a valid reason to give to the judge, Jason. Your speculation isn't going to convince him."

"And it shouldn't, but you do have cause. You have tire tracks that are distinctive and you have information that she has that particular brand of tires."

"Not enough," Burker maintained.

"And she was a past client of the deceased doctor."

He rubbed his jaw. "Slim. Very slim."

"You might point out," Zack offered, "that this is not an indictment of Stacey Ogletree. It's an attempt to determine if her car might have been used in the commission of a felony, since those tires are very rare in this area."

"Better." He picked up the phone. "I'll get a search warrant for the car and invite her to come in to answer a few questions."

"Get the warrant," I said, "and have someone available to serve it, but hold off a few minutes on bringing her in for questioning, because there's another possible scenario and another possible murderer to consider."

Chapter Fifty-Two

"Now comes the tricky part," I said after Burker put down the phone. "This next move will require some real finessing."

"What are you talking about?"

I took a deep, fortifying breath. "I found a copy of *Sweet Somethings.*"

He clutched the sweaty glass of iced tea Zack had just refilled. "You have the flick. Where'd you get it and when?"

"That's not important. What's important is what's on it."

Burker started to object. "Don't try to stonewall me, Crow. I'll decide what's—"

I hit the *Play* button and counted on the video, bad acting notwithstanding, to distract him from pursuing the matter for now. Over the next few minutes I observed the head of homicide as he tried to be nonchalant in watching young women dress and undress. His eyes widened and wandered when Keith made his first frontal appearance.

"Is it more of the same?" he asked, when we were about fifteen minutes into the video.

"Yep."

"Turn it off then. I've seen enough. More than enough."

I stopped the tape.

"If you hadn't already made a good case for Stacey killing her father, I would have said this was the motive behind his death," Burker said, "that the old man was blackmailing the preacher, and the preacher killed him."

"Bart didn't need the money," Zack pointed out. "He was a millionaire."

"It's not always about money, at least not completely," Burker replied, "but it is always about power. Ultimately that's what money represents, power."

Zack shook his head. "His own family."

Burker's laugh was short and cynical. "We've already established this family was dysfunctional."

"Dysfunctional, yes," I agreed. "But ironically Bart had a very deep sense of family loyalty, which I'll demonstrate later. He wasn't blackmailing anyone."

My old nemesis studied me a moment, waiting for further elaboration.

I wheeled away from the TV but left my hands on the rims.

"As far as we can tell, only two people knew about *Sweet Somethings*," I said. "Bart, who purchased it, and Manny Hollis, since he made reference to Rosa about the old man watching porn and whose fingerprints were all over the player."

"And who also happens to be dead," Zack pointed out. "The victim of murder."

"The question now is who Hollis was blackmailing," I summed up.

"Connors, of course. He's the most vulnerable and has the deepest pockets," Burker said, then added thoughtfully, "And his wife. Lisa has as much to lose as Connors if his former role as a porn star was to get out."

"There's a third party we can't forget." I pressed the Play button on the remote, then the fast forward until I came to the scene I'd earlier shown Zack. I slowed the tape again, then froze the frame I was looking for, the one in which the not-yet-saved Keith invited the tall buxom blond to join him on the stage.

"Study her face," I said. "Ever seen her before?"

"No."

"Look again," I urged.

It took him almost a minute of concentration. "Surely you're not telling me that's . . . well, she sort of resembles . . . but it can't be . . ."

"It is," Zack assured him.

"Notice the skin blemish on her arm," I said. "We saw it no more than an hour ago."

In a few short sentences I told Burker about our detour to Woodhill Terrace.

Burker's brown eyes shifted between me and the TV screen as he worked his jaw. "You're telling me the blond bimbo in this skin flick, the broad who's doing the reverend, is Rhonda Bartholomew?"

"She's fifteen years older now," I said, "at least fifty pounds heavier and a respected member of the community, but the skin blemish proves she's the woman on the screen."

"Shit."

"Of course, that doesn't make her the murderer," I reminded him. "We still have three candidates for that distinction. Keith, Lisa and Stacey."

"Four," Burker corrected me. "Don't forget Ned."

I wanted to. I was utterly convinced he had nothing to do with any of what was going on, but to give Burker his due, Ned had to be included in the list of suspects. I also realized I'd boxed myself in a corner. If I protested that my friend hadn't seen the flick before today, I'd give away that the source had been someone else, and that would put Harden in jeopardy. I had no doubt Burker would eventually figure out who my source was, but he wouldn't get any corroboration from me. I wasn't going to give him my brother.

"I'll get a subpoena for all their bank records," Burker reported. "I don't imagine payments were made by check, but an otherwise unexplained cash withdrawal or series of them could serve as a red flag."

"Hollis wasn't stupid," I said. "A one-time large payment or a series of large cash withdrawals might raise questions with accountants and bankers—and spouses. I suspect you'll find he received reasonable amounts, maybe from more than one party, which allowed him to live comfortably, if not extravagantly. His victims would be less likely to balk at modest payments they could afford in contrast to crippling extortion."

"You're probably right," Burker conceded, "but we have to start somewhere."

"I think we can already narrow the field. I presented the case against Stacey first, primarily because it all fits together. But she didn't know about the porn. If she had, you can be sure she would have drained her father dry. That narrows the field for Hollis's murder to four people. We can also eliminate Ned Herman for one very good reason. He was out of town when Hollis was killed.

"So we're down to three," Burker said. "Collins, Lisa and Rhonda."

"I have an idea how we might be able to cut to the chase with them," I said, "and get the goods at the same time."

Burker regarded me, his earlier anger at my peremptory summons forgotten for the time being. "I'm listening."

I began rolling forward and back, forward and back, wheelchair pacing. "We agree the key is Bart's video. So where is it now?"

"Destroyed, of course," Burker declared. "Isn't that why the killer went back to Bart's house when Rosa was there, to get the damn thing and destroy it?"

"Probably, but he or she could have put it somewhere for safe keeping."

"Why?" Burker's face took on a thoughtful expression.

"A souvenir, or maybe because disposing of it discreetly isn't all that easy. You can't just throw it in the trash. Burning it carries risks. Keeping it, on the other hand, can be good insurance."

"Insurance?" Burker gave me a rare *get-serious* glare.

"Think about it. Two people, Keith and Rhonda are in that flick, and a third, Lisa, has a vested interest in it. Suppose the person possessing it decided to use it to take advantage of one or more of the other two? The holder of the tape stolen from Bart's house could edit him or herself out of it and blackmail the others with impunity."

"Unless one of the others had an original copy," Zack contributed.

"Makes sense, I suppose," Burker acknowledged.

"Here's the tricky part," I said. "If the video was kept, and my gut tells me it was, either for blackmail or simply for old times' sake, it's been hidden. I think I know where in general but not specifically. We need to lure whoever took it into retrieving it."

"And how do you propose to do that?" Burker asked.

"Scare tactics."

Chapter Fifty-Three

Burker hung up the phone on my desk. "Connors was released from Clover a little while ago, against medical advice, by the way. The doctor wanted to keep him overnight for observation, but apparently the rev doesn't have much faith in hospitals."

"Where is he now?"

"According to staff personnel, his wife drove him back to Woodhill Terrace to get his truck. A couple of minutes after he arrived at Junior's house, a police patrol driving through the neighborhood reported he went to a neighbor down the street, borrowed a chain saw and cleared the driveway so Lisa's mother could get her car out."

"Stop her," I snapped, "before she dumps that spare tire." I was assuming she understood its significance. She'd seen me staring at it, so she might.

"She's not going anywhere," Burker replied. "We have a patrol car blocking the alley because of a downed power line."

"Will you be able to get the search warrant for her Mercedes?"

"The judge just signed it. Lambke will serve it. When he does, he'll also invite her downtown for an interview."

"She knows her legal rights. She'll refuse."

"Roy can be very persuasive."

I remembered the detective's sharp eyes from our brief meeting the previous week. I had no doubt they could be intimidating.

"You said you think the video's hidden in Hilltop Church," Burker reminded me. "Why not just go there and get it?"

"Because I don't know how to gain access to the secret compartment it's in."

His brows rose. "Secret compartment?"

Zack explained what he'd found and the legendary history behind it.

"We need whoever put the video there to show us," I said. "And we need that person's fingerprints on it exclusively. If any of ours are on it, it loses its value as direct evidence."

Burker nodded.

"As I see it," I said, "there are three candidates. Keith Connors, his wife Lisa and Rhonda Bartholomew."

"Connors claims to have no specific knowledge of a secret compartment," Zack added, "but then he would if he's using it."

"He's owned the building for eight years," I said. "Wouldn't it be odd if in all that time he never looked for it? And if he did, wouldn't he share the information with his wife? As for Rhonda, she was the source of the rumor about it. As a realtor, I can't imagine her not looking for it."

"That doesn't mean any of them found it," Burker pointed out.

"True. Zack says the cabinetry where we think it's located is exceptionally good."

"So what's your plan?" Burker asked me.

My scheme was simple. Arrest Stacey in front of the others, let them know the law was closing in, so the person who had the video would panic and retrieve it with the objective of destroying it. The plan wouldn't work, however, if Ned was the bad guy, since there was no reason to suppose he knew about or had access to the secret compartment, but I didn't seriously consider him a suspect, and apparently neither did Burker. Nor would it work if Stacey was the guilty party, but as far as we knew, she was completely unaware of the scandalous porn and had no personal stake in its existence or disclosure. Burker must have reached the same conclusion, because he didn't raise the issue.

He left. I tucked my .38 revolver in the back of my waistband, then rode the elevator down to the courtyard. Zack, as usual, took the stairs. I transferred to the passenger seat of his convertible. He folded my chair and stowed it in the narrow space behind me. We'd decided to take the Mustang because it was less familiar to the people we were chasing than my old pickup.

The storm a few hours earlier had cleared the air and left it cool and refreshed with the nighttime scent of clean vegetation. The stars were twinkling; the moon was full. A romantic night, except we were out to catch a murderer.

At the crown of the hill, only a few yards from the tiny front porch of the country church, Zack dropped me off. I wished I could have worn my prosthetics, and would have despite the delay in recovery time from the bruising I'd sustained, but they would have been so uncomfortable that they would have restricted my mobility instead of enhancing it. To add insult to injury, I couldn't use my wheelchair either. I would have had to get out of it to mount the three steps to the narrow vestibule under the belfry, and once inside, it would have restricted me to the center aisle. Nor would I have been able to get it up the one tall step to the choir without help. With no better alternative, I lowered myself to the ground and hand-walked to the small building. Zack ran around me, used our key to unlock the door, jumped back into his car and tooled out of sight.

Burker had been waiting around the side of the building and now came up behind me.

"Thought you'd like to know," he said, "Stacey Ogletree was arrested about fifteen minutes ago for assaulting an officer. It seems when Lambke invited her downtown for an interview, she became quite belligerent. The detective's calm attempts to persuade her to cooperate had an adverse effect which culminated in her hauling off and punching him in the balls."

"Ouch."

"No question now about holding her for cause."

"The others?" I asked. "Rhonda, Keith and Lisa?"

"Less than two minutes after Stacey was taken away in cuffs, the maroon pickup left. At last report, Lisa and Rhonda's cars were still in the driveway. If Connors is coming here, we don't have much time. Where's this secret compartment supposed to be?"

I moved down the center aisle and nodded to the right, to the vestry side of the choir. "We know it's there." I pointed to three vertical panels facing the congregation.

"So all we have to do is wait until somebody shows us how to get access." Burker scanned the barn-like space. "Where can we hide? This place is so small. No pillars, no pews. Unless we're blessed suddenly with dense cloud cover, there's enough moonlight coming in through the windows to read a newspaper."

My shoulder muscles shrieked as I lifted myself up the high step. "I have a hold card." I moved over to the pulpit, a large, three-sided vertical wooden box.

Burker looked at it, then down at me. "You're not seriously considering—"

I backed into the cramped space. He confirmed I was invisible from three sides.

Having ditched the Mustang, Zack unlocked the vestry door from the outside and joined us. Before he was able to say a word, however, we heard the crunch of tires on the gravel drive. There had been no flash or glow of headlights, which meant the driver had them turned off. Did that mean he knew we were here?

Zack ran to the nearest window and looked out. "The maroon pickup."

"Time to skedaddle," I said.

"I don't like—" Burker started.

I flashed my .38 to reassure him, tucked it into my waistband and heaved myself toward the pulpit.

"I still don't—"

I turned beside the podium and watched Zack push Burker out the vestry door. For a moment I was aware of sitting alone and legless in an eighty-year-old wooden building. The door through which my friends had just exited was my closest escape. I hoped I didn't need one.

I listened. The crickets had gone silent. No footsteps, but I did hear the front door handle being jiggled, a key being inserted into the lock. In the semi-darkness the sound was as loud as the afternoon's thunderclaps.

The squeak of a hinge. A black silhouette against the clear starry sky.

The shadow closed the door and disappeared behind the beam of a flashlight moving up the nave.

I slipped inside the podium. The beam swept across the choir stand I sat facing. I froze. The light passed from my left to right and back again.

Cautious footsteps creaked the old wooden floorboards to my right, near the compartments. Click. It was open.

I held my revolver with both hands. "Stop right there."

The next sound was a gunshot.

Chapter Fifty-Four

It was a cliché, but time stood still. My ears rang from the report of the gunshot in such a confined space. I tried to determine if I'd been hit and where, but nothing registered. Had I discharged my revolver without realizing it? Not likely. I'd been handling firearms since I was four years old, taught by my grandfather who was a tyrant about safety. My finger was beside the trigger guard as the rules dictated, not on the trigger, and the barrel was still cool.

The lights went on. I squinted in the sudden glare.

The person with the other gun stood less than six feet away, equally dazed. Unfortunately her finger was not beside the guard but inside it, the fleshy tip of her index finger on the trigger of a .45 caliber semi-automatic. Was it a hair-trigger? Was that why she'd fired? By accident? Or had it been intentional. Had she been trying to kill me?

"Put down the gun," I said reasonably.

Several seconds went by before she seemed to realize the voice was not at her height. She looked down, her eyes instantly drawn to my missing legs. I perceived the familiar reaction of shock and fascination.

"Put down the gun," I repeated more firmly.

Behind me the front door squeaked. Someone had entered the building, but I couldn't turn to see who it was. Did she have an accomplice?

"Drop it," Burker growled from beyond the step. He must have circled around from the vestry to come up behind her. "You can't escape. Drop the gun."

"Rhonda," I implored, like an old friend, "lower the gun and put it on the floor."

She continued to stare at me. Had I been standing I could have rushed and disarmed her before she knew what was happening. But I wasn't, and Burker, who probably had an equal assessment of the situation, was too far away.

"Rhonda, stop staring."

The boldness of my reprimand got her attention. Her gaze rose to meet mine. It was only then she realized I had a gun pointed directly at her.

"Do you really want to shoot me, Rhonda? Put the gun down. You don't need it anymore. You never wanted to hurt anybody. You just got scared when you saw yourself again on the TV screen."

"It was a mistake," she said. "For both of us. He was so young. Sixteen." She laughed. "And inexperienced. A guy like that, and he . . ."

I expected her hands to be shaking by now under the weight of the full-size Glock, but they didn't.

"He'd never had a girl, much less a woman. Can you imagine? I was his first. It was a very special moment. I couldn't let people see me like that. Not now. He . . . I . . . . No. I couldn't let people watch us."

In a level tone I said, "Rhonda, that gun must be getting awfully heavy. Put it down, please, and we can talk."

I sensed someone moving up the center aisle. Burker? How much time did I have to save her life, how long before that approaching person blew her away? It wouldn't be difficult. She was standing there alone. A single shot, properly placed, and she'd be dead.

"Please, Rhonda." I had the feeling this might be my last chance to implore her. "Please, put down the gun."

She gave me a slight nod, an ironic twist of a smile on her lips. Her eyes never left mine as she slowly crouched and placed the handgun on the floor. In less than three seconds, Burker kicked it away. I didn't know the fat man could move that fast.

I wasn't surprised at what happened next. Three men had her pinned to the wooden floor. Burker stood aside and observed dispassionately as her arms were pulled, non-too-gently, behind her back, her wrists cuffed.

Rhonda Bartholomew had cracked the skull of a kind, gentle woman who wished no one any harm. Had the murder attempt succeeded, she would have robbed a grandmother of years of watching her grandchildren grow, cheated her of the modest rewards of years of hard work and frugality, not to mention the heartache her family would have suffered, was suffering now. I had to remind myself of those things, lest I feel sorry for the middle-age woman whose face was being pressed to the floor.

"You okay?" Zack asked.

I hadn't been aware of him coming in, but I was glad he was there.

"I'm fine." It took all my strength to hand walk toward the storeroom side of the choir, out of the stampede of men and women racing past me. The right compartment was open, revealing a cupboard deep and wide enough to accommodate two stacks of liquor cases. I wanted to laugh.

"How did she open it," I asked.

"I didn't see her do it," Zack replied.

I shrugged. In the dark I didn't either. "It doesn't matter, at least not right now."

I watched a man in plain clothes wearing latex gloves carefully remove a video cassette from the open compartment. He slipped it into a paper bag, then pressed his foot against the kickboard to its left. The door opened. There was nothing inside that compartment or the third.

Burker came over. "You all right?"

I'd come within a gunshot of being dead. I nodded. "Why'd she shoot and where was she aiming?"

"She fired directly over your head."

I stared at him.

"She's a crack shot. She's familiar with the building, so she knew the podium was there. When you ordered her to halt she didn't realize it was you, maybe because being in the podium distorted your voice. But she knew the person was by the podium, so she fired at whoever was standing there and put a slug in the middle of the bookstand."

He didn't say any more. Zack remained silent, but I could imagine what they were thinking. A man standing at the pulpit would be dead now with a hole in his chest.

"Dig the slug out carefully," I advised. "I think you'll find it matches the one from Hollis's head."

"Has she made any statements?" Zack asked Burker.

"Only that she's sorry. She didn't specify about what."

A uniformed cop passing by handed me a canned coke. "Sorry it's not colder." He grinned. "Or a beer."

I thanked him and practically inhaled all twelve ounces in a single gulp. The sugar helped.

Burker stood in the front row of seats. "I've got a slew of questions."

"I hope I have answers to match them," I said, "but can they wait until tomorrow? Tell you what. If that slave-driving chief of police will give you a lunch break tomorrow, how about coming to the *Nest*. I'll buy you the biggest steak of your choice, along with a whole peach cobbler to take home."

"Can you make it one of George's peach crumbles?"

I laughed and realized I was in danger of becoming hysterical. "You're on."

When Zack brought the car around, I had to "walk" the length of the nave and endure the usual stares. My mind flashed back to the nightmare in which Michiko had no legs. She'd said they weren't important. It wasn't true. They were important but not as much as I'd once thought. She'd also said, "You'll get along without them." She was right about that.

I savored the trip home in the rain-cleansed night air. The Mustang's top was down. The wind buffeted my head and shoulders. The moon was full. The stars were out. I was on my way home to my beautiful wife and my beautiful children. It didn't get much better than that.

Chapter Fifty-Five

Burker showed up at the carriage house the next day, a few minutes after eleven for our twelve o'clock lunch. He struck me as tired, no doubt from a long night of interrogations, as well as relieved. Four homicide cases were now in the lap of the D.A.

"You held out on me." He clutched the mug of coffee Zack had automatically handed him when he came through the door. "You had that flick and didn't tell me."

"I had it less than twenty-four hours."

"I don't give a damn if you had it twenty-four minutes. It was evidence in a murder case and you withheld it. I could charge you with interference."

"Clyde," Zack drawled, "don't be an ass." He picked up the morning edition of the *Gazette* lying on his desk. The headline blazed: *Murderers Apprehended.*

He read aloud, "Clyde Burker, head of the Coyote Springs Police department's homicide division, announced late Tuesday evening the apprehension of two people suspected of murdering Mortimer Bartholomew, Erma Webley, Sylvester Webley, Manfred Hollis and the attempted murder of Rosa Garcia." He folded the paper and tossed it back on the desk. "Top of the fold story, too. Seems to me that's a nice cluster of feathers in your cap, Lieutenant."

"All right, all right, but you could have—Oh, hell, after seeing what's on that flick, I suppose I'd hesitate to turn it over too."

"That tape can destroy people's lives," I cautioned. "I hope it's being handled with discretion."

Burker snorted. "Hell, I'm not even allowed access to it anymore. There are at least three locally prominent citizens on that piece of film, Reverend Keith Connors, Rhonda Bartholomew and your friend Ned Herman. Then there's the fourth. It seems one of the other beneficiaries of the parson's largesse is the current wife of a state representative in Austin. So, yeah, this is going to be handled with kid gloves. The district attorney, I understand, is trying to find a way to prosecute the case without it, at least in open court."

"I hope he can," I said, "as long as politics doesn't allow Stacey and Rhonda to get away with murder."

When we headed over to the *Crow's Nest*, Zack locked the carriage house, something we'd rarely done when my father was alive, but the world was changing. Michiko, Nancy, Debbie, Aaron, Ned and George were waiting for us in the parlor. I rolled to my usual place at the head of the table. George sat at the other end.

"I hardly know where to begin," I said, "because nothing ever happens in isolation."

I waited until drinks were poured, and I had everyone's attention before I retold the story of Stacey's visit to her father; her not only failing in her attempt to blackmail him but being told at last who had really molested her; her stabbing him in consequence, then visiting Dr. Webley, arguing with her, Sylvester accidentally shooting his wife, and Stacey killing him to cover up her crime.

"I have to hand it to you," Burker said, "you got it right. One of the first things Stacey insisted on when we accused her of killing Erma was that Sylvester had shot her."

"How did you figure out it was Hazel who was abusing Stacey?" Debbie asked.

"The earliest clue was when Stacey insisted her mother knew nothing about what Bart was supposedly doing to her, that she'd never confided in her mother. My immediate question was why not? It would have been the most natural thing in the world for a little girl to go crying to mommy when daddy did something bad, but even as an adult Stacey refused to confide in her mother. That was the first red flag—or should have been.

"Another clue was that no complaints were ever lodged against Bart for misconduct of any sort. Sexual predators don't stop, and they don't remain static. They persist and progress in their levels of abuse. Yet Bart supposedly had been doing the same thing for forty-plus years. It didn't fit the pattern.

"On the other hand, a complaint had been lodged against Hazel by one of Bart's male students, that she not only interrupted him when he was using the bathroom, but that she made comments that were inappropriate. Bart was very protective of her, bought the complainant off. The boy never returned, suggesting there might have been a real problem.

"Then there was something my mother said, that she could usually tell what a friend was up to because she inevitably accused others of doing it.

"Lastly I asked myself the question Nancy had posed: what would possess a man to take the blame for such a heinous crime when he didn't do it? Only one answer came to mind. To protect somebody, and that left only one possible answer. His wife, Hazel. Bart had no close associates. No service buddies. No golf cronies. No lifelong friends. There was only one constant in his life for the past forty years of his supposed abusive behavior, his wife."

I drank iced tea before going on.

"He married her because she was pregnant back at a time when being an unwed mother was a social disgrace and sometimes resulted in shunning by family as well as friends. Whether she got pregnant on purpose—" I shrugged "—we don't know. According to a woman who knew her for years, Hazel admitted setting her sights on Bart for marriage. One reason was that he had a promising military career ahead of him. Then the war broke out. He was deployed overseas, and she was left alone with their child, Stacey. How the abuse started, we don't know and probably never will, but it happened."

"My question is," Nancy said, "why did he stay with her?"

"That's a tough one. I think it was a long time before he realized what his wife had been doing. He attributed Stacey's claim of molestation to Dr. Webley's influence. By the time he fully appreciated his wife's culpability, the kids had outgrown Hazel's unnatural interest in them. She wasn't involved with other kids, so it wasn't as if she posed a real danger to anyone else. I know, I know. The woman was sick and should have been helped, but look at it from his perspective. Dr. Webley was a professional counselor, a medical doctor and a psychiatrist, and she had been responsible for alienating his daughter from him. Who could he possibly turn his wife over to with any degree of confidence that he wouldn't again become the scapegoat? By staying married to her, he was at least able to monitor her activities and protect himself."

"When do you think Bart became aware that his wife was abusing their daughter?" Debbie asked. "And how?"

"He was probably overseas when it began, so he would have had no way of knowing it was going on. When he came home I'm sure the possibility never crossed his mind. It goes against the most basic human instinct for a mother to sexually abuse her own child, especially a daughter."

"The thought makes my skin crawl," Zack said.

"I'm sure it made Bart's, too, so it's understandable that he didn't even consider the possibility for a long time."

I scanned the faces at the table. All were downcast, all contemplative.

"I'm guessing," I went on, "that it wasn't until Stacey came to him as a teenager and accused him of having touched her inappropriately that he began to realize what was going on. I suspect having her husband home and the prospect of Stacey reaching adolescence convinced Hazel to quit, at least until she could evaluate the situation. Maybe, too, she'd switched her interest to her son."

"Jesus wept," Aaron muttered.

"I questioned Junior last night," Burker said. "He denies anything inappropriate took place between him and his mother."

"It would be difficult for a man to admit if it were true," Michiko pointed out.

"We have to be careful here," I warned, "that we don't create a gotcha. Believe him if he admits something bad happened, accuse him of being a liar or in denial if he doesn't."

"Are you saying," Debbie asked, "that Stacey stabbed her father to death because she believed he'd molested her as a child?"

I shook my head. "Stacey had believed that for forty years. What's important is that she didn't visit her father with the intention of killing him. I believe her violent reaction was provoked when he dropped the bombshell that he hadn't molested her at all, but that her mother had. At first Stacey would have been incredulous. It couldn't be, she'd say, except once the words were spoken, I think she knew they were true. So what was her reaction?"

"Anger at her mother," Aaron concluded.

"No," Debbie corrects him. "At her father. 'You knew Mommy was doing that to me and you did nothing to stop her?'"

"In fact he had stopped her and possibly saved Junior from being victimized as well," I added, "but Stacey wasn't listening. In her confused fury, she picked up the knife on the table and stabbed him."

A waiter came in with fresh pitchers of iced tea and lemonade, topped off glasses and left the room.

"I'm a little perplexed," Aaron said. "You're always questioning coincidences, saying real ones are extremely rare, yet here we have two murderers in the same family committing their crimes at nearly the same time. What are the odds—"

"Astronomical," I admitted, "if they were truly independent actions, but they weren't. Stacey and Rhonda acted alone but not in isolation. Had Stacey not killed her father, I doubt Rhonda would have attacked Rosa or killed Hollis."

"He's right," Burker contributed. "Rhonda told us last night Hollis claimed to be Bart's agent but didn't know why he was picking up money from her every month. When Bart informed her he was moving to Vegas, she figured the request for payments would cease. Then he was killed, and Hollis showed his hand and upped the ante. She knew it would never end, so she killed him."

"Why did Rhonda keep the tape?" Debbie asked. "Why didn't she destroy it?"

"A couple of reasons. I'm guessing here, too, but I imagine she wanted to watch it again and relive her youth. She may also have felt it wise to keep it as leverage, insurance if you will, against Keith, in case it ever became necessary."

"She didn't think he would reveal it, did she?"

"She couldn't take the chance. In her mind she had as much to lose by its disclosure as he did. In a sense she had more. He still had youth and good looks. She had neither. Just how much she'd changed was driven home when she met Keith as a real estate agent in Coyote Springs, and he didn't recognize her."

"Ouch!" Debbie said, and received nods of agreement from Michiko and Nancy.

"As Rhonda pointed out last night," I noted, "she was Keith's first sex partner. In her mind he should have been able to see past the fifty pounds, the fifteen years, the layers of makeup and colorful wigs. He should have felt eternal gratitude for that first exhilarating experience."

Burker spoke up. "Jason's right on target. She more or less confessed to all of this last night."

"Was Hollis blackmailing Keith too?" Michiko asked.

Burker shook his head. "I questioned the preacher last night. Hollis never approached him. The guy was smart enough to stay away from Bart's grandson-in-law, lest he alienate the old man."

"What about all the photographs?" Nancy asked. "Why did Bart want them and what did he intend to do with them?"

"I think they were just what they appeared to be," I said, "pictures of pretty little girls and boys. Nothing sinister. He'd once entertained notions of having a photographic studio where he would specialize in children's portraits. I think this was just a reminder to him of what might have been."

"What about the picture he was supposed to give to me?" Debbie asked.

"He miscalculated by waiting so long to take Livy's portrait. The last session. No time for follow-ons. According to Rosa he wasn't satisfied with the ones of Livy, and if you examine them carefully you'll see her pictures lack that magical quality that the ones he had on his wall possess. The old guy was a perfectionist. The portrait of Livy wasn't up to his standards, so he didn't send it."

"I'm glad," Debbie said. "I'd feel lousy about throwing it away, but I wouldn't want to keep it no matter how good it was, not under these circumstances.

"I agree." Aaron squeezed her hand. "It would be nothing but bad memories, best left forgotten." He addressed me. "So the only real coincidence was *Sweet Somethings* turning up accidentally among Bart's legitimate tapes?"

"Was it really by accident that the one dirty movie that featured the husband of Bart's granddaughter turned up with the musicals? Or did someone put it there?"

Burker nodded. "Hollis's apartment was full of porn. He seems to have been addicted to it. In all likelihood he found *Sweet Somethings* by chance, realized its potential and decided to use it for blackmail. He'd been getting quiet payments from Rhonda for a couple of years."

"Why even bother giving it to Bart?" Aaron asked.

"Because, like all abusers," I said, "he had to go to the next level. I imagine he tried to pull the same trick with the old man that Stacey had been using successfully for years. In this case, give me money, or I'll expose your precious granddaughter and her awe-inspiring husband."

"But it was too late," Zack remarked.

"By then Bart had learned he was dying," I said. "He was probably also fed up with being suckered. I imagine he told Hollis to go to hell. He wasn't about to give him a penny. Hollis undoubtedly underestimated his father."

"Whoa!" Debbie's eyes had gone wide. "His father? Bart had a black son?"

"He'd paid child support and sent money to the woman who bore his child for almost fifty years, and continued to subsidize his son after she died. Hollis, however, apparently showed no appreciation or gratitude. Another disappointment for the old man and maybe the reason he was vocally racist. In the end Bart didn't even bother to acknowledge Hollis in his will, much less leave him anything."

"What a sad family," Michiko said.

Epilogue

Sunday, July 4, 1976

"Brilliant program today." The mayor shook my hand with the energy of a contestant who'd just won the grand prize. "I have to own up. When you first presented it to the City Council, I thought it was too ambitious."

"I'm glad you enjoyed it."

"You pulled it off magnificently. Having someone read the entire Declaration of Independence at City Hall, then moving on to the County Courthouse for the Gettysburg Address . . . . It was really inspiring."

"Did you see how many people were lip-syncing it as it was being recited?" Zack asked.

His honor smiled. "I was one of them. We had to memorize it in school. Haven't thought about it in years, but when that high school kid started reciting it, it all came back. *That this nation, under God, shall have a new birth of freedom, and that government of the people, by the people, for the people shall not perish from this earth.* What an inspiring piece of oratory. I often wonder how different the aftermath of that terrible war might have been if Honest Abe had lived."

"We'll never know," I said. The game of *What if.* There were no winners, yet we kept playing it.

"And now this grand display here in our new mall. You've done a wonderful job, Jason. Thank you."

After the mayor stepped away other people, some of them complete strangers, came forward to offer their greetings and compliments.

"Great program, Mr. Crow."

"Really nice parade, Jason. Best ever."

"Good to see that old Packard out again. Your dad would have loved it."

After the explosion and fire eight years ago that had nearly destroyed the car—as well as Zack and me—my brother Leon had taken on the project of restoring Dad's '56 *Packard Patrician.* It was a museum piece now, something we brought out only for special occasions, like today's parade.

I was standing at the base of the three-level patriotic display area beneath the central atrium. The top level was a semicircle of American flags, from Betsy Ross's original thirteen stars—a new constellation in the firmament—to our present day's fifty above them all, the proud achievement of two hundred years of unparalleled liberty.

Colonel Bartholomew's baby grand piano, on special loan from his estate, sat on the middle tier. Lavinia Elsbeth, our Livy, had played patriotic songs and hymns on it for over an hour to the overwhelming applause by those attending and singing along.

On the bottom tier, just above the walkway, the longest and most sweeping of the three levels, I'd set up mannequins of men in various historic uniforms from the 18th century Revolution that had bought our independence from Great Britain, through the 19th century Civil War that had tested it, to its 20th century role as world leader. Small plaques acknowledged the names of the uniforms' contributors. Among them, of course, were the pinks-and-greens of the late Lieutenant Colonel Mortimer Bartholomew, United States Army.

The last uniform display had not been a single mannequin like the others but a group of five: an army soldier in a Vietnam-era field uniform, a Marine officer in blues, an Air Force pilot in a flight suit, a Navy sailor in bell-bottom trousers, and a female in nurse's whites. Behind them I had also placed on display: a wheelchair, a pair of crutches, a mechanical arm and hook, a pair of dark glasses and an irregular roll of barbed wire. I was surprised at the silent reverence with which people regarded the tableau.

It had been a strangely rich, warm, spine-tingling sensation, standing among friends, neighbors and strangers, listening to the final benediction and singing "God Bless America." There was a poignant moment of silence as "my home, sweet home" echoed off the brick walls and people applauded the conclusion of the formal program.

I gazed beside me at my wife in a sky-blue maternity smock, at our three children in their Sunday best, bright and enthusiastic.

To my right were Zack and Nancy and their two.

On my left my sister Debbie held hands with Aaron, surrounded by their other three children.

The kids were all anxious to get with their friends.

"You'll see them all at the *Crow's Nest* a little later," Debbie reminded them.

Negotiations inevitably followed and the mothers agreed that their kids could go talk to their friends, but that they had to be back at that spot in ten minutes. Michiko caught me smiling and grinned herself. I figured ten minutes would last at least half an hour.

I turned around and scanned the crowd. A few rows back, I spied Ned arm-in-arm with a young lady I'd never seen before. She was tall, with long mahogany hair and blue eyes. Her athletic build and self-confident grace made me wonder if he might have met her at a sports event. In any case, she was a knockout. I looked forward to meeting her later.

My brother Leon was here, too, just returned from sunny California. He'd brought the guy he'd been visiting in Silicon Valley with him. When the two of them got to discussing computer technology, which seemed to be most of the time, they were in a world largely foreign to me.

Still farther back, on the edge of the crowd, were several members of the Garcia family, including Felipe in his new wheelchair. He'd come out to the ranch the last two Sundays and gone swimming with me. The next step would be to put him up on a horse. The kid had challenges ahead, no question about it, but I was convinced he'd conquer them.

Standing by the entrance of Sears was Clyde Burker. At my urging and with Michiko's help other so-called experts had been asked to evaluate all the forensic interrogations. I say so-called because I would expect experts to agree, since they were all presented with the same data, yet their professional opinions were all over the place. Still, the net result of the critical reviews had been positive. Of the original twenty-three children who had claimed some form of molestation, only six were confirmed victims, not of Bart, but of other adult male relatives or family friends. They were currently receiving professional counseling.

Not far from Burker was the Reverend Keith Connors and his wife. I'd run into a little resistance from the Bicentennial Committee when I'd recommended he give the day's opening invocation, not because of a certain video in which he played a prominent part—politics in Austin had succeeded in quashing that—but because two members of his family were being held without bail for capital murder. I reminded the naysayers that the Constitution specifically rejects corruption of blood, that is, holding families responsible for the acts of their individual members.

The televangelist gave an inspiring invocation.

Burker and I had had several meetings with the reverend since the night his mother-in-law was arrested for patricide. What came out were real surprises. Indeed, things were not as they appeared.

Bart had shown Keith the video and demanded to know if he was still involved in pornography and if he had involved Lisa. Assured she was completely ignorant of his former role and innocent of any involvement, Bart agreed the skin flick constituted a major threat to his ministry. The question was whether there were any more videos of him out there. Bart had therefore been reviewing all the porn he could get hold of with the promise that he would buy and destroy any such copies. In hindsight it was naïve in the extreme, but the intention had been good.

Hollis had never approached Keith with blackmail or even to say he was aware of the film. Keith had seen him at Bart's house a couple of times, but they had never even been introduced. Keith was of the opinion that any attempt on Hollis's part to compromise him would have raised Bart's ire, since Bart, though not a member of Keith's congregation, was very protective of his ministry.

Keith had never met Ned. The version of the pornographic video he'd seen after making it had not included the bodybuilder sequences. He agreed that the likelihood of other versions was high, but he had to trust in the Lord to either keep them hidden from men's eyes or give him, Keith, the strength and wisdom to deal with the situation when they were revealed.

Finally, he thanked me for my discretion. "I've been the source of pain and injury to many people. I'm devoting my life to making amends for it."

"Thank you for including my father's uniform, Jason." I turned to see Junior. I hadn't expected to see him here. "I'm sure there were people who thought you shouldn't."

I had to sympathize with the man. His wife and his sister were both in jail awaiting trial for two separate murders. Junior had closed Bartholomew's Jewelry, at least temporarily. He looked terrible. I had to remind myself he was no innocent victim. I'd learned since Rhonda's arrest that he'd bribed Ethel Gartner, the spinsterish legal assistant of Nelson Spooner, Bart's attorney, for information about the old man's estate. She'd informed him his father was worth millions. What she hadn't been able to pass on was that he was no longer the executor of the estate, because Bart had handwritten that change and given it to Spooner without it ever going through her.

I had to shake my head in wonder at the wiliness of the old Army officer. Junior had subsequently run up gambling debts that would bankrupt him, and Ethel had found herself out of work. I heard she'd sold the ring and several other pieces of jewelry she'd come by dishonestly.

"I wish Dad could have been here to see it," Junior said. "I have so many questions I'd like to ask him, so many things I want to say to him, so much I should have said."

I wished mine could be here too. "Thank you for helping out the Garcias. You could have contested possession of the buttons."

"I saw them so many times as a kid," he said. "Held them, admired them. It never occurred to me they might actually be gold and not brass. I'm glad the money is going to good use."

It was more than enough to get Felipe his new wheelchair. I'd suggested the family use the rest of it on a hand-controlled vehicle when he was ready.

I saw a figure standing by himself on the edge of the crowd, excused myself and walked over to him just as he was about to turn away.

"Harden," I called out loud enough for everyone in the immediate area to hear me above the hubbub of the crowd and strode toward him with extended hand. "Thanks for coming."

His right hand went out, a reflex habit. He stared at it, as if he weren't sure how it got there.

"I appreciate you're being here," I said.

"Uh, yeah, sure. I'm glad I came."

Neither of us could be unmindful of the faces and eyes turned our way. I was almost as nervous as he was and not sure what to say next.

Zack came to the rescue. He joined us unobtrusively. "Hope you can make it to the barbecue at the *Nest* later."

If Bubba . . . Harden . . . was surprised at my overture in public, he was downright shocked at Zack's. "Uh, thanks. I'll try."

"Good." Zack said to me, "We're leaving now to help George, though he could probably get things done faster without us."

I chuckled. "I'm sure he'll appreciate your assistance. We won't be far behind you."

Zack nodded. "Take care, Harden," he said over his shoulder as he moved away.

"Have you thought about my offer?" I asked my brother.

"You sure you want me around?"

"I wouldn't ask if I weren't. It's hard work, work you may not like, but it'll give you a modest income and plenty of breathing space. When was the last time you rode a horse?"

He smiled. "I think I was six."

"You're going to have a sore butt then. The foreman knows who you are. He's okay with this, and so am I."

"Your old lady . . . . Sorry. Your mother—"

"Is fine with it. You're not likely to see much of her anyway."

"If you decide it isn't working out—" he was so earnest "—If I'm a problem for you, tell me and I'll leave."

"It's a deal." I again extended my hand. We shook with smiles on our faces.

As I turned to go I saw Brayton Spites standing by one of the exits. We made brief eye contact. I got the impression he wasn't pleased. He and his son had avoided each other all day. As far as I knew, they hadn't spoken to each other since Bubba's release from prison.

I rejoined Michiko. Ted and Livy were with her.

"They want to go with you," Michiko announced after giving me a peck on the cheek. "We'll meet you at the *Nest*."

Livy slipped her hand into mine. Ted was getting too old for handholding, at least in public. When we were all seated in the cab of my truck, I started the engine, pulled out of the handicapped parking space near the mall's grand entrance and set off for the <i>Crow's Nest.</i>

"I wish Colonel Bart could've been here today," Livy muttered.

I wasn't quite sure how to react. She knew he was dead, but did a seven-year-old understand what death was? "Any particular reason?"

"He would have liked to hear me play."

"Yes, he would. We all enjoyed it."

"I heard him tell Rosa the last time we were together that I was the best young piano player he'd ever heard, that Daddy was the best, but that someday I'd be even better than him."

Another surprise answer. "But didn't you say the last time you saw him he told you not to come back?"

"Because he was going away for good."

"Did he tell you why?"

She didn't answer immediately. Seconds went by. "He said . . . his time was up." She looked up at me. "He was sad when he said it. I didn't understand why. I told him he could come back anytime. He smiled and said this was his last P . . . P-something move."

"PCS move."

"Yeah. What's a PCS move, Uncle Jason?"

"It means Permanent Change of Station. That's when you pack up everything and go somewhere else to live."

His last PCS move. He was dying, of course. Did he realize he'd never make it to Las Vegas? When he called me that Monday night, he knew his daughter would be coming to see him the next day. Had he somehow anticipated her response to what he had to tell her? Had he called me when he did because he expected the next day to be his last?

If there was a life after death, I could picture my father and Lieutenant Colonel Mortimer Bartholomew, United States Army, retired, having a good laugh together.

"You know, Livy, I think Colonel Bartholomew was here today, watching and listening to you, and I think he was very pleased with the way you played. I also think he was right about you being a great pianist, too, that you'll make your daddy real proud. We're all very proud of you now."

Lou Flores caught up with me later at the <i>Crow's Nest,</i> where we were serving free mesquite-barbecued beef brisket to anyone who showed up. She reached up and placed her hand on my cheek. "Thank you for what you're doing for Harden, Jason. It means a lot." She raised herself on tiptoe and kissed me on the cheek.

"Where's Mom?" I asked before she got away. She was helping George in the kitchen.

"Left a few minutes ago. Had Leon drive her back to the ranch."

"Why? She was going to stay all day, said she was looking forward to seeing old friends."

"That's sort of the problem," Lou said. "The old friend she was really looking forward to catching up with was my brother. The last she'd heard Brayton and Dolly had broken up again. Your mother figured with him free and Harden working out at the ranch, he'd be paying a call from time to time. Then Brayton walked in with Dolly on his arm, making it clear they'd made up."

"Jason—" Michiko tugged on my arm "—let's sit down and eat." She rubbed her belly. "I'm starved, and so is your child."

About the Author

Ken Casper, aka K. N. Casper, author of more than 25 novels, short stories and articles, figures his writing career started back in the sixth grade when a teacher ordered him to write a "theme" explaining his misbehavior over the previous semester. To his teacher's chagrin, he enjoyed stringing just the right words together to justify his less-than-stellar performance. That's not to say he's been telling tall tales to get out of scrapes ever since, but . . .

Born and raised in New York City, Ken is now a transplanted Texan. He and Mary, his wife of thirty-five-plus years, own a horse farm in San Angelo. Along with their two dogs, six cats, and eight horses—at last count!—they board and breed horses and Mary teaches English riding. She's a therapeutic riding instructor for the handicapped, as well.

Life is never dull. Their two granddaughters visit several times a year and feel right at home with the Casper menagerie. Grandpa and Mimi do everything they can to make sure their visits will be lifelong fond memories. After all, isn't that what grandparents are for?

CPSIA information can be obtained at www.ICGtesting.com
Printed in the USA
LVOW07s2136120515

438294LV00001B/131/P